"Once again Brennan weaves a complex tale of murder, vengeance, and treachery filled with knife-edged tension and clever twists. The Lucy Kincaid/Sean Rogan novels just keep getting better!"

—*RT Book Reviews* (4½ stars, Top Pick!) on *Stalked*

"The evolution of Lucy Kincaid from former victim to instinctive and talented agent continues in Brennan's new heart-stopping thriller . . . From first to last, this story grabs hold and never lets go."

—*RT Book Reviews* (Top Pick) on *Silenced*

Praise for the Max Revere Novels

"Talk about grit and courage, Max never gives up."

—Catherine Coulter

"Buckle up and brace yourself for Maxine Revere."

—Sandra Brown

"Boldly drawn, psychologically complex characters, and a multifaceted plot distinguish this entry, which thoughtfully explores the different forms that family can take."

—*Publishers Weekly*

Missing

ALLISON BRENNAN

St. Martin's Paperbacks

Published in the United States by St. Martin's Paperbacks, an imprint of St. Martin's Publishing Group

For information, address St. Martin's Publishing Group, 120 Broadway, New York, NY 10271.

www.stmartins.com

ISBN: 978-1-250-83216-0

Our books may be purchased in bulk for promotional, educational, or business use. Please contact your local bookseller or the Macmillan Corporate and Premium Sales Department at 1-800-221-7945, ext. 5442, or by email at MacmillanSpecialMarkets@macmillan.com.

Printed in the United States of America

St. Martin's Paperbacks edition / February 2022

10 9 8 7 6 5 4 3 2 1

Dear Reader,

I am thrilled to present *Missing,* a Lucy Kincaid anthology featuring three never-before-in-print stories.

Each of these stories were previously available in ebook only. My publisher and I recognize that many people prefer print, and so we decided to combine these stories into one book.

When writing the digital-first stories, I take great pains to make sure that they stand alone, so that those who read only in print don't feel they have missed anything important in the series story arc. That said, these stories feature favorite characters in the Lucy Kincaid series, while also providing a good mystery in between longer books.

Occasionally, I come up with ideas I love, but that wouldn't fill a full-length novel. These I can turn into meaty novellas—stories between 30,000 and 35,000 words. I hope you find them just as satisfying as I do.

So where do I get these ideas?

Ideas come from everywhere, but it's usually a combination of things I see or read. It also helps if I connect a concept immediately to one of my characters.

The tenth Lucy Kincaid book was *No Good Deed,* which started with a prison break. I've always been intrigued by good prison-break stories—I even wrote an entire trilogy in 2008 about a prison break after an earthquake at San Quentin—so the concept of *Storm Warning* was in the back of my mind.

I had come up with the idea for *Cut and Run,* the sixteenth book in Lucy's series. It begins after a major storm unearths a grave with four human skeletons. I started thinking about the storm itself, and all the public safety problems that can arise during a major event. Then I thought, what happens if law enforcement is dealing with a typical situation—like a prison transport—and the storm creates issues?

I mulled over this idea for a while, until it clicked. I needed a reason for Lucy to be transporting a prisoner—it's not common for FBI agents to be responsible for this; it's generally the job of corrections or the US Marshals. But I had a plausible reason to need to move a federal suspect wanted for bank robbery who was arrested in a small, local jurisdiction—they couldn't hold him over the weekend. So Lucy and her partner, Nate Dunning, are sent to pick him up and bring him back to San Antonio.

Of course, because this is a Lucy story, the suspect's partners use the storm as a way to break him out of the van. Then it's a race against time to find him, his gang, and figure out what's *really* going on. Because things are not what they seem.

I hope you enjoy it!

Allison

Storm Warning

Chapter One

FBI Agent Lucy Kincaid hadn't experienced wind this strong since moving to San Antonio nearly two years ago. Old-timers said the storm was bad, but not the worst they'd faced. Last weekend, when the first downpour hit, Lucy and Sean's retired neighbors came over and spent hours drinking beer and talking about where they were during every major storm in the last thirty years. Sean thought the old couple was cute; Lucy would prefer an earthquake to 60-mile-per-hour winds and flash floods.

Thank God there were rarely tornadoes in San Antonio, or Lucy would be requesting a transfer, ASAP.

Right now, Lucy would rather be home in her warmest pajamas under three down comforters with a mug of hot chocolate—even though it was September. Seventy degrees wasn't cold, but it was wet and sticky and the wind wasn't exactly a warm breeze. The drive to Brady, Texas, had taken three hours when it shouldn't have taken much more than two, and she was relieved that Nate was driving. They'd crossed two sections of road that were partly flooded, and three times had to get out to remove debris from their path. If one of San Antonio FBI's Most Wanted wasn't sitting on ice in the small-town municipal court, they wouldn't have been out in this weather.

Hands down, this was the most miserable day of the year.

They pulled up to the rear of the municipal building and ran up the stairs. The employee entrance was locked, and Nate rang the bell impatiently. They were both dressed for the weather in khakis, long-sleeved shirts, and sturdy boots. Nate had left his jacket in the transport van; Lucy put hers on. Not that it did much good—her hair was still soaked from the last time they'd moved a tree branch from their path and it wasn't even raining that hard.

A minute later, an officer let them in.

"Nate Dunning, FBI," Nate said, and showed his badge. "Agent Lucy Kincaid."

"Glad you folks made it, I'm Police Chief Thomas Osgood."

"The chief answering doors, don't think I've seen it before," Nate said as they followed Osgood down a long hall.

"We have twelve sworn officers, and the same number in civilian staff. It's all hands this weekend—and then to have the basement flooded, on top of the trouble outside. We right appreciate your assistance. If it was just a bunch of drunk and disorderlies, we'd have let them go—in fact, I released two brothers this morning who'd been in a bar fight. I know them both, they're idiots, and when they get to drinking, they're even more stupid. Two thousand dollars in damage." He shook his head. "I know where to find them. But these two men—I can't just let them walk."

Brady, Texas, was a small community northwest of San Antonio, two counties over. It wasn't near any major highway. It was by chance and smart thinking that Brady police apprehended a wanted fugitive. They'd been going door to door yesterday morning in an area at risk for flooding, and the officer recognized Samuel Trembly from an FBI Most Wanted flyer. Trembly and his gang had committed five armed robberies—including three bank heists in South Texas—the last of which resulted in two dead, including one of Trembly's gang. That was a month ago, and the San Antonio FBI had bumped him to the top of their internal Most Wanted list.

The US Marshals had been scheduled to bring Trembly to the federal courthouse in San Antonio on Tuesday, since Monday was Labor Day. The small jail in the Brady Municipal Courthouse was sufficient to house the suspect for the long weekend. But last night the basement—where the cell was located—had flooded when a support wall cracked and the pressure resulted in severe structural damage to the 150-year-old building.

"I thought we were just bringing Trembly in," Nate said.

"This morning my officers responded to a domestic violence call out by the reservoir. Arrested a guy by the name of John Carr, though he has no ID on him. We've sent his prints in to confirm. His girlfriend's in the hospital. She doesn't want to press charges, but since Carr took a swing at one of my cops, we hauled his ass in. Hoping to convince the young lady to change her mind. Might not matter since we have two cops who saw Carr throw the girl across the room."

"And why are *we* taking him?" Nate asked.

"He can't stay here, and I can't let him go. I called Austin; they can't spare a car, and the 87 is flooded between here and San Angelo, so there's no easy way for one of their patrols to get out here. I knew you were coming in for Trembly, called down to Bexar County Sheriff's Office, and they said they'd take him. No way am I letting him out, when his first stop will likely be the hospital to terrorize his girl."

Nate didn't look happy about the change, and Lucy didn't blame him—they didn't normally handle prison transports, but with the storm, and local law enforcement working overtime on emergency calls, they didn't have much choice. Trembly was an FBI Most Wanted, and he was their responsibility.

"I should have tried to reach you, I'm sorry," Osgood said. "Last week we had a lot of damage, no flooding—but the ground is so dang saturated right now that there's been several flash floods. The reservoir sustained damage last week, and now our engineers are trying to prevent a major breech that could take out a community of three hundred folks. We may have to evacuate if they don't get it under control. I can't spare the manpower to watch these two outside of lockup."

"It's fine," Nate said. "But it took us three hours to get here because of traffic and weather, so we need to get going. I don't want to deal with this storm and nightfall."

It was nearly two in the afternoon, though the dark-gray skies made it appear timeless. Eerie and creepy was more like it.

"We have the paperwork ready. Do you have a good map of the area?"

"Yes," Nate said. He sounded snippy, which was unlike him.

As soon as the chief walked away, Lucy said, "What's going on?"

"I don't like changes. If I had known we had more than one prisoner, I would have brought in a second vehicle."

Lucy had never worked a prison transport, she didn't really know what it entailed, beyond what she'd learned at Quantico. And every transport was different. "You want to transport them separately?"

"No—I want a tail or a lead car, someone to watch our ass."

"We can call in backup. I haven't done this before, if you want to bring in a more experienced team."

"It's not you, Lucy. When Leo called me and said they needed two agents to come up here and transport Trembly,

I picked you. I like working with you, and I know you have my back. The point is, I've done transports before—in the Army. Albeit it was a different situation, we had shit going on around us, but we always had a minimum of two soldiers for every one prisoner. Preferably three, but since we don't generally have sniper fire or landmines in the US, two is sufficient."

"You're joking."

He shrugged. "Sort of a joke. The faster we get to I-10, the happier I'll be. I have a route I want to take that's longer, but it'll get us to I-10 faster."

"Whatever you think is best."

"I need to talk to the folks here, see what hazards we have. Get an escort. Just be alert."

The chief came back with two folders and a clipboard and said, "If you can dot the i's and cross the t's, you can get out of here."

Lucy took the paperwork and Nate said, "Chief, can I trouble you for some information on road conditions?"

"Absolutely. We have several road closures, mostly due to flooding or a risk to flood. You're not from here, are you? There's several creeks you'll need to be mindful of. And I'll give you our emergency channel for your radio, so we can communicate any changes." They walked down the hall with Nate asking questions.

Lucy filled out the transport forms, signed them with her name and badge number, then flipped through the two prisoner files.

Samuel Trembly, thirty-five, was the apparent leader of the gang of five, who had robbed three banks and two jewelry stores in the last four months in Austin, San Marcos, and San Antonio. They were also suspected of multiple robberies in the Dallas–Fort Worth area last summer. Trembly had landed on the FBI's radar because his prints had been recovered at the last bank robbery, four weeks ago, when he tried to save his partner, Reginald Hansen, who'd been shot and killed by a private citizen during the robbery after Hansen mortally wounded the bank manager. Trembly had a record—two misdemeanor charges years ago—that made him pop on the criminal database.

Once they had Hansen's identity, they quickly traced him to Austin, Texas, where he'd grown up and had a construction job until a few years ago, then connected him to his life-long friend, Trembly. Unfortunately, neither had a known residence in the city and Trembly's family had long moved out of the area.

According to the FBI file she'd read that morning, Trembly's father died when he was young and his mother raised four children by working two jobs. Samuel, the oldest, was in and out of trouble. He had two sisters and a brother, but there was next to nothing on them, either. All she had was names and ages, and none of them had been in trouble with the law.

Still, when someone was in trouble, the first place they often looked for sanctuary was their family. This wasn't Lucy's case, so she didn't know what the lead agent had already done. No Tremblys were reported as living here, in Brady, Texas—Trembly had been discovered in a trailer on the outskirts of town and it was just chance that the local police recognized him from the bulletin. The file indicated that the landlord had rented to him on the cheap with no background or credit check because he paid three months up front—starting three days after the last robbery.

The other gang members weren't identified, just Trembly and Hansen. Kirk Hansen, Reggie's younger brother, was wanted for questioning—he had a long rap sheet and the lead field agent for the investigation, Mike Crutcher, suspected he was part of the gang when in the course of his investigation he learned that Kirk and Reggie were practically inseparable. But Kirk was nowhere to be found.

It could be they used a different crew for every heist—Trembly being here in Brady alone supported that argument. Or maybe they had split up after the last robbery because it was the first time someone had been killed. But it wasn't the first time someone had been seriously injured. The third robbery—a jewel heist—left the store manager beaten and shot, but she survived. Witnesses said there was no reason for the attack, just that one of the criminals "went off" on the manager for no apparent reason.

The gang was bold, well organized, and had some skills and street smarts—they disabled cameras, wore masks and gloves, and communicated with hand signals instead of words, to minimize identification. Lucy suspected they were using sign language—which she knew well—or a variation, but she was relying solely on the thin report for the information and no one confirmed the use of ASL. The Dallas regional FBI office had passed along all the information from their robberies once Trembly's gang moved into the San Antonio jurisdiction. Crutcher, a senior field agent on the White Collar Crimes squad, had practically done a jig in the office when the Brady police chief informed the FBI that they'd arrested Trembly last night.

Why she and Nate were picking him up and not Crutcher and one of his people she didn't know.

The second file was even thinner—the booking sheet for John Carr, a copy of his prints, and a statement by the two officers. A neighbor had called 911 about a domestic disturbance. When they arrived they heard a woman scream, entered the apartment, and saw Carr push his girlfriend into a dining-room hutch, which shattered, and the girl was cut badly in the arm. He was arrested and the girl was taken to the hospital. There was no name in the file. Carr didn't have identification on him and he wasn't in the system—which immediately made Lucy suspicious. They found no ID in the house and there was no vehicle to search for registration or confirmation of his identity.

Nate returned a few minutes later and Lucy pointed out the discrepancy. "It's just a matter of time before we ID him," Nate said. "We need to get going quick—the rain is light now but will get worse before nightfall, and the winds are fierce. We could be dealing with road debris. It's really a mess out there. But the good news is the chief agreed to give us an escort to Fredericksburg, which is seventy miles down US 87, and the Fredericksburg chief agreed to give us an escort to Comfort, which is off I-10. Leo is sending a tactical team to Comfort to meet up with us and take Carr into custody, plus provide an additional escort."

"That's terrific."

Nate smiled. He didn't smile often enough, Lucy thought. Though they'd been friends for nearly two years now, she didn't know a lot about him, over and above his ten years of service in the Army and the fact that he was adopted when his parents were older and they were now both deceased. He was a good friend and a great cop.

A few minutes later, the chief had the two prisoners brought down from where they'd been locked under guard in a conference room. They wore handcuffs, orange jumpsuits, and their own shoes, minus shoelaces.

"This is Mr. Trembly," Osgood said. He looked a few years older than his driver's license photo, but his appearance wasn't substantially different—sandy-blond hair and brown eyes. He was physically fit and nearly as tall as Nate.

"And Mr. Carr," Osgood said. Carr had dark-blond hair and hazel eyes and was on the scrawny side. The only injury from his attack on his girlfriend was a bruise on his right hand.

An officer had two bags with Trembly's and Carr's personal effects. "We'll take these two outside for you," he said.

"One minute," Nate said. "I have a call coming in from my office." He walked away to take the call.

Trembly stared at Lucy. He was trying to intimidate her. She hated that he was partly succeeding. Fortunately, she had a great poker face and stared him down. Then he smiled and winked. "If I'd've known the FBI was hiring hot little chicas, I would have gotten myself arrested long ago."

She didn't respond—getting in a tit-for-tat conversation with her prisoner wouldn't be prudent. Unfortunately, the officer kicked Trembly in the back of his shin and he stumbled.

"Respect, boy," the officer said.

"He doesn't bother me," Lucy said firmly, silently admonishing the cop. She didn't need anyone standing up for her, it would diminish her authority in the eyes of the prisoners. They might think she was a pushover or weak and attempt something on the road; she had to exert her authority without exerting physical control.

Nate returned a few minutes later. "Let's go," he said.

The two Brady cops walked the prisoners out to the back. The rain was still coming down, and the wind whipped them. The FBI transport van was reinforced and bulletproof, the glass bullet resistant. The back had attached shackles, which could hold up to five prisoners. Nate first secured Trembly to the shackles on the passenger side, near the cab, then secured Carr to the shackles on the driver's side, rear. He double-checked them: waist, hands, ankles.

"Your boyfriend doesn't talk much, does he, sugar?" Trembly said.

Lucy ignored him.

Nate secured the doors, took the two bags of personal effects, and he and Lucy entered the cab.

"What was the call about?" Lucy said. Nate adjusted the camera that showed the rear of the van. There shouldn't be any trouble, but they could watch their prisoners on a camera to make sure no one was in distress or causing problems.

"Backup. Just wanted to clear a few things up with Leo before we head out. We have a three-hour drive ahead of us, half of it on a two-lane highway. Want to make sure we're being tracked the entire way."

"Do you want to wait until Leo can send a team up here?"

"We wouldn't be out of here until near dark, and traveling these roads in a storm at night is too dangerous. Plus, we have escorts all the way down to Comfort. I can't go the way I wanted—west to I-10—because Menard is knee-deep in water. So it's back along 87."

"That's more of a direct route, isn't it?"

"Yeah, and the road is better maintained, but there are several low spots and a dozen or more creeks and rivers we have to cross. The chief gave me a heads-up on where to watch out, plus I talked to the patrol escorting us. Officer Dominick Riley is local and knows the area well. We're just waiting on him to check out equipment. Do you have a good visual on our boys back there?"

Lucy could see both prisoners in the back through the dash camera. The cab was completely sealed off from the rear for agent safety. They had filled up with gas when they first arrived in Brady so had a full tank, and they had a radio, extra water, and emergency supplies.

"They're secure."

"Just keep watch. I searched them before they were taken out, not that I don't trust the cops here, but, well, you know."

She knew. Nate was a soldier through and through, just like her brother Jack and her brother-in-law Kane. They were cautious by nature, didn't like to leave anything to chance.

A large, burly black cop came out and waved to Nate. Nate

smiled and waved back. "Riley there was a Marine for six years. We're in good hands," Nate said.

"Why do I think you hand-picked him?"

"I would have, but he was the only one not out dealing with an emergency."

Riley jumped into a patrol truck, and a minute later Lucy heard his deep baritone over the radio. "Ready to roll, Agent Dunning?"

"Yes, sir," Nate said.

Riley laughed. "Call me Riley, all my friends do."

"I'm Nate, my partner is Lucy."

"I expect no real trouble, but there're a few creeks that will roll on over the road, should be passable, but we'll need to keep our heads on. I'll update you regularly."

"Appreciate it, Riley."

Nate started out, letting Riley take lead. He radioed into FBI headquarters.

"Dunning and Kincaid leaving Brady at fourteen hundred hours. Brady PD escort through to Fredericksburg"—he checked the GPS navigation—"one hour, forty minutes. Over."

"Roger that, Agent Dunning. Monitoring GPS for the duration, check in every fifteen."

"Thanks, Zach," Nate said, and signed off.

"Zach's monitoring the radio?"

"Yeah—all hands today. There are multiple teams out assisting SAPD and the sheriff's department. We're all wearing a different hat, I suppose. Kenzie may be called up if the storm gets worse." Kenzie was in the National Guard and trained monthly with her unit. She'd been deployed to Houston immediately after Hurricane Harvey for two weeks to assist in rescues and prevent looting.

"Did the chief get confirmation on John Carr's ID?" Lucy asked.

"They sent in his prints, system's overloaded right now. He'll let us know if there's anything we need to know. You read Trembly's file?"

"I read the FBI file this morning and the arrest file. He came in without putting up much of a fight. First tried to say they had the wrong guy, but when they got his ID, he just rolled over. Hiding out here for a month, it seems."

"Probably could have hid out here for longer if not for the storm."

"The police didn't search his place—there could be evidence."

"Well, shit," Nate muttered. "You sure they didn't search?"

"If they did, they didn't indicate in the report." She flipped through the file again. "Says they put a police lock on the door, but if the trailer floods, that's not going to help us."

"We'll talk to the lead agent and let him deal with it—this isn't even our case. They'd need a warrant anyway, and Crutcher probably wants to send an FBI team in to do the search."

"How did we get called for the transport? Neither of us is even on the task force."

"Office protocol demands that a SWAT-trained agent is attached to any transport, and apparently I was the only one available. White Collar doesn't have any SWAT agents. And you were on call this weekend."

"Lucky me."

"Lucky me. I could have gotten stuck with Lopez."

"Jason isn't that bad."

"Don't trust him, don't like him."

Jason Lopez had started out on the wrong foot with Lucy as well, but she'd made a point of getting to know him better, and he wasn't a bad agent. He tended to be a people pleaser, but he was diligent and personable. It did sometimes disturb Lucy that he was so close to their boss—and Nate's point about trust was well taken. It was known in the squad that anything Jason learned their boss Rachel Vaughn would soon know.

Riley called in on the radio. "We're making good time to Mason," he said. "Twenty more minutes or so. Talked ahead to a buddy of mine who has a cattle ranch down there—he says the Llano River, which is eight, nine miles south of town, is right up to the road—it hasn't gone over yet, but if it rises another foot we're going to have a serious problem. We should be past it by then, but stay sharp. I'll give you fair warning before we reach the bridge. There's a couple places where the road is partly flooded once we get past the Llano, but nothing impassable at this point."

"Thanks for the update," Lucy told Riley.

Nate firmly gripped the wheel to keep the van on the road as the wind hit them hard. Lucy was grateful Nate was do-ing the driving—she didn't particularly like driving, even in fair weather.

She looked at the two men in the back. They were jostled with the movement of the vehicle but otherwise looked re-signed to their situation, their heads hanging low. Good—they shouldn't give them too much trouble.

Nate asked, "How's everything going with Jess? He adjust-ing okay after all the bullshit with his grandfather?"

Jesse was Sean's thirteen-year-old son. Until last year, Sean didn't even know he had a child. Jesse's grandfather, wealthy businessman Ronald McAllister, had threatened to fight for custody after his mother died two months ago, but Sean and Jesse went to California to work out an arrangement that McAllister reluctantly agreed to. Lucy didn't know all the details—and Sean was still upset about everything that happened—but Sean had full custody of Jesse and McAllis-ter wasn't contesting his paternity.

"I think he's okay," Lucy said. "Started school last Monday.

Already found a soccer team that took him on. Jesse seems to be adapting well—stood up to his grandfather about wanting to live with us. I'm glad *that's* over. None of us wanted a court fight over custody."

"Sean is . . . well, he's not really himself these days."

"You noticed?" Sean tried to keep a positive attitude, but after Jesse's mother was killed, he'd had a hard time wrestling with guilt and anger.

"It's been nearly two months. I'm sure that Jesse is having a hard time—the kid lost his mom—but none of what happened was Sean's fault. It seems like he's putting all the blame on his shoulders."

"He is," Lucy said. "I talk to him, and sometimes he listens . . . I think he needs to know that Jesse is really going to be okay before he can let it all go."

"Is something wrong with Jess?"

"I don't know that anything is," she said cautiously, "but he hasn't really talked about his mother at all. A little here and there. I know grief is different for everyone, but he's a thirteen-year-old kid. I guess—I expected something else."

"Maybe it hasn't soaked in yet."

"It has. I think— Well, damn. It's just a mess."

"You don't have to talk about it," Nate said. "Seriously, I'm not pushing, I just feel for Sean and the kid."

"I know you do, and that's not it. After Madison died, Jesse learned that she was privy to many of Carson Spade's illegal activities."

"That's fucked," Nate said. "Poor kid."

"Sean wanted to protect Jesse, but he knew it would be worse if Jesse found out through someone else. So when Jesse asked, Sean gave him a sanitized version. But Jesse isn't an idiot. He read between the lines. Battling love and anger is hard for anyone, especially a teenager. And then the battle with Madison's father—that took its toll on Sean. So they are both dealing with some heavy emotional baggage, I think. And being Rogans—they don't share very well."

"But Sean has custody."

"Yes. Honestly, I think if Jesse wasn't one hundred percent behind Sean, there would have been a battle. Sean was willing to fight all the way, but McAllister has money and friends in high places."

"So does Sean, but I'm glad it didn't come to that."

Nate was right about that—Sean had dug up a lot of dirt on McAllister, and Lucy didn't know if he'd had to use it.

"I'm just glad they're home," she said.

Ahead of them, Riley was slowing down and Nate followed suit. The road wasn't flooded, but there was a lot of water on the roadway. The gusts of wind continued to jostle the heavy van, and Lucy looked at the camera. Their prisoners had barely moved. Carr, in the rear, was talking. Lucy could somewhat read lips, but the camera was partly distorted so that they could view the entire compartment and it was almost impossible to tell what he was saying to Trembly.

The radio beeped. "Nate, it's Riley."

"Trouble ahead? You're slowing down."

"We're coming into Mason. Serious accident in the center of town, so we're making a little detour. Nothing to worry about, I got word from the sheriff's deputy that the route I want to use to get back to 87 is clear. Just wanted to give you a heads-up. We'll be merging back right past town."

"Roger that. Thanks, buddy."

Chapter Two

The wind drove the rain from the east, gusts rocking the van. Nate's hands gripped the steering wheel tightly.

The detour took them a couple of miles out of their way, but they were back on 87 and only lost ten or so minutes. Lucy checked in with headquarters as soon as they passed Mason, and the FBI backup was already en route to Comfort.

"We're halfway to Fredericksburg," Nate said, and immediately slowed. "Holy shit!"

In front of them, Riley had slowed almost to a stop. The road had flooded, but he was rolling through it. It didn't quite reach the underbelly of his truck, which told Lucy it was less than a foot deep.

Lucy got on the radio. "Is this the Llano?" she asked.

Riley replied, "Comanche Creek. We're lucky we got through it—two hours ago it was practically dry."

"Does that mean Llano is going to be impassable?" Nate asked.

"Not necessarily," Riley said. "Llano is a deeper, wider channel. We should make it through—though I might be finding a different way back home if the Comanche continues to rise. We have to watch the creek that branches off of Llano, there's a bridge about a mile south of the river."

"We appreciate your help out here."

"I'm calling in road conditions as I see them, which helps everyone. Over."

They passed through the last of the water and picked up speed on the highway. Lucy glanced at the camera in the back. The men weren't talking, but Carr was restless. His hands didn't stop moving.

She tilted her head and leaned closer to the camera.

Almost time.

She looked at Trembly. His hands were also moving, though his signing wasn't as clear as Carr's because of the angle of the camera. She thought he signed, *Tomorrow night*, but she wasn't certain. The shackles made his movements short and jerky.

She said, "I think they're talking to each other in sign language."

Nate glanced at the camera in the dash. "How can you tell?"

"I learned sign language in high school—it's hard to tell what he's saying because it's a bastardized version of ASL. The only thing I clearly made out was Carr signing, *Almost time*. Trembly's gang used a variation of ASL to communicate during the robberies."

"Who is this Carr? Does he know Trembly?"

"Carr might not be his real name." The two men stopped signing but weren't slumped over as they'd been at the beginning of the drive.

Nate immediately got on the radio to Riley. "Hey, buddy, keep your eyes open. Seems that our prisoners might know each other, and I'm getting a bad feeling about this."

"Roger that."

To Lucy, Nate said, "Call it in. Have headquarters run facial recognition and rush Carr's prints—we need to know what we're dealing with."

Lucy got on the radio. "This is Special Agent Lucy Kincaid. Agent Dunning and I are on 87 south of Mason, approximately ten miles north of Cherry Spring."

Zach Charles, the VCMO analyst, came on the radio. "Roger that, Lucy."

"We have a potential issue. The prisoners seem to know each other and are using sign language to communicate, just like Trembly's gang did during the robberies. It reasons that Carr may be one of Trembly's gang." She hesitated, then said, "Either he's a complete unknown, or he's using a false identity."

"What are they saying?" Zach asked.

"They're aware of the time, it seems they're waiting for something. Trembly said something about tomorrow night as well. Nate's concerned that they may be planning a break."

"You still have backup, right?"

"Yes—a police escort. We're—Wow, that river is huge."

"What?"

"We're crossing the Llano River."

The water was right up to the bridge but hadn't spilled over. It was violent and the wind caused gusts of spray to hit them, making visibility difficult as they crossed.

"Can you contact Fredericksburg? They're going to escort us to Comfort, but we need backup now—they can meet up with us. Nate and I would feel a whole lot better if we had another patrol."

"Hold on," Zach said. "I'll contact them."

Lucy hadn't taken her eyes off the prisoners in the back. She leaned forward trying to make out what Trembly was signing. "I think Trembly is asking *how long* and Carr is just saying *not too long, road slow* or something . . . damn, they have their own style, and it's difficult to read."

"We know more than we did five minutes ago."

The signing between the prisoners stopped. Nate was both

looking in his mirrors and monitoring the road ahead. They hadn't passed a car or emergency vehicle in more than ten minutes.

Zach returned. "Two patrols from Fredericksburg PD are being deployed to your location—they say the road is a mess all the way down from your location to town. Watch for rising water, but you shouldn't have more than eighteen inches in any one spot. Power's out all over, don't leave the road—a lot of the side roads are impassable."

"We might not have a choice," Lucy said. She looked at the men in the back. Were they anticipating something or was that her fear? "Is Mike Crutcher in the office?"

"I'll track him down."

"Have him call me, on my cell, if he can get through. We need to keep the radio open."

Riley had slowed down, and Nate did the same. The winds continued to come in waves from hard to van-shaking, and it was all Nate could do to maintain control. "What are you thinking?" Nate asked.

"We need more information about the Tremblys. According to the file, I don't know if Crutcher talked to anyone in his family. He has a brother, couple of sisters. None of them have a record. What if the rest of the gang is family? According to the witness statements, they indicated that at least one of the gang was a woman. Trembly and Hansen have been friends since high school. Crutcher's people have been trying to find the other Hansen, his younger brother, who has a record, but he's also in the wind. They didn't kill anyone until the last robbery, but they're violent and aren't afraid to use fear and intimidation."

The radio buzzed and Lucy answered. "Agent Kincaid."

"Agent Kincaid, this is Officer Cliff Rabke with the Fredericksburg Police Department. I hear you might be having a spot of trouble. Whereabouts are you now?"

Nate responded, "We just crossed the Llano River."

"We're already out, we'll meet up with you probably about Road 648. Your office said you're in a tan van with government plates."

"Yes, sir. We're being escorted by Officer Dominick Riley with Brady PD."

"I know Riley. You're in good hands."

"Sir, we don't know what to expect with the Trembly gang, but they already killed one civilian."

"Stay alert. We should cross paths in about twenty, twenty-five minutes. We have two patrols en route to escort y'all back to town, and we have a nice, warm jail cell for your prisoners and a pot of hot coffee for you, until you can figure out what's what."

"Thank you, Officer," Lucy said.

"Over and out," Rabke said.

Nate nodded to the dash camera. "Anything else?"

"No, and they can't know exactly where we are—there's no windows back there. They have to be tracking the time, and they act like they're anticipating something."

Nate got back on the radio to Riley. "Be alert." To Lucy he said, "It wouldn't have been too difficult to figure out which way we were going once we left Brady. Or they could have been watching the jail—but no one has followed us."

"No one's passed us, either."

"They could be on radios or cell phones. You said there were several people involved in the heists, right?"

"Five according to the witnesses," Lucy said.

She alternated looking at the camera and looking at the roadway. The rain was still coming down at a sharp angle, the wind pushing water over the road. The asphalt was slick; drainage was minimal. They were driving through two, three inches of water across the entire highway. But there was no place for someone to hide. Few roads or driveways merged into this section of 87 and bushes and trees were set far off the road, most of the land flat and grassy. Then she saw the creek—which looked like a roaring river—that they were about to pass. The force of the water coupled with the strong winds pushed waves over the road.

Riley slowed to a crawl; Nate followed suit. They crossed over the bridge and Lucy breathed a sigh of relief.

Nate was monitoring the GPS, which was also attached to the dash. "We have a couple of roads coming up, looks like they don't go anywhere, and they might not even be paved, but it's a good place for— Shit!"

Immediately, he slowed down. In front of them Riley was hydroplaning, his car wildly skidding on the road as he tried to control it.

"It's a fucking spike strip!" Nate exclaimed. He tried to brake before he hit it, but he couldn't avoid it. The strip had been camouflaged just beneath the surface of the water covering the road, made more difficult to spot because of poor visibility. Fortunately, Nate hit it going much slower than Riley and was able to control the van into a stop.

Lucy had her gun out.

Riley spun around but kept his truck upright.

Nate hit the radio. "Nate Dunning, FBI, officer needs immediate assistance at this location! We've been ambushed!"

Immediately in front of them, a short individual wearing tactical gear and a ski mask converged on Riley's patrol. He had a shotgun aimed at the driver's door. Riley was effectively trapped.

A bullhorn cut through the sounds of the storm. That was when Lucy saw two more people running toward them, one with a shotgun, one with a handgun and the bullhorn.

"Try anything, we kill the cop," a male voice said. "Out of the van."

Nate didn't move.

Over the radio, Rabke said, "We're still thirty minutes from your location because of road debris. A patrol may be closer. Stay put."

Nate said, "We're surrounded by three armed gunmen. Three shotguns and one handgun visible. They're wearing body armor. Riley is pinned down."

To Lucy, Nate said, "I can get one, you can get the other, but Riley will be dead before we can get the guy on him."

Lucy concurred. Riley's truck was too far up the road to guarantee that they'd be able to make the shot in these conditions.

The gunman said, "I'm not fucking around here. Get out of the van and toss me the keys *now*. Five. Four. Three. Two." He put his hand up and the gunman next to Riley squared up.

Nate slammed his fist on the horn and got his attention. He cracked open his window. "Take the gun off the cop."

"You're not in a position to negotiate, Mr. Agent. Out."

"Cops are already on their way. We can wait you out."

"Your cop friend will be dead."

"Your friends will be tried as accessories to killing a cop and get the death penalty."

"I don't fucking have time for this bullshit. Do it!"

"No!" Nate shouted.

The bullhorn guy said, "Fair warning."

The short guy with a shotgun—Lucy thought *woman*—fired into Riley's engine.

"Get out, throw down your weapons, give me the keys, or the next one goes through his window."

Nate said to Lucy, "Be prepared to run—they've already decided to shoot." He glanced in his mirrors. "There's a car approaching. Shit, we can't get civilians in the middle of this bullshit."

Nate opened his door.

"The car may be their getaway," Lucy said. "Be careful."

He had his hands up—no weapon, the keys in his right hand.

"Get the gun off the cop," Nate demanded over the storm.

"Your partner needs to get out first."

Lucy opened her door. The wind nearly pushed her over as she climbed out of the van. She showed her hands.

The bullhorn guy motioned for the girl holding the shotgun to lower the weapon. She was reluctant, and there was a silent exchange. Lucy watched his hands. These people knew each other well.

Though the shotgunner put the gun down slightly, she could bring it up quickly and fire if she wanted. Mr. Bullhorn was in charge, but that girl was a wild card.

"Toss me the keys," Bullhorn said. "Nice and easy, big guy. I don't want to shoot your partner or the cop, got it? Just want to get my friends out."

Friends. If there had been any doubt, there wasn't now. Carr was definitely part of the gang. Lucy realized then that he intentionally got himself arrested. Why? To convey information to Trembly? To help with the breakout?

Nate tossed the keys. They landed at Bullhorn's feet, and the other guy picked them up and handed them to Bullhorn.

"Now, move away from the van. On your knees. Now! Both of you! Hands where my buddy can see them, got it?"

The guy holding the shotgun on Nate and Lucy was tall and skinny. He was shaking.

She. This is a girl, too.

Was she shaking from the cold or because she was scared? Two women, one man. But Lucy would never underestimate a female bad guy. One of the most vicious criminals she'd faced was a woman.

"Knees!" Mr. Bullhorn fired his .45 at Nate's feet and

dropped the bullhorn. "Both of you. Now." He shouted over the wind, even though they were just twenty feet away.

Slowly, Nate fell to his knees. Lucy could feel his rage, even though his expression remained staunchly blank. She dropped to her knees as well, her eyes on the woman in the distance, the one with the shotgun on Riley. Mr. Bullhorn retreated to the rear of the van.

"Nate," Lucy said. He didn't hear her, and she said louder, "Nate."

He nodded his head once.

"The car. Where did it go?"

He didn't say anything but tilted his body forward so he could see the roadway. They heard voices behind the van. He leaned back.

"It stopped," he said.

The woman closest to them said, "What are you talking about?"

Nate said, "You're not going to get away with this."

"We already have."

"We'll find you."

"Shut up." She glanced behind the van. She was definitely nervous.

Lucy looked over to the shorter female. Her shotgun was raised and aimed at Riley. She wanted to fire it. Her entire demeanor was excited . . . she enjoyed this.

The car that Nate had seen pulled up parallel to the van. It was a full-sized pickup truck. Carr was in the back, Trembly in the passenger seat. "Get in," Mr. Bullhorn said.

The woman couldn't wait to jump into the back seat.

The gunman faced them. He then turned to the van and shot up the radio.

It could be worse. They could have killed you and Nate.

Probably not—they both could reach their backup pieces—but Riley would most certainly be dead.

The gunman saluted them then jumped into the back of the pickup. They drove to where Riley was pinned down.

They couldn't hear what Mr. Bullhorn was saying over the wind, but it was clear he was arguing with the short girl, motioning for her to climb into the back of the truck.

She finally did and Lucy began to breathe easier. The truck pulled away, then the girl stood up and fired a shotgun round into Riley's patrol. The driving wind muffled the sound of shattering glass.

Nate was up and running, gun out as soon as the woman had aimed the shotgun. He fired even though the vehicle was more than fifty yards away. Lucy pulled her backup service weapon and ran after Nate, but she didn't have a clear shot. She thought she saw the girl fall to her knees but didn't know if Nate had hit her or not.

The masked girl fired the shotgun again at Riley's vehicle, but the truck was moving fast and shotguns had a short range. Buckshot pinged against metal.

Nate continued to fire. Lucy would take him over most everyone as her backup because he didn't miss, but at this distance and with the wind she didn't know how he could have hit her.

Nate reached Riley first. Lightning flashed across the sky, the echoing thunder making Lucy's heart skip a beat. She caught up to Nate as her partner pounded on the locked door. "Riley!"

The cop looked dazed and didn't unlock the door.

Lucy ran around to the side where the glass was broken and opened the door. She unlocked the doors from the inside and Nate opened the driver's door to inspect Riley.

"I'm fine," Riley muttered when it was clear he was anything but fine. Blood poured from his head.

"Where are you hit?" Nate said.

"Just glass. I think."

By the look of the wound, more than glass hit him. The side of his face was bleeding and it looked like glass or buckshot had pierced his upper right shoulder.

Riley tried to get up, but Nate ordered him to sit. Lucy looked through the back of the Bronco and found an emergency kit. Nate pulled out his cellphone and got out of her way so she could inspect Riley's injuries. She heard him first talking to Zach at headquarters, reporting exactly what happened and asking for immediate backup, then he swore, "We got cut off. Dammit."

"Try the radio," Riley said. "That little girl hit it, but I think it's still working."

Nate ran around to the passenger side and after a couple tries got through to Fredericksburg PD. He reported what happened, gave the make, model, and license number of the truck. "What's he look like?" Nate asked Lucy.

"I'm fine," Riley said.

"No, you're not." Lucy had patched up his neck, shoulder, and head, but he'd been cut up bad and there were at least three buckshot embedded in his upper shoulder. One was closer to his artery than she would like, and she feared it was nicked. She'd slowed the bleeding but couldn't get it to stop, and too much exertion would cause his blood pressure to rise. "Hold still."

She looked at Nate and shook her head. Riley wasn't going to die, but he wouldn't be walking to Fredericksburg right now.

Nate reported, "Officer hit, need ambulance at our location."

"We have to get out of here," Riley said.

"The van is toast, this truck isn't moving," Nate said.

"And you're not walking," Lucy added. "Don't move, Riley. I'm serious."

"The river," Riley said. "Look."

They looked back and saw that the creek had crossed the road and water was surging. It seemed to rise even as they watched.

"I heard on the radio, right before the attack, that the Llano had flooded 87. This is a major artery off the river. Damn, if I hadn't taken my eyes off the road to double-check, I might have seen the spikes."

"They had the spike strip under the water," Nate said. "No one could have seen it, not on a day like today."

Nate told Fredericksburg dispatch that the creek had flooded the road and they had to find higher ground.

The water had already topped the guardrails. Though the momentum kept the water mostly moving downstream, the wide space of the roadway gave it a lot of room to spill over. The van, which was closer to the river, had water up to the wheel well.

"I have to get our supplies," Nate told Lucy, and handed her the radio. "Give them a description of the suspects." Nate ran through the rising water back to the van. First thing he did was pull the spike strip from the road.

Lucy kept pressure on Riley's neck while reporting what she knew. "Trembly and the man known as John Carr were released from the van by four unknown suspects. A man and two women, plus an unknown driver. All masked in full tactical gear. White or Hispanic. The male was approximately six feet tall. One female was approximately five feet four inches, small, petite build; a second female was five foot ten, slender—I'd guess one fifty, tops. The shorter female is particularly dangerous, she fired a shotgun into Officer Riley's truck without provocation as they drove away. We fired in response, one of the suspects may have been injured in the escape."

"Status of officer?"

"Multiple contusions on his head, neck, upper right shoulder. Stable but needs emergency medical attention. We can't move him."

"I can walk," Riley said.

"Not far," she said.

"Repeat?" the dispatcher said.

"I'm telling Officer Riley that we need to keep him immobile as long as we can. But we might not have a choice—the water is rising and his vehicle is inoperable. At this rate we have five minutes before we'll have to move."

"Hold, I'll find ETA."

Lucy watched Nate retrieve their extra weapons and emergency pack from the van. By the time he was done, he was fighting water that had risen to his thighs, holding his M4 over his head so it wouldn't be submerged. The emergency pack was strapped to his back.

She'd never seen water rise so quickly.

The dispatcher came back on the line. "Agent Kincaid, it's Fredericksburg dispatch."

"I'm here."

"Emergency crews are on their way to your location, but we have multiple situations and flooding on the road. ETA unknown—at least thirty minutes. But we have a situation one half mile from you. A nine-one-one call came in from a house on Brandenberger Road, then was cut off. The timing coincides with the attack on your vehicles."

"They could be seeking another vehicle or medical care if the girl was hit. Can you play me the call?"

"Yes."

A half minute later, Lucy heard the recording. Nate was standing next to her.

"Nine-one-one what is your emergency?"

"Someone's breaking in. I can't get to the gun safe without

them seeing me. I tried my dad, but his cell phone isn't an-
swering."

"What is your name?"

"Bobby."

"Bobby, do you know your address?"

"Sixty-eight ninety Brandenberger Road."

"How old are you?"

"Eight."

"Are you home alone?"

"My sisters are in the barn with the horses. My dad is—"
The call ended.

A kid was alone in the house and Trembly's gang was breaking in.

"Go," Riley said. "I'll be fine."

Nate didn't look like he agreed. "Can you move? At all?"

"Yes."

"As soon as the water reaches the bottom of your grill, you need to get to higher ground got it?"

"Yes, sir," Riley said with a half smile.

Nate handed him a radio. "That's on our secure channel. The range is good for a couple miles. You call us if you need us, understood?"

Lucy told dispatch that they were heading to the house on Brandenberger. It was less than half a mile; she and Nate could make it long before the police.

Riley said, "Go get those bastards."

Chapter Three

Sean and Jesse spent all morning sandbagging their driveway and helping neighbors do the same. Olmos Park had terrific drainage and the basin could handle even the worst storms, but the amount of water coming down was fierce, and several of the storm drains had to be cleared of debris, which had caused minor flooding of lawns and driveways. Sean, Jesse, and a group of neighbors went through the neighborhood freeing the drains. It was intensive work and sometimes difficult, but they managed to complete the task in a few hours. It could be worse. Other parts of town had far more problems than a little inconvenience.

By the time they made it back home and showered, it was well after lunch. They collapsed in the living room, too tired to play video games.

"I'm starving," Sean said.

"Me too," Jesse agreed

Neither of them moved.

"Kane and Siobhan are coming up this weekend," Sean told Jesse. "They would have been here today, but Kane had to take care of something."

"Something cool?"

"What do you mean by that?"

"Well, he has like a totally cool job."

Sean snorted. "Job. Yeah—I guess you could say that. He and Siobhan are helping the Sisters of Mercy—the missionary group that Siobhan's mother had worked for—re-locate orphans from their current school that's falling apart to a new school they built in Arteaga, which is outside Monterrey. Kane and a couple guys from his team are just making sure there are no problems." And, Sean knew, Kane wanted to keep his eye on Siobhan. Now that he and Siobhan were living together, Kane feared his enemies would use her against him. It had happened once before. But convincing Siobhan to lay low was impossible. She always put others before herself—something Sean admired. He would have been down helping, except now he had other responsibilities— namely a son who had lost his mother eight weeks ago.

"Is it dangerous?"

"Probably not, but anytime you're dealing with outlying areas in Mexico, you have the potential for problems. The Sisters are usually left alone by the cartels and gangs—unless they go into the wrong territory." What they really needed was for law enforcement to take care of the most violent gangs and cartels and push them out of the communities so kids had a chance at a real future. But Sean had long ago realized the problem was bigger than one person. He thought at one time that Kane tilted at windmills because he kept fighting a losing war, then his brother did something like escorting orphans and nuns to safety, and that made everything worthwhile. One step at a time.

"Anyway," Sean said, "they'll be here tomorrow night if light aircraft isn't grounded, or Monday morning."

"Where'd Lucy go so early?"

"Up to Brady, a few hours away." Sean was surprised he hadn't heard from her. "She and Nate are bringing in a prisoner because the Brady jail flooded. A bank robber the

local cops caught up there that the FBI has been looking
for."

"That's cool, too."

"You want to be a cop?"

He shrugged. "I don't know. Maybe. I really liked talking
to that guy from the crime lab at our Fourth of July party.
Ash, I think his name was. He has a totally cool job, too."

Sean appreciated forensics. It required the same focus as
computer programming, and when you loved what you were
doing, the tediousness disappeared. "Fortunately, you're only
thirteen—you have time to figure it out. Let's make lunch. I
stocked up a couple days ago, so anything you want."

"Anything? Can you make those grilled sandwiches we
had last week?"

"You mean the Cuban sandwich?"

"Yeah. They were great."

"Sure—I don't have any more of the Cuban bread, but I'll
make do with French rolls. That's the only thing Lucy can
cook, but I'm still better." According to her family, Lucy had
never been proficient in the kitchen. However, sometimes
Sean thought Lucy cooked awful on purpose—so she didn't
have to be in charge of the kitchen. It was almost endearing,
a little sneaky, but he would never call her on it. He liked
cooking.

Together they prepared and grilled the sandwiches. They
were nearly done eating when his cell phone rang. It was FBI
headquarters.

"Rogan," he said.

"Sean? This is Rachel Vaughn."

Immediately, he tensed. Why would Lucy's boss be calling him? "Yes."

"First, Lucy is fine."

Not a good way to start the conversation. "Why wouldn't
she be?"

"The transport she was in was ambushed. Two prisoners were freed by four assailants. The police officer who was escorting them was injured, but both Agent Dunning and Lucy are fine."

"Why is she not calling me?"

"I don't have all the details yet—we're getting them secondhand from Fredericksburg PD. But we believe that one of the gunmen was shot and they are holed up in a private residence near where the ambush occurred. Last I heard, Dunning and Kincaid were heading there but have gone radio silent. I wanted to keep you in the loop."

"Where are they?" Sean asked.

"I can't have you in the middle of this, Rogan."

Sean wanted to hit something. "I want to come to headquarters and monitor the situation." He swallowed his pride. "Please, Rachel. That's my wife and my best friend."

Rachel agreed. "All right, I'll authorize it. Zach Charles is monitoring all radio transmissions, and Agent Proctor and a team are already en route. If you create any problems for Zach or my office, I will personally escort you out."

"Yes, ma'am." He hung up.

"What happened?"

Jesse looked panicked. Sean realized he needed to better control his emotions for his son. Jesse had just lost his mother—he was on an emotional roller coaster.

"Lucy and Nate are pursuing a group of fugitives. We're going to FBI headquarters so I know what's going on. But Lucy and Nate are the best at this sort of work. They're going to be fine."

They had to be fine. Lucy had to come home. Sean didn't know what he would do if he lost her.

Chapter Four

Sam had a great thing going with Reggie. There had been four of them, and they'd successfully robbed four banks and six high-end businesses last year in Dallas. Before that, Reggie and Sam alone had robbed dozens of places all through the South while they were trying to figure out what to do with their lives. They hadn't been caught, weren't even under suspicion of being involved. Of course, they had Reggie's little brother, Kirk, to teach them what *not* to do, considering he'd spent a few years behind bars.

Once they brought Amanda and Jacob into the mix, everything got better. Their method was brilliant. Amanda was calm and collected and had the technical skills to shut down security; Reggie had the intimidation act down pat; Sam was fast and light and could grab enough to keep them going while they planned the next big score; and Jacob was a fucking *brilliant* wheelman.

Then Sam's ma insisted they include Kirk and SueAnn. Sam should have stood up to her. He wanted to. He'd known it was a bad idea. But Sam couldn't say no to his own mother, and Reggie thought Monica Trembly walked on water. Probably because Sam's ma stood up to Reggie and Kirk's good-for-nothing dad years ago and said that if he laid one more hand on his boys she'd shoot him full of buckshot.

So Sam went along with it, against his better judgment. And everything went to hell. Because both Kirk and SueAnn were fucking *crazy.* Separately they were bad enough, but *together* they were like Bonnie and Clyde. Thelma and Louise, if Thelma were a guy. SueAnn was Monica's baby girl who could do no wrong. And his mother couldn't see how volatile the kid was. She was certainly her father's daughter, and there was no love lost between Sam and SueAnn's dad, who— thank the Lord—wasn't *his* father.

Or maybe Monica knew exactly who and what SueAnn was and just liked watching the fireworks.

With Reggie gone . . . damn, he *really* didn't want to think about it. He missed his buddy, who was closer than his own brother. Sam liked Jacob fine enough, but he wasn't Reggie. The kid was smart and stayed under the radar, always a good thing. Until now.

Sam was positive that the asinine idea for Jacob to get arrested came from Kirk. Jacob was smart—except when he listened to Kirk. Sure, having the inside information helped, but they could have figured out a better way to spring him.

Of course, flooding the basement had been brilliant. Sam wasn't surprised that the flood had been Amanda's idea.

And now they were stuck. SueAnn had been shot in the arm, and the truck was hot. Sam wasn't a violent man. SueAnn had wanted to kill all three cops, but Sam knew better. Robbing banks and breaking out of jail was bad enough—but kill a cop? Hell, they'd have every fucking law enforcement agency from the podunk Brady PD to the Texas Rangers out looking for them, and they didn't have enough money to stay hidden forever.

They had to lay low until tomorrow night when they'd score big; then they could head for their property in Mississippi. They had a place on the bayou, not in anyone's name—at least, no one that the FBI or anyone could trace to them—and they would have enough dough to live for a long time. Then he and Amanda could grieve properly for Reggie, and SueAnn and Kirk could fuck like rabbits, and Jacob might be able to win back his ex-girlfriend. And their ma? Well, Sam suspected she'd go right back to SueAnn's daddy up in Amarillo.

Fine by Sam.

But first, they needed a clean vehicle to get out of the area.

They'd found the girls in the barn, just down the road. Fifteen, sixteen—somewhere thereabouts. They were fighters, and one of them pulled a rifle out from behind a hay bale, but Sam grabbed it. Tied them both up with their horses, who were freaked out by the thunder and lightning. Made sure they didn't have a phone on them. They spilled the beans that their ma was long dead and their father was out helping a neighbor shore up his levee.

There was a pickup truck in the garage with a camper shell. Jacob got to work on it—taking off the plates and making sure it was in running order. Amanda stayed with him.

Sam went into the house with his ma, Kirk, and SueAnn. The door was unlocked. Two large black Labs came running to them. They barked once, then got excited at the visitors.

Stupid-ass guard dogs, Sam thought. He scratched them behind the ears and one ran over to a basket and brought him a rope to play.

"It don't hurt much," SueAnn said as she sat down on the couch and put her feet on the coffee table.

"Baby, we gotta check it out. You're bleeding." Kirk kissed her neck and she giggled. Sam rolled his eyes.

"Knock it off," Monica said. "Sam, search the house. Grab

anything you can to stitch up SueAnn. Take off your shirt, girl, let me see if the bullet is still in your arm."

Kirk helped SueAnn off with her shirt. Sam ignored them. He first locked the dogs in the mudroom, then found a fully stocked first-aid kit in a small bathroom. He handed it to his mother, then went down the hall and looked through the bedrooms.

Master room—masculine, a picture of the father and his now-dead wife on their wedding day on one wall. He must not bring other women here, it'd be right creepy to have sex with the dead wife looking down on him. But Sam verified that there were no women's things in the room—no perfume or clothing. He glanced at the pictures and did a double take.

Two girls. And a boy. The most recent picture looked like he was seven or eight.

Where was the kid? Was he with the dad at the neighbor's?

Sam pulled out his gun. He wasn't going to shoot a kid, for chrissakes, but he couldn't have him calling the police or getting his father. He looked in the closet. No kid, but a big-ass gun safe was front and center. *Well, shit.* The girls had a rifle in the barn, and now there were guns in the house? Did the kid have access to them? The safe was locked, but that didn't mean the kid couldn't get inside.

The police were already on the way because of the feds, but they had been listening to the police scanner and knew the roads were fucked up. Amanda was a planner, and they had created enough hazards in this storm to delay the cops for a while. Besides, they only needed a few minutes to stitch up SueAnn, grab supplies, and swap vehicles. Jacob had another truck waiting for them when they reached the main highway—and he and Amanda knew all the back roads. They just had to get going.

He left the master bedroom. "Kirk, get Jacob's ETA," he called down the hall. "I'm going to check the other rooms, but I want to be outta here in five minutes or less, under-stand?"

"Gotcha."

Sam continued down the hall and looked into each of the bedrooms. The girls' rooms shared a bathroom. One girl was all frilly and into pink and purple and had posters of country music stars like Thomas Rhett and Sam Hunt and a young clean-cut kid Sam didn't recognize. The other girl was a tomboy, had trophies up the wazoo—for wrangling. Impressive, for a girl. Junior this, junior that. Not a pink sock to speak of.

The boy's room had a space theme going on and an eclec-tic collection of Legos and comic books strewn everywhere. He didn't see the kid, but he now knew his name from schoolwork on his desk: *Bobby*.

"Bobby, you in here?" Sam called out. "I don't want to hurt you, kid, but I need you to come with me. Just to keep my eye on you."

Nothing.

The bunk bed was raised and didn't provide any place to hide underneath. Sam opened the closet, which overflowed with stuffed animals but no kid. Sam poked around, but the kid wasn't hiding in there.

Shit.

He went back to the living room. "There might be a kid around here somewhere," Sam told SueAnn and his mother. "I can't find him."

Monica had finished bandaging SueAnn's arm. His sister was drinking whiskey straight from the bottle. Sam grabbed it from her and slammed it down on the table. "No drinking on the job, dipshit."

"Don't call your sister names," Monica said. "The bul-let was stuck in there, I gave her the bottle to dull the pain while I dug it out." She showed him the bloody bullet she'd extracted.

"If you hadn't shot at the cops, they wouldn't have fired back."

"We should have whacked them when we had the chance," SueAnn said.

"Enough of this," Monica said. "Your brother is right about one thing: If you get branded a cop killer, all bets are off. We're already going to be the subject of a manhunt, we need to get out of here and finish what we started. We have one job to do, and we're going to do it, understand? No going off the reservation, hear me?"

"Yes, Ma," SueAnn said.

Sam hoped Monica could keep the brat under control, because they couldn't afford any screw-ups in the next thirty-six hours. He looked at his watch. They'd been here for twelve minutes. Not all that long, which was a good thing. But he'd wanted to be out in ten.

Sam peered outside. The rain was still a bitch. Branches and bushes that had been ripped from the earth littered the landscape, stopping only when they encountered a barrier. No cop cars. He could barely see Jacob and Amanda in the garage across the muddy gravel drive. Kirk was running back toward the house, not caring that he was drenched. He put his thumbs up when he saw Sam looking at him.

"We're ready," Sam told his mother. "Let's get out of here."

"Grab one of the girls, Sam," Monica said.

"No." Shit, what was his mother thinking? They didn't need a hostage. "She'd slow us down."

"We're behind schedule, if those feds are looking for shelter, this is one of the first places they'll find. I— What was that?"

Sam didn't hear anything.

Monica jumped up and stomped into the kitchen. Sam followed. A door vibrated, as if it had just been closed.

Monica opened the door and said, "There you are. You didn't look very hard, did you, Sam? You're getting soft."

Sam looked inside the pantry. A boy was crouched in the corner. He had a knife in his hand. Sam almost admired the kid.

"Bobby, right?" Sam said.

The kid didn't respond.

"Look, drop the knife. I'm not going to hurt you."

Monica pulled out her gun and aimed it at the kid. "Drop the knife or you're dead, boy."

Bobby dropped the knife. Monica grabbed him by the arm and pulled him up. "Got our hostage, let's go."

A gust of wind tore through the house and Kirk shouted over the storm, "We got company!"

This day could not get any worse.

Chapter Five

There wasn't much cover along the long driveway leading up to the house on Brandenberger Road, but Lucy and Nate had two advantages: First, the house was around a bend; and second, as they got closer there were more trees to hide their approach. So they ran in the open, then hunkered down behind a small woodshed as soon as they caught sight of the house. Lucy was so wet she didn't even feel it anymore. As they watched, a man—neither Trembly nor Carr—left the house and headed to what appeared to be a large carport on the other side of a barn. He wore all black with a gun on his hip and a rifle slung over his back.

Nate called into Fredericksburg on the radio. "Agent Dunning here. We're in position near the house. One hostile visible, possibly patrolling. The suspect's vehicle is in front of the house. ETA?"

"Dunning," a male voice came on the phone, "this is Rabke. We have a problem. Someone diverted a drain right onto the highway, and several cars are stuck and in danger of being washed off the road. We can't pass until we clear this."

"On purpose?"

"That's what my crew is telling me. And with the amount of water coming down, they have to fix it immediately."

"We have a young boy in immediate danger."

"We can't pass at this point. We're working as fast as we can—once it's clear, we'll be there in ten minutes."

"How can they get out of here?" Nate asked the local deputy. "The highway isn't an option."

"There are dozens of roads all through the area. At least four off Brandenberger, ranch roads mostly. With a truck they should make it. There's several places to cross Beaver Creek to the west. It's riding high, the bridges could be out. They're not feats of engineering. Some roads only go through when the creek isn't running. If they cross, they'll head to Hilda, where there are several roads going off to several highways. If they don't, they'll head south toward Loyal Valley—again, several ways out from there. We can't cover all of them."

"Contact my office. Send them a map of the area with all possible exits marked. Over and out," Nate said, and swore under his breath. "I hope we have the people to cover, but getting up here is going to be difficult, and we can't rely on the sheriffs when they have the storm to contend with. And we have to assume Trembly's gang has the kids. What did the kid say? Two sisters?"

"They were in the barn."

"We check the barn first, see what's going on, then head to the garage. If they've split up, it'll be easier to take them down. Ready?"

She nodded. Nate led the way to the back of the barn. They walked around, hugging the wood. The barn was in good repair, and they could hear horses inside jittery from the storm. There was a side door, which was good because if they walked around to the front they'd be visible from the house. Nate pushed. It was locked from the inside.

"We have to take the chance," Nate said. "It's only ten feet from the corner to the opening."

Lucy followed. Nate peered around the corner. He gave her the signal and then ran low to the opening of the barn, guns out, expecting to find a hostile.

No one, just four horses antsy in their stalls.

Nate went right, Lucy left, and they searched the barn.

In the first empty stall, Lucy found two teenage girls back-to-back, hog-tied, and gagged. She whistled and Nate came running.

"We're FBI," Lucy whispered, pulling the gags out of their mouths. "Don't make a sound." She started with the knots, but Nate said, "I got this, clear the rest of the barn."

Lucy did—no hostiles anywhere. A minute later she was back in the empty stall and Nate already had the girls out of their ropes much faster than she could have done it.

"Bobby, our brother," one of the girls said. "He's inside."

"We know. He called nine-one-one," Lucy said. "What happened?"

"We were soothing the horses, the thunder freaks them out. And then these two guys came in with guns and tied us up. Asked as about our parents—"

"Where are your parents?"

"Or dad is at our neighbor's ranch—they have to shore up part of the creek or we'll all flood. Our mom died five years ago."

"Bobby's eight?" Lucy asked.

"Yes—you have to help him, please. We didn't tell them he was in the house, we said we were home alone. Bobby's smart, he'd hide or something. But what if they found him?"

Nate said, "Did you hear anything else? Did they say something?"

The younger sister, about fourteen, said, "They want our truck. It's old, didn't start right away, but one of the guys said he could fix it. And if they can't, they were going to wait for my dad and— And, well, they've been here about fifteen or twenty minutes."

"Is there someplace in here that you can hide?" Nate said.

"The tack room. It has a lock on the door."

"Do it."

The younger girl ran over to the corner and picked up a rifle. "We tried to get to it, but they stopped us."

"Take it in the room. Law enforcement will identify themselves, okay? Don't shoot at the cops. Be safe, don't make a sound, until someone comes for you. If you hear anything, stay put."

"Just get our brother," the older sister said. "Please."

The sisters ran to the back of the barn and locked themselves into the tack room. Nate and Lucy went over to the opening of the barn—the doors had been secured open on the outside, so there was no way they could close them or use them for cover without making a lot of noise.

The sound of the old truck starting cut through the storm. "They have it running," Nate said. "We play this by ear— the priority is making sure the kids are safe, even if we have to let Trembly go."

"Understood," Lucy said. "If Bobby found a place to hide, we ride it out and then go get him."

"Exactly."

They peered through a slat in the barn and watched as the guy who had crossed the road five minutes ago headed back to the house. He gave someone a thumbs-up sign and jogged against the wind. When he got to the porch he stopped, leaned against the house, and lit up a cigarette.

"That's Kirk Hansen, Reggie Hansen's brother," Lucy said.

"You sure?"

"I saw his mugshot in the file—he has a record. Crutcher was trying to find him for an interview, he fell off the map."

"What was he in for?"

"Armed robbery, ten years ago. Pled and did a year back when he was twenty-one."

"Maybe he just hasn't been caught."

A calm fell over Nate. He reminded Lucy so much of her brother Jack, even more than Sean's brother Kane, who was always more intense. Jack and Nate could be just as intense, but when they were on a job, they had a calmness about them even at the height of danger. It reassured Lucy that they would find Bobby and bring him to safety.

"Our best bet is to go out the side door and around the back of the barn to the garage," Nate said. "Based on what we saw, there should only be two people in the garage with the truck. Likely Hansen is telling the others they're ready to go. They bought themselves some time with the flooding on 87, but they aren't going to want to wait around. Every minute they lose means we have a better chance of tracking them."

"We take those two out quietly," Lucy said, "we might be able to get the others as they come out."

"If they have the kid, you focus on him. Use those negotiation skills of yours. Bobby is our number-one priority."

"Got it."

They crossed over to the side door and out of the barn. They stayed as close to the side as possible, ran around the back, and Nate halted at the corner. "The girl is heading to the house. If we go around back, we should be out of sight of the door and surprise the driver."

Lucy followed Nate. Ten seconds later, he had his gun on John Carr, who was removing the license plate from the front of the truck. "Don't move," Nate said. "Don't speak. Search him." Nate kept watch on the house while Lucy searched Carr. He had a handgun in the small of his back, which she confiscated. That was it. He'd already ditched his orange jumpsuit for clothes.

Lucy cuffed Carr to the door handle of the old truck.

"Well, shit," Carr muttered.

"We're made," Nate said a moment before Lucy heard faint shouts and a door slam shut.

Carr said, "I'd suggest you skedaddle while you can. Sam isn't a violent man, I swear to the Lord, and neither am I. But the rest of our family? They're batshit crazy."

Lucy looked him over. She didn't see the resemblance to Sam Trembly, but Sam only had one brother. "Jacob Trembly, not John Carr," she stated flatly. It was a guess, but she didn't think she was wrong.

"Smart cookie. Now be smarter and get out of here."

Nate ignored him. "The girls are safe, we find the boy."

Jacob paled. "It wasn't supposed to happen like this."

"What'd you think was going to happen when you attack three cops, escape custody, and take a family hostage?" Lucy snapped.

She needed to ignore him, because right now they were at a standoff of sorts. They didn't know what the gang was going to do. The longer they stayed in the house the better chance backup would arrive, and that could put the boy in even greater danger.

"My guess is they're going to make a run for it," Lucy said to Nate. "That was the primary goal, and I don't think anything has changed."

"Okay. If the boy isn't with them, we engage. If he's with them, we negotiate."

They waited only a minute before the front door opened. Hansen stepped out half carrying Bobby, his left arm around his waist, Bobby's feet scrambling to find footing. Hansen had a gun in his hand. Three people emerged behind them, all women. An older woman and two young women. The short one had a bandage on her arm, blood seeping through. She was the one Nate had hit after she shot up Riley's patrol.

"Well, shit," Nate said. "Who's that older woman?"

"Jacob, help yourself," Lucy said. "You know we're going to find out."

"Our mother," he mumbled.

"And the girls are your sisters?" It was a guess, but it made sense as soon as Lucy said it. She'd read the file and knew that the Trembly family was close and Crutcher hadn't been able to track any of them down.

The Tremblys and Hansen were approaching their truck, the idea of stealing another gone. Unfortunately, they had Bobby with them.

"We can't let them take the kid as a hostage," Lucy said.

Nate took Jacob's cuffs off the truck and cuffed his hands behind his back. "We're going to track you down, all of you," Nate said into his ear. "But if that kid is hurt in any way, I'll shoot you." He looked at Lucy and nodded.

Lucy focused her energy on Bobby and defusing this situation before anyone got hurt.

They stepped out of the garage. Nate had Jacob in front of them, holding him tight with one hand, his gun in the other. Nate looked every bit the soldier he had been.

The gang was climbing into the truck from the house side, using the vehicle as a shield. The older sister slid over to the driver's seat.

"Stop!" Lucy shouted. "We'll trade your brother for the boy."

Hansen shoved Bobby into the back seat and followed him. The younger sister climbed in as well, the boy between them. Where was Sam Trembly? Still in the house? Was he circling around?

"Trembly's not there," Lucy said to Nate. She called out to the gang, "We're not playing games. All we want is that little boy to be safe."

Jacob's mother stepped in front of the truck. She showed

no fear that two armed FBI agents had a gun on her and held her son as prisoner.

"Chica, you bring my boy to the truck and I'll turn over the kid."

"I'll meet you halfway," she said.

"I don't like this, Luce," Nate said.

"Options? Anything?"

He had none. Neither did she.

She took ahold of Jacob's restraints and walked with him ten yards toward the truck. His mother stood smugly. Lucy was betting that family would win out, that they wouldn't shoot their brother to kill her. Jacob had gotten himself arrested to pass information to his brother—that was the only reason she could see that he would do such a thing—and they had this escape well planned. The flooded jail. The spike strips. Disabling a major road drainage system to prevent law enforcement from reaching them quickly. You didn't plan an elaborate escape only to kill your team.

She didn't give up her weapon; she didn't like this any more than Nate, but she couldn't forget Bobby's terrified and determined face. That kid was her focus, though he was now out of her line of sight.

She stopped twenty yards from the truck. "Your turn," she called out. "Let Bobby go."

"You for him," Mrs. Trembly said. "I'm not going to ask twice."

Lucy looked the woman in the eye. She didn't bat an eye.

"Let him out first."

"You're not in charge here. My son is unarmed. You can't shoot him."

"He's an escaped prisoner. I'll take my chances with the review board."

Mrs. Trembly's lips tightened. "You hurt my boy, you answer to me."

"Let Bobby go. When he's safe, I'll come."

She knew it was dangerous, but if she let them take a little boy into this storm, what would happen if they left him in the middle of nowhere? Or worse. They could kill him.

Or you.

"Time's up, Agent."

"Let Bobby out."

Someone was watching her. She had an odd sense, as she always did when something was amiss. This wasn't Nate—she knew how it felt now to be watched by someone on her team. This was different.

She glanced behind her a second too late. Sam Trembly was there with a gun on her back. "Drop your gun or you're dead."

She dropped her gun. She hadn't heard a gunshot, and she didn't see any blood on Sam. What happened to Nate? He'd been right behind her!

Sam grabbed her, pulled her extra gun from her ankle holster, and tossed it into the mud. Then he dragged her to the truck.

"Let the kid go. Please," Lucy said. "You don't want a little kid—"

"Shut up. Jacob, let's go. Get in the back."

Sam pushed Lucy into the back seat. Kirk Hansen took her arm and held a gun to her head. "Don't be a hero, because you'll be dead."

Bobby was cowering on the floor.

Sam got into the driver's side as the older sister slid over.

Suddenly Mrs. Trembly collapsed in the middle of the driveway. A drenched man Lucy had never seen before, with fear and anger etched into his face, ran toward the truck. He fired at the truck.

"Shit!" Sam said.

That had to be Bobby's dad. Sam sped out of the driveway full speed. Lucy looked through the side window and saw Nate staggering from the garage, his badge in hand. He was shouting at Bobby's father, but Lucy couldn't hear him. Sam sped around the bend, then turned off on a side road.

"Jacob's not in the back!" SueAnn said. "You left him!"

"That was the kid's father. Dammit, he got the drop on us. All this bullshitting around. I told you to let the kid go as soon as we had Jacob."

"Your ma said no," Hansen said.

"And now she's dead!"

Lucy didn't think that the woman was dead, but she'd been shot, and Lucy had no idea what happened to Jacob. All she saw was a blur as Sam drove away.

"Mandy! Get the map!"

Amanda Trembly was in the passenger seat trying not to cry. She fumbled for a map. Lucy looked over and realized it was extensive and someone had written a lot of notes along the roads.

"A hard right will take us to the creek. There's several roads through there, but with the storm Jacob said we might not be able to pass over. Most of the roads you can only use when there's no water, but there are two small bridges. One is just wood, the other is wood and metal, but it's old. Jacob checked them out yesterday morning, they were fine, but with the water—"

"Get me to the closest one."

"Let Bobby and me out," Lucy said.

SueAnn slapped her. "Who said you could talk?" She slapped her again. "That's for your boyfriend shooting me."

"Leave her alone!" Sam ordered. "Damn, someone's following us."

He made a hard right and Lucy had no idea where they were. The road wasn't paved—the rain had made the hard earth soft and muddy, but not muddy enough to get them stuck.

Lucy resisted the urge to rub her face where SueAnn had hit her. It was sore, raw, and she tasted blood.

Sam was furious and worried. Lucy couldn't shake what Jacob had said: that Sam wasn't violent. Was that the truth? Or just fast talking by an escaped convict?

"He's gaining, Sam!" Kirk Hansen said.

"Shut up and let me drive," Sam said.

"He shot Ma. What if . . . ?"

"She's fine. It hit her calf. We'll deal with Ma later, okay?"

"I can't believe you left her."

"What was I supposed to do? If we'd have just driven straight through, none of this would have happened, but you had to come up with some stupid-ass plan to swap cars when there was *no fucking need to*!"

"Don't yell at me." Amanda pouted. "I came up with the idea to flood the jail. I figured out how to divert the drainage system on the highway. And Jacob thought that swapping cars would buy us time. I was at that house this morning— they were packing up. I thought they were going on a trip, or to get away from the storm. How was I to know they didn't actually go?"

Sam took a deep breath, slowly let it out. He was wrestling with his anger. It was a very interesting sibling dynamic, Lucy thought. She was the youngest of seven. She could see this family, dysfunctional as it was, as a unit. And Sam was the leader. Even SueAnn, who—just like Jacob said—was half-crazy, listened to him.

"The breakout was brilliant, Mandy. I mean that. But sometimes you let your brains get ahead of you. Simpler is usually better, okay?"

"I'm sorry." She rubbed her stomach and shifted in her seat.

"Are you okay? Are you hurt?"

"No—just feel sick. We left Jacob."

"We didn't have a choice. I'll figure it out. I promise."

"I know you will, Sam, but—I miss Reggie."

"Me too."

Interesting, Lucy thought. *Had Amanda been in love with Reggie?*

Kirk said, "We can kill the hostages and dump them out."

"Shit, what did I say? Kill a cop, and everything is ten times worse. And I'm not killing a kid."

Sam followed the road as it sharply turned, then suddenly veered off the road—a tree limb had fallen across the path. For a second Lucy thought they were stuck in mud, then the gears kicked in and they spun out of it, and Sam turned back up to the road.

She held tight to Bobby. "It's going to be okay," she whispered in his ear.

"Don't lie to the kid," SueAnn said.

"I have an idea," Amanda said. "Dump them."

"Yeah!" SueAnn said with a wicked smile. "*Finally,* I get to shoot someone."

"No," Sam and Amanda said simultaneously.

Amanda continued, "Half a mile, we'll be close to the river. The first bridge isn't much farther. If we toss them out, the fed chasing us will stop to get them. It'll give us time to get away. Once we get over the bridge, we have five different ways we can go. They won't know which one, and they're not going to take the kid with them looking for us."

Amanda was actually very smart, Lucy thought. Nate wouldn't pursue armed suspects with a child in the car.

"We toss the kid only," Kirk said. "We need a hostage."

"No," Amanda said. "We keep her, we're going to be in

a whole lick of trouble. We need to travel light. We have a plan, remember?"

"Toss the kid, kill the cop."

"Shut up, Kirk," Sam said. "Okay. Next bend, throw them out. No guns, SueAnn, or I swear, I'll kill you myself."

"Party pooper," SueAnn pouted.

Lucy hated the plan. Not only because it was dangerous for her and Bobby, but also because she didn't trust Kirk and SueAnn.

As they rounded the bend, Lucy thought that Sam was bluffing. That he wouldn't actually have her and Bobby thrown from the truck.

She was wrong.

"Do it," Sam ordered.

Kirk opened the rear door of the truck and said, "Jump."

Lucy held tight to Bobby. "Don't—"

SueAnn pulled her gun. "Ten, nine, three, two . . ." She jumped numbers quickly.

She aimed.

Lucy said, "Slow down, please!"

Sam took his foot off the gas just a fraction.

"One!" SueAnn grinned.

Lucy didn't close her eyes. She couldn't, she had to know where she was falling. She held Bobby close to her chest and dropped away from the truck.

She hit hard in the mud and Bobby fell from her grasp. They started rolling quickly down toward the roaring creek. "Grab the bush!" she screamed but didn't know if Bobby heard her.

He clawed at the roots of a half-submerged bush and held on. She reached for the bush next to him. Touched it. Held on tight. Slowed her descent. The muddy creek slapped at her legs, seeming to rise with each passing second. Debris hit her

as it went past. Pain radiated up her legs even as they went
numb from the cold water.

The bush pulled out of the saturated ground and she started
down toward the surging water.

"Hold on!" she yelled at Bobby. "Help is coming. Hold
tight!"

Then the current took her downstream.

Lucy was a strong swimmer, but fighting the current to get
back to the side would quickly exhaust her. She let the water take her, focusing on keeping her head above water. Her
Kevlar vest weighed her down, but she couldn't maneuver to
get it off. She focused on staying above water.

The creek hadn't topped its banks yet, but it was close,
making it difficult for her to find anything to grab on to. There
were few trees, and those that were along the banks were
short, scraggly, and too far from the edge for her to reach.

She tried to see where she was going, but only saw water
and dark skies. A piece of fence rushed by her; she tried to
grab it to help her stay afloat but missed.

Lucy felt more than saw that the creek was turning. There
was a bend up ahead, and if she could stay to the left, she
might be able to hit the side and find something to hold on
to.

Her body ached as she fought to swim. She stayed with
the current as best she could while still moving left. Then she
saw the edge. She reached up, knowing that if she didn't grab
something she would be swept farther downstream, and
would most likely drown. She prayed that Bobby was still
holding on to that bush, that Nate got him to safety. A child
wouldn't survive this.

Lucy realized she might not survive.

You're not going to die today.

Her hand brushed against a bush and couldn't get it. The
bend was only thirty feet, she didn't have much time. She

clawed at the side of the creek; mud came off in handfuls. There was nothing to hold!

Her leg slammed into a rock beneath the surface and she cried out, drawing water into her mouth. She sputtered, willed herself not to panic. Then she saw the tree.

It was a small tree, low to the ground, with a trunk made up of several small trunks. The trunk was halfway submerged and the tree was leaning. Her weight might completely break it loose, but she had to try. It would at least slow her down and wasn't far from the edge of the bank. Against all survival instincts, she stopped fighting the current. She whirled through the water, her eyes on the tree. As soon as it was within her grasp she lunged to the left and grabbed the leaves. They were sharp and cut through her skin, but she held on. Pulled herself over to it and hugged the tree, one hand on the twisted trunk, the other on the branches.

She took a second to catch her breath. She was coughing and she'd swallowed some water, but she wanted to shout for joy: The tree took her weight. It was still rooted.

A minute later, she started moving around the tree toward the bank. She reached out to climb up, but the ground was too muddy and she couldn't. If she let go of the tree, she would be swept downstream. She was so close but so far!

"Lucy!"

She looked up. Nate was standing on the bank. She was at ground level—the creek was about to spill over into the fields. He tossed her a rope. She grabbed it and winced as the cuts on her hands stung. She wrapped the rope around her wrists in case she lost her grip but still held tight.

Suddenly she was pulled out of the water. Nate had attached the rope to a truck and someone was backing up. Ten feet later she was on solid ground.

Nate fell to his knees and unwound the rope. "Are you okay? Where are you hurt?"

"Bobby," she said breathlessly.

"We have him." Nate awkwardly hugged her. "Dammit, I thought you were gone." He held her for a second, then stood up. "Can you walk? Are you hurt?" he repeated.

"I'm okay."

She would be. She took his offered hand and he pulled her up. Her legs buckled and he put his arm around her waist to support her.

"We?" she asked.

"Robert Thomsen. Bobby's dad. He came with me."

Nate helped her into the cab. It was a tight fit with Lucy wedged between Robert and Nate. Bobby sat on Nate's lap, and his dad turned around and drove back to his house.

"The mother. Jacob Trembly."

"They're cuffed and Thomsen's girls have an eye on them."

"You left two teenagers to watch them?"

"My girls will shoot if necessary," Thomsen said. "But they're secure. I'm sorry about back there, I didn't know what was going on. Bobby left a voice mail about someone breaking into the house and I ran as fast as I could from the neighbor's house, across the fields because to drive it would have taken longer."

"He's your son," Lucy said. "I would have done the same thing." She turned to Nate. "Are you okay? You're bleeding."

"Trembly got the drop on me. The damn wind, I couldn't hear him come around behind me. He plowed me on the head. I should have known. I should have had your back."

She took his hand and squeezed. "You did. But right now, call Leo—I slid my phone under the seat in their truck, Sean can give him the GPS code to track it."

Chapter Six

Sean knew that Lucy was safe. That she was on her way into headquarters. But until he saw her—tired, wet, alive—he couldn't truly breathe.

And then there she was.

"Lucy."

He didn't know if he spoke, but she looked at him, and everything at once came crashing down. His fear. His anxiety. The knowledge that Lucy meant more to him than his own life. Without her, he wouldn't be half the man he was today.

He didn't care where he was or who saw. He strode over to her and pulled her into his arms without hesitation. Held her.

He never wanted to let her go.

"Lucy."

He breathed in deeply. She was wearing sweats that were far too big for her, and her long, thick hair was still damp. She had some cuts and bruises on her arms and face, but she was here; she was in one piece.

"I love you," she whispered.

He put his forehead against hers and breathed deeply. Truly breathed, for the first time in hours.

Nate walked into the room with a slight limp and stitches

across his forehead. Sean looked up at his friend. "Thank you," he said.

Nate didn't say anything. He clapped Sean on the back and sank into a nearby chair.

"Where's Jesse?" Lucy asked.

"When we knew you were okay, Zach went to get food for everyone. Jesse and Bandit went with him."

"Rachel let you bring Bandit into the office?"

"He's almost graduated from his search and rescue program. And he's already an official service dog, so she really can't keep him out. Besides, I think she's a dog person. Bandit has her wrapped around his little paw."

Rachel came out of her office. "I heard that, Rogan." She looked at Nate. "Agent Dunning, you're supposed to be at the hospital. I gave Leo explicit instructions."

He shook his head. "I let the paramedics check me out. No concussion. Nothing broken."

Rachel turned to Lucy. "You need to talk some sense into him. And why are you here? You were also supposed to be at the hospital."

"We're okay," Lucy said. "Really. Just cuts and scrapes, and frankly, I'm exhausted. But we wanted to come in and find out what was going on. Leo said they found their truck abandoned."

"That was quick thinking on your part, leaving your phone behind," Rachel said. "Unfortunately, by the time we arrived, they were gone. No surveillance cameras in the area, and it looks like two vehicles had been parked—by the time the ERT unit got there, there were no usable tire treads, but they're working with what they have."

"They had this well planned, except for stealing the car at the Thomsens' ranch," Nate said.

"They thought the family had left for the weekend," Lucy said. "Amanda Trembly saw them packing up. I asked Thomsen about it—he said they'd brought extra supplies to their church for people who were displaced because of the flooding. Food, sleeping bags, extra clothes, stuff like that. They were gone all morning."

"It was a good place for them to regroup—there were several back roads that they could use to escape, and difficult for the search because with no air support, it would be impossible to track them," Nate said. "They were lucky to get across the creek. They could have been caught up in a flash flood."

Lucy shivered, and Sean tightened his arm around her. She'd told him what had happened, and he suspected she'd sugarcoated the details.

Lucy said, "They knew every place where they could cross, what kind of bridge was there. Most were practically wooden planks, because most of the roads just went through the creek, which is dry most of the year." She gratefully took a bottle of water from Rachel, then said, "We told Leo and Agent Crutcher what we know. Bobby, the little boy, heard a lot when Trembly was in the house. Nate and I took his statement—he's a smart kid. He said they have something planned for tomorrow night. They never said what or where, but he heard Sam Trembly talking about sticking to the plan, that once they got through tomorrow night, they could retire. That was his exact word—*retire*. Their take from the last few robberies was good, but not enough to live on for years. I read the reports—quarter of a million estimate in cash and jewels, and jewels are hard to get rid of."

"Sunday during a storm? They have something planned?" Rachel shook her head. "We already have our analysts working double-time trying to figure out what would be big enough for them to hit. Because they seem to have access to heavy-duty equipment and some knowledge of engineering— based on their escape—we're specifically looking at any bank or jewelry store that might be vulnerable. But we're dealing with hundreds of potential targets in the greater San Antonio area alone."

"We can—" Lucy began, and Rachel cut her off.

"You and Nate are off duty for the rest of the night. I know it'll be impossible to keep you home for the next two days, and honestly, with this situation coupled with the storm we need all hands—but not tonight. You already sent in your report, and that's all I need right now."

Zach and Jesse walked in with two boxes of food from The Rib House. It smelled amazing. As soon as Jesse saw Lucy, he put his box down and ran over to her. He gave her a tight hug and said, "I'm so glad you're okay."

Sean blinked back sudden tears, then wrapped his arms around both of them. "Me too," Sean said. "Let's eat, then go home."

Bandit ran over to Nate and ran around in circles. Nate got down on the floor and let Bandit love all over him.

"You really have ruined my dog, Dunning," Sean said. "When he sees you, all obedience training goes out the window."

"He loves me more," Nate said.

Sean suspected that was true. "But he respects me." He went over to the boxes and started unpacking them, with Zach's help.

"There's enough for an army," Rachel said.

"We have an army," Zach said. "All the analysts are working overtime, and I told them it was Rogan's treat."

"I'll let everyone know," Rachel said and walked down the hall.

Sean turned to Nate. "Come home with us."

"I'm fine."

"It's not open for discussion, buddy."

Nate almost smiled. Sean had chiseled away at Nate's

shell over the last two years, but he was tough. In some ways tougher than Kane, because at least with his brother, Sean knew he was a hard-ass. Nate could be fun and socialize and seem almost normal, but Sean had been around enough military folk to know that Nate was still a soldier at heart, and his outward appearance was mostly an act. He harbored a lot deep inside and didn't let it out. It couldn't be good for him. Sean had talked to Kane about it, but Kane was hard to talk to. He simply said Nate was solid, not to worry about him.

Sean worried about his friend more than anyone.

At first, Nate looked like he was going to argue with him. And Nate's way of arguing was to remain silent and do whatever the hell he wanted. Now he said, "Bandit gets to sleep with me."

"You really *have* ruined my dog," Sean said. "He's not supposed to be on the furniture, but dog hair on the guest comforter doesn't lie."

Nate grinned. "You're a hard-ass, Rogan."

Lucy was so glad to be home.

She burrowed under the comforter and let Sean check the house and secure them for the night. She was so glad that Sean had asked Nate to stay tonight. He'd felt so guilty for something that simply wasn't his fault. They were in an impossible situation, and lucky that they weren't all dead. The Trembly gang could have killed them during the original breakout—bulletproof glass wasn't really bulletproof. It would break with enough force. And they could have easily killed Officer Riley, who was hospitalized after surgery to remove buckshot and glass from his neck. He was extremely lucky that the wild shot didn't hit a major artery.

Robert Thomsen had his children home safe. Monica Trembly was in the hospital under guard, and Jacob Trembly was in a Bexar County jail cell after being treated for

minor injuries. Crutcher had interviewed him tonight and
gotten nothing—and would go back at him tomorrow, now
that they were narrowing down the possible targets. It had
stopped raining, but the winds were fierce, howling around
the house.

Sean came in and said, "Jesse's out like a light, Bandit the
traitor dog is sleeping with Nate—on the bed—and it's just
you and me, finally." He dropped his pants and pulled off his
MIT sweatshirt. Lucy smiled. He looked so good standing
there in boxers and a threadbare gray cotton shirt.

"What are *you* smiling at, princess?" he asked.

"I can't say, you already have a huge ego."

He mock frowned and climbed into bed next to her and
pulled her close to him. At this moment, she wanted to stay
here for days. She sighed into his chest and held him close.

He kissed her head, her forehead, her lips. "Are you sure
you're okay? You have some nasty bruises."

"I'm going to make you turn off that light if you keep
pointing out my flaws."

"They're not flaws. They're badges of bravery. And I know
you're sore."

"The hot bath felt amazing. I'm waterlogged."

"You're beautiful." He kissed her. "Nate told me the truth
about what happened."

"I didn't lie to you."

"You skipped some important details."

"I didn't want you thinking about it while we were still
out there. I know you, Sean—you would have risked the
storm to come up to Fredericksburg when you wouldn't have
been able to do anything. I feel beaten up, but it's all just su-
perficial. I'm more worried about Nate because he took a
major hit to his upper back. I talked to the paramedics and
they think he should get X-rayed, but he refused. And Nate

knows his limitations, even if he regularly exceeds them. I'm glad he's here so we can keep an eye on him."

"Nate and Kane, two peas in a pod."

Lucy squirmed closer to Sean. "Enough about everything. I just want to be here with you."

"You are."

Lucy kissed Sean's neck. His chest. His biceps. His body relaxed against hers and she continued to explore. She had been scared today. Terrified, really. Not just that she would die—she'd faced her own death more than once, had accepted her mortality. But she had been terrified for little Bobby, an innocent kid caught up in violence that wasn't his making. Terrified of losing her family—Sean, and now Jesse. She didn't want to die—she had no death wish—but she mostly didn't want to leave the people she loved. The people who loved her. She had more now than she ever thought she'd have. More to love. More to lose.

She ignored her aches and bruises; she ignored her own discomfort. And as Sean gently held her, sweetly kissed her, pain disappeared as a wave of desire swept through her. It surprised her on one level and soothed her on another. That she could be here, love this man, make love to her husband.

"Lucy," Sean whispered as she ran her hands under his shirt, felt the heat radiating from his body. Her own personal furnace.

"I love you so much," she said. She ran her hands down his boxers, over his ass, holding him as close to her as possible. "You're all mine, and I never want to let you go."

"The feeling is mutual."

Sean maneuvered out of his boxers, then pushed down Lucy's sweatpants. He was gentle because he knew she was sore and bruised; he'd seen the damage when she got out of the bath. He wanted to coddle and care for her, put her in a bubble until she healed; instead, he hugged her and kissed her, let her explore at her own pace. A pace that was quickening as he kissed her stomach; as he spread her thighs and kissed between her legs, touching her, tasting her, savoring her.

Lucy gasped and held on to his shoulders, her fingers digging into his muscles as he pleasured her. He knew exactly what she liked, exactly what would make her explode. And he wanted to give her that pleasure, each and every time they made love. He wanted her to know that love and sex were entwined deeply, irrevocably. He pushed down his own deep desire for her, his own sexual need, to make sure that Lucy had the first bliss. Because nothing on earth made him happier than when Lucy fully let go.

"*Sean.*" Lucy could scarcely breathe; all she felt was heat pooling between her legs, hot blood filling her veins as she tightened her grip on Sean's shoulders. Her back arched, sweat dripped from her face, and when Sean touched her with his tongue and fingers in just that right spot, the wave washed over her and she let go.

He kissed her again, sending shivers through her body, and she came down off a peak that she knew would rise again soon. He kissed her thighs, her stomach, her chest. His hand teased one breast while his mouth teased the other.

Then he kissed her slowly. But she didn't want slow. She was already heating up again. She held his head to her and devoured his mouth as if she were starving. She loved this man, loved the way he made her feel, loved his heat, his passion for life. And when he fully entered her, she gave him her trust and her love.

"Oh, God, Lucy, I love you."

Sean was moving slowly, she felt the tension in his muscles as he controlled his body. Every sensation was exquisite, every movement designed to give Lucy these intense feelings of passion. She whispered, "I'm not fragile, Sean. Let go."

The switch flipped and he held himself deep inside her; withdrew and penetrated deep again; held it. Even in his passion, he thought of her first, she realized as the second wave threatened to take her over. Sean's arms wrapped under her legs, giving them both maximum contact, maximum pleasure. Then they both went over the top.

Sean lay on top of Lucy as his body relaxed. He kissed her over and over. "You okay? I didn't hurt anything?"

"Shh, I'm perfect."

They shifted, and Lucy spooned against Sean's body. He pulled the comforter up around her, and in minutes they were both asleep.

Chapter Seven

"We should have killed them," Kirk said as he poured coffee.

"Just stop already," Sam said. He was exhausted, and listening to Kirk bitch put him on edge.

"What? You're planning on killing that self-righteous bastard who shot Reggie, but shooting a couple of cops is *immoral*?"

"It's completely different and you know it."

Sam glanced at Amanda. It wasn't his idea to target the guy who killed Reggie. But Amanda had it in her head that they had to avenge him, and honestly, he didn't want to dissuade her. She had loved Reggie since they were all kids. But Sam also believed that as soon as they finished the score she would put retribution aside. They couldn't afford to make any mistakes, and Amanda was smart. She'd see the truth, eventually.

"Is not," SueAnn sulked. She'd been in a real shitty mood since they arrived at the safe house, and Sam was getting tired of her attitude as well. Honestly, when Kirk and SueAnn had joined their operation, that's when things started to fall apart. They didn't listen. They went off script. They were the reason Reggie had gotten killed.

Sam missed his best friend. Sure, Reggie had problems—like the fact that he trusted his no-good brother—but he was a good man. Loyal to a fault. He was funny and lighthearted, a great balance to Sam's moodiness.

He could go along with Amanda's plan of killing the Good Samaritan who had been treated like a fucking *hero* for murdering Sam's best friend. He wouldn't see it coming. *After* they settled in Mississippi and the heat died down. It was the only way it would work. He never should have told the others what the plans were. It was the week after Reggie had been killed and he'd been drunk. He didn't handle his liquor all that well, and he didn't drink much, but Reggie had been his best friend. Sam wasn't handling his death all that well, either.

But he hadn't had a lick of alcohol in three weeks, and he was clear-headed. He was not going to deviate from the plan. Sure, it was going to throw them off with Jacob in jail and Ma out of commission. He'd have to think about how to get them out later. Jacob hadn't really done anything, and nothing the police could prove. He might get out after a short stint. Of course, he didn't want his little brother in jail. He wasn't like Kirk; he wouldn't do well behind bars.

The important thing was that Jacob wouldn't rat them out. Sam trusted him. And even if he slipped up, it didn't matter much—no one, except Sam, knew the entire plan.

Problem was, now they didn't have a driver. While Amanda was capable, Sam needed her for the security system. She was the only one who could handle the electronics and that nonsense; Kirk or SueAnn could be the wheelman, but neither wanted to. They liked being in the middle of everything. And no way in hell was Sam going to let them go into the vault alone. He didn't trust either of them, family notwithstanding.

That meant changing the escape plan. It was the only way.

"We have to hit before Tuesday," Sam said. "No other option—it's this weekend or never. So we stick to the original plan, but everyone is responsible for getting themselves back here after the hit. And if this house is compromised—we meet up at the Dallas safe house in forty-eight hours. I don't want to go to prison—do you?"

"And neither does Jacob, but look where he is!" SueAnn countered.

"Walk away," Sam said. "I'll do this without you."

"You can't, and you know it."

"Don't tempt me, SueAnn."

She glared at him, but he held his own. You had to with SueAnn, otherwise she'd walk all over you.

"Now, are we done with the bullshit so we can go over the plans one more time?"

"We've been over them a hundred times," SueAnn moaned.

"And I'm sure you know them by heart, sugar," Amanda said, all sweetness to keep the peace. "But we still need to make sure we're all on the same page especially without Jacob. Then we sleep, because we need all our energy tonight."

Sam laid out his dad's old blueprints. He and Reggie had spent months planning this heist, doing recon, making sure nothing would be left to chance. And now Reggie was gone.

Reggie should be part of this . . . but thinking about him wasn't going to bring him back.

"Once we're inside," Sam said, "Amanda will take care of the security. Then we have sixteen minutes until the system fully reboots. Sixteen minutes and we have to be out. Understand? No fucking around. We get in, we grab as much as we can, we get out. We should be able to score between ten and twelve million dollars." He went through the danger of their approach, and the two ways they could get out.

"Because we don't have Jacob, SueAnn and I will go north, Amanda and Kirk will go south."

"I wanna go with Kirk," SueAnn whined.

"No," Sam said.

"You're mean."

"You'll be distracted."

"Because he's such a cutie," she said, and winked at her boyfriend.

"See what I mean? Now focus!"

He went through the dangers, the potential security, and showed them again how to use the specialized tools he'd also found in his father's belongings. Once Sam was confident they were both paying attention and wouldn't fuck this up, he told them all to go to bed and he'd wake them at nine that night.

He knew he should sleep, but he couldn't. He sat at the dining-room table of the cheap rental and thought about everything this gig had cost him. His best friend. His brother. His mother.

It had better be worth it.

Chapter Eight

There was nothing Lucy could say to convince Sean to stay home. Even Jesse conspired against her and insisted that he would be fine home alone. He even pulled her aside after breakfast and said, "Dad is really worried about you. I think you should let him come. He won't get in the way."

She couldn't help but smile. Jesse had a lot to learn about his dad, because Sean didn't sit quietly during a crisis, but she appreciated his concern. Plus, Sean had government clearance, so with the blessing of her boss, he could assist with the threat analysis. Most of the tech people at headquarters liked Sean and appreciated his skills, so it shouldn't be a problem.

The good news was that the storm had broken. Because of the updated flood protections in the downtown area, San Antonio came through with mostly wind damage and minor flooding in the suburbs. The rural areas had experienced the worst of the damage and there were still risks of flash floods, plus mudslides had devastated the hills. Many roads were impassable, and the creeks and rivers were being monitored closely. Kane called Sean in the morning and said he and Siobhan would be flying in late that afternoon. Sean filled him in on what was going on, and Kane said they would keep Jesse company.

Sean didn't want to leave Jesse alone all day, but Jesse convinced him he would be fine. "I'm thirteen, Dad. I've stayed home alone before. And Uncle Kane said he'd be here by five. Really—I'll do my math homework and then just play video games, okay?"

Sean and Lucy followed Nate to FBI headquarters at ten thirty. There was a task force meeting at eleven, run by White Collar Crimes agent Mike Crutcher, the lead agent on the Trembly case. By the time she and Nate had arrived at headquarters yesterday, he'd left to talk to Jacob Trembly at the jail. She was curious to find out what he'd learned, if anything. Lucy didn't think that he'd give up his family, but she could be wrong.

Sean clipped on his visitor badge and told Lucy that he was heading to Cyber Crimes, where the analysts were working on narrowing the field of possible hits. "Zach's there, and I'm already cleared, so don't worry about me."

He turned down the hall opposite to where Lucy's squad was housed. Lucy and Nate found Rachel in her office. "I didn't think you'd stay home," Rachel said. "The debrief is in twenty minutes. I heard your husband volunteered to assist Cyber Crimes. Normally I would say no because we have one of the best cybercrime teams in the country, but there's a lot of data and they haven't narrowed down whether they're going for a bank or a jewelry store. There are hundreds in the city, we can't cover all of them. Banks are closed—so Crutcher thinks it's going to be a jewelry store. But which one? In San Antonio or San Marcos or Austin? It could be anywhere."

"San Antonio," Lucy said. "Based on the conversation Bobby overheard, he thinks it's San Antonio."

"He's an eight-year-old kid who was held hostage at gun-point. His recollection may be clouded."

"He had it together," Lucy said. "What about Jacob Trembly?"

"Crutcher and his partner interviewed him last night and went again this morning; he's not talking. Denies there's any heist planned, says it's all a misunderstanding. We did figure out what happened up in Brady, his sister, the petite one—"

"SueAnn," Nate filled in.

"Yeah. She told the hospital she was Jennifer Smith. No I.D. She slipped out when the nurses turned their back. She wasn't seriously injured."

"We figured it was staged."

"And smart, too. Jacob goes into the jail cell, tells his brother what the plan is, the others flood the jail, they're transported out."

"But there was no guarantee that we'd pick them up, or that they'd be transferred together. And why not just break him out? Why did Jacob need to give him information?"

"Good questions," Rachel said. "Maybe Crutcher has an-swers by now. This is all on us—SAPD has their hands full with storm management, power outages, road closures. When we have a hard target we'll get backup." Her phone rang and she said, "I'll be in but might be late—I'm dealing with another issue right now. But I wanted to tell you—Robert Thomsen sent a note to the SAC last night commending you both for your actions in protecting his family. You rescued and secured his daughters, then risked your lives to save his son. Good job."

She picked up the phone, and Lucy and Nate stepped out and closed the door to give her privacy. "That's nice," Nate said. "We don't usually get a thank-you."

Even though most of the Trembly gang had escaped, Lucy

wouldn't have done anything different. A family was intact, and that was a win as far as she was concerned.

Lucy poured coffee and walked into the conference room. No one was there yet, so she sat down and looked over the report she'd sent to Rachel and Crutcher yesterday. She and Nate had written it together after Leo picked them up in Fredericksburg. Because of the urgency in this matter, formality went out the window—Crutcher needed all the information possible to do his job.

"He's late," Nate muttered. There were a handful of agents and analysts who had trickled into the room.

There was something in his tone that had Lucy wondering if Nate had a history with Crutcher, but she didn't say anything.

He finally came in with his partner, Laura Williams, nearly fifteen minutes late.

"Jacob Trembly isn't talking," Crutcher said. "I have ten minutes, then I'm heading over to the hospital to talk to the mother. When she realizes that her kids are all facing capital charges, she'll help."

Lucy disagreed. "She won't give them up. You might be able to trick her into spilling information. The harder you push, the less she'll give."

"I don't think you could possibly know that after spending five minutes with her," Crutcher said. "She's a fifty-five-year-old woman who has no record and we don't have much of a case on her—she talks, she gets probation."

Lucy mentally reviewed the family dynamic that she witnessed yesterday. The mother was a true matriarch. Based on what she witnessed and what Bobby had said, Sam Trembly was the leader, but everyone deferred to the mother.

And Bobby said she'd put a gun in his face. That was a cold woman.

Before she could comment, Crutcher went on, "Cyber

Crimes analysts are reviewing every possible target, but leaning to jewelry stores. There are dozens, but based on what
they hit before and the potential take in each store, we're
looking closely at about nine of them."

One of the task force members asked, "Why jewelry stores
and not banks?"

"Every robbery has been during the day and normal business hours. Banks are closed today and tomorrow, for the
holiday. If the intel is accurate and they're planning something for today—a Sunday—it's going to have to be a jewelry store. Of the stores on our list, one is definitely not going
to be opened—the street it's on was flooded, and while the
businesses are safe, it's shut down for at least forty-eight
hours."

"And," Laura said, "while they have someone well versed
in security, they haven't shown that they can take down a silent alarm system. Based on what we know of their previous robberies, all of which were well planned, they couldn't
have predicted the extent of the storm. It wasn't supposed to
come this far inland."

Crutcher said, "Laura and I searched Sam Trembly's trailer
in Brady early this morning and determined that he wasn't
using the place to stage his robberies. There were very few
personal items. The apartment where Jacob Trembly was
arrested for the alleged domestic violence wasn't even his
apartment—we're still trying to track down the renters, but
they're out of town. They may not have even known someone had broken in. Nonetheless, we confiscated the computer
in case Trembly used it. We have their phone records, but
their personal effects were lost yesterday."

He looked directly at Lucy. She'd heard that the FBI van
had been partly submerged and the weight of the water had
pushed it off the road and into muck. It had taken a construction tow truck to extract it, and it was being sent to the local

FBI lab to see if they could retrieve any evidence—though Lucy doubted anything was there, except maybe the recording of the escape.

She wasn't going to take his bait—she and Nate had done what they had to do to survive and protect Officer Riley. But she realized that there *was* a recording of the Trembly brothers for the entire drive. They could have communicated something that Lucy missed.

"They were using sign language to communicate—we don't have audio in the back of the van, but the camera would have caught their conversation. That's saved to the dashcam. There could be something on there that could help us."

"If it's salvageable," Crutcher said, "we'll have it. If you'd just grabbed it to begin with, we wouldn't have to cross our fingers."

Out of the corner of her eye, she saw Nate straighten his spine. This wasn't going to end well. She didn't know why Crutcher was being such a prick, but she was willing to dismiss it based on the fact that he likely hadn't slept last night. Laura looked uncomfortable as well and quickly jumped in. "We have contacted all jewelry stores in the area—plus made personal contact with the owners of the nine we believe are likely targets. They are on heightened alert. Six already employ a guard, and three are bringing in extra employees for the next two days."

Leo Proctor had walked into the room with Rachel a few minutes before and he'd maneuvered to stand next to Nate—did he sense the hostility between Crutcher and Nate as well? Leo was the head of FBI SWAT, which Nate also served on, and they were friends.

"We'll be on high alert for the next two days," Crutcher said. "We also have a team in Austin interviewing everyone who knows the Tremblys or the Hansens. They left Austin two years ago, but their last known address was a ranch outside of the city. They could still be in contact with some of their neighbors. Trembly and Hansen had worked in construction together, and we've already talked to their former employers and colleagues."

Lucy asked, "Do you know specifically what they did in construction?"

Crutcher stared at her blankly. "It was years ago, and it hardly matters. They built houses for the most part."

"What I mean is, the skills they had to flood the jail in Brady and divert the drains outside Fredericksburg to delay response when our transport was attacked, those skills may be put to use in this heist. We know that one of the people—I suspect Amanda Trembly, the sister who graduated with a degree in computer science—is the one who is handling the security systems."

"Which is all they need to do. Handle security. We have teams ready to mobilize, and we're tapped into SAPD to be notified as soon as any silent alarm is tripped or shut down—in case they're going after one of the jewelry stores that are closed. That's not likely, because the jewels are locked in a safe, and so far this gang hasn't been able to get into any of the safes—and not for lack of trying."

Lucy felt they were missing something, and then it hit her. "In all the reports, none of the jewels have been recovered. It's very difficult to fence stolen jewels, unless they have a private buyer lined up, but none of these people have those kinds of connections. And they haven't shown up on the market—"

"Agent Kincaid," Crutcher cut her off, "you handle violent crimes, let me handle white collar. Most jewel thieves hold on to the goods or sell them into a private market, where the buyer recuts or waits until the heat dies down. They move them outside of the immediate area to minimize the chance of being discovered. Many of these jewels end up in other countries."

"But none of the jewel heists yielded a payday," Lucy said. She was talking off the cuff, because there was something here that she wasn't quite seeing. "None of them scored more than twenty thousand in jewels, and that's retail—"

"Because we're not dealing with rocket scientists, Kincaid," Crutcher said.

She decided to keep her mouth shut. Crutcher was right, she didn't know a lot about white collar crimes, and she didn't want to get in the middle of it.

Crutcher glanced at his watch. "My team—monitor the jewelry stores. Keep me in the loop. I'm going to give Mrs. Trembly an offer she can't refuse, and maybe this will all be a moot point."

Okay, Lucy couldn't quite keep her mouth shut.

"Did you make that same offer to Jacob? Because while he's loyal to his brother, he is also worried about the operation and his family. He doesn't want them hurt."

"Hell no, we believe that he's one of the gang, which makes him an accessory to murder."

"Monica Trembly is involved as well. In fact, I think she's running this operation."

"There's absolutely no proof of that."

"About as much as you have on Jacob," Lucy countered. Why was Crutcher being so belligerent? "I don't think that Jacob will talk—at least not willingly. But lay out the full repercussions and he might give us something because he doesn't want anyone in his family to get hurt, especially his brother, Sam."

"Wow, you must have had a heart-to-heart with him before you let him and his brother escape."

Nate slowly rose from his seat. "Watch it, Crutcher."

"It was a simple prison transport in a fully armored van and you gave them the keys."

"Mike," Lucy said, trying to defuse the situation, "another officer was in immediate danger. They would have killed him."

"Oh, and I thought in your report you said that Jacob and Sam weren't violent? Changing your mind?"

"I said that *SueAnn and Kirk* were volatile and violent, and they—"

He waved his hand at her. "Be that as it may, backup was on the way and you blew it."

Nate took a step forward. "The roads were flooding and they sabotaged a drainage system."

"But you didn't know that at the time. You let them go. It's not important at this point—"

"You didn't read a damn thing," Nate said. "You think you know what happened? You know nothing. You weren't there. You were supposed to be my partner in this, but you couldn't be bothered. Thank God I had Kincaid with me, because you would have gotten either Officer Riley killed or that little boy killed, all because you have no idea what it's like to be on the ground."

"Get out," Crutcher said. "You're off this task force."

"That's enough, Agent Crutcher," Rachel said.

"Me? Dunning is a loose cannon, he's the one who should be reprimanded for the fuckup yesterday."

"Clear the room," Rachel said. "Everyone except Dunning, Kincaid, and Crutcher." When no one moved, she said, "*Now.*"

Everyone left. Lucy was frozen in place. She shouldn't have challenged Crutcher. She'd known that Nate was on edge from the beginning of the meeting when Crutcher accused them of screwing up the transport, she should have just let him continue without comment.

Leo was the last one out and he closed the door.

Crutcher said, "I don't have time for this. I have an interview scheduled."

"That can wait. This is your operation, Mike, but you asked for my squad's assistance, and they gave it and went above and beyond. I cannot allow you to disparage their service and sacrifice in this office. If you have a problem with how they conducted the prison transport, write it up and we'll fully investigate the situation. But you will not criticize or insult them in front of their colleagues. We're all cops here. We all know that split-second decisions are made when lives are on the line. Agents Dunning and Kincaid provided their reports last night, and they are being reviewed by ASAC Durant's staff. You were also sent a copy. I'd suggest you read it closely, file any complaint after that, and then we'll go from there. Understood?"

"Yes, ma'am," Crutcher said. He didn't look either Nate or Lucy in the eye, but he was furious. Lucy didn't care. She was both relieved and surprised that Rachel had stood up for them. Maybe she shouldn't have been surprised—Rachel had proven to be a more than competent boss, and after a few rough months at the beginning, Lucy had learned to respect her and believed that she had earned her respect in return.

"You can go," Rachel said.

Crutcher left without further comment. Rachel turned to Nate. "Don't bait him, Dunning. I found no fault with what happened yesterday, but this is Mike's investigation, and we're just assisting. He has seniority and the respect of his supervisor. Granted, he was an ass today, but he wasn't there, he has no idea what he's talking about, and I'll make sure his supervisor knows that. But you need to stay out of it."

"Yes, ma'am," Nate said. He was still angry, but Rachel had taken the edge off his anger.

"Lucy, I was interested in what you had to say about the family dynamics. If you feel comfortable writing up a basic profile beyond what you provided in the report last night, it would help."

"I will. I think the single most important thing to remember here is that this is planned to be the last heist. They want to quit—at least Sam does. So it's going to be big, and I don't see any of these jewelry stores—unless they have a high-value object—being the targets."

"But they're open, and the Trembly gang has never hit a closed business or bank. They use threats and intimidation to control the hostages, and they use the chaos as part of their escape."

Rachel was right, but Lucy thought they didn't have enough information.

"However," Rachel continued, "the analysts are still working on this. The jewelry stores popped because they most closely match the MO, but we can't discount that there may be a completely different plan in the works. They're looking at the previous crimes in new ways—and your husband is instrumental in helping them, though that fact I may withhold from Mike until he gets his head on straight. Sean understands security systems as well as or better than anyone here. We already knew that the banks and jewelry stores had a similar type of security system—not the same monitoring company, but the same programming. So we're going through our most likely targets and looking for systems with that same programming in order to narrow the field. Sean says it's a top-of-the-line system but flawed—each individual company that uses it is fixing the flaw, but it has to be done on-site and not every system has been updated. It's a lead, and they're running with it."

"Thank you, Rachel. And I'm sorry, I didn't mean to bait Agent Crutcher."

"You speak up when you have something to say, and I appreciate that. He was out of line. I know what happened yesterday, and based on what we know and the statement we received from Officer Riley and the Brady PD this morning—that's another reason why I was late—there was nothing else you could have done. But for now, stay away from Mike. Nate—you should take the day off."

"Is that an order?"

"No. You're still technically on call this weekend. But you can be on call at home."

"I'll stay."

She stared at him.

"I'll avoid Crutcher."

"Thank you."

She left and Lucy turned to Nate. Nate said, "That guy's an asshole."

"No argument, but let it go." She put her hand on his forearm. "Are you really okay?"

He stared at her, showing more emotion in his expression than she'd ever seen. "I thought I'd lost you yesterday in the floodwaters. And all I could think about was how I couldn't face Sean and tell him I let you die."

Her heart twisted. How could she make Nate understand? "Nate, that wasn't your fault. None of it was. You can't take the burden for everyone's safety on your shoulders. We did everything we could do, and we're both alive, and that's what matters."

He sat back down at the conference table; Lucy sat next to him. Nate said, "I was never close to my sister. Jenny's so much older than me. Smart, a scientist, and I guess because of age and interests, we don't really have anything in common. And my parents were in their forties when they adopted me. I loved them, they were good people, but I never felt like we were all that close. Like I had a family or anything, until the Army. For ten years, my unit was my family, and now you and Sean are the closest thing to family I have. I just wanted you to know that."

She squeezed his hands. He was still tense. "I know that," she said.

"Good. I'm going to talk to Leo about some stuff." He left quickly, and Lucy suspected that he had become more emotional than he wanted to.

Lucy went to her desk and read the file on the Tremblys again. Before yesterday's escape, they didn't have much to go on. They'd identified Samuel Trembly because of prints, and they suspected Kirk Hansen was involved because he had a record and no one knew where he was. But that was hardly enough to get a warrant—until yesterday when they had collected quite a bit of evidence from the Thomsen house. The gang hadn't worn gloves.

But there was nothing on Sam's sisters, his brother, or his mother. It wasn't until the escape yesterday that any of them had been put in the file. The only reference was that the attempt to locate them after Sam had been ID'd had failed—the family had long since moved from Austin and didn't have a known address.

She reviewed the first series of robberies from Dallas. Four suspects, none identified. Sam, Reggie, and who? Lucy would guess Amanda and Jacob. They were smart, calm, not violent. And none of the Dallas robberies had resulted in more than minor injuries. It wasn't until the last five locally that things got out of hand. They were also bigger, bolder, and had a larger score. But still nothing to retire on.

Whatever they had planned, it was big. It would need to be cash or something easily convertible, not jewelry. Crutcher may not put weight on the statement of an eight-year-old, but Lucy did. She'd met Bobby, talked to him. He had been hiding in the house and heard much of the Tremblys' conversation. He might not have understood the context, but Lucy had interviewed enough children to know how they processed information and how to determine whether they were interpreting or quoting. *Retire* was the key word. That implied one final act in order to have enough funds to get out of the business. To *retire*, they'd need millions for six people. They also had to have a place to regroup, a fortress or home where they were going to lay low after the heist.

She made notes about that—it probably wouldn't be in any of their names, but they could look at relatives and family names. They'd rented the trailer with cash; the apartment they'd either borrowed from friends or without permission; they no longer owned the property in Austin, but according to the real-estate records, they'd netted over three hundred thousand dollars from the sale and there was no corresponding purchase in the state of Texas. The property had been owned by Samuel Sr. and Monica Trembly.

But if they bought out of the state, eventually the FBI would track them down. Might take a few months and a lot of manpower, but they'd find the property and this family was smart enough to know that. Lucy put her bet on either property owned by a relative—likely a distant relative—or property they purchased with a false identity. Much harder to track. But she'd also double down on her bet that the money from the sale of their Austin property was used for the new purchase.

Crutcher was good with financial records, and those were as complete as possible. No one on the list had more than a few thousand dollars in any bank. The amounts and goods stolen were itemized—he was right, no score was over twenty thousand dollars. There was no set time in the day when they hit, but each business had been open.

The MO was consistent. They all wore masks. One person stayed in the car, in the rear of the building. Based on the visuals of those inside, Lucy guessed that Jacob was the driver. Five entered through the front. One person jammed the cameras—which was possible because of a security flaw coupled with technology that the robbers had access to and the ability to use. That had to be Amanda, with the computer science degree. There was nothing else about her in the files, but she hadn't been a suspect until yesterday.

Two in the gang manned the door and watched the hostages. Two grabbed the cash or jewels. They were fast and knew exactly where to go and what to do. No robbery took more than five minutes from breech to escape—except for the last one, where Reggie Hansen was killed. Sam went to his friend to try to extract or save him, but he was already dead or dying. There was only a brief period of time that their images were caught before the jammer went into effect, but Lucy could tell from their build that Kirk and SueAnn were the lookouts, and Sam and Reggie grabbed the goods.

But the final robbery showed that even in his grief, Sam was thinking. He ordered his gang to leave without him. Everyone exited through the back except Sam, who brazenly went out the front. The gang went north; he went south. One lone security camera picked him up at the corner; he turned east and disappeared. Police arrived at the bank ninety seconds later.

Were these robberies a rehearsal? To get enough money for tools and equipment for their big payday? A diversion? All of the above? Lucy didn't know. What she *did* know was that without Reggie, Sam might not be in complete control. He had exhibited some power over his family yesterday— Kirk and SueAnn would be *happy* to kill someone. Without Sam and Reggie, they both would have ended up in prison long ago—Lucy was certain of it. They didn't have much self-control.

Likewise, without Sam and Reggie, Amanda and Jacob

probably wouldn't have started down a life of crime or wouldn't have done anything violent. They might have been predisposed to be criminals—what about their father? Lucy suddenly wondered. Where did he fit into the picture, if at all?

There was nothing on him in the paperwork. SueAnn was at least ten years younger than her brothers and sisters—did they share a dad? Lucy was ten years younger than her next-youngest brother, but truthfully, that big of a break was rare with the same parents.

She turned and did a records search, dug around for a good thirty minutes before she found out that Samuel Trembly Sr. had been killed in a construction accident in San Antonio when Jacob—the youngest at the time—was five. Clearly, Sam Jr. had grown into the father figure. Monica Trembly had never remarried—or, if she did, she didn't take her husband's name. SueAnn was born five years later, which put her at twenty-two. She was named Trembly. Odd.

Lucy learned that there was no insurance payment on Trembly's death because he had been found to be intoxicated while working. The company was a major employer in the state of Texas and worked on several of the largest civil projects, many related to flood management. They often worked alongside the Army Corps of Engineers.

Monica had taken a couple jobs over the years, had kept her family afloat, and Sam Jr. had started working when he was sixteen. If they hadn't gone into a life of crime, Lucy would have had a lot of respect for them picking up after their world fell apart.

Amanda Trembly had gone to college on a full-ride scholarship. She had the highest SAT score in her high school and graduated with top honors. How did she get sucked into her family's criminal lifestyle? She had a ticket out—a college education, a good degree, and at one point had a job with a computer company that paid well.

Family. It was complicated, Lucy knew, and she felt for the girl Amanda used to be—until she decided to follow her brother.

The Hansens and the Tremblys had grown up together. They lived on adjoining properties. The Hansen family was split—parents divorced. Wife remarried and moved to California.

Lucy made a list of all the names she could find in both families—Monica Trembly's maiden name was Bane. Hansen's maiden name was Lorenzo. Lucy logged into an ancestry database and spent far too much time digging around. But she did learn that Monica's two grandmothers' maiden names were named Donovan and Shane; her dead husband's mother's maiden name was Richardson. She couldn't find anything else on the Hansens—no one in their family had taken the time to input the data. But this was a start.

Family was the core of their actions, the good and bad. That meant the mother was integral to their plans. Would they just leave her in prison?

Except . . . there was no evidence that Monica Trembly had committed any crimes other than helping to break her sons out of jail. She had no record. She was in her fifties. A halfway decent attorney would get her off whether she cooperated or not. Likely, she would say she didn't know anything about it, and all they would have was Lucy's and Nate's word that she was in the thick of things yesterday. She could argue she didn't know what her kids had planned. And Bobby Thomsen could testify, but Lucy didn't know how much weight the court would put on the testimony of a scared eight-year-old.

No way was Mike Crutcher going to get anything out of the woman. The way she interacted with her kids, how she dealt with Lucy . . . that woman was cold and calculating.

Jacob didn't want to turn on his family, but he might—because he had a conscience. He cared about his siblings, worried about them in a sense . . . what had he said? *"Sam isn't a violent man, I swear to the Lord, and neither am I. But the rest of our family?"* Did that mean SueAnn and Amanda were? His mother? Did it mean he would do whatever it took to protect his brother? Or that maybe it wasn't his idea?

Lucy didn't realize that more than two hours had passed since she sat down, and she jumped when Sean and Nate came up to her desk. "Sorry, princess," Sean said, and kissed her. "Didn't mean to startle you."

"Just doing some background work and writing a profile."

Nate said, "I just heard from Laura that they got nothing out of Monica Trembly."

Lucy raised an eyebrow and tapped her screen. "Yep, that was my educated guess."

"Not only that, she started crying and begged them not to hurt her kids."

"And her excuse for holding a shotgun on us?"

"She claimed she would never have fired, that she didn't realize until the last minute that her kids were planning the breakout. She helped because she didn't know what else to do."

"I wish I could have talked to her. She would have done the same thing with me, but I might have been able to make her mad enough to let something slip—especially since I was there and she likely blames you and me for her capture. But she won't talk now. Jacob Trembly will be hard, but I think it's possible. Or it was, before Crutcher played hardball. He won't trust any of us if we go to him with an offer now."

"So far, no one's been hit."

Lucy turned to Sean. "Rachel said you were reviewing all

the security systems, that there was a common security program?"

"Yeah, the same program, and it's a serious flaw. They know about it and have been working to fix it for months."

"What company?"

"Thursgood Security. They're pretty good for on-site systems, but this was a major software glitch. They've fixed about half the systems and are on track for fixing the remaining by the end of the year."

"Hmm." Lucy shot off an email to national headquarters to find out where Amanda Trembly had worked after college. "Amanda Trembly was a computer science major, maybe she had inside information." Or maybe she had been responsible for the "glitch" in the first place. But that meant that these robberies were planned long ago. "Did the Dallas hits have the same security flaw?"

"No," Sean said. "Completely different systems. And Trembly worked those old-school. Destroy the equipment, masks and gloves, grab the goods, disappear. Nothing as elaborate as the San Antonio jobs."

"And they had fewer people working those heists. Dallas FBI believes there were three, maybe four. Two and a wheelman, but they also suspected a possible ringer inside."

Nate said, "They're going through all the old security tapes to see if they have any of the other suspects as ringers in the Dallas robberies."

"I think it's Amanda or Jacob," Lucy said. "Likely in a decent disguise."

Sean asked, "Do you want me to call Thursgood? I know the owner. Did some work for them a while back."

Lucy almost said no but realized that the company could share any information it chose to share.

"And," Sean added, "I've talked to him twice today. He's already getting the FBI a list of businesses in the greater San

Antonio area that are waiting for a software upgrade. It might help narrow down the potential targets."

"Talk to your contact in Cyber Crimes and get his okay first, I'll shoot off an email to Rachel to cover my butt."

"And your profile?" Nate asked.

"It's basic because we don't have a lot of information, but in a nutshell, I think Sam Trembly is grieving over the death of his friend. They grew up together, worked together, they were practically inseparable. He might not be thinking clearly—which is a problem because SueAnn and Kirk are wild. They wanted to shoot me."

Sean put his hand on her shoulder, squeezed.

"I think they're two peas in a pod and feed off each other. Separate them and they might not be as violent, but together they will do anything, and I don't say that lightly. Amanda is smart. She doesn't want to be caught, she thinks everything through clearly. Sam listens to her, he depends on her. This entire escape was her brainchild. And if we're right about her computer background she has been planning this for a long time. She used the skills of her team to get it done, meaning she's good with asset management. She knows who can do what and sets them on the task. But she overthinks and she might get caught up in her own elaborate plans. They'll need to adjust the plans because Jacob is in prison, but they're capable of doing it."

"So the mother isn't involved?" Nate said.

"Not in the heists, but she's involved in the planning. The family dynamic at the Thomsen house—they deferred to the mother. Maybe humored her, but listening to her and seeing how she talked to them, she is definitely involved. They must have a safe house somewhere in the city—and I would guess relatively close to where they plan to hit. But they went up to Brady because Reggie was killed and they knew Sam was compromised. They wanted to regroup, let some time pass.

Whether they had additional robberies planned or not, we don't know, but this one—the one tonight or tomorrow—is the big one. The final act, and then they'll disappear. So I suggested that we handle this in a two-prong fashion—work to stop them, but simultaneously find their safe house. That's why I was making these lists of names. If one of them pops up in the investigation, we look more closely. Of course, they could be using a shell corp or a completely fake identity— but it's a start. And the mother is the protector—she will most likely be the one who set up the safe house and wherever they're going to retire."

"That's a lot in two hours," Nate said. "Good work."

Nate and Sean went back to Cyber Crimes, and Lucy sent her memo off to Rachel. She hoped she wasn't too far off, and she wished it weren't so vague. She didn't think there was anything here that would give their team enough time to locate the crew—or where they were going to hit.

But she was very certain about one thing: This next heist was going to be big.

Very big.

Chapter Nine

Mike Crutcher stepped into the small conference room that they were using to monitor the investigation. "You were wrong, Kincaid."

Lucy bristled, but before she could speak, Crutcher continued, "All the jewelry stores are now closed, they didn't hit tonight. We just wasted an entire day when my guess is they are long gone."

It was nearly dark. She was tired and sore and crabby and wanted to go home. Sean was in the middle of a complex security analysis with the head of the cybercrime unit, and she and Nate had been at desks all day making calls and analyzing information. Kane and Siobhan had arrived at the house an hour ago and were entertaining Jesse, but Lucy wanted to see her family more than sit here to be yelled at and ridiculed by a fellow agent.

"I'm not wrong," she said. "I've looked at the list Cyber Crimes put together, and there are two banks that meet the criteria—both downtown, and both with over a million dollars of assets in their vaults—not to mention whatever is in the safe-deposit boxes. Zach and Cyber Crimes are working on assessing the potential of those targets, and—"

He cut her off. "You mean your husband."

"I mean Zach," she snapped. "And Sean, with the permission of Cyber Crimes. Just because they haven't hit something this big before doesn't mean this wasn't always in their plan."

He looked at her as if she were an idiot. "Out of all the robberies attributed to Trembly's gang, they have never broken into a vault. Those two banks have the highest level of security, over and above the flawed security software system. And if either of them is the target, the hit won't be until Tuesday—and we can cover both of them. So go home, relax, and let those of us who have worked white-collar crimes for a few years do our job."

Nate was getting ready to jump on Crutcher, so Lucy had to do something and stand up for herself. "Agent Crutcher," she said, "I don't think you've read one word of our reports, but Amanda Trembly worked for the security company who designed the security for those two banks. They called in every one of their techs today to determine whether she might have created the software flaw to begin with—her supervisor said she has the skills to do so. And while there are more than three dozen businesses that still have the flawed software, those are the only two that have a big enough payday that the gang can retire."

"*If* that's their plan—you're relying on the memory of a scared eight-year-old. We have one of the highest-ranked white-collar units in the FBI. We've been doing this a long time, Kincaid."

"These aren't traditional white-collar criminals. You need to contact the bank managers and have them do something different—sending in private guards starting now would be a good start."

"Those two banks you mentioned are completely secure when they're closed. There's no way they can get in without every law enforcement agency knowing about it, software flaw notwithstanding. I talked to the head of the security company myself, and he assured me that the external security isn't compromised, it's only internal security. *That's* why they have to wait until the bank is open before they hit. One thing I've learned is that robbers rarely change their MO, that there is a reason that it works for them. And now you know."

"I think you're wrong."

"Noted," he said dismissively. "Tuesday morning, we'll be all over both of them—you can be a part of the solution, if you can learn to take direction."

"Maybe you should learn to take advice."

"From a rookie?"

"You're already on thin ice, Crutcher," Nate said.

"Go home, both of you," Crutcher said. "There's nothing more we can do tonight."

Lucy walked out before she said anything that would get her in more trouble. Fortunately, Nate followed—he was just as angry.

"He's an asshole," Lucy said.

"Yes, he is," Nate agreed. "I'll get Sean."

"No—I'm writing a memo. I don't want to go over his head, but I think this is one of those situations where asking for forgiveness is preferable to asking for permission. But if you want to talk to Daphne in Cyber Crimes—not Sean, because he'll back my play no matter what—do it. She's brilliant, and has a lot of respect here. I know she and Sean have had their heads together all afternoon. If she signs off on my memo, that'll give us more clout."

"I'm on it."

Lucy went to her desk and wrote out everything she knew as fact and her educated theory about why the Trembly gang was going to hit one of the two banks—one on Broadway, one on Commerce—tonight or anytime Monday, a national holiday. She didn't know how yet—while Crutcher was a prick, he was a smart prick, and Sean had confirmed that the external security was intact. How could they get inside the bank without compromising external security?

It might not matter if they knew how . . . Lucy was confident of the when. She tried to keep her personal opinion out of the memo and rely solely on the facts that they knew and her expertise when it came to criminal psychology. She also relied on the preliminary report that Daphne Goodall, the SSA of Cyber Crimes, had written. One thing Sean was good at was figuring out who in an organization had authority and making that person his best friend. It had worked with Daphne and the VCMO analyst Zach Charles, who both sang his praises. It helped that all three of them were smart and talked the same language—a language that often went over Lucy's head. She was more than competent with computers, but she much preferred working with humans than machines.

She finished quickly, because she had most of the information already compiled. She sent it off to Daphne for her review and asked if she would be willing to co-sign it with Lucy. Daphne read the message, then nothing . . .

And nothing for more than twenty minutes. Her memo was only three pages, how long did it take to read?

She was about to call Sean when Daphne responded with one sentence:

I need you here now.

Nothing more, and she didn't want to read anything good—or bad—into it. She went down the hall to Cyber Crimes, which was jumping with people. A map of downtown San Antonio was projected on the whiteboard with two red marks and some lines and notes that Lucy couldn't decipher.

"I sent your memo under both our names," Daphne said as soon as Lucy entered. "It's out of our hands right now—I sent it to Crutcher, and cc'd your boss and my boss." Because Daphne was an SSA, her direct supervisor was Abigail Durant, the ASAC who supervised several of the squads. "I added two important facts: The first is that these two banks we identified as being high-risk targets are both directly over the San Antonio River Tunnel. And I went through your initial report from this morning, Lucy, and focused on the fact that Trembly and Hansen both worked in construction. They've never had a job in San Antonio that we could find, but we learned that the *senior* Sam Trembly worked for the construction company that helped build the tunnel more than twenty years ago. It was under construction for ten years. He would have been privy to blueprints, maps, service tunnels—we don't have that information at our fingertips, but I already reached out to the Army Corps of Engineers and they're going to get back to me."

Lucy was floored. "So—you think they're going to use those tunnels?"

"Crutcher is right about the external security, and I asked Sean to run through scenarios and the response time is less than five minutes if they are breeched—maybe seven minutes with weather-related issues. Even if they created diversions like they did in their escape, there are too many potential access points to those two banks on surface streets to create enough diversions to prevent a swift response, even if they plan to escape underground. I have no idea how they're going to get in, but with the kind of information they may have had access to, it's certainly possible."

She guzzled half a bottle of water before continuing. "I asked that Crutcher put together two teams to stake out the two banks from now until Tuesday morning." She hesitated, then smiled and said quietly, "It will ultimately be Durant's call anyway, to deploy that kind of manpower on a hunch—however well documented and supported that hunch is."

"So what now?" Lucy asked.

"We wait. Durant is out of the office and I asked her

assistant to track her down, but it'll take time and she'll want to talk to me—I know how she thinks. She'll do it, I'm eighty percent positive. But we have a few hours. Go home, eat, rest—I'll call you. I want you there. You know these people." She glanced over at Nate. "You too, Nate. Get some rest, I promise to call you in."

"No objection here," Nate said. "I'm beat."

"That you admit it," Lucy said, "tells me that you're about to crash."

"One of the benefits of serving in the Army for ten years is that when I crash, I really crash . . . give me thirty minutes and I'll be as good as new."

Sean ordered Lucy to go upstairs and rest and Nate to hit the guest room. When he got no complaints from either of them, he knew they were wiped. He found Kane and Jesse in the sunroom playing pool. "Where's Siobhan?" Sean said after giving his brother a hug.

"Sleeping. The flight here wasn't all smooth sailing. A lot of turbulence. Not that bad, but you feel everything in the Cessna. Doesn't bother me, but Red has a more sensitive disposition."

"You sound like you enjoyed her distress."

He smiled. "I gave her a double shot of whiskey and told her I'd wake her up when dinner was ready."

"So you're cooking?"

"Put some steaks in my special marinade and pre-heated the oven for potatoes, but that's as far as I got. We're tied at two, and this kid has never been able to beat me before. You've taught Jess a lot of your tricks."

"Not tricks. Skills."

Kane snorted. "Cheating."

"I resent that. I don't have to cheat to win. And Jesse is a quick study."

"We'll finish this game up and I'll help you in the kitchen. Did I hear Nate's voice?"

"He's taking twenty in the guest room."

"Jesse told me what went down yesterday. Surprised the feds let Nate and Lucy come in today."

"Bruised and sore, nothing serious. They're tough."

They were down to the eight ball. As Sean watched, Jesse called his shot into the corner pocket. Sean knew he was going to miss it as he set up, but he didn't say anything. Jesse had to learn on his own.

Jesse missed and almost dumped the ball in the opposite corner because he hit a bit too hard. Kane called the shot and nailed it perfectly.

"I really thought I had it," Jesse said.

"Age and experience, kid," Kane said. "Next time I might not be so lucky."

"Dad, look what Kane gave me!" Jesse showed Sean a military-grade watch he was now sporting. "It's just like his. It has a compass built-in and is waterproof. Isn't it cool?"

"Totally cool," Sean said. "Especially since you keep letting your phone die."

"Cell phones are unreliable," Kane said.

"Not if they're charged."

"Easy to break. That watch is damn near indestructible."

"I like it," Jesse said. "Thanks again, Uncle Kane."

"Did you guys walk Bandit?"

"Yep, and fed him," Jesse said. "I finished my homework and did my laundry."

"You did your laundry? Well, damn, I'm impressed," Kane said. "I didn't learn until I was forced to do it in the Marines."

"Lucy said her mom made them all do their own laundry growing up and taught me how to use the washer and dryer. It's not hard."

"Just don't put a red shirt in with your socks," Kane said.

They went to the kitchen and Sean put potatoes in to bake, tasked Jesse with making the salad, and Kane was in charge of barbecuing the steaks. Forty-five minutes later Sean went to fetch Lucy. She was crashed in the middle of the bed, still fully dressed, even her shoes. Normally, he'd let her sleep, but she needed fuel. He knew she didn't want to sit out on any police action tonight.

He sat on the edge and rubbed her back. "Lucy, time for dinner."

"Umm," she moaned.

"You can sleep if you want."

"Now that I smell food, I'm starving."

"Well, come down whenever you want, I'll make sure there's something left over."

"I'm going to jump in the shower to wake up. I'll be down soon." She smiled and stretched.

He leaned down and kissed her. "Don't rush."

Three hours later they were fully fed, had dessert, and were catching up with Kane and Siobhan. It was close to midnight. Sean had tried to get Lucy to go back to sleep, but she didn't want to. She was waiting for a call from FBI headquarters—a call that might not even come.

But it did at 12:05 a.m. from Daphne. "It was a battle, but we have two stakeouts being set up. Crutcher was supposed to call you, but he's nursing his wounds. I'm leading one, Crutcher is leading the other. Can you and Nate be at the Broadway bank ASAP? We're leaving headquarters now, our ETA is ten minutes. Staging in two tactical vans across the street and one around the corner."

"We'll be there." She glanced at Sean. "Would you object to a civilian joining us?"

"If said civilian hasn't lost his government clearance in the last six hours, absolutely. The more the merrier."

Chapter Ten

"What's the plan?" Nate asked when Daphne cleared them to enter the main tactical truck.

"Rogan," she said without answering Nate's question directly, "Thursgood said you know his system almost as well as he does at this point. He developed a down-and-dirty program that can monitor the software remotely to detect when and if it goes down. I have Zach working on it, but he's on the phone with Thursgood himself, who's sitting with Agent Crutcher's team. Can you assist in that?"

"My pleasure," Sean said.

Lucy was glad. Sean liked being needed and having something vital to do—especially when he didn't have to ask.

"There's an unmarked white van kitty-corner to us."

"I saw the antennas," Sean said. "Discretion isn't really in the FBI playbook."

Daphne grinned. "No argument here, but we're not in line of sight to the main doors, so I'm hoping we're discreet enough."

Sean slipped out, and Nate said, "Why aren't we going into the tunnels and blocking any entrances into the building?"

"Pick your reason," Daphne said. "First, we don't know where they're going to enter. Second, we don't have access to the tunnels. The Army Corps of Engineers maintains the underground tunnels. The city doesn't have full access. I talked to the head honcho in Dallas and he's pulling together the team that works on it—they know everything about this project—but it's going to take until morning to get anyone out."

"How does Trembly have access?"

"We think his father might have had blueprints or maps and information on the security and specially keyed underground access points. The research Lucy did into the Tremblys showed that Sam's construction job gave him the skills he needs. It's likely his father, who worked on the project for five years until his death, had blueprints and information about the tunnels—possibly information that only those who worked here know. This isn't a water system that the average person knows about above and beyond some news reports. The only time it's mentioned is when there's a storm, and it's 'yeah, the underground river saved the River Walk once again.'"

"And we can't get into the bank?"

"We talked about it, but one thing Crutcher and I agreed on is that we'd spook them. If we're there, and the security isn't exactly as they expect, they could bolt. We have to assume they know the underground maintenance tunnels better than we do, and we could get lost. It's literally a maze down there. One of the original engineers who helped design the project went missing for three days because he became disorientated. Not to mention some of the passages haven't been maintained—crumbling rock, possible drops. I'm not risking going down unless we absolutely have to."

"So we're waiting until they break in."

"Exactly. According to Thursgood, if he's monitoring the internal security in real time, there'll be some sort of code or warning in the software program when Amanda Trembly takes it down—a log that's generated at that moment, even though she bypasses the alarm. Once they're in, we breech. We have the keys." She meant that literally, as she held up a key.

Law enforcement could access emergency boxes to enter secure buildings, just like the fire department. Getting the key early would save time when they went in.

"Based on what Rogan and Thursgood uncovered from the software flaw, there's a sixteen-minute window as the internal system reboots after it's disabled. It should never take that long—and they now think that Amanda herself may have tampered with the software before she quit last year. It's such a subtle change—one line of code in millions—that no one caught it before it was rolled out. And when they did, it looked like an innocent mistake, so there wasn't an urgency to get out the fix. However, these banks and six other businesses in San Antonio are scheduled for the on-site upgrade this week."

"Which means it's now or never," Lucy said.

"And with this plan," Nate said, "we'll catch them in the act."

"That's the hope. They try to escape, we pursue—much easier than figuring out where and when they're going to enter. We have city engineers working with us to identify potential breech points, but we won't have a complete list until later today. I just hope you're right that it's tonight, because I really don't want to do this again tomorrow—and I don't know that I'll get the approval for two nights of surveillance."

Daphne sat back in the command chair and monitored the video she had of the two bank entrances and rear emergency exit.

Lucy sipped bad coffee and waited.

And waited.

For the first time since Reggie was killed, Sam Trembly felt good about the plan.

They entered the underground tunnel system at 2 a.m., just as they had planned. There was an access point in a park a quarter mile from the bank. The service room was generic and barely protected—a lock, metal building, but nothing more.

Once inside, they removed the locked manhole cover. Sam and Reggie had done so many of these types of jobs—minus the bank robbery part—when they worked in construction. People never realized how much of construction work was underground. Pipes. Reinforcement. Testing the soil to make sure there was no chance someone's home or business would sink in the next big storm. Sam had done a stint for a company where he dealt with underground garages for businesses. Pipes, concrete, reinforcement—and once they'd contracted with the city of Austin and he'd spent an entire summer in the sewer system. Not his favorite job, but he learned a damn lot, all of which helped him here.

He wasn't in a sewer, but same principles.

He was relieved that SueAnn and Kirk were focused on the job. Maybe the sleep helped. Or the solid meal they had where they talked about being kids, free-and-easy teens who thought the world was theirs. Remembering Reggie and the good times. So they were all disciplined, focused, and didn't argue. They did their jobs and did them well. He needed Kirk to help him with some physical work and SueAnn to take care of opening a latch where no one else would fit. They were on schedule, and arrived in the bank's underground garage through a city maintenance door at 2:21 a.m.

Their planning and recon had paid off. Right on time.

An unused emergency staircase was easy to disconnect from the system, and Sam let Amanda handle that. Generally, if opened the door would set off an alarm and the fire department would be called. In two minutes, the alarm was disabled from a main control room in the garage and they were able to access the bank directly.

By 2:25, they were standing in the middle of the bank. They'd eluded all external security and now just needed to tackle internal security.

Amanda pulled out her mini-computer and ran through her program. A minute later, the internal security went through its reboot program—a program Amanda had rewritten when they originally came up with this plan two years ago.

The light turned green.

"We're in," Amanda said.

Sam started the countdown and they ran to the vault. He used a card key that Amanda had cloned and the door clicked open. The vault had a second level of security that required a code, which Amanda cracked with her computer in less than a minute.

"Fourteen minutes and counting," Sam said. "Let's go."

This particular bank had two dozen gold bars in their vault. They couldn't carry it all—Sam determined that they would each put two in the bottom of their expandable back-packs, each twenty-five pounds and worth a half-million dollars—then fill the rest with stacks of hundred-dollar bills. They could fit $1.5 million into the packs, which would weigh about twenty-five pounds. They'd all practiced carry-ing hundred-pound packs for the last year, so seventy-five should be easy.

That would give them a total take of $10 million. The gold would be harder to move, but Sam had some friends who could help. The cash would carry them for years.

Amanda monitored security while also filling her bag.

"Twelve minutes," Sam said.

"We can do anything!" SueAnn squealed. "Kirk, we can go to Hawaii! I've always wanted to go to Hawaii."

Sam wasn't going to burst her bubble that they wouldn't be getting on airplanes anytime soon. Maybe when they got new identities and some time had passed, but for the next year at a minimum they would be living on their ten-acre fortress in Mississippi.

But that was a fight for another day.

They were making excellent time and would be back in the tunnels long before their sixteen minutes were up.

Life was good.

Then he heard a sound.

"They're in," Zach alerted Daphne. "The system went into slow reboot one minute ago—you're on."

Daphne got on her radio. "All teams, proceed according to plan. Go-go-go!"

Daphne took the lead. Nate, Lucy, and an agent Lucy had never worked with before—Hank Christopher—were on the Alpha team. Beta would head immediately to the garage, Charlie team would back up Alpha, and the Delta team would cover external exits.

It took them four minutes to get into position, unlock the main doors, and then unlock the secondary door. The Beta team leader informed the group on their secure radio band that fire security had been disabled in the garage.

"Proceed with caution," Daphne whispered.

Earlier, they had reviewed the blueprints of the bank. The main bank had desks, teller stations, and a large lobby. The vault was to the right, at the end of a short hall off the lobby. Two private offices, with glass windows looking into the bank, were dark. Security lighting illuminated the entire area, and glowing red exit signs could be seen at key points.

They reached the vault and the gang was gone. How the hell did they get out so quickly? There had been a secondary vault with gold bars that was open—it was clear several had been taken. Money was on the floor as the Tremblys had been frantic in grabbing as much as they could before they were chased out by the FBI. This was potentially a huge hit—by far their biggest, and one of the biggest in San Antonio history if they got away with it.

Through their earpieces, they heard commotion outside. "FBI! Stop!"

A second later, the Charlie team commander said, "One suspect detained. One suspect fled on foot, Delta team is in pursuit."

Daphne ordered the Beta team to keep two agents in the garage to stand guard and send two up to the main bank.

A door clicked to the right. Immediately Lucy and Nate pursued. Daphne reported that one or more suspects had exited via the north fire exit.

"No one's here," Delta reported.

Lucy and Nate exited and ran into two Delta team agents. "Someone left through this door," Lucy said. "Were you here the whole time?"

"Just got here after securing the first suspect."

"They might have a minute lead," Nate said. "Fan out, be alert."

They had streetlights that helped with the search, and almost immediately Lucy looked down and realized exactly how they escaped. "Over here!"

One of the manhole covers was missing. Nate lay flat and put his ear to the ground. Everyone was silent and ten seconds later he said, "I hear someone. Proceed with caution—assume they know these tunnels better than we do."

Daphne ordered all available agents to fan out to every access point to the underground tunnels based on the Army

Corps maps. She pulled in Crutcher's team for additional support.

Nate, who had extensive experience tracking humans, took the lead. He sent four agents to the north, and Lucy and two agents followed him to the south. There was dull yellow lighting all along the maintenance tunnel, plus Nate had a tactical light attached to his Glock. He stopped periodically to listen and then continued in pursuit. Lucy didn't know how Nate differentiated the sounds when every movement created an echo.

Water seemed to be rushing everywhere; a dampness permeated the tight area, though nothing was wet. The sound of the storm water being drained, the sewage system—whatever it was, it was eerie and disconcerting. Lucy focused on following Nate. They were on a narrow walk with reinforced walls and several offshoots.

Zach came over the com. "Dunning, Agent Forsyth said you're leading the pursuit to the south."

"Roger," Nate said quietly.

"I've already given the north team the most logical egress for the suspects. I'm tracking you on my map. The walls are marked with numbers and letters every twenty yards. Where are you?"

Nate shined his light. "C-24."

"The most logical escape route is a door at C-32. The second is a tunnel to the right just past C-36."

"Roger that."

Nate said, "Kincaid, you're with me at C-32; Delta team, proceed to C-36."

They quickly covered the yardage and Nate let the Delta team pass them before he tried the door.

It was unlocked.

Nate motioned for Lucy to cover him as he stepped aside and opened the door.

A gunshot rang out from the space. From the sound, it came from a distance. Nate turned and fired his weapon three times. Listened.

There was no lighting in this tunnel, because either it had been disabled by the Tremblys or this wasn't a normal access route. Nate shined his light and no one fired back. They heard faint footsteps ascending metal stairs—they were some distance away.

Nate motioned for Lucy to follow, and he turned off his light. They kept close to the walls. Nate's sense of direction and space was second to none—as soon as they reached the stairs, he knew. He flashed his light up but stayed to the side.

No one fired at them.

They ran up the stairs two at a time. The heavy metal door at the top was secured from the outside, but Nate broke the handle and pushed it open, waiting a fraction of a second for a possible attack.

Nothing.

They were in a small utility room. The second door leading out was ajar. Nate reported that one, possibly two, suspects had exited the tunnel at his location. He pushed open the door, and two suspects were running in opposite directions. One was short and small, SueAnn, and one was tall and broad, either Sam or Kirk.

Nate motioned for Lucy to pursue SueAnn, and he went after the other. Lucy ran. She had on a Kevlar vest and full tactical gear, but she was gaining because SueAnn was hampered by a heavy backpack.

Did she actually think she could escape with all that money? If she'd dumped it they might have had a chance to get away.

Greed over common sense.

"FBI! Stop!" Lucy commanded.

SueAnn turned to face her. "You," she said with disgust.

"Drop your weapon or I will shoot."

SueAnn raised her gun and fired. It might have hit Lucy except that SueAnn's aim was off because of the weight on her back. Lucy fired three times. SueAnn went down.

Lucy ran over to her. She was struggling, trying to get up. One bullet had gone through her forearm, the other two had hit her shoulder.

Lucy kicked away the gun. "Suspect down, need an ambulance at my location."

To SueAnn she said, "Stop struggling! You'll live, but I need to slow the blood loss."

"You bitch! We were so close! Don't touch me!"

Lucy ignored her. She read SueAnn her rights while she searched her for another weapon. She had none. Lucy cuffed her, then put pressure on the wound. She didn't want another death on her conscience. It was a justified shooting, but she didn't want the girl to die.

Over her earpiece she heard Nate's voice. "I have Sam Trembly in custody. He gave up without a fight. Wants to know if his sister is okay."

"Tell him SueAnn fired at a federal agent and is lucky to be alive. She's injured but should survive."

"Roger that. Good work, partner."

Amanda Trembly was in tears when she arrived at the safe house. She half expected the police to be there waiting for her.

They weren't.

She waited, and still no one came. She waited for an hour, sitting on the front porch, her entire body aching and crampy from the panic, the running, the fear . . . hoping and praying that Sam had made it. She didn't care what happened to Kirk and SueAnn—Sam was right, they were to blame for Reggie's death. They had fucked up, so cocky and self-assured, and Reggie had paid the price.

When Sam didn't come, Amanda was ready to give herself up. She was exhausted and grieving and the $2 million she had in her backpack was nothing if she had no one to share it with.

You do. You have someone to share it with. You have to get up, get out of here. It's what Sam would want.

It's what Reggie would have wanted.

She shivered in the cold, damp predawn morning and finally went into the house. She dropped the backpack on the table and sank into the corner of the dining room.

She had to plan. She'd lost the man she loved last month, and her family over the span of two days, but she needed to focus on her future.

She put her hand on her stomach. She felt the small bump. No one knew about the baby. Sam suspected, but he hadn't said anything. Right now she wished that she and her big brother had just disappeared after Reggie was killed. But Ma wanted the money. She wanted the big score, and she pushed and prodded until they all fell lockstep into line.

Monica Trembly was a hard woman to say no to.

Without someone—Reggie, her brothers, her family—could she raise this child alone? Could she just disappear?

Yes, you can. Sam didn't tell anyone about the property in Mississippi—except you. And he trusted you with the key. Go there. Stay there until the baby comes and then you can figure out what to do.

She needed to eat, pack a bag, and disappear. She didn't know if the safe house was compromised—or if there was a way for the FBI to track it. She had to assume there was. They had two vehicles—she would take the truck, it was beat-up but ran well, and she would go straight to Mississippi. Drive through the day and night if she had to.

Resolved, she stood up. A cramp hit her in the gut with the force of a punch. She was sore, and she wanted to throw up. She had to protect Reggie's baby. But first she had to catch her breath.

She sat back down and that's when she felt something wet between her legs. She looked down and saw blood soaking through her jeans. And she knew. The tears stopped, the pain turned to numbness.

She had nothing to live for.

Chapter Eleven

After a nap and shower, Lucy returned to FBI headquarters late Monday morning as the office was abuzz at the success of thwarting a major bank heist. Though Amanda Trembly's disappearance was problematic and she had two gold bars worth a million dollars and approximately eight hundred thousand in cash to help her escape, they had everyone else in custody.

SueAnn Trembly would be in the hospital for a couple of days—surgery was successful, but she had lost a lot of blood. She wasn't talking, other than to curse the cops. She would be facing extensive charges over and above robbery: She had beaten up a clerk at one jewelry store and had shot and injured a civilian during the last bank heist. Not to mention attempted murder on Saturday by shooting at Officer Riley's patrol and earlier this morning firing at Lucy.

Monica Trembly would be moved to the county jail the following morning, if her doctor signed off. There had been no complications from her injury. She would most likely get off—which infuriated Lucy. Unless they could get one of her kids to testify that she was involved in the planning—or they found evidence that she had masterminded any of the heists—she would probably walk. They could build a case for the prison break and kidnapping of a minor, but she was already crying foul on that, that she had been pressured to help.

Jacob Trembly would be arraigned in the morning for escaping custody, facilitating a jailbreak, and using a false identity. But the truth was, they would have a difficult time tying him to the heists. He hadn't resisted arrest, and hadn't used a weapon when he escaped. If he pled and the AUSA was in a good mood, he might get a year in prison for conspiracy.

Kirk Hansen was a repeat offender and he had shot and killed the bank guard last month, plus injured two civilians. He wouldn't be getting out of prison anytime soon, and the AUSA was considering a capital case. Murder in the commission of a felony could mean the death penalty.

Sam Trembly had no weapon on him when he was searched after the robbery, and he'd surrendered peacefully. But he was facing serious charges, in addition to the prison break. Lucy didn't know what would happen—right now the man seemed defeated, and if he worked it right he might be able to plead out for a reduced sentence. Because he had never used a gun in any of the felonies, he might get away with ten years in a plea deal, if he cooperated. That was all out of Lucy's hands. She'd done her job and could sleep comfortably knowing she'd done it well.

Amanda Trembly was the wild card. She was educated, smart, and now had money. But she had lost her entire family in this scheme, and Lucy hadn't spent enough time with her to assess how that would impact her. Chances were that she had a bigger escape plan and that she would disappear from San Antonio and lay low. They'd continue to look for her, trace the money, use the research Lucy had done on property and family names to see if any of it led to the Tremblys. But for now, Amanda might be able to disappear.

Lucy was eating her second donut in the conference room

after the debriefing. She shouldn't, but they were so very good, and she had a weakness for chocolate anything. And these were chocolate crème donuts.

Agent Crutcher walked in with Nate. He said, "I already told Agent Dunning, and I'm telling you—I'm sorry that I was an ass about this case. I finally did read your reports in full, the final report from Fredericksburg PD, and I talked to Mr. Thomsen about what transpired at his ranch. I was wrong to put the blame on either of you—I jumped to a conclusion and was too stubborn to admit that I was wrong."

"Apology accepted," Lucy said.

Nate was grinning smugly over Crutcher's shoulder where the senior agent couldn't see. Lucy smiled. "I'll tell you this, your files were impeccable, and we used that information to figure out the Tremblys' plans. So we all did well."

"I've always been good with numbers and patterns. I took your research into the two families and we're expanding the property search. We even narrowed down the date—when Monica Trembly sold her property outside Austin, that money was transferred sixty days later to another bank, transferred again thirty days after that—and we'll find it, whether it's in some foreign account or used to buy property."

"Good. That's where Amanda probably is right now—or on her way. To a safe house, out of state."

"About that—I'm heading to the jail to talk to Sam Trembly. We really need to recover the blueprints and equipment he used to access those underground tunnels. I'm going to play nice with him because if we lose that, it could be a potential terrorist threat. Army Corps of Engineers is coming here to analyze any potential security threat, but that someone could move so freely down there with no one knowing—well, it worries us. Maybe he'll help us find Amanda."

"I don't think so," Lucy said. "Based on my understanding of his psychology—and that's minimal because I didn't

spend a lot of time with him—he's a protector. He's not going to give her up because she's the one who got away. He'll
be happy she got away, and content to spend time in prison.
However, I might be able to get some clues from him about
her plans. But he can't think we're trying to manipulate him,
so we'll be straightforward on the surface."

"Okay," Crutcher said. "You want to sit in, Dunning?"

"No, Lucy's got this. I'm taking the day off. We're taking
Jesse to the gun range and teaching him how to shoot, then a
certain Marine and I are having a competition."

"I'm sorry I'm going to miss that," Lucy said.

"Sean said he's going to record it. I need to have the proof
when I beat him. Army rules."

Lucy was going to have to watch that video tonight.

Crutcher drove them to the jail. It didn't take long, and
they were brought in to talk to Sam Trembly in a small interview room. He looked hollowed out, with dark circles under his eyes and a small cut on his cheek that had been taped
closed. He stared at Lucy, then shook his head and looked at
his hands. "Kirk wanted to kill you and your partner. I hope
maybe it helps some that I didn't want no part of that. I'm
not a violent man."

Almost verbatim what Jacob had said.

"I believe you," Lucy said.

"Mr. Trembly," Crutcher said, "we have everyone in custody and all the missing money, except for Amanda and her
bag. If you can help us find her, that will help you during sen-
tencing."

He shrugged. "I can't help you."

"You can, you don't want to. Where were you staying after you escaped on Saturday? You must have had a place
here, in town."

He didn't say anything.

"Sam," Crutcher said collegially, "you had access and information to a secure area. I'm sure you understand what could happen if those plans got into the wrong hands. Like you said, you're not a violent man. You're not a terrorist. You don't want to hurt anyone. But what if a real bad guy who wants to blow things up stumbled across the blueprints of the San Antonio River Tunnel? Or the tools you used to access the secure areas? We need to secure all that information."

"You'll find it," Sam said. "We rented a place locally for the last few months. When we don't pay rent next month, the landlord will find everything and that will be that. So I'm not really worried."

"You should be concerned about Amanda," Lucy said. "She loves you and your brother and what if she gets it in her head to try to break you out again? It's not going to go well for her."

"She won't. She's smart, Agent Kincaid. Real smart. She'll see that getting away with the money she has is the smartest thing to do. And I'm glad. Because I love her, and she was always the best of us."

They tried for a good thirty minutes, and while Sam was nice and friendly and even chatty, he didn't give them anything they could use. The only thing Lucy thought they could push on later was Monica Trembly's involvement. When Lucy mentioned her, she saw anger cross Sam's expression. He was angry with his mother, perhaps she could use that to keep the matriarch in prison.

But that was a conversation for the AUSA.

When Sam seemed to tire of the conversation, he said, "I think I'd like to talk to my lawyer now. I'm really done here."

They left him, and in the hall Lucy said, "Let's try Jacob."

"Go ahead. I have a hunch and I'm going to call Daphne and see if she can dig around in some property records for me."

Crutcher left her, and Lucy asked the guard to bring down
Jacob Trembly. He immediately said to her, "You can't talk
to me without my lawyer present."

"Technically, anything you tell me without your lawyer
here can't be used against you. And I can say anything I
want to you. I'm just waiting for my partner, but I wanted to
tell you what happened last night." She laid out everything,
from the brilliant plan to how Amanda got away. "There's
been something bothering me all day, and after talking to
your brother I know what it is. Both you and Sam said you
weren't violent men, and I believe you. Everything you've
done, Sam has done, proves it. But Kirk Hansen killed a man
and he will not be getting out of prison. SueAnn shot two
people, shot at me, shot at another cop—she won't be getting out of prison. But when I was in the truck Saturday, after your mother and you were detained, Amanda said and
did a couple things that had me thinking." Lucy was making
a lot of leaps in her reasoning, but as she had thought about
it, it made sense. "Was Amanda romantically involved with
Reggie? Because I think she's pregnant."

By Jacob's expression, Lucy knew that she was right.

"And she did all this because she wanted Reggie to get out
of the business. One big score and you can all walk away. You
and I both know Kirk and SueAnn are wild and irresponsi-
ble and they would have been caught sooner if it weren't for
you all keeping them in check. Nothing you or Sam has said
makes me think that you even care what happens to them.
Which is fine, because I don't, either. But Amanda isn't like
them. She's going to have a child—and now she's alone. Her
lover is dead, her brothers who have always protected her are
going to jail, and she can't go back to her mother—if Monica weasels out of this—because we'd pick her right up. For
Amanda, and for her baby, where is she going to go? I prom-

ise, I will do everything in my power to help her. If she turns herself in, and returns all the money, the AUSA will work with her—possibly even giving her minimal time or house arrest. So she *can* raise her child."

Lucy had no idea what the AUSA would do, but prosecuting a nonviolent pregnant woman probably wouldn't be on the top of her list of favorite things.

Jacob shook her head. "Even if I knew—and I don't—I wouldn't tell you. Amanda finally has a chance to break free of our cursed family, and I'm going to be rooting for her the entire way."

Crutcher and Lucy didn't talk as they drove back to FBI headquarters. They were both frustrated that neither brother would help—but confirming Amanda's pregnancy gave them intel they could use. Had she been to see a doctor? They wouldn't be able to access her medical records, but they might be able to find out if she was a patient. How far along? If Jacob knew, at least two months . . . maybe more. Had she known before Reggie was killed? Had he known? Was that why this one big final heist?

Crutcher's phone rang. He listened, then made an illegal U-turn, which freaked Lucy. She put her hand on the dash, then felt stupid. Crutcher sped up and said to the caller, "Send backup, Kincaid and I are on our way. You are brilliant, Daphne."

"That's why I'm the boss," Lucy heard Daphne say right before Crutcher ended the call.

"Daphne found their rental. The guy with the trailer in Brady? He owns a lot of property all over the area—including a house only two miles from the bank. He'll be dealing with his own legal mess, but Daphne sweet-talked him—or threatened him, don't know which—into confirming that he rented a house for cash for six months to Jacob Trembly and his sister. And better—Daphne is getting a search warrant as we speak."

Ten minutes later, they were in front of the small bungalow on a quiet street lined with small post–WW II houses. There was no garage and no car in the carport, but Amanda could have walked the two miles here from the bank.

"I know you don't think she's dangerous, Kincaid, but we wait for backup."

Lucy nodded. It didn't take long for a tactical truck to arrive, led by SWAT team leader Leo Proctor. He quickly cleared the house. "No one's here," he confirmed. "But I think everything you've been looking for is."

Crutcher and Lucy entered the house. Leo was right—the dining room was a war room, with all the blueprints and a bag of tools, the tools that hadn't already been recovered at the bank.

Sitting on the couch was a backpack that matched the three they had recovered. Lucy looked inside: The money and gold bars were there. She couldn't tell if Amanda had taken any cash with her. She frowned.

"She's probably coming back," Crutcher said. "Leo, get your guys out of here, station yourselves around the corner, Lucy and I will stay inside. Keep the coms open."

"Roger that, be careful."

Leo and his team cleared out. Lucy continued her search. In the bathroom she found bloody clothes and a towel on the floor. Had Amanda been hit by gunfire? Nate had shot into the dark hallway. Had Amanda been with SueAnn and Sam?

Lucy carefully unfolded the bloody towel. Inside was a small fetus, approximately six inches long. Four months into development.

"Oh, God," she said, and carefully folded the towel around

the dead baby. She said a prayer, for not only the lost child but also Amanda, who must be suffering right now.

"What? Was she shot? Other than you shooting SueAnn, only Nate fired."

"She had a miscarriage."

"Oh. Poor girl," Crutcher said with honest sincerity in his voice. "My wife had a miscarriage two years ago, it's dev-· astating." He put a hand on her shoulder. "Are you okay?"

She nodded but felt queasy. She didn't feel right leaving the towel on the floor. She put it gently on the counter. "We should get an evidence bag. Amanda might want to bury the fetus or something. She might not be thinking clearly right now."

Crutcher said, "And she left? Without the money? Why?"

"She could be sick, infected, grieving—she needs a doc-tor. Mike—please take me back to the jail. I need to talk to Jacob again." She took a photo of the fetus. She didn't want to use the picture, but she would if it would help her find Amanda.

Crutcher put Leo on the house in case Amanda returned, called Daphne about what they learned—she would be reach-ing out to local hospitals and clinics—and then he and Lucy went back to the jail. Lucy told Jacob exactly what they found at the house. "Your sister was four months pregnant. She lost the baby."

Tears clouded the young man's eyes. "You're lying."

"No. She folded the fetus in a towel. And then she left with-out the money. She's in pain, she could be sick, she needs medical attention. We're looking everywhere for her. But if you know anything—anything at all—you have to tell us."

He was wrestling with something. Guilt? Doubt? But he didn't say anything.

Lucy sighed and took out her phone. She showed him the picture she took only thirty minutes ago.

Tears clouded his eyes. He said, "If I tell you what I think she's going to do, promise me you won't hurt her. Please. I love my sister so much. She doesn't deserve any of this. She never wanted to be a part of this. Reggie and Sam talked her into it. She could have had such an amazing life, she's so smart. And we ruined her."

"I will do everything in my power to ensure she lives through this."

"Sam and Amanda both loved Reggie. And when he was killed, they talked about getting back at the person who killed him."

Lucy's heart sank. Crutcher said, "She's going after Peter Castillo? The guy who shot Reggie in the bank robbery?"

"I don't know—I think in her mind she wants to take from him what he loves the most. I never thought she would do it—except now." He nodded toward Lucy's phone. "Now she just might."

Crutcher and Lucy were both on the phone as they worked to track down the Good Samaritan, Peter Castillo, who'd saved lives during the bank robbery last month that took Reggie's life and the life of the security guard. He lived in an established old neighborhood with large lots and numerous trees, known as Shavano Park. They didn't see any sign of Amanda, but there were several cars in the long, wide driveway. They ran up to the door, rang the bell. A forty-year-old man answered the door wearing an apron. Several people were in the background talking and laughing.

"Can I help you?" Castillo recognized Crutcher. "Agent Crutcher—I remember you. Working on Labor Day? Follow-up? Can it wait until tomorrow? We're having a barbecue."

"Can you step outside for a minute? It's important," Crutcher said.

He did, closing the door behind him. Crutcher introduced

Lucy, then showed Castillo the picture of Amanda Trembly. "Have you seen this woman?"

He looked closely, shook his head. "I haven't. What's going on?"

"We apprehended the bank robbers last night that were involved in the robbery you helped stop last month. This is the only person who escaped, and we have reason to believe she may target you or your family. I've already called the sheriff's department and they are on their way to watch the house. You're having a party—is your family here?"

"Yes, my kids are—my wife left fifteen minutes ago to go to the store. I forgot hamburger buns, can you believe it? And she wanted more wine. And—I'll get her."

"You stay here and do not open the door to anyone. Ask your friends to come into the house; lock up. Stay here until we tell you it's clear. We'll get your wife—what's her name, what store, what car does she drive?"

"Maggie." He wrote down her car and license number and her cell phone number. "She'll be on De Zavala. It's almost a straight shot down to the store from here."

"Call her," Crutcher said. "Tell her if she's in the store to stay in the store. Then text me with her exact location, okay?"

"Yes, sir. Just bring her home safe. Please."

He went inside and they could hear him taking charge with his guests.

Crutcher called for backup. The sheriff's department had dispatched a patrol to the Castillo home and another to the store, but Lucy and Mike were closer. They were almost there when Mike got a text from Castillo. Lucy read it.

Maggie is hiding in the bathroom. I told her to alert security and she doesn't want to leave. She said she thought someone was following her from the house in a blue truck. Now she's scared. Please find her.

He also said he had her turn on her GPS location services.

"Smart guy," Mike said.

Lucy put in Maggie's phone number and immediately started tracking her. "The restrooms are in the rear of the store. What's the sheriff's ETA?"

"Five minutes."

"We need to go in. I can talk Amanda down."

"I hope so, because if she's desperate she may shoot first."

Lucy had gone through hostage rescue training and critical negotiations, but she was still new to it, and when someone was emotionally volatile and grieving like Amanda, it would be doubly hard.

They walked into the store and the manager immediately ran up to them. Mike and Lucy had their badges around their necks and FBI jackets on, so it was clear they were law enforcement. "I just called nine-one-one and they said two FBI agents were on their way. We have a situation in the back of the store. A woman is screaming and pounding on the bathroom, which is locked from the inside. She has a gun."

"We're on it," Mike said. "Get your customers out and into the parking lot away from all exits."

Mike and Lucy ran down an aisle, then paused at the back of the store. They could hear Amanda sobbing and banging. "Let me in! Let me in!"

"Cover me," Lucy said. She revealed herself to Amanda. "Amanda, it's me, Agent Lucy Kincaid. Do you remember me?"

Amanda was partly shielded by the alcove. She flattened herself against the wall so Lucy didn't have a shot even if she wanted. "Go away!"

"Amanda, I was at the house. I know what happened."

"You don't know anything. Go *away*!"

"You're grieving. You lost Reggie. Your family is in jail. You lost your baby. Let me help you. Put down the gun and kick it to me."

"It doesn't matter. It doesn't matter anymore. I have nothing," she sobbed. "I have nothing and no one!"

"You have more than you can imagine. You have two brothers who love you and would do anything to protect you. They helped us find you because they don't want you to die. You have to put down the gun."

"I thought I had everything. And I lost my b-b-baby."

She sobbed. Lucy risked getting closer.

Amanda saw the movement out of the corner of her eye. She held up her gun, aimed it at Lucy. Lucy still didn't have a clear shot. "Stop!"

Lucy kept coming forward, slowly.

"Amanda, you have never hurt anyone. I've read every report from every robbery, and you never hurt anyone. That was all SueAnn and Kirk. I know it. The courts will know it. Jacob isn't going to do much jail time. He might even get out in a year or two, and then you two can start a new life, far from here."

"You're lying."

"No. He helped us find you, and I'm going to tell the court that. That without his help, we would never have known you were grieving so much you wanted to punish the person you blame for killing Reggie. He did the right thing. He's never been in trouble before. Neither have you. That means something. I will help you as much as I can, I promise you that."

"I don't believe you." But her voice was weak. She sank down onto the floor. That's when Lucy saw blood on the floor.

"Mike," Lucy said, "she's hemorrhaging. Call an ambulance, stat."

Lucy had to risk it, because if she didn't get Amanda to drop the gun, she would be dead.

"Amanda, I'm coming to help you. You're bleeding."

She stepped closer. Amanda waved the gun, but she was so weak, her arm dropped.

Lucy ran over to her, kicked the gun out of her hand, and laid her down on the floor. "Mike! I got her."

"The ambulance is on its way."

"Maggie Castillo?"

"Yes?" a voice said from behind the door.

"Stay put for a minute, but you're safe. Call your husband and tell him you're safe."

"I heard everything," she said. "I'm a nurse, I can help."

She opened the bathroom door and got on her knees. Amanda was pale and half-conscious.

"She had a miscarriage four to six hours ago. There was a lot of blood at her house."

"She's going to need blood and most likely surgery. Keep her legs elevated."

Mike said, "ETA on ambulance is four minutes."

"Send them right back here," Maggie said. "Honey, you're going to be okay. Just hold on."

"Let me die," Amanda moaned. "Let me die."

"No," Lucy said, holding her hand. "We're not letting you die. You're suffering. I know how you feel."

"No one knows."

"Yes. We know. I've been where you are." Lucy had never been pregnant, but she had lost her uterus to an infection that could have killed her. She grieved for the children she could never have. She felt Amanda's pain, her despair. "I promise what I said before—I will do everything to help you and your brother. I know you never shot anyone. I know you didn't want to hurt anyone. I know how these things get way out of control, especially when family is involved."

She closed her eyes, tears rolling down her cheeks. "I'm so sorry."

"I know you are. Tell the court that. Okay?"

Mike brought the paramedics to the rear of the store and they took over. They whisked Amanda off and Lucy thanked

Maggie. "That must have been hard on you, knowing that she threatened you."

"That girl was in so much pain—helping her was not hard."

Chapter Twelve

Lucy was glad to be home and relaxing. It had been a tumultuous weekend, and she just got off the phone with Mike Crutcher—he had gone to the hospital and waited until Amanda was out of surgery. They'd stopped the bleeding and given her blood and medicine for uterine atony, and the doctors expected her to make a full recovery, but she couldn't be moved for at least forty-eight hours. The hospital put her under a suicide watch based on what she'd said and done, and Lucy was glad—once she got over this despair, with help she could make a full recovery, physically and mentally.

But it would be a long road. And no one was out of the legal woods yet. All Lucy could do was hope that making the right choice in the end would help some of the Tremblys get their lives back—even if it took a few years of jail time in between.

Lucy was sitting in the backyard listening to Kane and Nate argue about their gun range competition. She turned to Jesse. "Were you there, right?"

"Yeah, it was bad-ass."

"Who won?"

"I did," Kane and Nate said simultaneously.

Jesse laughed. "I'm not getting in the middle of it."

"There has to be a score."

"It was a tie." Sean came up behind Lucy and rubbed her shoulders.

"He cheated," Nate and Kane both said.

Siobhan walked up with Rachel Vaughn. "Sorry to disturb you," Rachel said. "I was on my way home and wanted to give you a file, since you're taking the day off tomorrow."

"I am?"

"It's an order," Rachel said.

"Thank you very much, Agent Vaughn," Sean said.

Lucy took the file. "What's this?"

Rachel glanced around, and the others walked out of earshot. "They didn't have to go, but it's kind of sensitive. Remember the guy who was killed off Farm-to-Market Road five weeks ago?"

"Not really."

"Well, it'll all be in there. There was some media, they billed it as a robbery, but it wasn't. He was beaten, then shot in the face."

"I remember now."

"There's now a second, and the Bexar County Sheriff called Abigail and asked if we could assist. Not take over, but they think there may be a serial murderer, and they're worried about more victims. It's their case, but right now you're all I can spare. I already assigned Nate to work with Kenzie on a big case, and everyone else is juggling. You just finished the CHR case and wrapped it up with a bow for the AUSA, so you're available—not to mention if we are dealing with a serial murderer, you have more experience there than the rest of the team."

"I can come in tomorrow, it's not a problem."

"No—just maybe put some time on the file tomorrow, there's a lot of information to absorb, but stay home. You have family visiting, and you put in extra hours on a three-day weekend."

"You don't have to twist my arm."

"Sometimes I think I do."

Lucy glanced over toward the barbecue, where Kane and Nate were still arguing and Sean was laughing with Jesse. "No, you really don't," she said with a smile. "Do you want to stay for dinner?"

"No, I don't want to intrude."

"Seriously, no shop talk, just have a beer and be social."

"Well, okay, thank you. Though I think I'd rather have what you're drinking."

"Yes, it's very good. I'll get you a glass."

Lucy walked into the kitchen and poured Rachel a glass of the Pinot Noir she had been enjoying. Sean followed her inside. "It was really classy of you to invite Rachel to stay, after all the shit that went down earlier this year."

"She's my boss, and she really had our back on this case."

"So I heard. Well, I guess I can bury the hatchet."

"It's going good, Sean, I'm willing to accept it."

"I was surprised."

"I don't think I was. She's very predictable. It just took me a while to figure her out."

She watched through the window as Nate sat down and Bandit was immediately at his feet. Nate had been struggling with a lot lately—and Lucy was worried about him. Not that he would do anything rash, but just . . . she wanted him to be happy. She didn't know if being a cop made him happy.

Sean wrapped his arms around her and said, "Penny for your thoughts."

"My thoughts are worth far more than a penny, Mr. Rogan."

"They're priceless, sweetheart."

"Just thinking about our friends."

"I'm worried about him, too," Sean said, knowing exactly what she was thinking. "But Nate will figure it out. And he has us."

"That he does."

Sean kissed the back of her neck and whispered, "When would it be tacky to kick out our guests and take you to bed?"

"Mr. Rogan!" she admonished with a laugh.

"I'm serious."

"I think we should eat first. And my boss is here. And I promised her this glass of wine."

"Party pooper."

"I have tomorrow off. Jesse has school. Just you and me all day. Alone."

"You? Me? *Alone?*" He laughed, then kissed her.

"What's so funny?"

"You don't remember that you invited Kane and Siobhan to stay all week?"

"Oh. No. I guess I didn't."

"Well, they can entertain themselves. I, for one, am going to pamper you all day."

"I can hardly wait," she said, and kissed him. "You can start now by fetching me another bottle of wine from the wine fridge—this bottle is empty."

"Your wish is my command."

He bowed and she laughed, watching him walk down the hall to the pantry.

She was so lucky to have Sean. He'd rebuilt her foundation after she was barely holding her life together. She was so much stronger now than before, and she owed it all to Sean's love and faith in her.

If he was killed—like Amanda lost Reggie—she might fall down that slippery slope of despair. Depression. Grief was complicated and no two people handled it the same way. She didn't want to face it. She didn't want to think about the possibility. Because she didn't know who she would be without her anchor.

"Lucy."

She turned. Jesse stood there with Bandit on a leash. An overwhelming sense of love washed over her. Jesse wasn't her biological son, but she loved him as if he were.

"Hey."

"I'm going to walk Bandit. Want to come?"

She shouldn't leave her own party . . . but a short walk would be good. She could clear her head and spend time with her stepson.

"Absolutely."

Sean returned with her wine. "Where are you going?"

"We're going to walk Bandit," Jesse said. "Come with us."

"We have a houseful of people."

Jesse waved at the laughing crowd outside. "They won't miss us for fifteen minutes."

Sean ran out and gave Rachel the glass of wine Lucy had already poured, the full bottle, and the opener. He said something, then ran back in.

"You're right. No one will miss us. Let's go."

Dear Reader,

The story behind *No Way Out* is a bit different than my other novellas. In *No Good Deed*, when we first meet Siobhan Walsh, I alluded to a backstory between her and Kane related to why Kane could no longer go into a certain part of Mexico. I wanted to explore that story more, and a wedding novella seemed a good place to do it. So the first chapter is what happened then, which sets the stage for the current story.

No Way Out might be my favorite of all my novellas. I know, I shouldn't pick favorites, but there are three things I particularly love about this story.

First, Sean and his brother Kane are the ones in jeopardy. Sometimes I get tired of the woman-in-jeopardy trope, even though it's popular and fun to write. Having two of the strongest male characters I've created be held captive and Lucy needing to find a way to save them before they're killed was a different twist. I've had Sean in jeopardy before, but this was very different.

Second, I was able to explore Sean and Kane's relationship, and how it has changed over the years. What they each admire about the other, and how they work together against all odds to save each other made me happy. These are two brothers who had ups and downs and don't always agree, but will always have each other's backs.

Finally, I enjoyed bringing in a full cast of characters at the end. This was supposed to be a quiet wedding for Siobhan and Kane . . . but clearly, nothing is easy for the Rogan/Kincaid clan!

Happy reading,
Allison

No Way Out

Prologue

Though Kane Rogan was no longer active military, he was still a soldier and a commander. He expected everyone to obey his orders because he knew how to keep people alive.

And his gut told him Siobhan Walsh had done something stupid. Something really, really stupid.

He and Blitz, his partner in this rescue operation in Tamaulipas, Mexico, sat in the courtyard of the Sisters of Mercy girls' home. Only girls were allowed inside, and Siobhan had nearly taken his head off when he said he didn't trust her.

"Half these girls have been trafficked and abused. The other half are nuns and missionaries. I will not have you terrifying them with your attitude and your arsenal. Wait here. I'll be ten minutes!"

She'd turned and walked into the building without looking at him.

Siobhan Walsh was Trouble with a capital T. Why had he let Andie talk him into this? He should have said no. He should have sent Ranger in with Blitz. He could have tapped someone else at Rogan-Caruso to lead the rescue. But because Andie had once been his commanding officer and he respected her, he'd promised to bring her younger half sister back to the US alive.

Damn bleeding heart. Know who you can save and who you can't, that's the only way you stay alive.

It had been five minutes.

"I should never have let her out of my sight," Kane mumbled.

Blitz glanced at him. "You think she's running."

"She didn't listen to a damn word I said."

Kane had a good relationship with the Sisters of Mercy because he'd helped them in the past, but he was still an outsider, and Siobhan's mother had been a missionary with the group. That gave the fiery redhead the upper hand.

"Wait here," Kane told Blitz, and followed the path Siobhan had taken into the mission.

The building was cooler than outside, the stone structure providing reprieve from the heat.

He listened. Silence.

He walked toward the front. He didn't want to scare any of the young women seeking refuge here, but Siobhan had used that against him, and she would pay for her deception.

He'd met Siobhan years ago through Andie, when Siobhan was still a teenager and he was still in the Marines. Though he was enlisted and Andie was an officer, they had become friends, largely because Kane had once served under her father's command and respected him tremendously. Andie had the same leadership skills as her dad. On base, he was the subordinate; here, he was a friend.

Siobhan had certainly grown up since he'd last seen her a decade ago. Why Andie couldn't keep tighter reins on her sister, Kane would never know.

Like you could keep tight reins on your family?

At least they did what he said, and if he said don't go to Tamaulipas because it was too dangerous, they would listen to him. This was his world. If he said stop, they would stop. If he said run, they would run.

And Siobhan Walsh had ignored the advice of her wise sister and walked right into the danger zone anyway. It took him two days to track her down, right outside Felipe Juarez's house, where she nearly got herself spotted by his patrol.

Juarez ran a criminal gang, mostly kidnappings for ransom or thugs for hire to transport drugs from point A to point B. Because he never ventured into the States, he wasn't on Kane's radar. He stayed in Tamaulipas and didn't traffic in humans. Kane focused on the battles that would have the most impact on the drug trade (which didn't pay much) or the jobs for hire that earned him enough money to go back to the low-paying battles.

Kane understood Siobhan's position. He'd seen far too many child brides over the years. But there was nothing they could do about it, and why she couldn't see that, he didn't understand.

You can't save everyone, Red.

Kane spotted one of the nuns that he fortunately knew by name. She was surprised to see him inside the mission. "Sister Jeanette, where is she?"

The sister didn't answer.

"Siobhan!" he said, louder than he intended. He lowered his voice. "She's going to get herself killed. Tell me where she is *now.*"

Sister Bernadette came into view. "Mr. Rogan, you will not yell at my girls."

Kane wasn't Catholic, but Sister Bernadette scared the bejeezus out of him.

"Siobhan," he said, keeping his voice so low it was almost a whisper.

"I told her to tell you."

"Tell. Me. *What.*"

"But she said you were making her leave. I don't think you understand the situation."

It took all his self-control not to lose it. "Getting involved in the personal lives of a criminal is never the smart move," Kane said. "Juarez runs a criminal gang and he stays local. We can't go in and dictate morality and justice in how they treat their family. I'm sorry, Sister, but kidnapping his daughter is not an option."

"She's thirteen years old and being forced to marry a man three times her age."

"Not my problem. If Juarez finds out you were helping her, he could cause you and *your* girls untold trouble. Worse, Siobhan is going to get hurt. Do you want her blood on your hands?"

He didn't mean to speak so forcefully with the nun, but he had to make her see the truth: that Siobhan was in way over her head and Felipe Juarez would kill her in cold blood.

"I will tell you where she went if you promise me you will save Hestia."

Well, fuck.

"She put you up to this." It was now as clear as day. He'd been played.

"Mr. Rogan, sometimes we need to do the right thing even when there is great risk."

Sister Bernadette didn't need to lecture him, and she knew it. He risked himself on a daily basis to do the right thing, but he always did a cost-benefit analysis. Not financial—he didn't give a shit what it cost. It was up to his business partner JT Caruso to manage the money. But the risk versus the odds of success. Half the girls here at the mission Kane and his team had rescued, and the Sisters were in the process of returning them to their families where possible. That was a justifiable risk.

Going after Juarez's only daughter was not.

There was no way this was going to end well. Even if they did save the girl, what could they do with her? She couldn't stay with the Sisters; Juarez would find her. She couldn't stay in Mexico, because she had no one to protect her. She was a kid, for chrissakes. That meant smuggling her into the US, getting her papers, putting her somewhere safe. Violating the law didn't bother Kane, but he didn't need another enemy in Mexico. He had plenty of those to go around.

Juarez was low-level in the grand scheme of things, but if Kane did what Siobhan wanted, it would cause untold problems for Kane and Rogan-Caruso, now and in the future.

Sister Bernadette stared at him and Kane felt increasingly uncomfortable. Guilty. How did she fucking do that? He had to weigh the risks versus the rewards in every operation, and the risks here were too great.

But there was no way he could face Andie and tell her he turned his back on her sister. If saving Siobhan meant getting Hestia Juarez out of this arranged marriage, then he'd have to do it, consequences be damned.

Fuck fuck fuck!

He hated being manipulated like this, and when he saved Siobhan and brought her and the kid back to the US, he would deliver her on Andie's doorstep in handcuffs and tell his long-time friend to keep her sister under lock and key because he wasn't going to rescue her again.

Then he'd have to let shit settle down or he'd never be able to set foot in Tamaulipas again. Hell, shit may never settle. If Kane had a kid, and someone took her, he wouldn't forgive or forget. He'd hunt them down to the ends of the earth and make them pay.

"I'll get them both," Kane said through clenched teeth. "Tell me where."

"Our Lady of Guadalupe. Felipe Juarez moved up the wedding. It's today."

* * *

Siobhan Walsh didn't have much time. She had to grab Hestia before she started down the aisle. She'd only have a small window of time where Hestia wasn't under her father's watchful eye.

Kane didn't understand. She'd had everything under control until her sister figured out what she was doing. Why had Andie sent a soldier down here in the first place? Sure, Kane was no longer a Marine, officially, but once a Marine, always a Marine. Siobhan knew that from her family. She loved her family, respected them more than they could know, but when it came to individual human lives, sometimes they had tunnel vision.

Siobhan had tried to explain the situation to Kane when he caught up with her, but it was a lost cause. He was a big-picture guy: burn a cocaine crop, shut down a trafficking organization, rescue the kid of a billionaire in order to pay the bills. Siobhan respected his vision, his path—why couldn't he respect hers? Why couldn't he see what she saw? Why didn't he care about a thirteen-year-old girl in a low-level crime syndicate being married off to a forty-year-old pervert? Because she wasn't an American hostage? Because Juarez didn't move enough drugs for Kane to care?

She would never forget what he said this morning.

"The risk isn't worth it."

How he could think that way, she'd never understand. One girl—a child—wasn't worth the risk? The risk to what? To whom? Kane Rogan risked his life every day, but he wouldn't risk it for a young girl? How could Andie be friends with a guy like that?

Siobhan had thought Kane Rogan was different. She'd heard stories of his heroics from her sister as well as the Sisters of Mercy. He'd saved two POWs under Andie's command. He'd saved a group of international scientists after a major earthquake south of Mexico City caused a mudslide and cut them off from civilization. He'd helped Sister Bernadette relocate one of their orphanages after they'd been unknowingly caught in the middle of two warring drug cartels in Guatemala. All those operations had been extremely dangerous. Was it the numbers? Eight nuns and twenty children were worth the risk, but one girl was not?

She might never understand how he thought. At this point, she didn't care anymore. She pushed aside her feelings—she'd been half in love with Kane Rogan since the day she met him when she was fifteen, but none of that mattered. She had a plan, and while it was dangerous, it could work. It *had* to work. She didn't yet know how she was going to cross the border with Hestia, but she'd worry about that later. She had friends who would help.

Not if they find out you kidnapped Felipe Juarez's daughter.

They wouldn't. Siobhan would be swift, so word wouldn't carry faster than she could travel.

Though it was the priest, Father Paulo Rodriguez, who initially alerted Sister Bernadette about the impending wedding, he couldn't be trusted. He lived in fear of the Juarez family and aided and abetted them in their criminal enterprise. He would perform the ceremony, unless Siobhan succeeded.

How he could balance the two lives, Siobhan didn't know, but now she was on her own.

Siobhan parked her truck as close to the church as she dared. She could see the people walking in, dressed in their Sunday best.

She looked at her watch. She had fifteen minutes. She said a prayer, slowed her racing heart, and hoped that Gino the altar boy did what he was supposed to do.

Siobhan did everything she could not to stand out, though that was difficult. She had a baseball hat so faded that only up close could you see the Washington Nationals insignia, and it did little to hide her curly red hair that she'd braided down her back. Not to mention she was tall, skinny, and pale. She couldn't tan to save her life. She hadn't had time to change—she knew Kane would be suspicious as soon as she left the courtyard at the mission—so she still wore jean shorts and a black tank top. All she had was some money, the truck, and her wits.

She hid the truck and crept along the bushes that grew thick along a dry creek bed on the backside of the church. Our Lady of Guadalupe was right off the main road into town, a pretty little stone church that was always full on Sundays, and half-full every other day of the week.

She'd been to the church several times before, and Gino had given her the inside scoop on where everyone would be. The biggest problem, aside from Juarez's patrols, was Christina Juarez, his sister, who would be with Hestia until her father came for her. Christina was dangerous. Hestia's nanny might also be there, but she was an old woman and Siobhan hoped she wouldn't try to stop them.

Too many variables. But what choice did she have? She'd never be able to live with herself if she didn't even try to save the girl who had begged her to take her away.

Siobhan watched as four armed guards patrolled the church grounds. They were focused on the church, not the rectory behind it, which was closer to the stream and where Siobhan was hiding. She knew from Sister Bernadette that a tunnel went from the rectory to the church. Gino had promised he'd unlock the door on the church side—Siobhan had to believe that he had done it.

Because the guards were focused on the main entrance, the rectory and trees shielded her approach from the south. Siobhan slipped in through the back door, the coolness of the rectory surprising her. The stone floors and adobe walls kept the place comfortable, even on hot days. She hesitated, listened.

"*Señorita*," a small voice said.

She turned and saw Gino. He was eight, Hestia's cousin and best friend and an altar boy. Juarez wouldn't kill him, but he might punish him if he learned that Gino had helped her.

"I told you just the door—you can't be involved with this, Gino."

"I want to help."

"It's too dangerous. Go back to the church."

He shook his head. "My *padre* left me at home. Said I was too young. I snuck out so I could open the door."

"*Go home.*" She didn't know if both she and Hestia were going to die today, but Hestia at least knew what she was doing. She had told Siobhan she would rather die than marry Francisco. She understood the risks; Gino did not.

He frowned.

"Now, Gino!" she said. "I don't have time to argue with you. I'll make sure Sister Bernadette tells you what happened and that Hestia is safe, okay?"

He frowned, but left.

She waited until she saw him hop on an old bike before she relaxed.

The rectory was small—two rooms and a kitchen. She went to the bedroom and opened the closet. The door to the tunnel was in the back of the closet. Gino had left the key in the lock for her, and if he'd done everything he'd promised, the door on the other end would be unlocked.

Dank air drifted out when Siobhan opened the door. The tunnel was dark and narrow. She turned on a small flashlight attached to her keychain.

A ladder went straight down.

"You can do this," she whispered.

She didn't like small, dark spaces.

She took a deep breath. Then another. She descended the ladder. At the bottom she listened.

Silence.

She shined her light down the passage. It was only fifty yards to the church, but the tunnel wasn't straight. She couldn't see to the end.

Siobhan looked back up the ladder. The faint light from the closet beckoned her. A powerful urge hit her, to go back up, to avoid the darkness, the unknown; her fear nearly undid her. She could tell herself that she was Hestia's only hope, that she *had* to go to the church this way, it was the only way, but telling herself and doing it were two different things.

She bit the inside of her cheek so hard she drew blood.

Then, faintly, she heard organ music.

She didn't have time to fear. If Hestia was to be saved from an awful fate, Siobhan had to act now.

Battling her urge to run back to the light, Siobhan turned into the dark, her small flashlight faintly illuminating the narrow passage. There was barely room for her. Bugs, spiders, any manner of creepy-crawlies touched her skin and it was all she could do not to scream. Tears burned as she made her way through as fast as she could . . . until she reached a dead end.

Was she lost? Had there been two passages? Had she missed a turn? She didn't think so. There had been no fork in the tunnel, unless she missed it.

She shined her light up. There was the ladder, a rope ladder that ended just above her head.

She reached up and grabbed the bottom rung. Siobhan was in good shape, but it took all her strength to pull herself up until her feet were able to rest on the bottom rung.

A very faint light shone through a crack above her. That was the door.

The organ music was louder, but it wasn't the wedding song yet. Voices, people talking and chatting as they waited for the ceremony.

Siobhan climbed quickly now that she could use her feet, held on, and listened.

She heard movement in the room, and then a female voice said, "Hestia, your groom is ready."

That was her aunt. Christina. Not a woman Siobhan wanted to face, but she might not have a choice.

"I need to use the bathroom," Hestia said, her voice small. "I just need a few minutes, please, *Tia*."

"You should be grateful," Christina said. "This marriage is going to bring wealth to our family. You will be able to produce an heir, unlike your mother, who produced only you."

"I am grateful," Hestia said.

Another voice said, "I'll make sure she is ready."

Rosita, Hestia's nanny. She hadn't wanted this marriage, either, but she feared Juarez and his reach.

"I'll tell your father you're coming. Do not delay, Hestia, you will embarrass our family, and most certainly be punished by your husband."

A door opened, closed.

This was Siobhan's only chance.

She pushed at the door. It yielded. Stuck. She pushed again. It opened.

Siobhan climbed out of the small closet, a flicker of a childhood memory, of her mother reading her *The Lion, the Witch and the Wardrobe*, and Siobhan wished she could transport Hestia to Narnia, where no one would find her.

But this was real, not fantasy.

Siobhan wiped off the cobwebs and dirt. Wide-eyed,

Rosita shook her head. "You can't be here! They'll kill you, they'll kill me!"

Hestia said, "I cannot marry that man. I would rather die than be his wife."

"Darling, don't say that. It won't be that bad."

"You can come with us," Siobhan said. "I'll take you to the US with Hestia."

"No. Hestia, I love you like my daughter. Please don't run. He'll find you. I fear for you. Your father is a powerful man. Francisco is a powerful man."

Rosita wanted Hestia to stay, but she wasn't doing anything to alert the guards.

Siobhan pulled zip ties out of her backpack. "To protect you," she said to the nanny.

Rosita had tears in her eyes, but she nodded. "Hit me," she whispered.

"I can't."

Rosita picked up a wood carving and hit herself. The sharp edge of the base cut her cheek and blood dripped down. The older woman staggered and fell to her knees.

Siobhan stifled a gasp, then used the zip ties on Rosita's wrists. "I'm sorry," she said.

"Go fast. Go fast or you will die."

Siobhan gently laid her to the floor, then stuffed a rag in her mouth and grabbed Hestia's hand.

They couldn't go back down the tunnel—too obvious, and they would be trapped. The only way out was the window, and it faced the back of the rectory.

"We get to my car and we go, no looking back," Siobhan said.

"Thank you, Siobhan. Whatever happens, thank you."

A guard passed by the window but didn't look inside. As soon as he disappeared from view, Siobhan pushed the frame open and helped Hestia out. The wedding dress was simple, but long and white, which stood out against the stark green-and-brown scenery. Fortunately, Hestia was in flats— satin ballet slippers—which would help her run.

Siobhan climbed out after Hestia, closed the window, and ran low, away from the guards, away from the church. Hestia held her skirt up with one hand while Siobhan grabbed the other and pulled her along.

No one saw them, and they made it to the first set of bushes, which obscured them from view of the church. The next open stretch was twice as long, and they'd be even easier to spot.

It was seventy-five yards to her hidden truck. Shorter than a football field, but just as open. If they were spotted, Juarez had the vehicles and people to follow them. The only thing Siobhan had was . . . damn. Her whole plan was dependent on tricking them. Of making Juarez think she went one way, but going another. Because they went out the window that faced that rectory, Juarez hopefully assumed they'd be going in that direction, to the north. So that even if Juarez didn't go to the rectory, he would be looking in the wrong direction. Just long enough to buy them the time to escape.

Dear God, please help us. Please help us get to the truck safely.

Then there was a shout. She looked, saw no guards.

Please let them look north first. Please.

"Now," she said.

Hestia ran with her over the open space. Siobhan didn't hear anyone pursuing them, but she didn't slow down or look.

Breathless, they reached the truck. Siobhan jumped in and started the ignition. Hestia climbed in next to her. It was a small, cramped two-seater but had a full tank of gas, thanks to the Sisters.

She pulled out, heading away from the church, her heart racing. They'd done it!

She drove parallel to the stream until she was forced by the terrain to turn northwest, which would take them to a dirt road. She willed the truck to go faster. She couldn't see anything behind her because of the dust that her wheels kicked up. But they were gaining speed. Not far now!

She reached the road, turned west, and a hundred yards later slammed on her brakes.

Two jeeps blocked the road. Four men stared at Siobhan, all with guns, all aimed at her.

These weren't Juarez's men. They were Francisco's men, the groom. They hadn't been here when Siobhan came in. Were they patrolling? Had they been alerted?

"Out," one of them ordered.

Hestia bit back a sob.

Siobhan put the truck in reverse. They wouldn't shoot; they didn't want to risk hitting Francisco's child bride.

She drove straight back, then curved until she almost fell into a ditch, braked, then put the truck in drive and spun around. There was another way out, but time wasn't on their side.

Another truck raced up to her, boxing her in.

Felipe Juarez jumped out. He had a gun aimed at Siobhan.

"Hestia! Come here!"

"Don't," Siobhan told her. "I'll—" She was going to say she'd think of something, but she didn't know what to do.

"I'm so sorry, Siobhan. I'm so, so sorry."

"This is not your fault," she said. She looked behind her. Francisco's men were still there.

"I'll beg for mercy, for my father to spare your life."

"I have one more idea. Trust me."

"I'm scared."

"So am I."

Siobhan had to believe that Juarez wouldn't shoot at his

daughter, or they would both die. She took a deep breath, then pressed the gas and turned the wheel sharply to the left, across the dirt field. She kept going, knowing they would be followed, but she didn't hear gunshots. She drove around the backside of the church, past the rectory, the truck violently bouncing up and down as she sped over the rocky terrain. Her head hit the roof more than once, but she focused on the land in front of her and prayed as hard as she'd ever prayed before.

Don't get a flat tire. Don't get stuck.

She spared a quick glance in the rearview mirror. They were following her. She glanced at Hestia, who clutched a Rosary bracelet, silently mouthing a Hail Mary.

The field dipped as they headed toward the main road, and the truck picked up speed. For a moment Siobhan thought that they had a chance, at least to get to the road and an area she was more familiar with. If she could get out of their range, out of sight, they would hide in the woods and cross the land on foot until she found a vehicle to steal. Anything to get away from the brutal Felipe Juarez—and get Hestia away from being forced to marry Francisco Duarte.

Out of the corner of her eye, she saw another vehicle come at her from an angle. It hit the back corner of her truck, forcing her to spin out and stall.

She was going to die.

Two men got out of the car. Thugs. They had their guns raised and shouted for her and Hestia to get out.

"Siobhan," Hestia said, biting back a sob.

The report of a rifle sounded, and Siobhan thought she was dead.

Kane gave Blitz the signal. Ten seconds later, through his binoculars, he saw the two men with guns on Siobhan and the girl fall dead to the ground.

Yes, Blitz had been a damn good hire. Elite snipers who could make a head shot on multiple targets were hard to find.

He watched as horror crossed Siobhan's face, but then she quickly restarted her truck and headed away from the church.

Good girl.

He had been lucky to find the boy on the road. Gino told him Siobhan's plan. She clearly wasn't thinking. How the hell did she think she could get the bride out of the *church* with two dozen armed men inside and out?

He radioed his pilot. "ETA."

"A good afternoon to you, too, Kane."

Kane wanted to throttle the kid.

"Twelve minutes," Sean said, without Kane having to ask him again.

"Nine," Kane said.

"Don't see how that's possible."

"Nine minutes and counting or you'll be transporting home a couple of corpses. Understood?"

"Yes, sir," Sean said, and clicked off the radio.

Damn kid. If he wasn't the best pilot Kane knew outside of the military, he'd never use him. But he wanted to keep Rogan-Caruso a family business, and that meant using Sean's unique skill sets—planes and computers. But he wasn't a soldier, he was a fucking kid genius with a degree from MIT. He treated these rescues as an adventure, a fucking *game*, and Kane wanted to knock some sense into him but didn't quite know how. Nothing he seemed to do or say got through to him. If he wasn't so damn good, Kane would have banned him until he acquired a healthy dose of fear.

Siobhan approached where he'd pulled off the road. She slammed on her brakes when she saw his Jeep, and was about to put the truck in reverse when she recognized him.

He motioned for her to get out.

"Faster, Red," Kane said, his mouth clenched. Damn, Juarez's men were too close. "Get in and stay down," he ordered.

She and Hestia climbed into the back seat and made themselves as small as possible. Kane waited a count of three, then detonated the explosives he'd set. The explosion shook the ground, but he didn't fall. He jumped into the driver's seat and sped off.

"That'll buy us a few minutes," he said. He glanced down at Siobhan, furious and relieved all wrapped into one. "Do you have a death wish, Red?"

"You could have helped from the beginning."

"You don't listen."

He didn't care if she was angry with him. Not his problem. And as soon as he got her back to the States, she'd never be his problem again.

Eight minutes later, they were in a small field. Sean's plane was landing. Kane stopped the Jeep, told them to get out.

"Are you injured?"

"No," Siobhan said. She had her arm protectively around Hestia.

Kane looked at the girl. She'd been made up like a doll, too much makeup on her young face. Her mascara had streaked and her eyeshadow was smudged, and at some point she'd wiped her lipstick off with the back of her hand, and it had smeared across her cheek. But she didn't look a day over thirteen, even with the glitz and glamour. His anger rose. At her father, at Francisco Duarte, at the reality that no girl should be forced to marry anyone against her will.

Hestia spontaneously hugged him. "Thank you, Mr. Kane. Thank you for saving my life."

Kane looked at Siobhan over Hestia's head. Caught her eye. Forced his expression to be as blank as possible.

Hestia was now his responsibility, as much as Siobhan was. And he wouldn't let either of them down.

Blitz came out of the woods from the right, and the plane stopped just short of their Jeep. Sean opened the door and smiled. "Anyone need a lift?"

Blitz said, "Move it, Little Rogan, they're almost here."

"Thank you," Siobhan told Kane quietly.

"You lied to me and manipulated me."

She glared at him. "I didn't lie to you. I told you I had to get my things. One of those things was Hestia. And I would do it again."

He knew she would. And he knew he would move heaven and earth to save her.

"You're impossible." He helped Hestia up into the plane, and then Siobhan. "Siobhan, my brother Sean. Get us out of here, kid."

Chapter One

Kane tipped his cold beer toward Sean. "Thanks for coming down."

"I wouldn't miss this for anything," Sean said. "I expected you to elope."

Damn, the kid was perceptive. "Siobhan wanted Andie to be here. It's not like I could refuse." Kane drained half his beer. He had never felt so . . . *content*, he supposed the word was. He'd never expected to settle down, though he didn't know how *settled* he and Siobhan would be, considering that she wasn't giving up her career as a photojournalist, and he had made it his life's mission to keep her safe.

Hell, he'd expected to be dead by now. Forty-five was old in his line of work. For the last year, especially after being shot in the back and losing a kidney, he knew he had to slow down. It was time for Sean and Lucy's brother Patrick to take RCK in a slightly different direction, focusing on corporate and computer security instead of international kidnappings and Kane's special causes.

Though he wouldn't give it up completely. He would simply be more selective in the jobs he took.

And he'd be lying to himself if he said he didn't enjoy his relationship with Sean. For years he'd used his brother's insanely talented piloting skills without really getting to know him. Partly out of self-preservation. Kane's life was dangerous, which by extension made Sean's life dangerous.

But recently, Kane had explored the idea that family was important. That Sean, and his wife Lucy, were as important to him as any of his brothers-in-arms, as important to him as the woman he'd fallen in love with. And while he liked—needed—his solitude out here on the RCK ranch in Hidalgo, Texas, he enjoyed knowing he could pop up to San Antonio for a couple days and catch up with his brother.

"Jack said that he and you were training a new crew for rescue missions. I never thought you would retire, but it's a good choice."

"Retire?" Kane laughed. "Hardly. We'll call it a semi-retirement. Blitz and Ranger are both more than capable of being team leaders."

Ezra, the caretaker who'd been at the ranch since long before Jack signed it over to RCK last year, walked up the porch steps. "The bunkhouse is ready for Lieutenant Colonel Walsh. Need anything before I head out?"

"Thanks for staying an extra day," Kane said.

"I'm sorry I'll miss her. If I didn't have this trip planned I would have stayed."

Ezra was old-school military, a veteran of both Vietnam and Desert Storm. He'd turned sixty-eight this year but had no intention of leaving the ranch. Jack Kincaid had brought him on when Jack left the Army, and Ezra had been here ever since. He lived in a two room cabin on the other side of the airplane hangar and kept to himself when Kane was around, but mostly made sure the ranch was functional when first Jack, then Kane, left on a mission. Took care of anything that came up, and he was a magician with planes and trucks.

"Tell the Lieutenant Colonel semper fi from this old Army sergeant."

"I will," Kane said.

"I left a little something for you and Siobhan in the house."

"Thanks, Ezra. For everything."

Kane watched as his old friend waved and drove off in his Jeep.

"Where's he off to?"

"Reunion with his squad. They meet in Denver every year." Ezra had never married, had no children, and his squad was his family—as well as the Rogans and the Kincaids.

Kane glanced over at Sean. "Stop thinking about it."

"What?"

"Jesse. In California. There's nothing you can do. You made the agreement with McAllister, live with it."

"Screw you."

Kane didn't take offense. He knew Sean was going through a rough patch right now. It was the first time his son, Jesse, was in California staying with his maternal grandfather without Sean in the picture. Kane would have been willing to fight, but he understood that Sean feared losing Jesse if it went to court. McAllister had the time and money to dig deep into Sean's life, into Lucy's life, to find ways to hurt them. So letting Jesse spend a couple days here and there with his grandfather was the compromise. It was Christmas break and now was as good a time as any. Sean had legal custody and the court had recognized that he was Jesse's biological father. Jesse had willingly changed his last name to Rogan. Kane didn't know why Sean was so worried.

But he didn't say anything. It took a minute, but Sean said, "McAllister is going to say *anything* to turn my son against me. I know it. I just have to trust Jesse not to listen to his lies."

Sean was more trusting than Kane. Jesse was a good kid, and he loved Sean, but he was thirteen and impressionable. Sending him for a week to stay with a man who hated Sean was borrowing trouble. But Kane didn't say anything—it was clear Sean wasn't comfortable with the whole thing, and had probably thought of everything Kane would say.

Still, Jesse was a strong kid. He'd already faced more in his young life than most thirteen-year-olds, and Sean had done a great job getting him through the rough patches.

Though Kane didn't put anything past Ronald McAllister, he said—mostly to give Sean hope—"Jesse isn't going to believe bullshit, Sean. He's your kid, he'll talk to you. You've only had him for a few months, but you've done good."

Sean didn't say anything.

"If you want to go to California, I understand," Kane said.

"The deal was McAllister gets Jesse the week after Christmas and two weeks in the summer. I put him on a plane yesterday before Lucy and I drove down here. He'll be home Friday night."

"Then get rid of the long face, kid. I'm getting married. Never thought I'd say it."

"Never thought I'd hear it."

An alarm went off, then stopped. Kane frowned. Looked at his phone, which Sean had hooked up to the security system. "Western perimeter. Could be nothing—these things go off weekly. Animals, kids, a few times the cartel moving drugs—I nipped that in the bud. They know to stay away from this place. But with Ezra gone, I need to go check it out."

"Siobhan and Lucy won't be back for a few hours, I'll join you."

"Stay alert."

Kane sounded more serious now.

"Is there a new threat?" Sean asked.

He glanced at his little brother as they hopped into his truck. "There's always a threat," he said as he drove west down the dusty road. "Jack and I have been thinking of expanding the ranch here, using it for training. The bunkhouse where Andie will be staying has a large living area and another large sleeping area. Kitchen and bathroom are functional, need updating. Ezra's been working with some local contractors on planning a redesign. We can convert the sleeping area to four two-man rooms, add a second bathroom, update the kitchen. JT likes the idea—we don't have the facilities in California, and it's gotten way too expensive there to house our field team, not to mention all the rules and regulations. Jack signed over all two thousand acres to RCK. We want to use it for RCK."

"Eight men on site?"

"Or women. I don't have any female veterans on staff right now—but we have in the past. I was talking to Andie last week. She has a female enlisted soldier who is transitioning out, thinks would be a good fit for RCK. Trilingual, seen action, sharp on her feet. I'm going to meet with her after her debrief. If she works out, she'll have her own room—if Ezra can get the bunkhouse in order that fast."

"Sounds like a lot of changes."

He shrugged. "Ranger has his own place in Laredo, he's not moving. Blitz will, I've talked to him. Maybe Lucky. I like the idea of having backup here."

"It sounds to me like you're expecting trouble."

"It won't matter if I take an ad out in every major international newspaper in the western hemisphere that I'm retiring—which I'm not—there will still be scumbags who want my head. I'm okay with that."

"Maybe you should leave the area. Here, you're only fifteen miles from the border."

"I'm not moving."

"Just saying Montana or Wyoming have a lot of land and might be safer."

Kane glanced at him. "I hate snow."

Sean laughed. "I never knew that about you."

Kane pulled up at the western fence. The entire ranch was

surrounded by split-rail fencing, but much of it was decades old. The cost to maintain and repair was steep, though they kept on top of it as much as they could. Sean had installed sensors where a breach was most likely to occur—along the roads, generally. The property was surrounded by farmland, with a two-lane road separating them from their neighbors. The Santa Ana National Wildlife Refuge was to the south.

"You can always move to San Antonio," Sean added.

"Let's put it this way, Sean. I haven't had roots since I enlisted in the Marines when I was eighteen. Now I do. I'm not digging them up."

Sean considered what Kane said. Kane had more than earned peace in his life, and he wasn't actually retiring—though Sean wouldn't question it if he did. Six years in the Marines followed by twenty years as a mercenary, soldier-for-hire, whatever you called it. When he and JT founded Rogan-Caruso—which had become Rogan-Caruso-Kincaid eight years ago—they created a business that filled a void in the market, as well as a void for them, as veterans. Sean was one of the few who hadn't served in the military.

But Kane seemed to be a cat on his last life. Losing his kidney and nearly dying last year had been a wake-up call. It wasn't his first serious injury, but it had been bad. Then he had reconnected with Siobhan and realized that he was more than his job. Sean was glad Kane had found a balance, and he hoped it lasted.

Sean and Kane got out of the truck. Kane stood and surveyed the area with binoculars, while Sean went over to the sensor that had tripped the alarm.

He squatted to inspect the small device. It was cracked, which was what had caused the alarm to ping in the first place. He'd had to play a lot with the sensitivity of the sensors—he didn't want them going off in the wind or if a coyote slipped under the railing. But what had caused it to crack? The light breeze that had built up that afternoon couldn't send rocks or debris at the velocity necessary to break the sensor.

Sean stood and looked beyond the fence. "What road is this?" Sean asked Kane, gesturing to the one-lane paved road that was on the other side of a drainage ditch.

"It leads down to the Dickersons' farm. They farm sorghum, primarily for livestock feed. Good people."

Which meant in Kane-speak that one or more of the family had served honorably in the military.

"Do they use this road a lot?"

Kane shrugged. "I haven't talked to the family in a while, but they generally harvest in October. I don't know if the recent storms impacted them, though we didn't get hit like San Antonio did."

"Something hit the sensor. It could have been a rock from the road, but that seems like a one-in-a-thousand chance."

Kane took another look with the binoculars. "Nothing out of place."

There was no place for a sniper to hide, one of the benefits of having wide, flat property. The buildings were clustered on the southern end of the property, and that barrier was far more difficult to traverse because there was no road—only the 1,800-foot-long runway they maintained. Plus, Sean had heightened the security on the southern fence because he could use the power from the house and hangar.

"Since you're going to be living here full time with Siobhan, you might want to consider cameras."

"What's that going to cost RCK?"

"It's only worth doing if you're going to do it right."

"So a small fortune."

"I need to look at the power structure, see what I can tap into, see if we need to run any lines. These sensors work off solar power, but the camera needs a direct, dedicated, and closed intranet connection for real-time—"

"I don't need details. Work it out with Duke, but cameras are overkill."

"What happened to 'always be prepared'?"

Kane didn't respond. He did a third survey of the terrain. "I'll talk to Ezra about the Dickersons when he returns, see if they're working out on this part of their property. We might need to adjust the sensors if there's more traffic."

"If someone is going to breach here, they can."

"*You* can't fix it?"

"I can, but I need a new sensor, then I need to hook it up to the network and test it. I'll do it on Sunday, before Lucy and I head home."

"I haven't heard of any serious threats in the last few months," Kane said as they climbed back into the truck. "I still keep my ear out. RCK has a lot of people listening for chatter, and not just people who want to get back at me."

Kane drove slowly along the fence, to see if there was anything out of place. There wasn't. Sean ran a quick diagnostic on his phone of all thirty sensors around the perimeter and nothing else was broken.

Maybe Kane was right and it was just a fluke.

"You're not usually this paranoid, kid."

"It's been a wild few months."

"True. Did anything change after my last visit to St. Catherine's?"

"They're still on track, no problems Mateo and Ruth can't handle."

Kane had stayed involved with the orphan boys at St. Catherine's who they'd rescued nearly two years ago from a cartel using them as drug mules. When the older brother of one of the boys made contact and tried to recruit him into a gang, they'd all had to work together to protect the kids. The oldest was fourteen and the youngest was ten. Their families were either in prison or dead, and all they had was the home that Sean had built for them, run by a priest Sean and Lucy had befriended during the original investigation.

Sean was glad that Kane was more involved. He elicited respect from the kids, and they needed firm guidance as well as understanding. Kane knew what demons they lived with, and he was honest and blunt. Sean didn't have the tough love gene that Kane had. He was more the big-brother type who helped with homework, taught them computers, and cheered at their soccer games. It worked, though—the boys had adjusted and were doing well across the board.

Twenty minutes later, they were back at the main house. Out of habit, Kane checked the security system. "All is good. Another beer?"

Sean looked at his watch. "Shouldn't we be getting ready for the rehearsal?"

"Rehearsal?" Kane laughed. A real laugh. "This is going to be quick. Andie is walking Siobhan down the aisle. You and Lucy are standing up for us. Padre is going to say the prayers, then tell us we're legally married. And married under God in a Catholic Church, which is important to Siobhan, so who am I to say the Big Guy in the Sky doesn't exist? What do I know, anyway?" He handed Sean a beer. "Relax."

"You're far more relaxed than I was when I married Lucy, and I didn't have any doubts."

"I won't have a church full of friends and family watching. I don't have to entertain anyone. You had nearly a hundred people at your house—I don't think I could handle that kind of invasion. After the wedding, Siobhan and I are flying to Colorado. Plane is already fueled and packed. Thank you for the week at your place there."

"It's yours anytime."

"Then we go to Ireland."

"Have you ever been?"

"No. Can't say I want to, either, but Siobhan's grandmother insisted."

"I went once, when I was in college."

"I know."

"You know?"

"Kid, you think I didn't know where you were at all times? You're a Rogan. I always kept tabs on you."

Sean supposed he should have known that intuitively, but he didn't think about it back then, when he and Kane rarely saw each other. He hadn't told Duke he was going to Europe. When Duke sent him to MIT after he was expelled from Stanford, it took Sean years to forgive him. And to this day, though Sean and Duke had a much better relationship, that time was still a sore spot.

If Duke hadn't sent him away, Sean would have known Madison was pregnant. He would have been in Jesse's life from the day he was born.

And chances are you would never have met Lucy. You would never have become who you are today. Don't play those mind games, Sean. They are never productive.

Siobhan was a great influence on Kane. He had mellowed, at least a bit. He smiled more. He'd never lose the edginess he had—too many years as a soldier—but he'd found a sense of peace that Sean was grateful for. For too long, Sean expected to hear that his brother was dead or missing. Now, Kane restrained himself from taking every case that crossed his path.

Sean wanted the time with his brother. He wanted Jesse to have time with his uncle. The Rogans had never done "family" well. Sean didn't pass along blame—their parents had many wonderful traits. They were smart, inquisitive, patriotic, and free spirits, of a sort. Sean never doubted that his parents loved him, but he'd wondered if having kids had been unexpected and unplanned. They hadn't grown up as a tight family unit, and then his parents were killed in a plane crash and his life was upended.

"Since we're not doing a rehearsal," Sean said, "I'll get dinner started. The girls should be back soon."

"That's why I invited you, kid," Kane said, laughing. "You can cook."

Chapter Two

Lucy had a lovely day with Siobhan. They picked up Siobhan's wedding dress—a family heirloom that her grandmother had sent over from Ireland and Siobhan had altered. Instead of a full-length gown, because of Siobhan's height, she had it hemmed to hit mid-calf and took off the train so it didn't look funny. But the Irish lace was exquisite, and the antique white complemented her curly red hair.

Lucy had brought a nice cocktail dress, but Siobhan had picked one out for her that she wanted her to wear. "Andie will be in her dress uniform, and so will Kane. I made sure Sean was bringing his tuxedo, so please, let me get this dress for you."

Lucy could hardly say no when she saw the classy, calf-length sleeveless dress in a rich blue, somewhere between royal and navy. It fit perfectly, and Siobhan admitted that she'd had Sean send her dress size.

Siobhan refused to let Lucy pay for it. "I'm just *so* happy that you and Sean could come down. I don't think Kane would have waited much longer, and Andie isn't able to easily get time off."

"Once Kane sets his mind on something, he doesn't like to wait," Lucy concurred.

They were having a drink in a café in McAllen, where they were relaxing while waiting for Andie's plane to land. One of the benefits of being a Marine was that Andie could often grab a free ride. She had flown from Quantico to Lackland Air Force Base in San Antonio earlier, and a friend of Kane's was flying her down to Moore Airfield. Her ETA was five thirty.

"I'm glad Padre refused to marry us last week," Siobhan said. "We were coming back from Arteaga—we'd helped the Sisters with a project—and drove by Padre's church. Kane said, 'Let's get married.' I didn't answer—I was, well, in shock."

"Your ring is gorgeous. It looks like an antique."

She smiled and showed off the simple round diamond with two sapphires on either side. "Kane bought it spontaneously months ago, he told me. For a man who can strategize and execute any military operation without hesitation, he was so nervous. When I could finally speak and said *Of course I'll marry you*, he made a U-turn and went back to the church." Siobhan laughed. "I didn't mean right that minute, but Kane did. I really wanted Andie here. Kane did everything to talk me into it, but Padre sided with me, and Kane gave in. He called Sean and I'm so glad you two could make it the same weekend that Andie could take leave."

"We are both so happy for you."

Siobhan beamed at her ring. "It's been a good year. I don't think Kane really cares whether we're married or not, but deep down I wanted to. I never said it—but I guess Kane picked up on it. I'm a little more traditional than I thought I was."

"Sean and I were happy living together, but marriage is a commitment. A deeper bond. And being Catholic, that deep-seated guilt of living together out of wedlock doesn't really go away."

Siobhan smiled in understanding. "Amen, sister."

"I'm thrilled to have you as a sister-in-law. I'm close to Dillon's wife Kate, but they live so far away. I miss them a lot."

A chill went up Lucy's spine. It was the feeling she had when someone was watching her. She looked around the café. There weren't many people there in the middle of the afternoon. Three women chatting at the bar drinking colorful cocktails; two men, who looked like a father and son, eating sandwiches in the corner. A group of coworkers who'd come in shortly after Lucy and Siobhan. A very affectionate couple in the corner. So affectionate it made Lucy blush.

"What's wrong?"

"Nothing."

None of the people in the café were watching them. Lucy looked out the window and saw a man sitting in a dark brown sedan across the street. He didn't seem to be staring at her, but what if he had been? She couldn't see the license plate from here, but she burned his image in her mind. Dark, thick hair, light-brown skin, mustache, tattoo on his left arm that was hanging out the window. She couldn't make out the design.

"Lucy?"

"Just my cop instincts working overtime."

"Kane says you have sharp instincts. You should listen to them."

"I will. It's that guy—don't look!—across the street. I think he was looking at us."

"Maybe because we're two attractive women and he's a cad."

"Maybe." Except they were inside. Sitting at a window, but would he be able to easily see them?

Siobhan leaned over the small table and squeezed Lucy's hand. Lucy wasn't a touchy person—she valued her personal space—but she accepted the reassurance.

"What do you want to do?"

Lucy wasn't sure. She sipped her drink—barely tasted it—and watched the street. A minute later, a second man—same basic appearance as the driver, but older and with military-short hair—got into the passenger seat and they drove off. She breathed easier; she caught the license plate number as they drove by and wrote it down.

"They're gone. Sorry."

"No apologies."

"I really enjoyed Thanksgiving at your place," Siobhan said. "I love your family as if they're my own."

"I'm glad. They *are* your family now."

Lucy missed them. She'd been becoming nostalgic of late. She loved San Antonio, and she loved her job, but she didn't like that half her family was on the East Coast and half her family was on the West Coast. Even though she was halfway between them, it didn't seem to help. But if she moved west or east, half her family would still be a continent away.

She glanced at her watch. "It's nearly five thirty."

Siobhan paid the small tab—they'd both had a glass of white wine and split a fruit and cheese plate. Shopping had made Lucy famished, and she was still hungry.

"Talking about family," Siobhan said as they walked out to her car, "I haven't seen my grandmother in more than a year. I'm so looking forward to going to Ireland, then we'll have a long layover in Virginia to spend time with Andie, since we're not going to get much time now. I love that she's not deployed anymore, so she comes home every night."

"It sounds like a great and well-deserved vacation."

"If we went anywhere else, Kane would be half working. It's his way. He never truly relaxes. But my grandma lives in a small village in Killarney and after a few days he'll realize that there's nothing for him to do. Either he'll go crazy with boredom or he'll finally take it easy and enjoy the peace."

"It sounds lovely," Lucy said.

"We'll have to plan a trip there, you and I. You would love my grandma."

Siobhan pulled away from the curb, changing the subject from her trip to a new spread she was photographing. She was a photojournalist and much of her work was done to raise money for the Sisters of Mercy and bring awareness of worlds outside the US border. It was grueling, dangerous, and rewarding.

Lucy thought she saw the brown sedan again, but it was down a side street moving away from them, the license plate too far to read. She wasn't positive it was the same vehicle, but she'd been on alert ever since she'd felt that creep looking at her.

Crime was a problem in the area. Mostly car thefts, muggings, property crimes. Violent crime was higher here than in other parts of Texas, but it was fairly stable, and daytime was generally safe. Still, predators often saw women as easy marks.

Lucy would not be an easy mark.

By the time they arrived at Moore Airfield—a private aviation field—Lucy had pushed the vehicle to the back of her mind. Not out of her mind, though—she had learned to be cautious. She and Siobhan had been shopping, had carried bags to the truck—it was Kane's decked-out Ford. More than a decade old, but in excellent condition. If the thugs were watching them, they might think about jumping them for their stuff, or stealing the truck. If that was the case, she shouldn't see them again.

Siobhan looked at her phone as soon as she stopped. "She's here!"

Lucy smiled. Siobhan sounded like a little kid.

They walked over to the small building that separated the

main airfield from the parking lot. Andie came in through the double doors. She was dressed in her everyday military uniform, her dark-blond hair pulled back into a tight, smooth bun.

"Andie!" Siobhan rushed over and hugged her before her sister could put down her garment bag.

"It's good to see you, too, sis," Andie said with a surprised grin.

"Lucy! This is my sister, Lieutenant Colonel Andrea Walsh."

Lucy extended her hand. "Pleased to meet you."

"Lucy Kincaid, I've heard so many great things about you, and not just from Sean and Kane."

"Well, thank you." She didn't know who else would talk about her—Jack had been Army, not the Marines, and she didn't know anyone who worked on the military base.

Andie said, "You're thinking. I know your sister-in-law Megan really well. Years ago—gosh, twenty years now. Megan was a new agent, and I was deployed to Kosovo as part of a protective detail when the FBI was working a crime scene after the civil war there."

"She worked under Dr. Hans Vigo," Lucy said. She had been expecting Andie to say she knew Kate, who worked at the FBI Academy at Quantico, so hearing about Megan surprised her.

"Yes, I remember Dr. Vigo. He was in charge of the unit."

"Small world."

"Indeed. Nice to finally put a face to the name. I wish Sean had introduced us when you were at training in Quantico."

"Do you have everything?" Siobhan said. "Sean's cooking and I'm starving."

"Some things never change."

Andie slid into the back of the extended cab and they left

the airfield. It was nearly an hour's drive back to the outskirts of Hidalgo. By the time they were on the road, the sun had set, casting an orange hue over everything.

"I'll let Kane and Sean know we're on our way," Lucy said.

Kane answered Sean's phone. "It's Kane. Sean's making a pie. If the security business goes south, he can open a restaurant."

"Ha ha," Lucy heard Sean in the background.

"Tell me it's chocolate pecan," Lucy said.

"Apple," Kane said.

"Second best."

"Chocolate pecan?" Kane groaned. "Sounds awful."

"It's amazing."

Kane said, "Sean said he'll make it when you go home."

"I'm counting on it." Lucy loved anything with chocolate. "We picked up Andie and are on our way back."

"Padre's coming by for dinner. He has some questions for Siobhan and me. I don't see what he needs to know."

"Humor him," Lucy said. "We'll be there in about forty minutes."

She ended the call and looked over at Andie in the back seat. Lucy was about to say something when she saw the dark-brown sedan again, following them at a distance.

"Lucy?" Andie questioned.

"I saw that car twice before. Once for certain, they were outside the café where Siobhan and I had a drink, then I thought I saw it turn off the road a few minutes later."

Andie looked. They were far enough back, and in the rapidly falling sun, neither of them could see the driver or if there was a passenger.

Lucy called Nate Dunning, her colleague and friend. He was staying at their house with Bandit, their dog, while they were here. "What's up?" Nate said.

"Can you run a license plate for me?"

"I'm not at headquarters, but I can get it done. Give me a few minutes. What's going on?"

"A car I've seen a couple of times. Might be following us." She read off the number. "Texas plates. It's an older car, a brown Ford sedan, but I'm the first to admit I don't know car makes well."

"I got it. I'll call you back."

Lucy held her phone and considered calling Sean, but they didn't know anything yet. As soon as she had the information from Nate, she'd give Sean the heads-up.

"Are you sure it's the same car?" Siobhan asked.

"Yes," Lucy said. "The same as outside the café for certain. But they're staying far back. I don't know what they're up to. I think we should lose them."

"I don't know that I can," Siobhan said. "I was going to turn right at the next street. Ware's a straight shot down to Hidalgo."

"Don't turn. Go to the next street, then turn right. If they follow, I'll navigate."

Siobhan was tense. Lucy didn't want to scare her—and maybe she *was* being paranoid—but she wasn't going to take any chances. She understood Kane's lifestyle and that his life could bleed into Siobhan's. Kane had made it clear to Siobhan that she could be at risk, and he didn't have to tell the same to Lucy.

Not to mention that Siobhan had upset the apple cart when she exposed a black-market baby operation and helped reunite the stolen babies with their birth mothers. It was how Lucy and Siobhan first met, and Lucy had liked her immediately, even before she knew Siobhan was close to the Rogan family.

Siobhan turned at the street past Ware. Lucy looked behind them. The sedan didn't follow.

"They went straight," Lucy said.

Siobhan's grip loosened on the steering wheel. "False alarm."

Lucy wasn't going to make that call, not yet. There could be a second tail, or whoever was following them suspected their destination was the ranch.

Two minutes later, Nate called Lucy back. "The car is registered to Juanita Zapalo of Edinburg. She's seventy-two years of age."

"A Hispanic male of about thirty was driving."

"Want me to run Zapalo?"

Lucy almost said no, then changed her mind. "Might get us in trouble, I don't really have cause, but my gut tells me something is odd."

"I'm on it. I'll call you as soon as I know anything."

"Thanks."

Lucy then called Sean's number. It rang four times, then voice mail picked up. She left a brief message. "Sean, it's Lucy, call me back. We're about thirty minutes out, but I need to talk to you."

She called Kane's number.

He didn't answer, either. She didn't leave a message.

"Now I'm scared," Siobhan said.

"They're probably outside barbecuing," Lucy said, not wanting Siobhan to panic. "Kane hates his phone."

"Sean doesn't," Siobhan said, stating the obvious. "Sean dependably answers his phone, day or night." She sped up. "Grab my phone and call Padre."

Lucy caught Andie's eye. Yeah, they were all worried. "Siobhan, don't go the normal way home, okay? Go a completely different route."

"But it'll take longer."

"Do it," Lucy said. Her phone beeped. Nate had run a quick search on the vehicle owner. She'd died a year ago and had no known family. The car could have been sold by the court, given to a friend, stolen, and they wouldn't know without more investigation. They didn't have time for that now.

She called Padre—Father Francis Cardenas—and he answered on the second ring. "Siobhan? I'm on my way. Mass just ended."

"Father, it's Lucy Kincaid. Siobhan and Andie are here with me. We just tried calling the ranch and neither Kane nor Sean is answering. How far out are you?"

"I'm leaving the rectory now. Fifteen minutes. Do you have a reason to be concerned?"

"A car followed us earlier today, and then I saw it again. Kane said there were no known threats."

"Nothing new, at any rate. Where are you?"

Lucy told him. "It's about twenty minutes, but we're going an alternate route."

"I'll meet you at the ranch."

Lucy ended the call. Her stomach flipped.

Something was definitely wrong.

Chapter Three

Sean never cooked until he started dating Lucy—other than spaghetti—but he found that he was good at it. More, it relaxed him.

Baking was a new thing, however. He and Jesse started with cookies, and then Sean tried a few pies—including the chocolate-pecan recipe that was now Lucy's favorite. Apple pie was easy, though he cheated with premade crusts. When he was done, he popped it into the preheated oven and turned his attention to the kabobs he and Lucy had prepared that morning. A full tray of steak, green peppers, and onions; and a tray of chicken, red peppers, and pineapple. Perfectly marinated. The barbecue was almost ready, but the kabobs didn't take long to cook, so Sean would wait until the girls were back.

He picked up his phone to call Lucy and had no signal.

"Kane, is there something wrong with the cell repeaters I installed last time I was here?" Because they were far outside of town, reception was sketchy. Sean had set up a series of repeaters around the property to tap into three different cell towers in three different directions.

"The storm that blew through last month screwed with one

of them. I've had a little trouble, but only when we're in the hangar. I haven't had problems in the house."

"You should have told me."

Kane shrugged.

Sean shook his head. "I'll go take a look. I had one mounted on the west side of the hangar, which gets the best signal from the tower in town. If it's just knocked out of alignment I can fix it in two minutes."

Sean would be miserable with unreliable cell service or internet, but Kane didn't care. Half the time he didn't even answer his phone, and he never called just to talk to someone. When Kane called him about getting married, Sean almost thought he'd dreamed the conversation, it was so short.

"It's Kane. Siobhan and I are getting married a week from Saturday. Padre's church. We'd like you and Lucy to stand up for us."

"Wow, Kane, that's terrific! Thank you, we'd love to. But ten days? Isn't that kind of short notice for everyone?"

"It's just you and Andie. Thanks."

And he'd hung up.

Sean had sent Kane a message that he might want to at least call their family and friends, let them know what was going on. He suspected Kane didn't want a party—he didn't relax easily, and he didn't like crowds. He'd disappeared shortly after Sean's wedding because there were too many people in Sean's house, where they had the reception.

An hour later, Sean was copied into a message that went to the RCK board, a few other staff that Kane worked with, and his core field unit.

Siobhan and I are getting married. We'll be in Ireland for three weeks and I'm not taking any jobs until after Feb 1.

Kane didn't do "social" well.

Sean took the ranch truck over to the hangar. It was two hundred yards from the house, so he could have walked, but the wind was picking up, tossing tumbleweeds around.

It wasn't a working ranch. They kept the land cleared and maintained the airstrip for small planes. The hangar could hold two small planes if necessary, though usually only Kane's was stored there. There was an unused eight-stall barn that needed some work; Siobhan had mentioned to Sean that she'd love to have a couple of horses. Jack had put in a gun range that Kane had upgraded, but most of the space was open.

At one time, before Jack Kincaid bought the property, it had been part of a much larger farm that grew sorghum and raised cattle, but these 2,000 acres hadn't been used in some time. Jack knew the owner, got a good deal, and used the place for more than ten years as his home base—convenient since much of his work, before and after he joined Rogan-Caruso-Kincaid, was south of the border. He'd recently signed the property over to RCK because Jack was settled in Sacramento with his wife, but Kane had been using it on and off for years—especially since last summer, when he'd lost his kidney and needed time and space to recuperate.

Sean stopped the truck at the southwest corner of the hangar. He kept the headlamps on because of the setting sun. As soon as he got out and looked up, he saw the problem: the repeater wasn't there.

He looked down and found it on the ground, clearly damaged. He might be able to fix it with enough time and patience, but they weren't that expensive to replace.

Still, this inoperable repeater shouldn't have denied him cell service in the house. He looked at his phone. Still no service.

He heard a buzzing noise and looked up and around; at first he didn't see anything in the twilight.

He recognized the sound. It was a drone. As he looked, he could make out the moving machine, heading toward the house.

It appeared to be a simple unit with a camera, a high-end toy. But Sean couldn't risk that it was innocuous or that it was just a kid messing around.

Sean jumped in the truck and sped toward the house. If it wasn't a kid, it could easily be someone working surveillance on Kane. If Sean had a signal, he could hack into the drone and figure out where the person who controlled it was standing; the newer models could be worked well over a mile. One that Sean had tested had a five-mile radius. Military drones had far more abilities.

As he got closer to the drone, he realized that it wasn't a camera mounted on the front. What the hell was it?

He parked next to the house, and when he got out of the truck he saw that there was more than one drone flying around the property. He detected movement more than distinct shapes. What the hell?

"Kane!" he shouted.

Kane stepped out onto the porch, holding his gun. Before he responded to Sean, he saw the drone. He immediately fired his weapon and the drone fell to the ground. By the sound, at least two other drones were circulating.

Sean ran over to the fallen device. He inspected what he had first thought was a camera. "This is why we have no service—these drones all have cell blockers. We're dead in the water here."

"Get inside," Kane ordered.

"We need to leave. Get in the truck," Sean said.

"We leave, we're exposed. Get inside."

Sean wanted to argue with his brother, a rarity. Kane was almost always right about tactical situations. But this time . . . something wasn't adding up.

"We need to warn Lucy and Siobhan. They'll be here soon, and we have no fucking way to warn them!"

A low-level alarm rang in the house.

"Someone rammed the gate," Kane said. "Get in the truck."

Now he changed his mind. Sean took the driver's seat while Kane went back inside the house. What was he doing?

Sean looked down at his phone. He still had no reception, but he typed out a text message for Lucy and hit send. His phone would keep trying until the message got out.

In the distance, Sean saw dust kicked up by multiple vehicles before he saw the vehicles themselves. They all had lights off. Looked to be at least four trucks or SUVs, all heading toward the house.

"Dammit, Kane!" Sean mumbled.

Kane finally emerged with weapons and his go-bag. He jumped into the passenger seat and Sean did a one-eighty, heading away from the oncoming trucks.

They headed toward the west side of the property to the service gate. He'd have to ram the truck through it, but the truck had a reinforced front end. He'd make it. Halfway there, Sean remembered the broken sensor. It had been intentionally destroyed, and now Sean knew why.

Three vehicles, all with multiple armed men, waited for them on the other side of the gate—which had been forced open. One man, in his fifties, with a round stomach and a rifle, stood on the flatbed of a truck.

Sean was about to turn left, to cut across the field and hope to get to the main gate, or at least buy them time to figure something out, when the men started shooting. They were aiming at the tires.

They hit the engine and the truck screamed in protest as Sean tried to turn. Then his front right tire blew. At the speed and angle he was going, Sean could barely keep control, but he managed to keep the truck upright as it stalled.

He turned the ignition. Nothing. Again. Nothing. Shit.

Kane had his gun out; Sean did the same.

Over a bullhorn, a booming voice said, "Kane Rogan. Get out of the vehicle. Drop your weapon. I don't want you dead, not yet."

Kane didn't budge. Neither he nor Sean had a clear shot of the man speaking from the back of the pickup on the other side of the fence.

The four trucks that had pursued them now surrounded them.

That's when Sean noticed Kane had a grenade in his hand.

"Felipe Juarez," Kane muttered. "Fuck."

Juarez was the man who had nearly got Kane killed the year before. His men had been pursuing Kane and shot him, and Sean had been part of the rescue team deep in the Tamaulipus region of Mexico.

But that wasn't the first time Kane had had a run-in with Juarez.

"Plan?" Sean asked. He had to trust Kane, because right now they had twenty men with guns pointed at them, sitting in a dead car. The grenade could take out either the men on the other side of the gate, or the men to the east. And they would be sitting ducks.

Kane didn't speak. Never had Sean known his brother not to have plans up the ass—contingencies for contingencies.

Juarez spoke in the bullhorn. "I only need you, Kane. I will spare your brother if you throw out your weapons and get out of the truck now. I will not ask twice. We're on the clock."

"Kane, we can't give in." Sean tried the truck again. Dead. He hit the dashboard.

"I'm not counting," Juarez said. "Out *now*. If you don't give me what I want, I'll get it from your girlfriend. I have men following her as we speak."

Kane's grip tightened on his gun. "Fuck fuck fuck!"

Kane opened his door and tossed out his gun.

"No! Kane, you can't—"

"He won this round, he won't win the war," Kane said.

But he didn't say *trust me*.

Kane didn't know what was going to happen. He didn't know that they were going to get out of this alive, or that these men wouldn't be waiting here for Lucy and Siobhan. He had lost his confidence, Sean realized, because he hadn't seen this coming.

Kane looked at Sean. The fear in his eyes wasn't for himself. "First chance, get away. I'll figure it out."

Kane climbed out of the truck and knelt on the ground, his hands behind his head.

This couldn't be happening. Kane never gave up without a fight. He was practically Captain America. He could do anything . . .

And yet he was on his knees, surrendering.

Four of Juarez's men approached Kane, and four more approached Sean.

A heavily armed man tapped on Sean's window with the barrel of his rifle. "Don't be a hero," he said with a heavy accent. "Out."

Sean didn't have a choice. He could fight and most likely die—or he could bide his time and find a way to escape.

But if Kane thought Sean was going to run without him, he was a fool.

Sean opened his door, keeping his hands visible. The men roughly pulled him out of the truck and pushed him to the ground. They searched him and tossed his weapons back into the truck. His wrists were tied behind his back, and then four rough hands yanked him up, forcing him to walk toward Felipe Juarez.

He and Kane stood side by side. Kane didn't take his eyes off Juarez. Sean assessed the force against them. Two against a dozen. Real shitty odds.

"Good boys," Juarez said. "Pete, take the brother. The soldier will come with me. I don't trust either of you, and certainly not together. *Vamanos!*"

Sean was pushed into the back seat of a rusty old blue Chevrolet and forced to lie down. Two gunmen sat with him, and two men—boys, really—were in the front. Kane was taken in Juarez's truck. But not before Sean saw Juarez coldcock him with his handgun.

Sean winced, then vowed to find a way to escape and find his brother.

Chapter Four

The front gate had been rammed open.

The ranch was fenced all the way around, but it was still relatively open—people could hop the fence, but someone had chosen to break through the main gate.

"What happened?" Siobhan said, a hitch to her voice. "Why aren't Kane and Sean answering? Are they—no. No."

"Stop," Lucy said firmly. Her stomach was twisted in knots, but she couldn't afford to let her emotions dictate her response. "Proceed with caution."

She pulled out her Glock, then glanced in the back at Andie. "Do you have a sidearm?"

"Yes, ma'am, in my bag." Andie retrieved her pistol.

"Siobhan, as soon as I tell you to stop, stop."

The house was visible a minute later. Padre's Jeep was parked out front, but Lucy didn't see him. No other vehicles could be seen.

Fifty yards from the house, Lucy said, "Stop."

Siobhan stopped and Andie jumped out. Lucy told Siobhan to stay put and followed Andie.

Lucy and Andie approached the house cautiously but quickly. There was no way to conceal their approach—a small grove of trees encircled the house and provided shade, but most of the ranch was flat and open.

Padre stepped out onto the porch. "They're not here," he said.

"Father, what happened?"

He shook his head. "I got here five minutes ago. The gate was mangled, and I came right here—I found that." He pointed to a drone on the porch.

Lucy didn't touch it, but inspected the device. It had been shot down. The box on the bottom, which should have held a camera, had something else instead. "I think this is a cell blocker. That's why we couldn't get through." Or they were already gone.

"I just got off the phone with the sheriff. He had calls about gunfire out here fifteen minutes ago. People don't call when they hear guns go off—this is the country, people shoot all the time—but this was more than target practice."

Siobhan drove up to the house and got out. "Padre—where's Kane?"

"I don't know."

"The ranch truck isn't here. He and Sean must have fled. Was there—blood?"

He shook his head. "No sign that anyone was hurt."

"We need to search the property," Lucy said. She didn't want to. The very real fear that she was going to find Kane and Sean executed hit her hard.

"Andie and I can do that," Padre said.

"I will. Andie?" Lucy said.

Andie nodded and Lucy took the keys from Siobhan. "Padre," Lucy said, "see if they left a note or clue about what happened. Search the place again, look for booby traps or anything out of place."

"Kane's go-bag is gone," Padre said. "It was the first thing I looked for."

That was a good sign, Lucy thought, and by the expression on Siobhan's face, she was relieved too.

"Padre, do you have someone you can call? To keep an eye on things?"

He knew what she meant. "The sheriff will assign a car."

Padre and Siobhan went inside, and Lucy steeled her fear and got into the car.

"Did you see the tracks?" Andie asked.

"A chase." There were multiple tire tracks on the dry earth, certainly recent. As if there had been a car chase through the property. She followed the tracks and saw Kane's truck in the distance, and no other vehicles. She was fixated on the truck—both doors were open.

Andie said, "The side gate is open."

Lucy looked at the western gate, which accessed a narrow, unmaintained road that both this property and the farm next door used primarily for heavy vehicles. It was a dead end to the south, but merged with the main road to the north.

She was more worried about what she would find when they reached the truck.

She stopped the car behind the truck. No bodies on the ground. She didn't see any blood on the windows, but bullets had riddled the metal. All tires were flat.

But no blood. She almost breathed easier.

She looked inside the cab. Kane's go-bag was on the floor on the passenger side. Sean's gun was on the driver's seat—along with his backup gun, knife, wallet, and cell phone. The keys were still in the ignition. A grenade was on the passenger seat.

"Andie, you know grenades." She pointed.

Andie carefully inspected it without touching, then picked it up. "He didn't pull the pin. I'll secure this. He shouldn't even have it in his possession."

Taped to the steering wheel was a note addressed to Sio-bhan.

Lucy pulled on gloves she always kept in her purse—she couldn't rush through this, though she was desperate to know what had happened. She had to preserve evidence in case . . . She didn't want to go there.

She unfolded the paper. It was written in Spanish, but Lucy was fluent and read it with ease.

> If you want to see your boyfriend alive,
> you will pick up your phone at exactly 7:00 p.m.
> If you don't pick up,
> he will die.
> Do not doubt me.
> F Juarez

No mention of Sean. Just Kane.

But there was no blood, no body. That meant Sean was alive. It *had* to mean Sean was alive.

Juarez. That name was familiar, but Lucy didn't know why.

Andie had walked around the perimeter of the truck and came back with Kane's handgun. "One bullet missing, recently fired."

Lucy showed Andie the letter and checked Sean's guns. He hadn't fired them.

"They were trying to get away," Andie said, "but there were multiple vehicles involved—not just the vehicles chasing them, but it's clear there were several trucks parked along that fence. I didn't find any blood."

Small blessing. Did that mean they were alive and well? Or being tortured?

A lot of people wanted Kane Rogan dead, and getting Sean would be icing on the cake for some of them.

A chill ran down Lucy's back. She could *not* think that way.

They weren't dead, not yet. This note would likely turn into a ransom demand.

She was about to call JT Caruso, one of the principals of RCK, to find out what she should do. She knew what to do as an FBI agent, but every principal of RCK had ransom insurance. She looked at her phone; still no service. Maybe the drone hadn't been disabled, and the blocker was still operating.

"Juarez," Andie said with distaste.

"Who is he?"

"Nine years ago Siobhan and Kane rescued his daughter, relocated her. She was going to be married off to another criminal family—she was thirteen."

Lucy frowned. "I never heard about that."

"Remember last year when Kane was trapped in Mexico, after he rescued Siobhan?"

Then it clicked. "Juarez took the contract."

"Right. He kidnapped Siobhan in order to get Kane down there. I think that put them both back on Juarez's radar."

They had taken his daughter—likely they'd never gone off his radar, Lucy thought.

"Then why not kill him?" Lucy said. As she said it, she realized. "They'll torture him."

"I can't say, but there has to be a way to track them down. That many vehicles—that many men? Kane has a lot of friends, as well as enemies. We need to get the word out and gather information."

"Let's talk to Padre. He knows this area better than anyone."

"I don't trust Juarez, but he would know that when he calls, Siobhan will demand proof of life. And Siobhan isn't going to turn herself over to him. I wouldn't let her, and Kane wouldn't want it. He's resourceful, and I hear Sean is the same way."

"Sean isn't military."

"But he's smart."

True.

They gathered up all the weapons from the truck, and Lucy unlocked Sean's phone. The screen was cracked, and like her phone, had no service.

But she saw his unsent text messages for her.

Multiple drones with cell blockers. Gate breached. We're heading to west gate, stay away until clear. Don't know who or why.

The second message was shorter.

Juarez. We're surrendering. No injuries. TX-TSB223 JBB197

"I love you," Lucy whispered.

"Excuse me?" Andie said.

Lucy showed her the messages. "These are Texas license plate numbers, and six digits, so they're from the nineties. Trucks most likely. Probably stolen or unregistered, but this gives us something to go on, and we might get lucky. We need to disable all the cell blockers and call in this information."

They drove back to the house. Andie secured the weapons in Kane's safe, and Lucy showed Siobhan the note.

She stared at it.

"Juarez?"

Her voice was a squeak. She began to shake.

"Why would he come after you now?" Lucy asked.

Siobhan shook her head. "It's been nine years . . ."

"But you and Kane went to his territory last year," Andie said. "It would take him time to plan an operation like this."

"But if he wanted to kill them," Lucy said, "it would have been smarter to wait until they were together."

She looked at her watch. It was six thirty. "If he's telling the truth, we have thirty minutes. Padre—did you learn any-thing from the sheriff?"

Padre shook his head. "He's reaching out to his trusted sources, has all deputies on alert."

"I need you to do the same. They are going to stay local, is my guess. Border security has been beefed up here along International Road, and it would be nearly impossible to get Sean and Kane out quickly." Though Lucy could think of half a dozen ways to take them south, because smuggling out of the US was much easier than smuggling into the US. "My guess is he has a safe house in the States. Sean sent the text messages at five twenty-seven and five thirty-two, they just didn't go through. They have about an hour head start."

"He wants me," Siobhan said. "He hates me because I took Hestia. He thinks I brainwashed her. She wanted to go. She wanted to escape. She said if she had to go through with it, she would kill herself. She didn't want to—to be married to that pervert."

"Stop," Lucy said. "We don't know why he's doing what he's doing, or what his endgame is. It could be revenge, but I think if that was the case we would have found their bodies in the truck."

Siobhan shivered, and Lucy probably should have been more sensitive. Except . . . she had to think like a cop. She had to work the case and forget that the man she loved more than anything in the world was being held captive by a bru-tal criminal who wouldn't hesitate to kill him.

Andie had brought the drone inside. She dumped it on the table. "Cell phones should work."

Lucy looked at hers. Suddenly, the two messages from Sean popped into her feed, and she blinked back hot tears. Swallowed. Forced herself to regain her composure.

She called JT Caruso. He would know where to start.

Padre got on his phone and started to spread the word and work his contacts.

Andie said, "I have a couple of people I can call." She stepped outside.

They would find Sean and Kane and they would be alive and well.

Lucy had to believe it.

Chapter Five

Kane didn't know where they took Sean. He could be in another vehicle following him, or he could be taken to another location. He had to trust his brother to get himself out of this mess, because it was clear Kane was the primary target.

Or Sean was already dead.

Kane couldn't think about that. Not if he wanted to survive. Emotions, grief, made even the strongest of men weak.

Mourning would come later.

After vengeance.

They'd been on the road for thirty minutes. Though Kane's head ached, he kept track of every turn, which were few. Based on the speed and road quality, they were on route 281 heading east, away from Hidalgo. He knew these roads well and the small towns that branched off them. He counted the times they slowed, the sound of traffic, and based on his memory, they turned north just before they hit Santa Maria. Less than five minutes later they turned left twice. This was all farmland up here. Open and spacious. Did Juarez have property here? Was he working with a local thug? Or had he found an empty warehouse?

The problem with open space, from a prisoner's perspec-

tive, was that it would be easy for Juarez's men to see someone coming for a rescue, and it would be difficult to find
cover if Kane managed to escape.

But he would put money on his ability to escape and elude.

He was hauled up and out of the back of the truck. No
blindfold or hood—so clearly they didn't care if he knew
where they were, or they planned on killing him.

Both, Kane figured. Whatever reason Juarez had for not
killing him on sight didn't mean that he didn't plan on killing him as soon as he got what he wanted.

Kane saw nothing but open fields, though far to the south
he could make out the lights in a couple distant houses. But
here, rows of neatly stacked hay, two high, led to a large
barn. Solar-powered security lights faintly illuminated the
entrance. They pushed him inside, which was lit only by two
portable battery-operated lamps. There were tools to one side,
a large harvester and tractor near the rear. No electricity. The
lock on the large doors hadn't been broken, which told Kane
that someone who worked for the farmer, or the farmer himself, had given Juarez the key. Kane's guess based on the
visual and the fresh smell of cut dried grass was that the
field had been recently plowed, possibly even that morning,
the hay bundled and left to be collected. Tomorrow? Monday? Maybe it wouldn't matter to Juarez. Whatever he had
planned, he would do it quickly.

They didn't bring Sean in, which concerned him. Juarez's
men restrained Kane to a support beam in the middle of the
structure. They didn't take any chances—his wrists were
bound, then his arms tied behind the beam. His ankles were
bound, then they doubled up the rope around his body and
secured it behind the beam.

Kane just stared at Juarez.

Juarez backhanded him. He looked smug, satisfied. As if
he had won.

He knew something that Kane didn't know, and that deeply disturbed Kane. Because in the nine years that Juarez had hated Kane, he had never made a move against him, until last year when his gang had been hired by a drug cartel to kidnap Siobhan to lure Kane in, because the cartel thought Kane had information they needed.

Something happened between then and now that gave Juarez the balls to come after him.

"I've waited for this day for years, but now your death will mean so much more. I will have my daughter back, and you will die knowing your girlfriend will suffer for her deception and lies."

Kane stared at him, didn't react. Giving Juarez any reaction was foolhardy. He didn't bait him or play him. There was no way that Juarez knew where Hestia was. Even Kane didn't know. He'd turned her over to one of the few federal agents he completely trusted. All he knew was that Sonia had successfully obtained Hestia a new identity—name, Social Security number, birth certificate—and placed her with a family that Sonia trusted. He didn't know where, he didn't know her new name, he didn't know anything—and he preferred it that way. And there was no way that anyone could find out that Sonia was involved at all—her name wasn't on any paperwork because nothing was official.

If Juarez thought Kane or Siobhan knew where Hestia was, he was mistaken. And if he tried to beat the information out of them, it would fail, because there was no information to gain. Torturing him or Sean wouldn't give Juarez the information he needed because they didn't have it. And they didn't have Siobhan, not yet. Not at all. Kane trusted Lucy to keep Siobhan safe.

Lucy and Siobhan had picked up Andie, one of the most decorated US Marines still active today. Andie would put her sister in a high-level military prison if she had to until this situation was resolved. If she got a lead, Lucy would certainly go after Juarez. If Juarez left men at the house, Lucy wouldn't walk into a trap.

Maybe that's why they separated him and Sean. To use Sean as the bait.

But Lucy wouldn't turn Siobhan over to Juarez to save Sean.

Love makes even the smartest people stupid. Don't forget that.

Kane trusted Lucy to do the right thing. But this whole situation was fucked; worse, Kane had no idea what Juarez's end game was.

He has a secret. He knows something.

Kane hated that he didn't have all the information he needed to formulate an actionable plan.

Juarez looked at his watch, still smirking. "Ten minutes. Ten minutes and you'll realize that your redheaded whore is a liar like every other female. I will enjoy watching you fall, Kane Rogan. I will enjoy it very, very much."

As soon as Sean was taken into the small, dark, moldy house he knew that Kane wasn't there.

Sean wished his Spanish were better, because he didn't understand everything the men were saying, but the part he picked out was that Kane was being taken to "the barn," wherever the hell that was.

They'd only driven about fifteen minutes before they stopped. There were voices around him, but he couldn't make them out. When he tried to adjust his position to look, one of the two guards sitting in the back of the truck with him kicked him in the ribs.

Then the voices stopped and the truck started moving again, bumping on a deeply rutted road. They only drove for a minute before stopping again. Sean was pulled out of the truck and taken into the sagging structure. It had once been a home, but storm damage had rendered it uninhabitable.

There were several other similar manufactured homes that were barely a step up from dilapidated trailers, scattered through the area, but no one was close enough where Sean could call for help. And why would anyone help him? Juarez could have paid off the neighbors, or maybe they just didn't want to get involved with a bunch of men with guns.

Only two vehicles had come to this trailer with Sean, which meant the others had either been left at the ranch or had followed Juarez, who had Kane.

One thing Sean had going for him was there *were* two trucks outside. He could hotwire most anything, especially older vehicles. And there *were* other houses in the area, where he might be able to find a vehicle or a phone or someone to help. He needed to get out, get away, and get to a computer. Kane still wore the watch that Sean had hacked. Sean could find out exactly where he was at midnight or noon.

He hoped it didn't take that long. He prayed Kane was still alive. That this wasn't just some elaborate plan to torture and torment him.

Sean's captors tied him to a chair. The trailer stank of rotting wood and furniture. It had clearly been flooded and only partly cleaned out. The windows were open or no one would be able to breathe in here; as it was, the place remained a serious hazard.

The chair was metal, and maybe his captors didn't know that he was as good—and sometimes better—than his brother at getting out of bonds, because they didn't secure him well. Nylon rope around his wrists, tied behind his back, ropes around his ankles, and they'd tied a couple of loops around his middle and the back of the chair.

Fools.

He just had to wait until they left. Two minutes and he'd be free, but only if they weren't watching.

The two young men—hell, Sean didn't think they were yet eighteen—stayed outside. He didn't see any guns on them. The two men with guns stood inside the doorway, letting the breeze come in through the open door. They didn't talk to him. Didn't tell him what they were or weren't going to do. They spoke in Spanish, but he didn't know if they came with Juarez or if they were local. Considering that southern Texas was 90 percent Hispanic, he suspected local. Juarez probably brought in his key team members from Tamaulipas and hired the bulk of his crew locally.

He listened as best he could. A few years of high school Spanish didn't really help him understand the fast-spoken dialect. Lucy could interpret virtually any Spanish out there, from high Spanish to regional Spanish. Kane was fluent—at least in conversational Spanish. Siobhan was fluent. But Sean was better with machines than language, and he'd never quite caught on.

He needed to work on that, because he really wished he understood what they were saying.

He closed his eyes. Focused. He heard a few things, specifically girls' names, and soon realized that they were talking about their girlfriends and what they were going to do with the money they were making.

Yes, definitely local.

Sean didn't know if that would help him, but it was best to have all the information available. And if they were local, they didn't have loyalty to Juarez. They might be enticed to run or disappear if things got heated.

He stared at them and waited, willing them to leave him alone.

I just need two minutes. Two minutes and I'll be free.

Chapter Six

Siobhan's phone rang at exactly 7:00 p.m.

She reached for it, but Lucy grabbed her wrist. "Remember what I said," Lucy said.

Siobhan was on edge. Lucy understood that, but both Sean's and Kane's lives were on the line, and they needed to play this right.

"I know. I know."

They hadn't had enough time to set up an FBI trace, and JT hadn't wanted to call in the authorities just yet—he wanted to make sure this wasn't a pure hostage situation, which RCK specialized in.

Fortunately, Lucy had enough technical skill to use Sean's computer to run a basic trace program, and she had set it up with Siobhan's cell. Siobhan would answer through the computer, which put the call on speaker. It wouldn't give them an exact location, but they could narrow it down, and then look at the region and find the most likely place they might be held hostage.

Lucy nodded, and Siobhan hit the enter key, which started the call and the trace program.

"H-hello?" Her voice cracked.

"Siobhan Walsh, this is Felipe Juarez. You took my daughter; you will return her."

"I saved her from a disgusting pervert. You should be ashamed marrying her off to an old man! She wanted—"

"Stop. Stop," he said over and over, until a gun went off.

Siobhan screamed.

"That's your only warning. The next bullet will go through your lover's head instead of in the wall."

"I—"

"You are a liar, Ms. Walsh. A liar and a kidnapper. When I learned the truth, I wanted to find you and break you. But I know you are strong. You would die with your secrets. But you are not strong enough. I will make Kane Rogan suffer. I will make him curse you and beg to die. I know he is strong. It will take days, weeks, to break him. But I will break him. I will send you tapes of his screams. I will send you videos of his blood flowing into the earth. All because you are a liar."

Tears ran down Siobhan's cheeks.

"I—I—I—p-please."

"*Please*. Please what, Ms. Walsh? Please spare him? He's going to die. You know I would never let him live after what he's done, so I won't even pretend. But the difference between weeks of pain and suffering and a bullet in the back of the head? That's on you."

"I don't—"

"Do *not* tell me you don't know where Hestia is! I know you do! You think you were so smart? Think again. She just graduated from college. From University of Arizona. And guess what? You were there. Oh, she's a smart girl, and you are a smart girl, but her friends, not so smart. I saw the truth. *Hazel Lopez.*" He spat out the name. "You will bring Hestia to me. You have twelve hours. At seven a.m. I will call this number again. Either Hestia answers, or the torture begins. Do you understand?"

"Y-yes."

He ended the call. Siobhan sobbed.

She hadn't asked for proof of life. Lucy had wanted it, needed it. She hadn't asked about Sean.

But at least they knew why this had happened.

"Who is Hazel Lopez?" Andie asked.

Siobhan couldn't speak. She had a hard time catching her breath. Lucy gave her water, but couldn't coddle her, not now. She was watching the computer as it narrowed down the area Juarez had called from.

A minute later, the computer beeped that it had a location.

A two-square-mile location in the middle of nowhere. The closest town was a small place called Santa Maria.

But it was a place to start.

She sent the data to JT in Sacramento, and he would work on narrowing the information down. It wasn't enough, but it was more than they'd had.

"Hazel Lopez," Lucy repeated.

Siobhan took a deep breath and pulled herself together. "I'm sorry, I'm usually better than this, but that man—he is evil. I know he'll do everything he said he'll do. I was a fool nine years ago, I should have done it differently."

"No second-guessing. Why does he think you know where his daughter is?"

"Hestia called me in May. She was graduating from college and asked if I wanted to come. And . . . I knew I shouldn't, but she had a new name, a completely new life! I don't know how he found out I went there, or that I went for her graduation, or anything! I don't know. But I don't know how to find her. Her name is Hazel Lopez now, that he has . . . he might be able to find her, I have to find a way to warn her, but I don't even know how to do that! All she told me was that she was going back home after graduation, that her family didn't live in Arizona. I met them and they are so wonderful, so proud of her. A wonderful family, and she has brothers and sisters and—"

"Siobhan, focus."

She said, "Only Kane knows who got her papers in order and how to reach out to her. He told me once that he didn't want to know, that he trusted this person—said she was in ICE, that she had been trafficked and would know exactly how to make Hestia disappear in all the right ways."

"Sonia Knight," Andie said. "She married a fed."

Then it clicked. Sonia had married Dean Hooper, the ASAC of the Sacramento FBI office. Dean and Sean were friends. "I know how to reach her," Lucy said. But this information would, by necessity, need to be kept confidential. She didn't want to know where Hestia was. But she would likely have to get a new name and identity if they couldn't stop Juarez now.

Lucy stepped outside and called JT Caruso. She gave him all the information she'd learned, not only about the call but the reason Juarez was coming after Siobhan and Kane now. JT was already working on tracing the call, and he said he'd talk to Dean and Sonia.

"Just get her protection," Lucy said. "Juarez hasn't been able to find her. My guess is when he learned her name and the college she graduated from in May, he tried and failed to track her down. That's why he took Kane—if he took Siobhan, Kane would mount a rescue. Taking Kane, Siobhan doesn't have the training or resources to find him, especially with this tight time limit."

"You're right, but I know Sonia and she's not going to turn the girl over to her father. Kane wouldn't want her to." Lucy heard voices in the background, but couldn't make them out. Then JT said, "I'm getting Sonia on the phone now. We'll get the girl protection, but if we don't find Kane and Sean before seven in the morning, we need to buy time. I'll figure out if we can patch Hestia in to Siobhan's phone, or forward the call to her location."

"We can't put her at risk."

"We won't. But when he calls again, we'll have the FBI trace it. I've already talked to Rick." Rick Stockton was one of the assistant directors of the FBI in Washington and JT's and Kane's closest friend. Rick and JT had been in the Navy SEALs; Kane had been a Marine. But they had worked more than one joint operation and seemed to be bonded for life, a bond that Lucy was grateful for now. "Rick's putting together a small tactical FBI team. They'll be there to trace the call at seven in the morning, but if you get any information about their location, call Rick directly—you'll need backup."

"I will." Lucy would take all the help she could get at this point, because twelve hours—eleven hours, forty-two minutes—wasn't enough when she didn't know where to start.

"I'll listen to the conversation as well—thanks for recording it. If I come up with anything, you're the first to know. Jack just left, but it'll take him eight hours to get there. He'll fly straight to the ranch, so he'll definitely be there early in the morning to help with any rescue. If this ends up being a hostage rescue, you'll want Jack."

"You don't have to convince me," Lucy said. "My negotiation skills aren't going to come in handy this time."

"But you can work on buying time. Use your strength, Lucy. And remember—Sean and Kane will do everything they can to get out of this. Be ready."

Lucy ended the call and took a deep breath. Padre had come out to the porch while she was talking.

"Jack's coming," Lucy told him. Padre and Jack had been friends for more than two decades.

"I expected nothing less. We'll find them, Lucy."

She had to believe it, or she would fall apart.

"JT is going through the maps, but—"

"I know this area. You'll just have to show me how to use that computer of Sean's. I'm technology challenged." He gave her a spontaneous hug and mumbled a prayer in Spanish. It comforted her like nothing else had.

She said, "Let's get started."

Chapter Seven

The sun was long down; the rotting house was dark.

The four men rotated in and out, but for the last thirty minutes, they all sat in the back of the pickup truck, talking. Complaining, it sounded like. From what Sean could figure out, they hadn't realized they'd have to sit on him all night. Maybe no one expected him, or if they did, they hadn't planned on grabbing him as well. Two of the guys had plans they canceled.

Sean recognized that he was lucky to be alive. They wanted Kane, for whatever reason. It would have been easy to kill him, especially since they'd separated him and Kane. Yet, if they needed leverage, they'd be able to bring Sean in. To torture or kill, it wouldn't really matter. Kane was strong, but would he bend—or break—if Sean was being tortured? Siobhan?

So far, though, other than a few bruises, Sean was in good health.

By now, Lucy and Siobhan would be back at the house. They'd know something was wrong, call for backup. If Lucy found his phone, she'd at least have the basic information of what happened. Sean hadn't seen any of the men go back and take their guns or phones. They had tossed everything in the ranch truck.

But he had no control over what Lucy had found or not found; he just needed to find a way to get out of here and call for help. Now that it was fully dark, he had a better chance.

They were checking on him infrequently, probably because the house reeked. It should be completely razed—it would cost far more to save it than it would to build it new. But the door was open. They'd hear if he made too much noise.

He'd mentally seared the image of the living room into his mind. He didn't know if there was a window he could crawl out—quietly—in the back of the house, but that was his best bet. Still, he had to make sure that he had a few minutes, and no one had checked on him for the last thirty.

"Hey, guys!" Sean called out.

No answer.

"Guys! I have a question!" he shouted.

He heard grumbling, then one of the four walked up to the doorway. "What?" he snapped.

"Can I get some water? I can hardly breathe in here."

He laughed. "Screw you." He walked away, said something to his friends in Spanish, and they all laughed.

Sean waited a few minutes in case one of them decided to bring him water, but no one came.

Two minutes later, he was out of the ropes. He sat there for a second, made sure no one was coming.

The open door was going to be a problem, but he would have to risk it.

Be smart. Be fast. Be quiet.

Sean slowly stood, stretched because his feet were asleep. The last thing he needed was to trip because he had no balance. He glanced out the door as the pins and needles

worked themselves through his body. He couldn't see his captors from this angle, but he could still hear them talking and
laughing. He stepped forward. The rotting floor creaked.

He hesitated, but didn't hear any change from outside.
They were still talking and laughing, and he heard a couple
bottles rattle.

No other noises in the neighborhood. No parties or cars
or voices. No kids playing or televisions blaring. Was the entire neighborhood empty? Were all the trailers abandoned,
like the one Sean was being held in?

He glanced out the door. Now that it was completely dark,
he couldn't make out the people in the truck, though two
of them appeared to be smoking, the small orange embers
from their cigarettes moving in the black night. They likely
couldn't see him, but they might be able to sense movement.

Sean took another step; another creak. The sound seemed
unbelievably loud, but that could be his adrenaline pumping.
He took six steps forward and two to the right—he knew
from staring at this place for the last three hours that there
was an overturned recliner that partly blocked the hall. His
left leg brushed against it, but he didn't trip.

He listened. The guys were still chatting.

He didn't know what was in the back of the trailer—
from his observations he had seen four doors, leading to
rooms or bathrooms. The stink was worse back here, as if
the septic tank had busted and no one had cleaned it out. The
last door was the largest bedroom and the door was missing.
But there were two windows—one facing front, one facing
back.

He felt around. Everything he touched had a gooey, slick
residue. His hand brushed against metal blinds. They would
make a racket if he tried to remove them. Shit. He found the
strings and prayed he could pull the blinds up without noise.
He held the bottom with his left hand and slowly pulled at

the string with his right. At first they didn't budge, and he yanked firmly. They rattled and he winced, but he couldn't stop now.

When the string locked, Sean felt the edge. The blinds were slanted, the right side all the way up, the left side still down because the string had broken. The window was a simple aluminum frame, and there was a safety bar to prevent the window from being opened.

He yanked it out, metal grating on metal, and if those bastards outside were listening at all, they would certainly hear that.

But now he had a weapon. It wouldn't stop a bullet, but he could use it to fight.

He forced the window open, then heard one of the men shout, "Hey, quiet! I heard something."

At least that's what Sean thought the rapid Spanish meant.

As he climbed out the window, the entire sill crumbled under his weight. He tried to hold on and control his landing, but he fell hard on his ass. The metal blinds came crashing down.

Sean jumped up and ran as fast as he could across the field. The night was nearly black, no street lights out here, the moon was a tiny sliver high in the sky, and the stars gave the faintest of illumination, but it was better than nothing. His eyes were already adjusted to the dark, and it was amazing what the senses could do, especially when fear coursed through your veins. One of the trailers to the south had lights, but his captors would go there first, likely thinking that's where he would seek help.

Instead, he ran, praying he didn't step in a hole and break his ankle.

He had to find a phone and call in the cavalry.

Then they could search for Kane.

* * *

Kane had been tortured before. He'd been well trained, thank you to the United States Marine Corps, and he endured.

Didn't mean he wasn't in pain, but he separated his mind from his bruised body.

And honestly, Juarez's men didn't know how to torture anyone effectively. They beat on him, and he would pay for it later. His body was getting old and worn. But right now they were just bruises. Nothing was broken, though one of his molars was a goner—he'd spit it out.

They had quickly grown tired. These were Juarez's men, but Juarez was the one with the grudge, not them. They did what they were told, but it was primarily to keep Kane here—too hurt and slow to mount an escape.

At least, in their minds.

What he was most concerned about was the call that Juarez placed to Siobhan earlier in the evening.

He had never known that Siobhan was in contact with Hestia. Had he, he would have put an end to it. It was foolish and emotional. And while he loved Siobhan for her compassion, that same compassion was going to get her killed.

How had Siobhan found her? Sonia Knight was the only person who knew who had adopted Hestia. Kane had introduced Sonia to Siobhan at Sean's wedding, but in no world could Kane imagine that Sonia would tell Siobhan anything about Hestia.

Maybe he was wrong. Maybe Sonia hadn't realized how serious the threat from Juarez was.

Don't be ridiculous. Sonia more than anyone would have protected Hestia from her father, and that meant keeping well-meaning Siobhan away from her.

Dammit.

There was no way that anyone would bring Hestia into this situation, even if they could locate her. Yet . . . if Hestia were anything like Siobhan, if she knew that someone would die if she didn't act, she would act.

He hoped that she couldn't be found. They had risked everything to save her from the arranged marriage, a marriage that would likely have resulted in an early death, or at minimum sexual servitude in a criminal organization. If what Juarez told Siobhan on the phone was true, then by now Hestia was back home with her adopted family and Juarez hadn't been able to find her—hence this plan to force Siobhan to talk.

Kane's binds were too tight to slip off, and Juarez wouldn't fall for a standard trick that might fool his minions.

Kane would have to keep his eyes and ears open—and think of an uncommon ploy. A way he could escape—trick Juarez—that he wouldn't be expecting.

He wished Sean were here. His little brother could be annoying as hell, but he was the smartest guy Kane knew, and he always seemed to have a trick up his sleeve.

I hope you're not dead, Sean. If anyone hurts you, they'll pay for it with their blood.

Chapter Eight

The Hidalgo County Sheriff, Eddie Consuelo, had been elected when Jack still lived at the ranch, and reelected two years ago. He had a good working relationship with the FBI and the DEA, and he knew Kane personally. He quickly pulled the registration records for the two trucks Sean had identified and offered to interview the owners, but Lucy wanted to do it herself.

Consuelo sent a deputy to sit on the ranch to keep an eye on the property, and Lucy asked Padre to join her in the interviews. Padre knew half the town, the benefit of being the pastor of the lone Catholic church in a small town.

The devout had a very hard time lying to a priest.

Andie promised to keep an eye on Siobhan. Siobhan didn't want to sit out, but Lucy and Andie convinced her that if she was easy to grab, Juarez would grab her.

However, Lucy realized that if Juarez wanted Siobhan, he could have gotten to her. They had been shopping today, their guard down until Lucy spotted the two men outside of the café and became suspicious. She wondered if Juarez simply wanted to keep tabs on Siobhan but planned on grabbing Kane from the beginning. Siobhan was more likely to cave in to Juarez's demands if he had her boyfriend tied up, and Kane *wouldn't* cave. Not only that, but Kane had resources that Siobhan might not easily be able to access. If Siobhan's life was threatened, she might still keep her mouth shut about Hestia's location. Using Kane made Siobhan more pliable.

Even though Lucy had no doubt that Juarez fully intended to kill both of them when he found his daughter.

The first truck was registered to Morris Jergens, an elderly man who didn't know his truck was missing. He lived in a small house on a large piece of property. His truck was supposed to be in his barn, but he rarely drove anymore because of his poor eyesight. He spoke loudly, as if he was hard of hearing. Lucy made sure she kept her voice clear and spoke a fraction louder than normal, but not too loud to embarrass the man. He had on one hearing aid, but it looked worn and old, and she wondered if it even worked.

Lucy asked about family who had visited him recently, and he kept shaking his head. He didn't have family in the area. She asked about neighbors, or anyone who came to help him on the property. It didn't look like the property was well maintained, though the house itself was clean, if cluttered.

"I have two boys come by every week to do chores. Brothers, Laredo is their name. Michael . . . Michael and I think Juan, but I don't remember. Michael was the older brother. Good boys, they've been helping me out for the last couple of years, since they were in high school."

"When was the last time you saw them?" Padre asked. It was clear that he knew who the man was talking about.

"I call Michael when I need help. I think they were here Tuesday—no, Wednesday. I had the big trash pickup, and they cleaned out my storage shed."

"Have you used your truck since Wednesday?" Lucy asked.

"I—um, no, I haven't driven since Sunday, when I went

to church. Lifepoint Christian, up in McAllen." He looked at
Padre. "Sorry, Father, I left the church long ago."

"No apologies necessary," Padre said with a kind smile.

"Would you mind if we looked in the barn?" Lucy asked.

"Go right ahead, but there are no lights in there," he
said.

"I have a flashlight," Lucy said.

She and Padre walked to the barn and went inside. The
truck, a ten-year-old Ford F-150, wasn't there. The barn was
clean, with containers for recycling, a few lockboxes, some
old, broken equipment, and a relatively new tractor. Tools
were lined up along one wall, and from the look of things
the Laredos primarily did gardening and cleanup work.

"Smart enough not to use their own vehicle, but not smart
enough to use a truck that can't be traced back to them," Lucy
mused.

Padre said, "There's no evidence that it's the Laredos."

"You know the family?"

"I do."

"We need to talk to them."

"Their parents are hardworking people," Padre said.
"Good people."

"I'm not saying they aren't."

"Let me talk to them, okay? I doubt these boys knew what
they were getting into."

"Maybe not, but they still had a choice."

"And I might be able to convince them to make a different choice, if they see that they have options."

"Not if Kane or Sean are dead," Lucy snapped.

Padre hardened. "I understand what's at stake."

"I didn't mean—"

"Yes, you did. And I understand your position. Your
brother Jack has been my best friend for more than twenty
years. I love him like a brother, and I love Kane like a brother.

I know that you're running on fear and training. And if this goes south, I will be at your side. But let me help prevent tragedy. These are good people, in their heart, and I can convince them to do right."

Lucy nodded. "We'll do it your way, Father." *For now.*

"Drop me off at the Laredos' house, and you look into the second address."

Lucy and Padre thanked Mr. Jergens and Lucy let Padre navigate to the Laredos', in the heart of Hidalgo. She looked at her phone and realized the second identified truck was registered to Regina Quezada, only a mile away. "I'll pick you up here," Lucy said, and drove off.

Regina Quezada was a large woman in her fifties with a cherub face. There was no garage and no truck—according to the registration a fifteen-year-old blue Chevrolet—under the carport.

Lucy identified herself, and Ms. Quezada wasn't intimidated by a federal agent, which relieved Lucy. In fact, she seemed pleased to have company and invited Lucy in. The house smelled amazing, of a rich Spanish stew, and Lucy realized she hadn't eaten anything since the fruit and cheese that afternoon.

"May I get you anything? Water? Coffee?"

"No, thank you," Lucy said. "I don't want to trouble you, but your Chevrolet truck was possibly used in a crime. A witness wrote down the license number and I'm following up."

She sat down heavily. "Oh, no."

"Do you know where your truck is now?"

"My baby—my youngest son. He knows better. He's a good boy."

"I'm sure he is." Lucy made a leap. "Is he friends with the Laredos?"

"Yes, Juan. They are both seventeen, both good boys. They help me, help others, they're going to college next year."

"We believe that someone may have offered a substantial amount of money for these boys to help them."

She looked torn about talking. "Dangerous?"

"Unfortunately, it could be. We believe they were hired by a criminal organization run out of the Tamaulipas region of Mexico." She didn't want to say kidnapping. Not yet. "I want to help them, but there are some lines they can't come back from. Right now, if they cooperate, I can put in a good word. But if they don't, I can't make any promises."

The woman blinked back tears. "Peter is the youngest of five boys. All my boys have done so well. Two went to college—I never went to college. One is a police officer like yourself, in McAllen. He's a good man, has a family, I love his wife like a daughter. My oldest is a soldier, in the Army. Serves our country. I—I can't have anything happen to my baby. He wouldn't do anything wrong."

"Is there a reason he might want money? Money that he might think is easy to earn?"

"I don't know. He's a smart boy, he wants to go to college. College is expensive, but he can get a scholarship, like his brothers. He—sometimes he thinks there are easier ways, but I say no cutting corners."

"Is there any way you can reach him?"

She still looked like she didn't know what to do. "What do you think my boy did?"

"I don't know that your son is involved, but we have reason to believe that he joined with the criminal group to kidnap two men. Possibly for ransom." She didn't want to go into the full story about why Kane was a target, but she needed to explain the severity of the situation with Ms. Quezada.

"I need to talk to Joseph," she said. "Joseph will know what to do."

She didn't want to lose this lead. "I can call Joseph for you."

"No, no, no, I will call him. Please. My son—he's seventeen. He's never been in trouble. He has straight As. He's in honors classes. He's a smart boy. Please leave."

Dammit! Lucy should have had Padre with her. They were going to lose valuable time.

She handed Ms. Quezada her business card after writing her cell phone number on the back. "Call me, or have Joseph call me," she said. "But I will tell you this: the kidnappers spoke to the fiancée of one of the victims and said that he would kill him if she didn't do what he wanted. We're on a time clock here. I can help Peter—he's a minor. But if some-one dies, he'll be an accessory to murder, and I can't do any-thing for him then."

Ms. Quezada was shaking, but Lucy steeled herself against feeling any guilt. There was no doubt in her mind that Juarez would kill Kane as soon as he had his daughter—and if he thought he couldn't get his daughter, he would kill him sooner. Time was not on their side.

She drove back to where she'd left Padre. He was standing out on the street. "How did it go?" she asked, as he climbed into her car.

"They don't know where their boys are. Didn't seem con-cerned, and said that Mr. Jergens lets them borrow the truck all the time. They were very certain that they weren't up to anything illegal. Michael is in his twenties, has a good job. Juan is a senior in high school."

"And friends with Peter Quezada, who is driving the other truck."

"Ms. Quezada. I know her. I know the whole family."

Lucy turned onto the main road, heading to Padre's rec-tory because she didn't know what else to do, where else to go. "She was very helpful, then kicked me out. Said she's calling her son, I assume the son who is a cop in McAllen."

"Joseph. I married him and his wife. They're good people, Lucy. This is going to be difficult on them."

"Those boys are seventeen. I will do everything in my power to get them off if they haven't done anything other than driving for Juarez. But if Sean and Kane are dead—"

"Don't say it. We'll find them, alive."

Lucy was at her wits' end. She wanted to go back and pressure Ms. Quezada—she was pretty certain she could get more information out of her. Instead, she said, "I'm calling the sheriff and telling him what we've learned. Maybe he can help, put a deputy on both houses, tell us when the boys return home."

"Do that, and in the meantime, I have one more idea."

"What?" She pulled up to the curb around the corner from the rectory.

"Trust me, Lucy. I'll call you if I learn anything."

He got out of her car. She rolled down the window. "Where are you going?"

He waved at her and repeated, "I'll call you." Then he walked down the street, away from the church, and out of view.

Chapter Nine

Sean didn't regret escaping, but he was now stuck.

Two of the men had followed him on foot, and one went back to get a truck. Sean didn't know where the fourth guy was, but he had one big advantage—these guys weren't experienced. The two older men—older in that they were in their twenties and not teenagers—were locals. They easily moved from Spanish to English and didn't have heavy accents. They might know the area, but they wouldn't be skilled in tracking, especially in the dark.

When Sean realized one of the three had gone back for a truck, he knew he had to find a hiding space. The dark helped hide him; headlights would expose him if he was in the open. He circled around and slipped behind one of the other trailers, the one that was directly across from where he'd been held captive—though directly across was relative, as there was at least half a football field separating them. He was partly shielded by a large, handmade garden toolbox. It was locked, and he didn't have any tools with him to pick the lock. He'd lost the metal rod when he fell out the window, and he needed a weapon to defend himself.

A stick wasn't going to defend against a gun.

He didn't know if all four men were armed, or only the

one he'd seen with a handgun. He didn't trust they wouldn't shoot him, especially since they were amateurs and might fire out of fear. They had clearly been waiting for something or someone—orders, perhaps, to bring him to Kane, or to kill him.

Sean didn't think you could tell a killer by their eyes, but if you could—none of these four had ever killed anyone. Maybe that's why they were sent to watch Sean instead of stay with the men holding Kane.

He could hide here indefinitely, but if those searching for him called in reinforcements, he would be stuck. If Juarez sent someone smarter, someone who had a history of tracking prey, they might realize he'd circled back.

He considered breaking into the trailer. There was no one inside; no car in the carport, no sounds he could hear. He didn't even know if anyone lived here, though there was some garbage and broken furniture lying between the house and the small drive.

He looked around the vast space. There were only a dozen manufactured houses out here, and he didn't know if they were employee housing or individually owned. All around this small development were fields—sorghum, melons, Sean didn't remember what kind, maybe cantaloupe—and cotton. People often thought that because Texas was hot and dry that the entire state was a desert, but in truth, there were a lot of thriving agriculture crops. Not Sean's area of expertise, but he knew enough to get by in conversation.

The storm over Labor Day weekend in San Antonio had caused damage all throughout central and southern Texas, and he wondered if all these places were now abandoned, at least temporarily. He saw a couple of lights in the distance, but he didn't trust that he'd be able to reach them without being seen. The truck was driving slowly through the fallow field with its high beams on.

Sean realized he could hide indefinitely from this crew of inexperienced thugs, but he couldn't hide from Juarez's people if these guys called them in.

He needed a distraction, and then he needed to get to the other truck.

Sean tried the windows in the back of the trailer. They were all either locked or stuck. He climbed onto the back of the wooden box to reach a higher window and looked inside. He couldn't see anything in the dark, though this appeared to lead to the kitchen. He couldn't tell if anyone was inside, but it didn't feel lived in. He hadn't seen or heard anyone in the hours that he'd been held captive.

He pushed and pulled at the window. It budged, but didn't fully open. It was such a dark, quiet night he feared if he broke the window, the guy waiting across the way would hear him.

He jumped down and peered around the corner, through the carport. He couldn't tell if someone had stayed with the second truck, but he had to assume someone was there. He couldn't see or hear the other vehicle.

A door from the carport led into the house. It was locked. He used his elbow to break the glass above the knob. A sharp pain told him he wasn't as good at breaking and entering as he used to be. He unlocked the door and entered.

The trailer was mostly empty. A few pieces of furniture, but nothing recently used. A thick layer of dirt and grime covered everything, and the same moldy stench as in the trailer across the way filled the place.

He searched. No weapons, no phone. Some old cleaning supplies under the kitchen sink. He searched the drawers. Most had been emptied—no plates, utensils, or glasses. But in a junk drawer he found mostly junk—and a couple of matchbooks.

Bingo.

He needed a distraction to get the kid away from the truck.

He took a nearly empty jug of bleach and a nearly empty bottle of generic window cleaner. Bleach wasn't generally flammable, but many glass cleaners had alcohol or ammonia in them, and mixing those with bleach created a noxious gas, which—depending on the concentration—could be flammable.

He just needed a distraction, he didn't need to burn down a house.

He tore through the bathroom and found a filthy facecloth in the back of drawer. It was stiff from whatever had dried on it. He was glad he could barely see because he heard rats and other creatures scurrying as he moved through the place, and he didn't want to see a giant rodent close up.

He took a cushion off the couch and brought everything outside, to the back of the trailer. He put them in the carport, so they would be visible faster, but that also risked him being seen, so he had to be quick.

The inside of the cushion was foam, which helped. He mixed the chemicals in the bleach jug while holding his breath, then poured the remainder of the glass cleaner on the rag. He tucked the jug into the cushion and pushed the rag in, then lit it.

It took him several matches to get the rag to smoke, and he wasn't certain it was going to stick.

He lit another match, and stuck it into the matchbook. As it burned, it should ignite the other matches, and he hoped it would start a big enough fire to distract the kid.

Sean ran to the opposite side of the trailer so he could see both the house across the street and the smoldering cushion behind the carport.

At first, all he got was smoke. Right when he thought the entire thing was going to fizzle out, there was a loud pop and a flame shot up.

Sean looked over at the Chevy truck. The kid was looking at the fire, but not moving. Well, shit!

Sean didn't have another idea. He would be calling his
friends. Sean could take out one kid, but not four.

While the fire distracted him, Sean ran in the dark toward
the Chevy. In the distance, across the field where Sean had
first fled, he saw the headlamps of the second truck bouncing on the rough dirt.

The kid walked away from the house and was halfway between the Chevy and the small fire. Sean was almost to the
truck when the kid spotted him. "Hey!"

Sean didn't respond. The kid didn't shoot or even say he
had a gun.

"Hey!" he called out again, running toward Sean. "Stop!"

Sean jumped into the driver's seat. No keys in the ignition. Dammit!

The kid stood in front of the truck. He was so young, sixteen or seventeen. This whole situation was fucked.

Sean got out of the truck, cautious. He didn't think the kid
had a gun, but he couldn't be sure.

"Give me the keys. Please."

"They'll—I didn't know what was going on. I swear. I was
just asked to drive. This has gotten way over my head."

"Come with me. I'll get you help."

"I can't. They have my best friend, he vouched for me, if
they think I helped you, they'll . . . I think they'll kill him."

The kid sounded scared—genuinely scared. Sean knew
how kids got in these situations—he'd done some stupid
shit when he was a teenager. Not kidnapping or any serious
crimes, but he could have. If the wrong people had talked
to him when he was young and angry, he could have led a
much different life.

"Kid, I want to help you and your friend, but they're going to be back, and we don't have time to argue."

"I'll give you the keys, but you have to hit me. Hard. Make it bleed or something. I—I can't just leave Juan here. I swear to God I didn't know what was going on. They told me they needed my truck to move someone. I thought, like, furniture or something. Or—you know—people. Gave me a hundred bucks, said I'd get another hundred when it was done. I would never do anything like this . . . but then it just happened."

Sean sympathized with him, and the fear he faced when he realized that he was party to a kidnapping.

"You can still come with me."

"I can't. Juan's my best friend. He didn't know what was going on, either. I think his brother did, though. Please, hit me, I'll give you the keys. My brother's going to kill me anyway. He's a cop. This is so messed up."

"Do you know where they're keeping my brother? The other guy with me?"

"No—I'd tell you, but Juan and I were sent here with the other two guys. I heard it was an abandoned warehouse or something. Maybe a barn."

Sean didn't want to hit the kid, but he saw the lights of the other truck coming across the field, gaining speed.

He hit him hard in the jaw, felt something crack, and immediately felt like shit. The kid went down. "What's your name?" Sean asked.

"Peter," he whispered, and spit out blood.

"Stay down. And call your brother, tell him the truth." Sean searched his pockets and found the keys, then ran back to the truck.

He sped away with his lights off, hoping to buy time, and worried about that kid he'd hit.

But he could only help Peter—and Kane—if he was free.

He bounced in and out of a deep rut and realized he had no idea if he was still on the unpaved road, so he was forced to turn on his lights. A dark house loomed in front of him, and he spun just in time to avoid crashing into it.

Shit, he would have gotten himself killed. He put on his seat belt and turned back on the gravel and dirt road. It, too, was in poor condition. He couldn't see any lights in the distance, but it was late, he was out in the middle of thousands of acres of farmland.

Sean glanced in the rearview mirror. The truck pursuing him was still a good hundred yards back, and Sean was by far a better driver, so he picked up speed. Once he hit the main road, he'd really fly.

His headlights reflected off a sign in the distance, indicating that he was reaching a T in the road. Excellent! These roads were all cut perpendicular, so he would have to slow down to make the turn or risk going into the ditch and flipping.

As he neared the road, he saw two cars approaching from the north, moving fast. And his gut told him these weren't civilians.

They called in your escape. Well, damn.

Sean had to risk the speed. He turned onto the road going far too fast, spun out in the opposite ditch, but had enough momentum and wherewithal to turn the wheel sharply to the right and pull back onto the road.

Then he floored it at the same time as he was rear-ended.

If he hadn't put his seat belt on, he would have hit the windshield. As it was, his head banged against the steering wheel and he saw stars.

He tried to speed up, but the collision had screwed with his drivetrain, and then he was hit again.

Gunfire rang out and suddenly he was spinning. It was all he could do to keep the truck upright as it drove into the ditch. He hit his head again and tried to open the door to run, but his hand would not cooperate.

Then the world went black.

Chapter Ten

Lucy was still driving back to the ranch when her phone rang.

"Agent Kincaid, I'm Officer Joseph Quezada from McAllen. You spoke to my mother. Scared her to death."

"It's about your brother, Peter," Lucy said.

"My mother is upset and not making sense. Is Peter hurt? In trouble?"

"The blue Chevy registered to your mother was used in the commission of a crime, and your mother implied that Peter had taken it out. He wasn't at home, so I can only assume that he's involved with the crime."

"My brother has never been in trouble. I've made sure of that."

"Can you say the same thing about his best friend, Juan Laredo? Juan and his brother borrowed a truck without permission from a neighbor. That truck was also used in the commission of a crime. So help me help you."

"Peter would never do anything wrong." He paused. "Michael Laredo has some criminal ties. I thought Juan was keeping it clean. If I thought he was going down the same path, I would have told Peter to cut ties."

"How long have they been friends, Officer?"

"Since they were little," he said quietly. "Look, I'm on my

way to my mother's house. Is this about the attack out at a ranch in the east county? I heard about it on the radio."

"Yes. Two men were kidnapped at gunpoint. We're not positive of the motivation, but we know that the organizer of the attacks runs a criminal organization in Tamaulipas, Mexico, and he believes that the men have information he wants." Not exactly true, but close enough, and Lucy wasn't giving everything away until she could assess Joseph Quezada face-to-face.

"I'll be there in fifteen minutes. I'll call when I arrive, and I'll try to find out what's going on with Peter. But please, he's a kid."

She wanted to read this cop the riot act, but instead she swallowed her fear and anger and said, "I understand. But this is a serious situation, and my job is to bring those two men home alive."

By the time she drove back to the ranch, it was well after eleven. She was tired and crabby and very worried. She had a terrific lead—the trucks—but so far, they hadn't found them or the kids who had taken them.

She sat in the car in front of Kane's house and put her head on the steering wheel, feeling overwhelmed. Sean and Kane were missing, taken by a brutal criminal who told no lies: He would kill Kane. He hadn't mentioned Sean, he hadn't even hinted as to his fate. Lucy wanted to believe that she'd know in her heart if he was dead, but she just felt numb, and she didn't put much stock in supernatural feelings. She considered herself spiritual, she believed in God and in justice and that evil would be punished, but she didn't *know*, in her heart, whether Sean was dead or alive.

Then the anger seeped in, the deep anger that she'd been keeping at bay all afternoon. That she and Siobhan had been followed for the purpose, she believed, of instilling fear into them. There was nothing those men did that suggested they planned to grab Siobhan . . . why? Why not grab her? Siobhan was the one with the answers. She was the one who put all of them at risk.

Yes, she was angry with Siobhan. She loved her like a sister, but what had she been thinking? Hestia wasn't in witness protection, she had been taken from her home country, brought illegally into the United States, and given a new identity because her father was a criminal. And while Lucy didn't fault Kane or Siobhan for their decision—there were some people so evil that you did what you could to protect the innocent—Siobhan should have done what Kane did: put Hestia out of her mind and never see her again.

Lucy had compassion for those like Hestia—or the boys that she, Kane, and Sean had rescued nearly two years ago, who had been imprisoned and forced to work for the cartels. She wanted to help those she could, especially the children who, through no fault of their own, had found themselves in the middle of violence. But sometimes, you had to remember that you don't save them for *you*, you save them for *them*. For their future. Sometimes, you don't get to know what happens to them. They go into the system and you have to trust that they will survive, that they have the hope of something better than they had before.

So yes, Lucy was angry at Siobhan for violating the unspoken rule. And Lucy was angry at herself for being mad at her future sister-in-law. And she was angry with Felipe Juarez, who used teenage boys to commit crimes. He was no better than the cartel leaders who used children to transport drugs and weapons in and out of the country.

She pounded her fist on the dashboard and pain shot through her arm, jolting her back to the present.

It was nearly midnight. Sean and Kane had been missing for more than six hours. They had seven hours to find them, or they would die.

Lucy believed that—if they weren't already dead.

Her phone trilled and she jumped. She grabbed it without looking at the number. "Kincaid."

"Lucy, it's Dean Hooper. I'm here with my wife, Sonia."

"Dean." She shook her head to clear it. "I'm in the car. Sorry. Distracted. You talked to JT."

"Yes, and Sonia reached out to Hazel—Hestia, but we don't call her that anymore. None of us are going to allow her to risk her life and her freedom to go to Texas and meet with her father, but we've figured out a way to get her on the phone and he won't know that she's not in Texas. She's an amazing girl, Lucy, you would like her very much. She is willing to give herself up for Kane and Sean, but you and I both know that Juarez would still kill them."

"I know," she said quietly.

"I'm having Hazel brought into FBI headquarters, where we have the technology to pull this off and can control the situation, but I'm hoping you'll find them before we have to do this."

"So do I." But at least this would buy them a little time, and she was grateful.

"I didn't know that Siobhan went to Hazel's graduation," Sonia said. "I've kept tabs on her and her new family, and Hazel said that she's the one who reached out to Siobhan. She emailed her and told her about her graduation and asked if she could come, because none of this would be possible without her. Hazel feels like this is her fault, and it's going to take both Dean and me all of our skills to convince her not to go to Texas. That's why I don't want her on the phone. She has a huge heart, and if she believes she can save Kane—who she thinks is in danger because of her—she'll promise anything."

"We don't want her to do that," Lucy said. "But thank you for getting her on the phone. I hope we find them first, but this is a good backup plan."

"I know you're worried, Lucy," Dean said, "but there's no one more resourceful than Sean and Kane."

"Thank you," she said.

When she ended the call, she surprisingly felt better. Not because she was less worried, but because Hazel's selfless act to help, even at risk to her physical and emotional safety, reminded Lucy that there were still good people out there, everyday heroes like Hazel who put others before themselves.

Lucy would do everything in her power to avoid Hazel having to talk to her father. The man had tried to force her into marriage, he was no better than a human trafficker, and he didn't want her back because he loved her or wanted her forgiveness; he wanted her back to punish her or use her for his own personal gain.

Lucy didn't want Hazel to have to face such an impossible choice: of death or servitude. Which meant she had seven hours to find Kane and Sean.

Chapter Eleven

Kane thought Sean was dead.

Two of Juarez's men dragged Sean over to the middle of the barn and dropped his limp body next to Kane. Dark, cold rage filled him. He stared at his brother's unmoving body, saw the blood on his head, and in that moment believed he'd been shot.

Then Sean moaned.

Relief flooded through him, then anger. He didn't say anything, only glared at the men watching them.

One of the men said in broken English, "Bastard tried to escape and sealed his own fate. He'll die with you."

Kane didn't respond. He needed Sean to wake up. He'd been mentally working on a plan, but it was contingent on Juarez wanting to hurt him. He needed Juarez to get close to him. He always had a knife on his belt. Kane couldn't free himself, but if he could get Juarez close enough, he could grab the knife and slice through the ropes. It was risky, because it depended on being fast after being beaten; depended on a clean slice with a knife whose sharpness he didn't know. It depended on the element of surprise, and getting the knife to Juarez's neck before someone shot him or tackled him.

Too many what-ifs.

But with Sean here . . . maybe. Maybe they had a chance.

They hadn't tied him up, but Kane didn't know how badly his brother was hurt.

The men stayed on the far side of the barn. They all had guns, except for the two younger boys, one of whom was sporting a broken nose and bruised jaw. Had Sean fought the kid when he escaped? Or had the kid been punished because he was supposed to keep an eye on Sean?

The teens looked scared. They were clean-cut, dressed better than the others. Hired, Kane figured. Lured in by promises of quick money.

It was because of boys like them that Kane did this job. It was why he fought the cartels and the traffickers. He didn't want teenage boys to feel they had no option except to work for criminals. It was a surefire way to die young.

Maybe they were a lost cause. Maybe they could be saved. But right now, they were not Kane's concern. They had made their choice of their own free will. They had driven two of the trucks. They were the enemy, until they proved otherwise.

Kane's concern was Sean.

Kane cleared his throat. Sean slowly turned his head and looked at him. The side of his face was bloodied from a cut on his forehead. He had multiple bruises.

"Hey," Sean said, his voice rough.

Rage burned in Kane that Juarez had had Sean beaten.

"They'll pay for this," Kane said, his voice low.

Sean winced. "Me."

Kane stared, having no idea what Sean meant.

"I stole a car. They ran me into a ditch."

"Anything broken?"

"No."

But Sean was in pain, it shone in his eyes. Concussion. Maybe internal bleeding, a cracked rib. But as long as nothing was broken, they had a chance.

"Stay with me, kid."

"Um-hmm."

Dammit, Sean was worse off than he looked, and he looked pretty pathetic.

Juarez himself had left with half his men two hours ago. They hadn't returned, and Kane didn't think that they would, at least until he was ready to call his daughter.

Kane planned on being long gone.

He closed his eyes and listened to the men talking in the corner. The teens sat on one side, either being punished or sulking. The other four men were in a semicircle, facing Kane, but in a heated conversation. One of the men was clearly American—he had no accent, but spoke Spanish well. He was doing most of the arguing, and it seemed to have something to do with one of the younger boys. Then he heard the word *hermanos* and realized that one of the kids was his brother, and his brother had screwed up, but ultimately it would be up to Juarez as to what the punishment would be.

Men like Juarez used systems of rewards and punishments to keep his people in line. Rewards were generally access to women and booze, and punishments were beatings. If the older brother was trying to get into the gang—though why, Kane didn't know, since Juarez worked south of the border exclusively—then Juarez would cut them both off. He didn't like incompetence. When Kane had eluded Juarez's men eighteen months ago in their own territory, he'd heard through the grapevine that Juarez killed the two in charge as an example.

Kane had stayed away from anything Juarez did, mostly because of the situation with Hestia, but he would have heard if he was branching out. It didn't make sense, but Juarez had to have contacts here in order to recruit locals who knew the area.

Juarez could have reached out to one of the local gangs, and they brought in the young Americans. Definitely the most likely scenario. Money talked, after all, and some people wanted the easy money.

And some people were desperate.

Little did they know that nothing was easy when working for men like Juarez.

"Sean," Kane said in a low voice. He didn't want to draw attention to them, and the fact that they hadn't tied Sean up.

Sean didn't answer.

"Kid," Kane said, slightly louder. Sean groaned.

"I'm here."

"You're not going to be able to escape."

"I will. I just need a few minutes."

Kane hoped Sean was right.

"I have matches in my pocket," Sean said. "And a knife. Right front."

"Okay. Wait for my cue."

Kane had to make sure that Sean could run. He wasn't leaving him behind, so he'd give him a little time.

But not too much. Because if they were still here when Juarez returned, they would both be dead.

Chapter Twelve

Two agents from the local FBI satellite office had already been to the ranch and left, setting up the phone and computer so that when Juarez called in the morning, they would hopefully be able to trace the call. They tested the connection with ASAC Dean Hooper in Sacramento to make sure that they could seamlessly bring Hazel Lopez into the conversation without any telltale clicks. Once they confirmed everything worked, they left, and promised to return before the morning call.

Now, Lucy, Siobhan, and Andie were studying maps and aerial photos of the surrounding area trying to figure out the most likely place that Juarez could keep hostages, but the area was too big for an effective search. And because they assumed, based on the tire tracks, that there were at least half a dozen men—and probably twice that—as part of Juarez's force, they needed a strong counterforce, otherwise they'd risk getting the hostages killed. The FBI and Sheriff's Department were working to put together several SWAT teams to go in—once they had a location. They, too, would be on standby.

A knock on the door had Lucy and Siobhan both jumping

out of their seats. It was after two in the morning and middle-of-the-night visitors were always bad.

Andie answered the door. She had a gun in hand, partly concealed at her side. She'd been a rock, and Lucy was so glad she was there. Not just because she was trained and competent, but also because she kept Siobhan calm and focused on the task at hand.

A police officer in uniform stood there. He was thirty, trim, with broad shoulders.

"I'm Joseph Quezada, from McAllen. I spoke to Agent Kincaid earlier."

Lucy motioned for Andie to let him in. "I'm Lucy Kincaid. This is Lieutenant Colonel Andrea Walsh and her sister, Siobhan."

"I got a call that the Chevy registered to my mother was found in a ditch off a county road northeast of Santa Maria, a tiny town about thirty minutes from here. No one was there—the truck had been hit from behind and the initial report indicates it was a high-speed collision. Not far from the accident are a dozen trailers that were flooded in early September. They're owned by one of the melon farms, housing for ranch hands, and everyone moved out. It's the only thing out there—I'm heading there now, thought you'd like to join me. If there was an accident, and my brother is wandering around injured . . ."

His voice trailed.

"May I call you Joseph?"

"Joe, please. My mom is the only one who calls me Joseph."

"Joe, we have to bring in a team." Lucy wanted to run out there herself, but she knew that would be foolhardy. "We can't do this alone, because we don't know what to expect. If they are holding Kane and Sean at those trailers, they have a minimum of half a dozen armed men."

"A deputy is out there with the truck," he said. "He didn't see any activity in the fields."

Lucy didn't think Joe recognized the seriousness of their situation.

"The man behind this already intends to kill his hostages once he gets what he wants—which he's not going to get."

"Maybe you'd better fill me in."

She didn't know if she could trust him, but he was a cop, and he knew the area. Plus, he also had someone he cared about in a dangerous situation. If his brother was as good a kid as Joe seemed to think, maybe the cop could talk to him.

Lucy glanced at Siobhan, as if asking what she thought. Siobhan immediately started talking. "It's my fiancé and Lucy's husband who were taken. Kane rescued a young girl nine years ago and Felipe Juarez is her father. He is cruel and abusive and I made a huge mistake in visiting the girl now that she's all grown up and graduated from college. I should have stayed away—it was my own stupid fault."

"Siobhan," Andie snapped. "What did I tell you?"

"I can't help it! I didn't think, okay? She has a new name and a new family and she's happy. And I should have known that Juarez would be watching me for the rest of my life, hoping I would lead him to her. And now he took the man I love because I never think about the consequences!"

Lucy said to Joe, "Kane Rogan is a well-trained mercenary who specializes in hostage rescue south of the border. Sean, my husband and Kane's brother, is a computer security expert. Juarez knows this, so he has certainly restrained them. We don't know what is going on with your truck, but I definitely want to inspect it. I can get a team ready quickly."

At that moment Jack walked in. Lucy had never been so happy to see anyone. She gave him a hug and introduced him to Officer Quezada.

"Where are we?" Jack asked.

"We found one of the trucks used in the kidnapping crashed about twenty minutes from here. It's registered to Joe's mother, and his brother may have been driving."

Joe explained, "I promise you, he didn't know what was going on. Since we talked on the phone, Lucy, I pulled Michael Laredo's record. He's twenty, been in and out of trouble, and I feared for a while that his brother Juan was following in his path, but Juan seemed to want what Peter wanted—a college education, a way out. They're both smart kids. I have to find a way to get my brother out of this before it goes south. He'll listen to me, I promise you that."

Lucy was sympathetic, but wanted him to understand the stakes. "You can come with us, but Joe, you have to realize that Juarez's people do not negotiate. They are brutal and they're not local. That's both good and bad—good in that you know the area; bad in that they don't have allegiances. They will kill and disappear. We are on the clock—Juarez is calling at seven a.m. expecting to talk to his daughter. We're setting it up. But he'll kill Kane either way. All that does is buy us time to find him." Though in the back of her head, Lucy couldn't help but think that Kane was already dead.

She turned to Siobhan. "I'm going with Jack and Joe, and calling in the FBI SWAT team to meet us at the accident site. If we don't return before seven, you must get proof of life before you let him talk to Hazel. No compromise on that. Proof of life for both Kane and Sean."

"I hope it doesn't come to that," Siobhan said. "Do you think you can find them first?"

"I hope so. But proof of life is nonnegotiable."

Andie agreed. "I'll be here the entire time. We'll get this done."

"I think they're still alive because Juarez knows we'll have no incentive to turn over his daughter if Kane is dead. It will also keep him on the phone longer, and give our people time to trace the call."

Siobhan hugged Lucy. It felt awkward and Lucy couldn't relax. "I'm sorry, Lucy. I'm really sorry."

"That's enough," Lucy said, and stepped back. "Andie is right. You didn't marry off a thirteen-year-old to a forty-year-old pervert. You saved her. And we're going to find them. If Padre calls or returns, have him call me." She knew that he was a former Army Ranger and that he had street smarts, but he was still a Catholic priest who hadn't been out in the field for years. "I have no idea what he's doing, and I don't want him going out on his own and getting caught in the crossfire."

Lucy contacted the FBI SWAT team out of McAllen about the new information, and they indicated they could be on-site in two hours, an hour earlier than the previous schedule, and would attempt to deploy earlier. Unlike on television, most SWAT teams didn't sit around waiting for action. They had regular law enforcement duties, they trained regularly, and they couldn't work unusually long hours, because of the high intensity of their operations. They needed a location and actionable intelligence before they'd stage for engagement.

Jack and Lucy were following Joe Quezada in his patrol car as he headed out to Santa Maria. "Have you slept?" Jack asked her.

"Have you?"

"Yes. Megan's brother flew me out. He's sleeping in the bunkhouse and will be up at oh-six-hundred if we need him."

"You didn't tell me."

"Just need to know that you're not going to snap. Sleep deprivation is serious. I'm trained for this, but I'm older now and can't always trust my reflexes when I'm overtired."

"Fortunately, I'm a lot younger than you." She was trying to make light of the conversation, but it sounded more confrontational. "I'm worried. And I have to keep it to-gether. Not just for Siobhan, but because I'm a cop. I can't fall apart because my husband is missing. He needs me to be smart and focused."

"You don't fall apart, Lucy," Jack said. "That doesn't mean you can't be worried. Tell me about Quezada."

She told him what she knew, about the kids involved in the kidnapping, and how they traced the trucks. Her conversation with Peter's mother, and then Joe. Finally, about Hazel being willing to talk to her father. "I don't want her to have to do that," Lucy said. "We need this to end before seven."

They had less than five hours. It seemed like forever—and it seemed woefully short.

"Thank you for coming," Lucy said.

"Everyone's a little ticked off that Kane planned on get-ting married without us."

"You did the same thing. Went off to Hawaii and married Megan."

"It was spontaneous. And even though it was eight years ago, Megan's brother is still mad at us about it. But I'm stick-ing around for the wedding, and Kane is just going to have to deal with it."

Jack's unspoken optimism that there would be a wed-ding calmed Lucy. They would find Kane and Sean and take down Felipe Juarez and everything would be fine.

The deputy who'd found Peter's truck had put out flares because the tow truck hadn't arrived and a portion of the smashed truck blocked the road. The headlamps from the squad car shined bright on the crumpled metal frame.

Lucy surveyed the damage as Deputy Ynez spoke. "About quarter, half mile down the road there's signs of a broken headlight. Whoever rammed the truck lost at least one beam. It seems they hit them again, then spun the vehicle off the road. They were going fast—at least that's my guess based on the skid pattern—but I'll leave that to the crime scene experts. They'll be out at dawn, with the tow truck."

Lucy looked in the cab. There was blood on the airbag, and a few drops on the ground. Probably a head injury or broken nose. The force of the airbag could easily cause a bloody nose, even if it wasn't broken. Only the driver's door was open, but that didn't necessarily mean anything.

Had Peter Quezada fled his partners and been hunted down? Or had Sean and Kane escaped, only to be pursued and re-captured? She was betting on the second scenario.

"Can one of you stay here, and one come with us to search the flooded housing?" Lucy asked.

Ynez left his partner with his cruiser and the truck and hopped into Joe's squad car.

The entrance to the melon farm's employee housing was a mile down the road, just past the initial broken glass. The road into the field had about a dozen trailers spread far enough apart to give some privacy, but not too far that they had to put in additional roads.

They pulled into the center of the plot and looked around. There were no vehicles, and the place was quiet. Ynez knew the history because his nephew, one of the field hands, had lived here. The farmer who owned the property had a thousand acres of melons; fortunately most of the land hadn't been seriously damaged, and he had another lot to put in temporary housing, according to the deputy.

"It's a good gig," Ynez said. "I worked for the same farm out of high school. My brother and I had our own place out here, worked for two years. Hard, honest work, paid pretty good. Then Mick joined the Army and I became a cop."

Ynez was chatty, and Lucy blocked him out. They shined the lights of the two vehicles around and from the depressions and fresh dirt, quickly determined that two trucks had been parked outside one of the trailers.

She was grateful Jack hadn't told her to stand aside as they approached the trailer with guns and flashlights out. She knew that there could be bodies inside. She braced herself as Jack went in first, and she stepped in behind him.

The trailer reeked of mold and dirt. A rat scurried across the floor, startled by the light. To the right was a small kitchen, rope strewn near a chair. The rope was too clean for this place; it was new.

Jack searched the rest of the trailer. "Someone escaped through the back window," he said when he returned.

"Only one person was here," Lucy said. "One chair, one rope."

Joe called out. "I found something!"

Lucy and Jack walked over to a trailer fifty yards away.

Joe said, "The door has been busted, this glass hasn't been here long." He shined his light on the ground. "And smell that?"

"Chemical fire?" Lucy asked.

"Yeah, of sorts." Joe shined his light to a burned cushion. A blackened plastic jug lay shriveled beside it. "I didn't want to touch it, it smells pretty bad."

Either Sean or Kane could have done something like this, but she knew who it was.

"It's Sean," Lucy said.

"Why?" Jack said.

"We know there were six vehicles at the ranch. By the tire patterns, two were left here, including Peter's truck. If you were holding a computer guy and a mercenary, who would you assign more men to guard?"

"Point taken," Jack said. "So they separated them." He was about to say something else, but didn't.

"Because Juarez wants to torture Kane. Or wants Kane to think that Sean is dead. Or because he thinks together, they might have a better chance of escaping. If Sean was driving that truck, he's injured. He had to have had the key. It's a newer model, no sign of hotwiring, and Sean didn't have his electronics to possibly bypass the ignition chip. So either Peter gave him the keys or Sean stole them, or maybe Peter left them in the car." She looked at Joe. He clearly wanted to say something, but didn't. "Sean wouldn't hurt a kid," Lucy said. "Not unless his life was in immediate danger."

Ynez had been looking behind the other trailer, and came back to them and said, "It looks like someone set off on foot that way"—he pointed east—"and a truck followed him. He must have circled back, and the truck made some donuts out there, then came back this way."

"It's smart," Jack said. "One truck pursues him, the other stays here. Sean steals the Chevy, the other truck follows, rams him, drives him off the road."

"So where did they take him?" Lucy asked. "If they wanted to kill him, wouldn't they leave him in the truck?"

Her voice cracked at the end, but she didn't break.

"We need to search the Chevy, top to bottom," Jack said. "Maybe there's some clue as to where they have been holding Kane. It's going to be someplace close by."

"Why would you say that?" Joe said.

"They need a remote location, one where trucks coming and going in the middle of the night aren't going to attract attention. And they need no interruptions through tomorrow morning. They could be using an abandoned barn, a warehouse, a farmhouse, flooded trailers like these."

Joe said, "I need to look at a map."

"I got one back at my car," Ynez said. "I know what you're looking for. This is my town. I was born and raised here. There are probably less than a dozen properties that meet those criteria in a five-mile radius."

* * *

Lucy's cell phone rang as Ynez and Joe were looking over a map and making notes. She wanted them to find something, but the truth was, they didn't have the team to go in hot at even one place, let alone half a dozen or more. She and Jack had searched the Chevy, but there was nothing that pointed to where they had Kane—or where they'd taken Sean.

"Kincaid," she answered.

"It's Frank Cardenas."

Padre. "We found where they were holding Sean. He's gone."

"I don't know where Juarez is keeping them, but I know where Juarez is staying."

"What do you mean?"

"Juarez hired a small local gang out of Hidalgo to help him. Michael Laredo is part of the gang. They mostly do petty crimes, sometimes get paid by the cartels to move product, but it's small potatoes compared to other entry ports. The gang leader is a guy by the name of Ralph Gomez. He's well liked by his men, but not the sharpest tack. His girlfriend has a house in Santa Maria, she lives there with his two kids. According to my source, Juarez is staying there."

"Gomez is letting him stay with his family?"

"The kids are young, Lucy. Eight and ten. He could have paid or threatened Gomez, but I'm leaning toward paying. Hire a local criminal gang to work with your core team. It makes sense. But Juarez is not going to want to leave any loose ends, and now I'm worried about Gomez's family. I'm not saying to let them off, Lucy—I'm saying that they probably didn't know what they were getting themselves into. They've never been violent. I've worked with some of the kids before—Gomez doesn't retaliate if someone walks away."

"So?" she snapped. "They took this job, they knew they were kidnapping two people."

"And Juarez could have told them anything he wanted, and Gomez probably believed him. I'm already on my way there. I have an idea."

Jack was listening to the conversation as well, his head close to Lucy's. When Padre was done explaining, Jack said, "It'll work."

"Will it?" Lucy said. "They could have seen you, Padre. Juarez could know you and Kane are friends."

"When I wear my collar, people don't see me as an individual, Lucy. Trust me—just give me a little time."

"We don't have time."

"We have enough."

Chapter Thirteen

Lucy hated Padre's idea. Fortunately, Jack kept quiet as they sat down the street from Gomez's girlfriend's house. It was five thirty in the morning and the sky hadn't even started to lighten. The last three hours had been somewhat of a blur between searching the trailers, inspecting the crash site, and studying maps. And right now, Padre's idea was the best they had, no matter how many ways Lucy could see this going wrong.

FBI SWAT was stationed at a business a quarter mile away, keeping a low profile, but ready to deploy. An un-marked FBI vehicle with two agents parked on the opposite end of the street from where Lucy and Jack waited. A second SWAT team was waiting at the sheriff's substation to the east, if needed. Joe and Ynez had stayed at the flooded field in case someone returned. Joe was worried about his brother, and Lucy didn't blame him. If Peter had given up the keys to Sean—voluntarily or involuntarily—he could be punished by Juarez or his people.

Juarez didn't condone weakness.

Padre drove up to the house in his personal vehicle, an older Ford truck. Lucy used binoculars to see better. He stepped out, his cleric's collar bright white in the dark. He knocked on the door, waited. Knocked again. A moment later the lights went on, and a woman answered. She wore a modest bathrobe that she held closed.

They'd wired Padre, and he had a safe word. One word and Jack and Lucy would come.

"Ms. Doreen Chavez?" Padre said. "I'm Father Cardenas from St. Rose's in Hidalgo. I'm sorry to disturb you so early in the morning."

"Is something wrong? My mother?"

"Not your mother, but we need to talk. It's important."

"Of course—I— Okay."

He stepped into the house and she closed the door. Lucy had no visual, but the wire was working.

There was only one truck parked on the street that wasn't registered to any resident, and Lucy suspected it belonged to Juarez or his men—if Padre was right and he was staying here.

"Would you like some coffee, Father?" Doreen asked.

"No, thank you. I'm here because a mother in my parish is very worried about her son. Peter Quezada is seventeen. His truck was in an accident only a few miles from here, and there was some blood on the steering wheel, but Peter wasn't there. The police called Mrs. Quezada, but she doesn't trust them and she called me. She wants to find Peter, make sure he's okay. He's worked for Ralph Gomez in the past, and Ralph's mother told me you and Ralph are friendly."

"Yes, he's the father of my children. But why come here, Father? I don't understand."

"I first went to Peter's best friend's house, but he's missing, too, and his mother thought he was at Peter's. Peter's mother thought Peter was at Juan's house. You can see the issue, now that Peter's truck was found. It was seriously damaged and his mother is gravely concerned. I'd hoped Ralph was here, that maybe he had hired them for a job and that's why they were out so late. Mrs. Quezada does not want the police involved, and I want to respect her wishes. I need to find these boys and bring them home, safe."

Lucy wished she could see the woman's face. She was much better at reading expressions than she was tone.

"Juan Laredo?" she asked.

"Yes," Padre said.

"I know him. Michael, his older brother, is friends with Ralph. But I haven't seen either of them. Ralph was here Wednesday to see the kids. He'll be here tomorrow, we always go to church together." In a slightly different voice, almost guilty, she said, "I know we're not married, but it's okay that we go to church, right?"

"Of course, Doreen. You're doing right by your children."

"Ralph just sometimes . . . well, if he's not here, I don't know where he is. Sometimes he takes jobs out of town."

"Is something wrong?" Padre asked.

"No, of course not."

Lucy straightened. What did he see that she couldn't hear in the conversation?

"Doreen, what are you scared of?"

"N-nothing."

Now Lucy heard the fear in her voice.

A little girl with a sleepy voice said in the background, "Mama, where's Bobby?"

"Christina, go back to bed."

"I heard voices. And Bobby isn't sleeping in his bed."

Padre said, "Ms. Chavez, where is your son?"

"You need to leave, Father. Please. Just go. Go, go now."

"I can help you."

"No, no you can't! He has my son!"

"Ralph?"

"I asked you to leave."

"Was a man named Felipe Juarez staying with you for the last couple of days?"

Silence.

"I know he was, Doreen," Padre said quietly, but firmly.

"My son," she wailed.

"Mama?" the little girl said.

"Doreen, are those bruises on your wrists? Your neck? Did someone hurt you? Did Ralph do this to you?"

"Ralph has never laid an unkind hand on me! If you don't leave, that man will find out, he will take my boy."

"I will get your boy back."

"You can't. This will all be over in a few hours, then Bobby and Ralph will be home."

Lucy had listened to enough. She got out of the car over Jack's objections. She trusted her brother completely when they were in the field, when planning an operation, but when it came to questioning an unwilling subject, Lucy trusted herself the most.

She approached the house and knocked loudly on the door. Padre answered it. He didn't look happy with her, but Lucy didn't care.

She closed the door behind her. "Ms. Chavez, is there anyone currently in this house other than you and your daughter?"

She shook her head.

Lucy showed her badge. "I'm FBI Special Agent Lucy Kincaid, and if you want your boyfriend and your son to survive to see the sunrise, you need to tell me right now where they are."

The woman shook her head. Christina began to cry, and Lucy pushed aside the guilt that the little girl was scared.

"You are an accessory to felony kidnapping and assault. If you don't help us, and anyone dies, you will then be an accessory to first-degree special-circumstances murder. That means you will go to prison and you will not see your children before they graduate from college."

"Kincaid!" Padre said sharply.

Doreen was sobbing.

"We did it your way and your way didn't work," Lucy told Padre. "Now we do it my way."

"They'll hurt my boy," Doreen said through tears as she clutched her daughter.

"I will do everything in my power to return Bobby to you safely. But right now, Bobby is in far more danger if you remain silent."

"An old dairy barn, up county road 503," she said with a loud sob. "I don't know exactly where, but all Ralph was supposed to do was find a remote place that had privacy. He brought that man here Wednesday—said it was only for a few days—but I haven't seen Ralph since then. Then that awful man took Bobby. Woke him up an hour ago after he got a call, I don't know why or who. I said no, he hit me. And he just took my baby. Told Bobby that he could see his father, that it would be fun. But that man isn't doing anything good, and I'm scared. He told me if I was good Bobby would be back this morning. That's all I know, I swear to God, Father, that's all I know!"

Lucy reached into her pocket and retrieved one of her business cards. She stepped forward and handed it to Doreen. "I know what he did to you. Call me and I can help."

"Nothing. He did nothing." But she wouldn't look Lucy in the eye.

"Doreen," Lucy said quietly, "I know. Don't bury the pain, don't deny it happened, don't blame yourself. Call me," she repeated. "I will find you help."

"Just get my son back. Please. Bobby's only ten years old. He's a little boy. I . . . I need to hold my son."

Lucy turned to Padre. He was looking at her differently, and she wasn't certain he wasn't still angry with her. "Can you stay here with them?"

He nodded.

"Thank you," she said, and left.

Chapter Fourteen

Shouting woke Sean up.

He startled awake, sat up quickly, every muscle in his body sore and aching. But nothing felt broken, thank God.

"Be still," Kane said quietly.

Kane was tied against a support beam in the middle of an old barn. Tied well, it seemed—he hadn't been able to loosen or get out of his restraints. Likely because of the noose around his neck—if he moved too much, it would tighten.

"You brought my son here? How dare you!" a man was shouting. "How dare you touch my child!"

"Watch your tone with me, Gomez," Juarez said.

The men were near the front of the barn. With them was a boy about ten wearing jeans and a pajama shirt. He looked scared, tired, and cold.

"You brought me incompetence! I was told you had a good crew, a smart crew. You're all idiots." Juarez pointed to Sean. "Why is he not tied? Do it!"

Juarez pointed to one of his own men and motioned for him to go with Gomez.

It was now clear who was who. Gomez, the two teenagers,

and three other guys were part of a local gang, separate from Juarez. They didn't have any serious gang tats, nothing Sean recognized. That didn't necessarily mean anything, he wasn't well versed in street gangs. But they weren't one of the major violent gangs, and they all sounded American, even when they spoke Spanish. The two teens had been tasked with watching Sean, along with two other Gomez goons. Sean figured because Kane was the more serious threat, the better-trained soldier, and the real target. Sean was just icing.

Juarez had at least six of his own men. Most were patrolling outside, but Juarez's right hand was keeping tabs on them—he had a radio and was getting regular reports. He stood off to the side, heavily armed, watching everyone. And then the thug came over to tie Sean up.

They dragged him to the other side of Kane, where they were back to back. Damn, he was sore, mostly his chest, but he didn't think a rib was broken. Maybe cracked, but more likely just sore from the seat belt when he crashed. It was his head that really throbbed, and he was pretty certain he had a concussion. Dried blood clogged his nose and he breathed through his mouth.

Right now, the most interesting—and troublesome— dynamic was the kid. From what Sean could piece together, Juarez had been staying at Gomez's place, and after Sean escaped, he grabbed his kid and brought him here. As leverage, perhaps, or a threat. Sean would kill Juarez himself if he harmed the child, who was both confused and terrified.

They didn't search Sean, which was a big plus—he'd found the knife in Peter's truck and it was now buried deep in his front pocket. He exaggerated his pain, hoping that they wouldn't truss him up too tightly. Gomez did an adequate job, but Juarez's guy tightened the knots.

Jerk.

When they left them, Sean whispered to Kane, "Do you have eyes on the boy?"

He felt him nod.

"What's the plan?"

"I'm thinking."

That wasn't good. Kane always had a way out, even in desperate circumstances.

"I have an idea," Sean said.

"I'm listening."

"We need Peter."

Silence.

"The kid with the green Vans shirt. He helped me after I escaped. He came along because of his friend, had no idea what was going on. From what I gathered, his friend is the other teen, in blue. And one of these guys is his brother. They all work for Gomez, though the kids—I think they were duped."

"They're too scared to act."

"Maybe, maybe not."

"If you get him, what next?"

Sean hadn't gotten that far.

"If he can get the kid out, I have an idea," Kane said.

Sean knew he'd have a plan. He said, "I can cut through my rope, but yours are thicker."

"I can get out of them."

"Why haven't you?"

"It took me a couple hours to think it through. All I need you to do is loosen one knot that I can't reach, near my neck. I'll do the rest."

The dairy barn was in the middle of a wide-open field. There was no place to hide, no way to recon without being seen, according to SWAT. The head of the FBI SWAT team out of McAllen, Eddie Jones, said, "Six men patrolling outside, two solo drivers on foot and vehicle. All appear heavily armed. We couldn't get close enough to use the heat sensors, so we have no idea how many are inside."

"Are you saying you can't breach?" Lucy asked.

"I won't go in blind. We can take out the patrols, but it won't be silent, and that puts the hostages at risk."

"Even though it's still dark?"

A very faint blue had started to rise on the horizon.

"We have maybe fifteen minutes before visibility improves," Jones said.

"They used drones with cell blockers at Kane's ranch. Can we get a drone up with a night camera?"

He smiled. "Damn, I think we can. Let me get on it."

It was just before six in the morning. They were staging in the only area that didn't have line of sight of the dairy barn. Juarez had picked the location well—there was no easy way to approach. The fields surrounding the barn were fallow. They could possibly have gone in during the cover of night, but by the time they arrived and set up, they didn't have the time.

"Drone. Smart," Jack said.

"I only thought of it because one of them was shot down at the ranch. We don't even know if they're alive, Jack."

"They're alive, until he talks to Hazel. We have time."

"Not much."

"We'll get them. They're going to be thinking the same things we are."

"If they're conscious."

"Can't I get a little optimism out of you, sis?"

"I'll try." She glanced at her brother. "I think Padre's angry with me."

"He'll get over it. I heard everything. You know what you're doing."

"I hope so."

"You do."

Jones wasn't back, and Lucy didn't know if that meant her idea didn't work, or if they didn't have the tools. The sun was working against them now, and so was time. She paced, unable to relax. Jones had gone into the tactical van, but he hadn't come out—and neither had anyone else. But she couldn't see what they were doing, if anything.

Her cell phone vibrated. It was Siobhan.

"Are they there?" she asked without saying hello.

What did she say? "We believe so, but we haven't had confirmation."

"I just spoke with Hazel and Dean Hooper in Sacramento. Hazel's ready. She knows what to do."

Lucy didn't want her to have to do this, but there might not be another choice. "Siobhan, this is really important. You need to get proof of life before you let Juarez talk to her."

"I will. I know I messed up last time, but this time—I won't forget. But—will it matter? Juarez still plans to kill him. How—"

"We're working on it," Lucy said. "If it comes to it, Hazel will keep her father on the phone."

"Agent Hooper briefed her. She knows what to do. She's strong. I just wish she didn't have to do this at all."

"Me, too, Siobhan. Hold tight. We're going to get them out."

"I trust you, Lucy. Let me know as soon as you know anything."

Lucy ended the call and continued to pace.

Then she saw Jones coming toward her with a tablet.

"We have it," he said.

"Have what?"

"A drone. Better, we have it parked on the roof and we have a live feed. Not visual, but heat signatures." He turned the tablet so she and Jack could see.

They studied the image. "These two are Sean and Kane," Jack said. They were close together, looked like they were tied back to back.

Ynez and Joe approached. "Crime scene is at the crash site, we though you could use help," Joe said.

And, Lucy figured, he wanted to be where he thought his brother was.

Ynez stared at the tablet. "I know this place," he said. "That's the center of the barn, there are several support beams there, they're probably tied to one."

"Good to know," Jones said.

"Here," Jack said, "is the kid. He's the smallest one, by himself, sitting on a chair. Who are these?"

Two other men were sitting down, up against a wall. They couldn't tell if they were part of the gang or tied up, but they weren't walking around.

That left four additional hostiles, all standing.

Eddie said, "There's no guarantee if we breach that the hostages will make it. The boy is right in the cluster of targets and could easily be used as a shield."

"We might have to wait until Juarez makes contact with his daughter. It'll distract him, at least long enough for us to get in position."

"Are you sure?"

"No," Lucy admitted. "But he hasn't spoken to his daughter in nine years. We've briefed her. She knows that we found Kane and Sean, but she's prepared to talk to her father. Siobhan will demand proof of life. That will help us know who is who—Juarez will have the phone. Once we have that proof of life, Hazel will get on the phone and talk to her father. She knows she needs to keep him talking."

"We have to take out the external security quickly," Eddie said. "We're working on a plan for that. But it would be best to get Juarez out of the barn, separate him from his team, and we can breach from the rear. There's an unused door in the back. We don't know if it's locked, but we'll assume that it is. We'll go in simultaneously, front and back, with tear gas. Two of my men will go directly for the kid. The rest of my team will go in two three-man formations. My men are the best-trained in the state, and our goal is no casualties. But if someone aims a gun at one of my people or the hostages, they will be put down."

Lucy had to let this go. She had to let Jones and his SWAT team do their job.

"However," Jones said, "we don't have the recon to go in, not yet. We don't know if there are booby traps at the doors, and it bothers me that no one is manning that rear door, which makes me think there's something blocking it. We also have a truck that can go in through a wall, separate the hostages from the hostiles, but the problem there is that the child is with the hostiles. We haven't identified any external cameras on the barn, however, so I don't see how they could be watching from the inside. There's no working electricity. The lights they have must be coming from battery-operated lanterns or a small generator."

Jones looked from Jack to Lucy. "I know you're worried, and we're taking every known fact into account. But without solid intel, we don't know what we're facing."

"Just be ready for Sean and Kane to help themselves," Lucy said. She watched the feed. It looked like they were moving slightly, but the edges of each human shape were indistinct.

"I have two men doing recon now. They should be back in the next few minutes, then we'll have more information."

He left the tablet with them and Lucy watched the screen carefully. What were they doing? Because it looked like Sean and Kane were up to *something*.

Joe said, "I need to do something."

He had gone from concerned to extremely worried as he learned more about Juarez and the hostage situation.

"SWAT is putting together a plan," Lucy said.

"That's my baby brother in there. Our dad died when he was eight; I'm the oldest. I'm more like a father to him than a brother. I need to save him."

"Hold tight," Jack said. "You can help, but right now we need more intel. Without knowing exactly what we're dealing with, we're not going to save anyone."

"I want to be involved in the raid. I can get Peter and Juan out safely. They won't fight me on this."

"We'll bring it up with Jones," Lucy said. "But ultimately, it's his call."

Chapter Fifteen

Sean was facing the back of the barn, and even if he turned his head he couldn't see much. Kane quietly gave him instructions, since he had the best line of sight to Juarez and the others and they had developed a rhythm where Sean would slowly saw the rope when no one was looking, and stop moving when anyone turned their way.

In the last two hours, since Juarez had brought Gomez's son into the mix, tensions were high, but no one was talking. The teens had fallen asleep against the barn wall; the younger boy was sitting on a chair, his head resting on his arms on a broken desk in the corner. Gomez was sitting on the ground next to him. Juarez had gone into a stall and was out of sight, but two of his goons stood sentry by the door.

Sean had his binds cut almost completely through and they were now loose enough that he could shed them quickly. "Okay, I need to work on the knot," Sean said to Kane.

"Hold."

They were going to have to readjust so that Sean could get his fingers into position, and that might draw attention.

Sean had a great sense of direction, but not as good a sense of time. It still seemed like it was dark outside, but with the lanterns on the east side of the barn and the lack of windows,

it was nearly impossible to tell. All they would know was
that at seven a.m., Juarez would call Siobhan to talk to his
daughter.

If they didn't get out then, they'd be dead. And probably
Gomez's entire gang. Sean didn't like petty criminals, but
from what he'd seen, this wasn't what they'd bargained for,
and the fact that Juarez had grabbed the kid, that told Sean
he didn't trust Gomez or his team. The kid was for leverage.

"You're tense and antsy," Kane said.

"What time is it?"

"About six fifteen."

How did Kane know that? They'd taken his watch.

"There's a SWAT team outside."

"How the hell do you know?" Sean hadn't seen or heard
anything.

"I heard a drone. It landed on the roof directly above us."

"Juarez was working with drones."

"I heard a click of a mic in the back. It wasn't Juarez, he
doesn't have short-wave radios. Between Lucy and Padre,
they'll have tracked down the local gangs. Lucy will have
called JT, who called Rick, which would jumpstart SWAT
action. You left the license plate numbers, they will have
traced them, that was a win for us. SWAT will come in front
and back, we need to be prepared to take cover. You get to
the teens—neither are armed—but if they hesitate or fight,
leave them. I'll get the boy."

"I hope this will work."

"Trust me. Just loosen that knot so I don't choke myself."

Finally. For the first time, Kane sounded like he knew what
to do, and that alone comforted Sean. The earlier Kane, the
one without a plan, without the vision of success, had scared
him. Because if Kane didn't know what to do, no one did.

"They'll probably wait until the call," Sean said.

"Yep. Adjust your position, but don't start on the knot."

Sean stretched, taking care that his binds didn't drop prematurely.

Juarez's head thug looked over at him through sleepy lids. "Settle down over there," he called out, but didn't come over.

"Any chance for some water?" Sean called over to the guy.

"Shut up."

The maneuver helped Sean move his fingers to the central knot that Kane needed loosened. It felt like a mess, but Sean closed his eyes and let his instincts take over. The rope was coarse and thick, and his fingers were already sore and raw, but he had to get this done. This was their only chance.

Juarez entered the main barn. "It's time."

It was seven already?

Juarez pointed to his main right hand. "Get the kid."

"No!" Gomez shouted.

Juarez hit him and disarmed him simultaneously. "You're a fool, Gomez. Your kid will be fine, he's insurance, and a lot more pliable than the Rogan brothers." To his other goon, "Wait for my call. If Gomez doesn't cause any trouble, he and his crew can live. Kill the Rogans and meet at the safe house. I'll leave Rod here inside, and the others will guard the door. I don't expect any trouble, but with that one"—he jerked his head toward Kane—"you never know. Anyone walks in through that door, put a bullet in their head. Understood?"

"Yes, boss."

Juarez walked over to Kane and took a picture of him. "In case your little whore needs to see you before you die. Just know, I will kill her too. She took from me the only thing that I cared about."

"You sold your daughter to a pervert," Kane said through clenched teeth.

"Daughter? She was my property! Her betrayal cost me my reputation, half my territory, and made me a laughingstock!

It took me years to rebuild what I had. I want that traitor to know that she will never be safe, that I will find her, find the people she loves, and kill them all. I want her to know that I punished those who helped her. That my nephew is dead because of her! That the old fool woman who raised her is dead because of her! She will beg my forgiveness, and I will not forgive. Actions have consequences."

He hit Kane. Kane took the punch. He spit at Juarez. "You will be dead before sundown."

Juarez laughed and walked over to the main entrance. He pulled Bobby up from the desk.

"Do not take my son. Please, I beg of you."

"That's a start. Do as I say, your boy will be fine."

"The truck's out front," Juarez's guy said.

"Let's go."

As soon as Juarez left, Gomez started to pace. He was worried about his kid, and he should have been. Juarez had left two of his men in here, and all Gomez had were the two teenagers, who looked like they had no idea what was going on.

But only Juarez's men were armed.

"Now," Kane whispered to Sean.

Jones came running out of the tactical truck. "Juarez is leaving with two trucks—two men in each truck, and they have the boy."

"Leaving? It's only six thirty!" *Why would he leave before the call?* Lucy wondered. Worried that she missed something.

"He wants to be closer to the ranch," Jack guessed. "He either thinks his daughter is there, or he's planning another attack."

"That would be foolhardy," Lucy said. "He should know that Siobhan would have protection."

She looked at the heat signature still coming from the drone on the barn roof. "Kane and Sean are getting up—Jones, they're making their move."

Jones called on his radio. "Go go go!"

"We have to go after Juarez," Lucy said. "He has Bobby."

Jack didn't need any convincing, but Jones said, "Take my number two, Fernandez. I'll radio him, he's at the end of the road in an unmarked truck." He started giving orders and reassigning a field leader.

Lucy was torn—going after Bobby was the right thing to do, but she still worried about Kane and Sean. Yet, Jones had this operation locked down, and damn if Lucy was going to lose that little boy.

When they got to the end of the road, Fernandez—who went by Dez—introduced his partner, Paul. They had been monitoring the situation from the opposite end of the main staging area. "The suspect passed by three minutes ago. There are not many ways to get out of here."

"We believe he's heading toward Hidalgo, to a ranch on the east side, outside the city limits."

"Rogan's ranch."

"Yes."

"I know the place. Kind of hard to miss considering he has his own runway."

"My brother here built it."

"You're Jack *Kincaid*? Friends with Frank Cardenas, from the Army, right?"

"Yes, sir."

"I've known Frank for years. Good man."

"He is."

"Have you heard anything from Jones? Do they have the hostages?" Lucy asked.

"No word yet. We're monitoring right now, they've breached the barn, waiting for reports from the team leader.

The Commander is good. Trust him. There's the target. Paul, you got him?"

"Got him."

They were watching a map as well as the road.

"Is that GPS? You have a tracker?"

"Yes, ma'am. Paul here planted it when he had the opportunity. To cover all our bases. Jones says you're in hostage rescue, which puts you in charge here since our HRS chief is at the barn. What's the plan?"

Lucy had anticipated this, because FBI protocols were fairly standard from office to office, but this was a precarious situation because of Juarez's motivation.

"Juarez will use the boy. He doesn't care about his life, or the lives of anyone else, even his team," Lucy said, drawing on all her criminal psychology training and what she learned during hostage rescue training. "At this point, he's motivated primarily by revenge, but it's tainted by his sense of betrayal—from his daughter—and his self-worth, his honor. He wasn't able to live up to his agreement when he promised his daughter to a man in order to unite two crime families, and that likely cost him. I don't think negotiation is going to work."

"Not even a promise to see his daughter?"

"I don't think he wants his daughter back home; I think he wants to kill her. An honor killing. He thought she was lost forever to him, and that's festered for years, turning into something even darker than the psyche that had him selling her off in the arranged marriage. He'll want to see her only to kill her. But that's not on the board right now—she's not in the state. She is, however, prepared to talk to him. That's when he'll be distracted, and that's when we'll need to act. We get Bobby out of harm's way, but don't expect Juarez to surrender."

She watched the blip on the truck that they were pursuing

at a safe distance. She hoped her profile was right. If she was wrong, Bobby Gomez would pay the price.

Sean broke his ropes, thanks to his being able to cut them nearly all the way through. How Kane slipped out of his binds was a trick Houdini would be proud of, and Sean didn't have time to inspect the knots to see how his loosening just one had worked.

Later, he'd have to ask Kane how he did that.

When they jumped up, all eyes were on them. Sean hoped that Peter and his friend were with them, because it was going to get ugly if they weren't.

"Down!" Sean shouted.

He ran toward the teens, heard a gun go, then a grunt. He didn't think it was Kane, but he couldn't be sure.

Peter and his friend laid flat down as the gunfire continued. Sean jumped behind a low stable, which wouldn't do much good as protection, but at least they were out of direct sight.

Wood splintered all around him.

"Peter, stay down!" Sean ordered. "Do what the cops say."

Sean peered out and saw that Kane was on the opposite side of the barn. He'd thrown the knife he'd retrieved from Sean's pocket at one of the gunmen, and it hit him in the leg. He was down, but he was still armed. Sean couldn't see where Gomez and the other two guys were.

"Police! Hands where I can see them!

SWAT breached from both the front and back of the barn, just as Kane predicted. Two teams of three came in.

The gunman who Kane knifed raised his weapon but didn't get a shot off before he was dead.

Every other man put his hands in the air.

"Rogan!" one of the SWAT called out.

"Here," Sean and Kane said simultaneously.

Sean slowly rose, kept his hands visible. He was the hostage, but it was still best not to make any sudden moves around trained officers packing serious firepower.

The five men—including the two teens—were all handcuffed. The dead shooter was checked and disarmed, and it was called in to the team leader.

A deputy in uniform came in behind one of the SWAT teams.

"Peter!"

"Joe?"

Peter was cuffed with his friend. Joe ran over and hugged him. "Thank God you're alive. Thank God."

"I'm so sorry. I'm so sorry, I didn't know this was going to happen."

"I know you didn't."

Sean walked over to them. "Peter helped me escape, and he paid the price for it." Sean motioned to the bruise on his jaw. "I'm going to put that in my statement. Maybe it'll help."

"Thank you," Joe said, holding his brother.

"It's my fault," Juan said. He was near tears. "Where's Michael? What happened to Michael?"

"He was captured out front. He's okay. What happened, Juan? How did you get into this mess? Michael?"

"He didn't know—he just thought it would be something quick and easy and we'd be home by midnight. And then—it just got weird."

"You're both going to give your statements. You're going to be arrested, but I'll do everything in my power to get you probation. If you lie, all bets are off, understood?"

They nodded. Sean became distracted when he heard shouting on the other side of the barn.

"You have to let me go!"

It was Gomez.

"Hold still, sir," one of the SWAT officers said.

"He took my son! He took my boy!"

If SWAT was in here so fast, they had to know that Juarez left with the kid.

Sean walked over to where Kane was talking to a guy with the name JONES on his breast.

"Eddie Jones, commander of this SWAT unit," he said. "You must be Sean Rogan."

"Yes, sir."

"Your wife is following Juarez and the hostage. You need medical."

"I'm fine."

"You look like shit," Kane said.

"So do you."

"Just get looked at, okay? An ambulance is already here, we had them standing by. I say this is a success. One hostile dead, no injuries to my men, and you two look like you'll survive."

"Thank you."

"You're welcome. Thank your wife and her brother."

"Brother?"

"Jack," Kane said with a half smile.

"You knew Jack was here?"

"No, but I knew when Lucy called JT that he'd call in the cavalry."

"Yes, sir. I even had a call from Assistant Director Rick Stockton. *That* doesn't happen every day," Jones said.

"What time is it?" Kane said.

"Just about seven," Jones said.

"We need to get to my ranch. That's where Juarez is headed."

"We have visual on him."

"I'm leaving. Sean?"

"I'm with you."

"You'll need a ride," Jones said. "Lucy left your truck here

when she went with my number two to follow the target."
He handed Kane the keys. "Be careful. Neither of you is one
hundred percent."

Juarez didn't go to the ranch, but went to a small house across
the main road that was in line with three other small houses.

"Who lives there?" Lucy asked Jack.

"It's owned by the Dickersons—they own everything
north and west of us—but that's not their primary house.
Those would be for ranch hands, the foremen. I know the
Dickersons—they're good neighbors. They would never be
in league with someone like Juarez."

"Where are they? Could they be hostages?" Lucy prayed
not. It was bad enough to have the boy, but an entire family . . . what if they were already dead? Cold spread through
her veins.

Dez spoke up. "The Dickersons left before Christmas to
visit their kin up in Amarillo. They won't be back 'til after the new year. They have a caretaker, but he lives on the
other side of the property. The rest of the staff is off, though
I can't say for certain no one is in any of those houses."

"He could have found out which were empty through Gomez," Lucy said.

"He'll have line of sight to the main driveway," Jack said.

"There's a squad car there, and two agents at the house,"
Lucy said. "They won't get close. But we need to know when
he's talking to Hazel. That's our window."

"I know how to get in through the back," Dez said. "We'll
go in on foot, the storage barn will help block our approach."
He looked at his phone. "The raid was successful," he told
Lucy and Jack. "One hostile down, no other casualties. The
Commander says that the Rogan brothers are headed our way.
But it'll take them twenty, twenty-five minutes even if they
haul ass."

Lucy was relieved, but she wished they would stay away—they had to be dehydrated and injured and if Juarez saw them, he would know his plan had failed.

That put Bobby at greater risk.

She called Andie's cell phone. It was almost seven.

Andie answered immediately. "Walsh."

"Kane and Sean are fine. They're on their way to the ranch."

"Good."

"Is the call set up?"

"Yes, we're waiting."

"Juarez is in an empty bunkhouse north of Kane's property line. He has a ten-year-old boy hostage. I'm with a small SWAT unit and we're going to go in hot while Juarez is distracted. I need to know exactly when he calls."

"Stay on the phone."

Lucy put Andie on speaker. "Dez," she said, "what's your plan?"

"Seems like you already figured it out. We go in hot, like you said. You're in the rear, ma'am. No offense, it's not because you're a girl—one of my best team members is a girl, beats my ass at the range nearly every time—but because you don't have the training."

"Understood. I'm going for the boy."

Jack stared at her. He didn't want her to do it.

"Don't play my big brother on this."

"I am your big brother."

She almost smiled, and if she hadn't been so tense she would have laughed. "I can do this. They're not going to be expecting us, so we have to be fast."

"I agree," Dez said, "but we'll get in position and first identify the location of the hostage. Those bunkhouses are small and functional with identical floor plans."

"I'll follow your lead."

"Grab a vest, both of you," he said. "There should be one that fits in the back. And a helmet. No one leaves here unprotected."

Andie said, "He's calling."

Dez said, "On my count."

Chapter Sixteen

Siobhan's hand was shaking when she answered the phone. She willed it to stop. She had two FBI agents here, her sister, and they didn't even need the equipment to track Juarez because he was right across the street. And she *knew* that Kane was alive and well.

Yet, she was still scared that something was going to go wrong.

"Hello," she said. She cleared her throat. "Felipe?"

"My daughter."

"I have her here. But you can't talk to her until I have proof of life. I have to know that Kane and Sean are okay."

"Check your phone."

She did. She saw a picture of Kane and Sean tied against a beam. Kane looked more than a little angry, but there was blood on his shirt and his face was swollen and bruised. Her heart ached. She couldn't make out Sean behind him, but assumed that second man was him.

"Hestia. Now."

"You won't get away with this," Siobhan said.

He laughed at her. "I already have, you foolish woman. Three. Two. One."

"She's here! Stop!"

He laughed again.

Siobhan took a deep breath, then another, and realized she was practically hyperventilating.

"Hazel," she said.

"Hestia!" Juarez screamed. "You can't change who she is. She's Hestia Maria Louisa Juarez, and she belongs to me!"

"Papa," Hazel said, "my name is Hazel Lopez, and I belong to no one."

Silence. Complete and total silence and for a second Siobhan thought that the call had been dropped, or something happened and Juarez heard the click that merged the calls. "Tell me something to prove it's you. The dog you had."

"Blanca? The sweet mutt that you kicked when she barked at you? Or Pal, the dog Mom fed and you ran off?"

"You will come home with me."

"Never."

"Do you know what you did to me? How I suffered?"

"I'm sorry, Papa, but you should never have sold me to that man. He was awful."

"You would have been a princess."

"I would have been a prisoner."

"So? That's what you were born for! Your mother couldn't give me an heir, just a girl, and that's what you could do for your family, marry and join two families together. Yet you were selfish, selfish like your mother."

"I know you had her killed, Papa. I followed Ricardo to the river where he drowned her. And I knew that would happen to me when I no longer served my purpose. Siobhan gave me freedom."

"And she will die for it. Just like Gino. Just like Rosita. They are dead because of you."

"N-no," Hazel said, her voice cracking. "They are dead because of *you*."

Siobhan wished she could hold Hazel as she suffered

through her father's diatribe. She knew she was with Sonia and Dean in Sacramento, that they would care for her,
but Siobhan wanted to fix it. She wanted to fix everything,
which is how they got into this mess in the first place.

"I will come for you, daughter, and you will suffer for your
dishonor—"

The call suddenly ended.

"Hello?" Hazel said. "Is anyone there?"

One of the FBI agents said, "The call disconnected on his
end."

"I'm here, Hazel," Siobhan said. "Don't listen to that man."

"I'm okay," she said. "I'll be okay."

Hazel was a strong young woman, and Siobhan was glad
she had saved her.

She prayed for Lucy and her team. Because Juarez was on
the warpath.

Lucy took the cue from Dez, who had a calm, almost joking, command presence. Paul had reconned the building—
two guards outside in the front, which meant Juarez, two
guards, and Bobby in the house. Paul had them all located in
the main room. There were two entrances—front and back
through the kitchen. The house was filled with durable furniture, which could be a help or hindrance.

Paul said, "The boy is on the couch in the living room, up
against the south wall." He drew on a piece of paper. "The
kitchen is here on the north—this door opens into the eating
area. The living room runs the length of the kitchen plus the
nook. The couch is dead center on the wall. You won't be able
to see the boy when you first enter, until you go through the
nook."

Dez said, "I'll go left through the kitchen, you go right
through the nook. Take the shield, Lucy—it works."

She hadn't wanted to carry the shield. It wasn't that it was too heavy—sixteen pounds, Dez had told her—but it was awkward because she hadn't trained with one before.

But she took it without argument.

They approached the house from the back. All the blinds were drawn; Paul had observed the layout through a broken slat.

Jack didn't want to leave Lucy, but he did, because Dez teamed him with Paul to take out the two guards at the front. Lucy was relieved he hadn't argued. He was lucky he was being included as it was, considering he wasn't a cop—military training notwithstanding.

For a big guy, Dez was soft on his feet. He was listening through his earpiece to Paul's report from the front and as soon as the external guards were contained, they entered through the back door. Dez broke the lock and pushed in, Lucy right behind him.

The set up was exactly as Paul described.

Juarez was shouting, ". . . you will suffer for your dishonor . . ."

Lucy saw Bobby as soon as she stepped to the edge of the breakfast nook.

Juarez was distracted, his back to the kitchen, but his guard saw or sensed movement and turned. He fired at Dez, who came in larger-than-life from the kitchen. Dez dropped him before he could get off a second shot.

"Police! Hands where I can see them!" Dez shouted.

At the same time, Lucy ran to Bobby, her shield up. She felt and heard a loud ping, then more gunfire from the kitchen.

She threw her body over Bobby, the shield covering their heads and most of Bobby's body.

There was a grunt, then three gunshots in rapid succession. Lucy didn't dare move. Bobby was frozen beneath her. She could feel his hot breath on her neck.

He was breathing.

He was alive.

"All clear, Agent Kincaid."

Slowly, she lowered the shield. Juarez and his two goons were dead on the floor. Paul had handcuffed the two men outside. Jack came in, looked from Dez to Lucy, then nodded.

Lucy said, "Bobby? Are you okay?"

"I—I—I want my m-mom."

"We'll get you home to her right away."

He hugged her tightly. He was shaking, but he was alive and uninjured. And that, ultimately, was all that mattered.

Kane walked into his house and the first thing he saw was Siobhan. He walked over to her and kissed her hard. He didn't give a shit that Andie was there or two FBI agents or his brother; all he needed was this woman.

She was muttering something, but he didn't know what it was.

He kissed her again, and she stepped back. She was crying.

"I'm okay," he said. Why was she crying?

"I was so stupid, Kane. I'm so sorry. When Hazel emailed me—I should never have gone. You could have died. You and Sean and—"

"Shut. Up." He kissed her again. "I never want to hear you say you're stupid. That conversation is over."

"But—"

He took her hand and pulled her to their bedroom and shut the door. He didn't need an audience right now. He was surprisingly emotional. While his life had been at risk, he hadn't truly believed that he would die. Maybe because his life had been at risk a multitude of times, and death didn't scare him.

What scared him was Siobhan's fear. Which he felt rolling off her, even now, when she knew they were all safe.

He kissed her, because physical connection was how he showed he cared. He didn't have the words. He wasn't like his brother Sean, who always seemed to know what to say. Kane was a man of action, and kissing Siobhan said more than any word he could think of.

And she was still crying. He felt her tears on his cheeks and he sat her down. "Please don't cry, I can't—I don't know what to say."

"I'm so relieved. I thought—I thought there was no way out of this. That a spontaneous decision nine years ago took you from me today. I love you so much. I can't—I don't want to think about losing you. And today—I just—I just—"

"Shh. Why talk? You should never feel guilty for doing the right thing. And Hestia reached out to you because you gave her hope, something she hadn't had for years. I don't blame you, and you damn well better not blame yourself. This was all on Juarez, don't forget it." He paused. "I talked to Jack right before I walked in. Juarez is dead. He pulled a gun on SWAT and he went down. It's over."

"Oh, thank God. And that poor little boy?"

"They're taking him home to his mother right now."

He kissed her again, even though his face hurt. Hell, his whole body ached.

He forced her to look at him, smiled, though it felt like he was scowling. That hurt, too. "One more thing, Red. No secrets. You should have told me about Hestia—Hazel—whatever her name is. I would have handled security if you really wanted to see her."

"No more secrets." This time, she kissed him. "We were supposed to get married today."

"At two. We can do it."

She stared at him and shook her head. For a minute Kane thought she was calling it off.

"Tomorrow. At sunset. I already talked to Padre. You need

to sleep, you need to eat, and I need—I need my heart to slow down."

"Tomorrow. I'm holding you to that."

An hour later, Lucy walked into the house. The FBI agents had left, Andie was in the bunkhouse sleeping, and Kane and Siobhan hadn't emerged from their room. Sean sat there knowing Lucy was okay, but desperately needing to touch her.

She and Jack had taken Bobby back to his mother. Bobby hadn't wanted to let go of Lucy, and Lucy couldn't bear to put him in the back of a police car for the ride to Santa Maria. They'd talked, but Sean had to wait an hour to see the woman he loved.

At least he'd had time to shower and put on clean clothes. He threw his other clothes away—they still smelled like mold from the trailer he'd been held in.

She looked exhausted. Sean got up, ignored his sore muscles and the pain in his head, and hugged her.

She hugged him back tightly, then maneuvered him to sit down on the couch. "I know now that you were in the truck that crashed. You have a concussion."

"Mild."

"You're in pain."

"Just sore."

She stared at him. "Sean, this was a close one."

He didn't have an answer to that, because there were a few minutes back there at the barn where he didn't see a way out.

"I love you, Lucy. God, I love you."

She put her head on his shoulder and a minute later, she was asleep.

Sean kissed her head and closed his eyes.

Yes, it was too close.

Chapter Seventeen

Padre never married anyone on Sundays, but today he made an exception.

It was late, at sunset, an absolutely gorgeous evening for the last day of the year.

Kane said he didn't need anything official. That he was tired and just wanted to have some peace and quiet with the woman he loved.

Padre simply looked at him, and he was silent.

Because this—this sacrament, this promise, whatever they called it—was important to the woman he loved. Siobhan would happily share his home and bed for the rest of their lives, but for her he would make the final commitment. For her, he would declare in front of his friends and family—and the God Siobhan firmly believed in—that he would be by her side now and forevermore.

And maybe he had a little more faith today than he'd had for the first forty-five years of his life. Maybe today be believed in miracles. Because even luck and training and police work couldn't explain everything yesterday. Even the heaven and earth Lucy had moved wouldn't have found them in time. It was a combination of so many different factors. Lucy's investigation, Padre's faith and intuition, Sean's escape and recapture, and Hestia—Hazel—taking the call at the right moment for them to act in unison—when no one knew that the other pieces were in place.

Training? Yes. Faith and God? Maybe. Just maybe.

At least he was willing to entertain the notion.

Kane looked at his brother. Sean was bruised and sore, one eye black and near swollen shut, but he stood there with him and Kane had never been so proud of him as he was now.

"I love you," he said.

Sean stared at him. Not moving, not blinking. Maybe Kane had never said it before. Hell, he hadn't. Sean was his brother, what did he need of his love?

With a half smile, Sean said, "I know."

But the tears in Sean's eyes told Kane everything he needed to know. And that everything was going to change. While Kane feared it would change for the worse—how could the world survive without him fighting its battles?—he knew now that it may actually change for the better.

The door opened and Kane did a double take when JT Caruso, Rick Stockton, and Matt Elliott walked in. The four of them had been closer than brothers when they were in the military. The three were Navy SEALs and Kane, the Marine. They'd shared more than one intense deployment . . . and were forever blood, forever bound.

"Only you, Kane Rogan, would think you could get married without us," Rick said bluntly.

"Only you would crash a wedding, Spike."

Rick laughed at a nickname he hadn't heard in years, then hugged Kane and slapped him on the back. "You won the jackpot with that one," he said.

Kane winced at the pain but Rick didn't show any remorse for the hug.

"No arguments," Kane said.

"Duke is here," JT said. "He wasn't certain you would be happy, since none of us were invited."

"Because I didn't want a thing."

It made him distinctly uncomfortable.

"But," he continued, "I'm glad you're here."

"Then you won't be upset that Ranger, Lucky, Blitz, and Dyson are all in the church too."

He stared at his closest friend and didn't say anything.

"They moved heaven and earth to be here tonight," JT said. "They wanted to be."

Kane felt surprisingly blessed—yes, blessed, he thought wryly—that he had so many close friends.

Padre stepped into the small rectory. "Time to get this party started," he said. He looked at Sean and frowned. "You okay?"

"Nothing a week of sleep won't fix."

Kane looked at his brother. He wasn't 100 percent, and that he was here with him meant everything. He hoped his present would arrive in time—he looked at Padre for confirmation.

Padre nodded.

Good. Jesse had made it. It was cutting it close, but Kane had sent someone he trusted to retrieve Jesse, have a conversation with his grandfather, and ensure that there would be no one coming between Sean and his son ever again.

Because they were family, and family was everything.

"You're . . . wow," Lucy said when Siobhan walked in. "Beautiful is an understatement. It's perfect."

Siobhan wore the same dress her grandmother had worn seventy years ago. Beautiful antique Irish lace, off the shoulder, shorter than most wedding dresses because her grandmother had been five feet tall. She'd taken it to a seamstress who had kept it mostly same, just minor changes, and she was so pleased with the result. It was simple, classic, and exactly what she wanted.

History and love all rolled into one.

"Ready?" Lucy said.

"One minute," Siobhan said, taking a deep breath. "I can't believe how many people are out there for a wedding we didn't send invitations for."

Andie glanced at Lucy. "Can you give us a minute, Lucy?"

"Of course," she said and stepped out.

Siobhan frowned at her sister. "What's wrong?"

"Nothing. Why would you think anything's wrong?

"I just—" She sighed. "I never really talked to you about Kane. I know you were his commanding officer, and this is probably all weird for you."

She laughed—something that she rarely did. "Honey, I was Kane's commanding officer nearly twenty years ago. And yes, I'll always be his superior." She smiled. "And I love that he's marrying my sister and he knows I'm always his superior officer."

Siobhan smiled, though she didn't quite understand what her sister meant.

"Anyway, something completely different." She took a deep breath. "I'm being promoted."

"Promoted? Really?"

"Yes, to Colonel. They told me last week, and there will be a ceremony."

"For your eagle wings."

"You're the last of my family, Siobhan. It would mean everything to me if you would pin on the eagle."

Siobhan teared up. "Stop. My mascara."

Andie smiled, but she, too, had tears in her eyes. "Dad would be so proud of you," she said quietly. "I don't say it, because sometimes your actions—well, I'm proud and worried and angry all rolled into one. But Dad—he was lost when my mom died. And then he found your mom and he was reborn. I'm not religious, not like you, but I really believe there was a higher power out there looking out for him, and giving him your mom. And you. If you weren't here, I would have nobody. My mom died when I was young, then my brother died in Desert Storm, and then our dad died . . . and I have you. You are the light of my life, Siobhan. I love my country and the Marines and will always serve them to the best of my abilities. But because you're here, I do it also for you. You could not have found a better man than Kane Rogan. He's hardly perfect, but there is no one more loyal on this planet."

Siobhan couldn't stop the tears, but she didn't care. "I love you so much, Andie."

"I'm proud to walk you down the aisle. And to remind Kane that if he breaks your heart, he answers to me."

Dear Reader,

Cold As Ice, book seventeen in the Lucy Kincaid series, left Sean dealing with both physical and emotional trauma. He healed physically, but is still suffering mentally. He has a hard time asking anyone for help—even Lucy. Sean doesn't even understand why he can't just "get over" what happened.

I thought a long time about how to craft the next story, *A Deeper Fear.* People like Sean—smart, strong, tough—don't always deal with trauma well. He feels he's weaker because he hasn't been able to get through his pain. Lucy wants to help, but Sean is now avoiding her, making it difficult for both of them.

Lucy and Sean attend a law enforcement conference in Sean's hometown of Sacramento, where they're staying with Lucy's brother Jack and his wife Megan. Jack knows something is eating at Sean, but he doesn't know what to do about it, either. But when a friend at the conference is attacked and left for dead—and her proprietary drone stolen—everyone comes together to solve the crime, and in the process Sean regains his confidence.

Writing a more emotional story for Sean wasn't easy, but it was an important part of his journey, and I'm very happy with how it turned out. Lucy and Sean continue to build a solid foundation for their future.

If you enjoyed these novellas and want to read more in the Lucy Kincaid series, visit my website at allisonbrennan.com for a complete list of books and novellas.

Thank you for reading!

Allison

A Deeper Fear

Chapter One

Jack Kincaid offered his brother-in-law Sean Rogan a beer. Sean accepted, twisted off the cap, and sipped.

"Like the new place." Sean stared out the picture window. "Great view."

Jack opened his own beer and motioned for Sean to follow him out to the back porch. They sat on chairs that boasted the best view of the property. Late May, warm but not too hot. They could see the rolling hills to the north and the sunset to the west. He liked this place more than any other he'd lived in. Probably because he shared it with the woman he loved.

Jack and Megan had moved into the house after the first of the year, but the beginning of the year had been hectic for everyone and this was the first time Sean and Lucy had been out to visit.

For years Jack had lived with Megan in the condo she'd owned before they were married, in downtown Sacramento. Jack hated it. Not the condo, which was surprisingly spacious, but being in the middle of the city. When the FBI moved their headquarters from Sacramento to Roseville and Megan had a forty-five-minute commute on good days, they'd started looking for a new place. It took time—because of their schedules—but finally they found this five-acre spread in the small rural community of Newcastle and Megan's commute was cut to less than fifteen minutes.

Sean looked out at the yard. "That your barn down there?"

"Yep, it's falling apart. That's low on my list of things to do."

"Hmm."

"I don't think I slept a full night in eight years living downtown. Since we moved here, I sleep like a baby." Still woke up at five thirty every morning without an alarm, but that probably would never change.

Sean nodded, but Jack realized he was only half listening.

"I have a lot of work to do on the place before we get to the barn, but we got a great deal. The owners retired to Arizona, a cop and teacher. The house came with a gun safe—I thought that was a plus."

"Um-hm."

"We talked about moving to Texas."

"Huh."

"What's going on, Sean?"

"What?"

"You're not listening. I just said we almost moved to Texas."

"Oh? But you just bought this place."

Jack cleared his throat.

"What?" Sean said.

"Your mind is a million miles away. You okay?"

"Sure."

"Don't lie to me, kid."

Sean shrugged, sipped his beer, then said, "It's been a tough month."

He clearly didn't want to talk about it.

Jack wasn't a shrink. That was the world of his twin brother.

But Sean hadn't talked to Dillon when he and Lucy were in DC two weeks ago. Normally, Jack didn't interfere in the personal lives of his family members, but this was one time when Dillon had asked him to find a way to get through to Sean.

"Lucy and Sean will be in Sacramento for a crime conference," Dillon had said. *"You need to get him to talk."*

"That's your expertise."

"This time it's yours. I tried to discuss this with Kane, but he's as communicative as a rock."

"You think I'm better?"

"With Sean, yes. He respects you, Jack. What happened with Paxton has him twisted up inside. I don't think he's shared everything, even with Lucy."

"He'll talk to her before me."

"Not this time."

Jack wasn't a shrink, he didn't want to be a shrink, but he understood PTSD. He'd been a soldier for fifteen years. He had friends who had blown their brains out or drugged their brains out—same difference in his book, one fast, one slow—because they carried baggage that would make Goliath stumble and wouldn't, or couldn't, share the load with anyone.

Jack didn't know how to approach this. He didn't play games, so he just spoke the truth. "Dillon's worried about you."

Sean shook his head. "I told him to leave it alone. I don't want to talk about it. Some things are better left in the past."

"I don't disagree," Jack said. "Just make sure that this is one of those things."

"I am."

Maybe he was right. Jack didn't know. He watched Sean as he stared at the land. Yes, he was quieter than usual. He'd lost weight. The outward injuries had healed, but Jack knew better than most that the most painful scars were those that couldn't be seen.

Time to change the subject, though Jack would keep a close eye on Sean while they were here. "What's Jesse doing this week? He couldn't come with you?"

"He has two more weeks of school, which he can't miss because of finals and a bunch of activities, then eighth-grade graduation the Friday before his birthday. I finally convinced Nate to move into the rooms I built above my garage and get out of the dump he calls an apartment, so he's there keeping an eye on Jess." He paused. "I considered staying, letting Lucy have some time to herself with you and Megan, but she said she'd cancel and stay home. I didn't want her to do that, especially since she has a presentation and everything."

Jack hadn't known that Sean wanted to stay home. That was definitely cause for concern—he'd been looking forward to coming out here up until last month.

"I, for one, am glad you came." He glanced at his watch. "We should get going. I promised Megan I'd join her for the meet and greet."

"I can't," Sean said. "I told Lucy I was going to Duke's."

"Want me to drop you off?"

"I have the rental car, I'm good. Thanks."

"I'd join you if I could, but then Megan would be mad at me." Jack didn't like crowds. They made him itchy.

"No, go, it's okay."

"Don't forget—tomorrow morning is the Pride Tactical presentation, and you know how Ellen is."

"We worked out all the bugs months ago."

"She's a friend. You told her you would be there to answer questions."

"I'll be there. But it's going to be fine."

Sean was usually all over any new tech, and up until his arrest last month, he'd been excited about this project. Pride

Tactical had hired RCK and Sean to test a drone, and he'd uncovered and solved half a dozen glitches. He generally liked bragging about his accomplishments, and this was one that he should brag about.

"After the demonstration we're meeting for lunch at De-Vere's Pub."

"I miss that place. There's only one decent Irish pub in San Antonio, but nothing like DeVere's."

"Agree with you there, buddy." Jack stood, clapped Sean on the shoulder and went inside.

Yeah, something was up with Sean, but Jack hoped a few days with nothing on his plate would help.

The Bi-Annual California Multi-Jurisdictional Law Enforcement Conference, sponsored by the FBI and open to all sworn officers, was the smaller version of the national FBI conference. Someday Lucy would love to attend the national conference, but space was limited and only six agents from the San Antonio office were attending this summer. She couldn't really complain about not being chosen, considering that all those attending were senior agents with more than five years' experience. This smaller conference was the next best thing, even though Lucy knew that her sister-in-law Megan had something to do with Lucy's presentation. Lucy was speaking on a panel about psychology and modern interrogation techniques.

The only thing that put a damper on this week was that Sean was still out of sorts after his ordeal, which had ended only four weeks ago. She'd offered to skip the conference—she thought maybe they could spend a long weekend at their house in Vail, where they'd have the privacy to talk, just them, but Sean said no, he didn't want her to cancel. If he'd insisted on staying home, however, she would have, because she could tell there was something up with him.

Nate, her partner and their closest friend, had moved into the apartment above the garage at Sean's suggestion. Lucy liked having Nate close by, but it meant they didn't have as much privacy. It was almost as if Sean had Nate eat dinner with them every night . . . play video games . . . go out with Jesse . . . to *avoid* being alone with her. Yet . . . he was so *quiet*. Very unlike him. Dillon thought he should talk to someone—a professional—but Lucy knew Sean wouldn't. Right now all she could do was be there when he was ready to talk.

He'd told her a lot about what happened after his arrest last month. The interrogation by the police for a murder he didn't commit had been emotionally exhausting and humiliating, as well as infuriating. She'd seen the interrogation tapes—thanks to a friend of Nate's in the Houston FBI—and they had been difficult just to watch, so she could only imagine how Sean felt living through it. Then being in jail overnight. He talked about it—his feeling of being trapped, helpless, unable to convince the police that he was innocent of the charges. In fact, he was very open about the first twenty-four hours of his ordeal, the anger and the fear and the frustration.

But he wouldn't talk about what happened to him at the hands of former senator Jonathan Paxton, who had orchestrated the whole thing. He wouldn't talk about how he felt when he learned that one of his oldest friends, Colton Thayer, had helped Paxton set him up. He only vaguely mentioned what happened between him and Paxton. Instead he gave details about the prison break to the authorities, about how they traveled, about Paxton killing Jimmy Hunt. A lot of detail—almost as if to downplay what actually happened *to Sean*.

The only thing he'd said was, "*I escaped at one point— late Saturday night. Early Sunday morning, maybe. That's when they locked me in the cage. Colton wanted to kill me, I know that, but he didn't.*" He claimed he didn't know why or what they'd had planned for him. Colton Thayer wasn't talking or even trying to negotiate a plea deal.

Sean also claimed he didn't know Paxton's motive, or why he hadn't killed Sean, though he'd had ample opportunity. He vaguely mentioned revenge, since Sean had been largely responsible for Paxton losing his US Senate seat after Sean helped uncover Paxton's devious plan to poison prisoners. But he'd never sounded convincing, at least to Lucy.

Lucy hated that she thought Sean was lying. Maybe to spare her . . . she had an idea of why Paxton had gone after Sean. She'd even told Sean what Paxton shared with her, some foolish nonsense about Sean putting her in danger, which was asinine. But there had to have been something else that had deeply affected Sean, and she couldn't figure it out. The senator loved to talk, especially when he felt he was morally justified. She of all people knew that. He would enjoy explaining his motives to Sean. Why wouldn't Sean tell her?

She tried to dismiss her anxiety and enjoy the meet and greet, but her mood must have been off-putting because she'd been standing in the corner nursing a glass of wine for the last thirty minutes and no one had approached her. She recognized a few people in the ballroom—mostly from the Sacramento field office, where her sister-in-law Megan served as a supervisory special agent.

Over four hundred were registered for the conference in total, and half that number were socializing here tonight. Lucy would have preferred a much smaller group. Sean was the social butterfly, but he wanted to catch up with his brother, which she thought was a great idea. But she realized she missed Sean's natural gregariousness, his way of making everything fun.

Megan was halfway across the ballroom talking to her boss Dean Hooper, one of the three ASACs of the Sacramento office. Lucy knew Dean well—they'd even recently worked on a case together—but she didn't want to intrude. As if Megan could tell, she waved at Lucy and motioned for her to approach.

Reluctantly Lucy put a smile on her face and walked over. "Great news," Megan said, "Dean and Sonia are coming to the barbecue on Saturday."

Megan and Jack were having a party of close friends and family the day before Sean and Lucy left.

"I haven't seen Sonia since Sean and I got married," Lucy said.

"She's looking forward to it," Dean said. "We both are. Is Sean here?"

"He's visiting Duke and Molly tonight," Lucy said, referring to Duke's two-year-old daughter.

"Probably didn't want to be around all these cops," Dean said. "I wanted to run something by him, cybersecurity-related. Might have a great consulting assignment for him if he's game. I'll catch up with him on Saturday at the party."

Lucy didn't know what to say. Dean had hit the nail on the head, and she felt so stupid that she hadn't realized why Sean hadn't wanted to come to the conference in the first place. It was a *law enforcement* conference. He'd been arrested for a murder he didn't commit, broken out of prison by a criminal gang, considered an escaped convict, chased by the police, his name and image spread across the news. It didn't matter that he was completely cleared of all charges; Sean had always had a simmering distrust of authority, and the events last month didn't help.

She needed to talk to him, tell him she understood. Why hadn't she thought of it before? Was she so blind to her husband's fears?

Fortunately, her sudden silence wasn't noticed, because several people from the Sacramento FBI office had come up to talk to Megan and Dean. Lucy politely excused herself and found the appetizers, two large tables in the center of the ballroom. She put together a plate and was nibbling when she saw her brother approaching, beer in hand.

"Showing my face and getting out of here as fast as I can," Jack said.

"You must really love Megan."

"She definitely owes me one." Jack looked around the room with eagle eyes. Then he did a double take. "I have to introduce you to someone."

Lucy followed Jack to the edge of the room, where a woman dressed in black, her long blond hair braided down her back, was wearing a name badge that read ELLEN.

"Ellen Dupre."

She grinned widely. "Jack! You're the last person I expected to see at a law enforcement conference."

"My wife." He jerked his finger over to the opposite corner, where Megan and Dean were still talking in a group.

"Right, she's the SSA of violent crime. Damn, I totally forgot, we met last year during a tactical training drill. Um . . . Megan, right?"

"That's it. And this is my sister, Special Agent Lucy Kincaid, out of the San Antonio office."

Ellen shook Lucy's hand. "Sean's wife! I'm so happy to meet you."

Jack explained, "Ellen and I did basic training together."

"Shush, she'll know how old I am."

"Older than me," Jack laughed.

"One fucking year," she said. Ellen turned to Lucy and said, "I'm here with Pride Tactical. A vendor."

"*With* Pride Tactical?" Jack shook his head. "You own the company."

"Fifty–fifty, with my ex."

"Ouch."

Ellen laughed. "Marc and I are still friends. In fact, we're better business partners than marriage partners."

"I'm just glad to see a friendly face that doesn't have a badge. No offense, sis," he said to Lucy.

"Doesn't RCK have a contract with Pride?" Lucy asked. "I see your logo on a lot of Sean's gear."

"Only the best for our company," Jack said.

"I appreciate it," Ellen said. "We mostly service law enforcement, but of course high-end security companies use our gear. I'm demoing the drone software tomorrow. I asked Sean to do it because we hired him to test it and work out the bugs. He probably knows it better than Marc and me, but he said no."

Lucy glanced at Jack, but he didn't comment about Sean. He said to Ellen, "I look forward to it. Morning?"

"Oh eight hundred, right here. We're doing the drill outside, I have Sac sheriff's all-in. We'll be livestreaming it so everyone can get the full effect—I tested the AV equipment before they set up for this. It's going to be totally awesome." She glanced at her watch. "In fact, I should go. I'm recording a night drill so everyone can see our awesome night-vision camera and the amazing quality of the images. Good to meet you, Lucy. Later, Jack." She left.

"Sean didn't tell me he was asked to participate."

"He does a lot of work for Pride, which is why we get such a great discount on their equipment," Jack said. "And they pay him, so it's a win–win for us."

"Dean said something earlier—that Sean probably didn't want to be here because of all the cops. After what he went through, I should have realized. I shouldn't have made him come at all."

Jack squeezed her elbow. "He's working through it, Lucy.

I'll keep an eye on him, and he's planning on being here in the morning for the demo."

"Maybe we shouldn't push him, Jack."

"Sometimes we all need a kick in the ass, Luce. But I'll appeal to his geek side. This drone software project was his baby, so to speak. He's proud of it—should be proud. He needs to be here, if only to make sure everything is functioning the way it's supposed to."

"I feel like Dillon and me and you, we've been, I don't know, pressuring him. Talk, don't talk, go back to normal, nothing will be normal again. It's not only conflicting messaging, but I think it's constantly reminding him of what he suffered."

"Sean went through hell and he won't talk about it. That's fine, to a point. But I think you're coddling him."

She frowned, shook her head. "I'm not coddling him."

"He knows you're not going to push him, and neither is Dillon—which is why Dillon wanted me to talk to him. But I can't—I tried. It's not who I am. I can, however, get him to work. I can piss him off, make him angry, and maybe he'll finally talk about what's really bothering him. Or maybe he won't. But RCK is a business, and I can use that to push him out of his head."

Lucy didn't know the right answer, but she didn't have a better idea.

"I trust you."

"Just be there when he falls."

When, Jack said. Lucy thought Sean had hit bottom last month when she found him locked in a cage, beaten, bloodied. How much did he have to suffer before he was healed? It hurt not to be able to help him, to fix the problem.

Lucy looked over Jack's shoulder when a familiar face entered. "Excuse me," she said to her brother.

"Abandoning me?"

Lucy gestured to where Megan was watching them. "I think Megan wants you to rescue her."

Jack looked over and grinned. "Should I?"

"Of course."

Lucy left him and approached Nora, Duke's wife and also an FBI agent in the Sacramento office. She looked like she didn't want to be there, either. Lucy didn't know her well, but when they had spent time together, Lucy appreciated Nora's down-to-earth common sense.

Nora looked relieved when she saw Lucy. "I didn't want to come, but Dean said I needed to show my face tonight. One hour is all I promised." She looked over to where Dean and Megan had drawn a much larger crowd than when Lucy had left them. They were both extroverts and used to socializing; Lucy preferred the one-on-one conversations.

"Wine?" she asked Nora.

"God, yes." They walked over to the cash bar and waited in the line. "I assume Megan told you about the party on Saturday."

"She did."

"I don't generally like parties, but this one will be fun, and I haven't seen their house since we helped them move in months ago. I know they've been doing a lot of work."

"It looks great," Lucy said. "The kitchen still needs updating, but Jack said they were going on vacation this summer and letting the contractors rip everything out."

Nora laughed lightly. "Jack? Vacation? I don't think he knows the meaning of the word."

"That's why Megan is good for him."

They reached the front of the line. Nora ordered white, Lucy stuck with her preferred red, and they moved away from the crowd.

"How's Molly?" Lucy asked. "I hope you're bringing her on Saturday."

"Of course, she's the joy of my life," Nora said. "I love my job, but I hate leaving her every day—though Duke is a terrific dad. He's now working from home almost every day, and when he has to go downtown to RCK he takes her, or we have a terrific babysitter we can call. I can't believe she's already two years old."

"JP—my nephew—will be two next month, and Carina had a little girl last week. Grace. Sean and I are going back to Texas by way of San Diego on Sunday so we can see her."

"I don't think a second baby is in the cards for me—but that's okay. I didn't even expect to have Molly, considering I was forty when I got pregnant."

"I'll bet Duke and Sean are having fun with her."

Nora tilted her head. "Sean?"

"Sean said he was going over to your place. Maybe you missed him."

"Duke is at Fort Bragg working on a security fix for one of their systems. He won't be back until Friday. It was last-minute—they called this morning. I had our sitter come over for a couple of hours so I could show my face here. If I'd have known Sean wasn't coming tonight, I totally would have tagged him to babysit."

Lucy was speechless. Why would Sean lie to her? Or maybe he didn't know . . .

He would have called Duke before he went over. He would have known Duke was out of town.

She didn't say anything, and fortunately at that moment a colleague of Nora's walked over and started talking to them.

Lucy couldn't focus on the conversation. All she could think about was why Sean had lied to her and Jack about his plans tonight.

Chapter Two

Pride Tactical owned a state-of-the-art van that rivaled most law enforcement tactical vans. Ellen used it for demonstrations because she could also use it as a command center, of sorts. She had permission to park outside the convention center for the duration of the law enforcement conference. It looked official, though there was nothing that screamed *police* on the outside. It was black and sleek with the Pride logo discreetly painted on the doors.

She finished checking the drone—twice—and did a trial run without the camera to make sure everything worked before Marc knocked on the rear door.

She opened up the back. "When I said nine, I meant nine."

"I texted you that I would be late."

"A few minutes, you said. It's well after."

She knew she sounded nasty; what she'd told Jack earlier was mostly true. She and Marc *did* get along better now than they had before the divorce, but the things that had irritated her when they were married irritated her as business partners, too. Marc could not be on time to save his life. She was punctual even before she enlisted in the army. She had to be, taking care of her two little brothers because her parents were

too lazy or wasted to do it themselves. She was running the
house by the time she was thirteen.

"I'm sorry, babe."

"Don't." She hated being called babe even when they were
together. He knew it.

Except . . . this was Marc. For him, it was an endearment.

He ran a finger down her arm. Sometimes, she missed him.
Really missed him. They'd been through so much together
and it wasn't all bad.

"I was meeting with Steven at the bar," Marc said.

"*What?*" She jerked her hand back. "Are you fucking with
me?"

"Hear me out."

"No! I *told* you we're not selling."

"Just *listen.*"

"Pride is my company. I love this company. We're doing
great."

"That's the best time to sell—and this new drone technology you've developed is going to double our worth."

"I'm. Not. Selling."

She couldn't believe what Marc was saying. Marc had
wanted to sell the company when they divorced, but she'd
talked him out of it. She couldn't afford to buy him out at
the time. The company had grown since, and he was right—
the drone tech was going to catapult them to the top. They
had five full-time staff members that handled contracts, programming, working with vendors on production, shipping—
and everyone was overworked. With this tech they could
double their staff and give everyone raises. All they would
need were a few contracts and they'd be set for *years*.

"You work more than eighty hours a week. It's why we
divorced."

"No, we divorced because you fucked our accountant. Literally. Then I fucked Steven. Then you fucked—"

"Stop."

"And then you meet with the guy who's trying to steal our company?"

"Hey, you slept with him!"

"Screw you."

Marc grabbed her arm, and she karate-chopped his wrist and walked to the other end of the van and sat in her chair. She needed to breathe. This was her baby. Her company. She wasn't selling. She liked working eighty hours a week. What else was she supposed to do?

"I'm sorry," he said quietly. "I miss you, Ellie."

"You miss a fantasy."

"It was *real*. We had a great marriage for years. But then all you cared about was this company. And I went along with it. I thought it would be like this for a while, we'd build it, then hire others to run it. But you have to do everything yourself. You're a fucking *control* freak. I knew it marrying you, it's one of the reasons I loved you, but it's one of the reasons I ended up hating you. Because you can't control everything."

That was true. So damn if she was going to give up the one thing she *could* control.

"I want what we once had," he said.

"That's long gone, Marc."

"It doesn't have to be. Steven is making a huge offer. A preempt. You like him. You trust him. Hell, the fact that the three of us are still friends even though you slept with him shows we get along."

She rolled her eyes. Yeah, she and Marc had a really unconventional divorce. It almost made her smile. Instead she said, "He's our competitor."

"He has a plan to keep the Pride line in his company as high-end tactical equipment. Our logo, our designs, our vision—his company. And if you want to work for him—"

She spun the chair around. All humor she might have felt disappeared. "Work for *Steven*?"

"He has ten times the staff and resources. And we—I don't know. I'm not saying we can get back together, but dammit, I want to try."

She couldn't be hearing him right. "What?"

"I love you, Ellie."

"You're living with another woman."

"Monica moved out two months ago because she knew that I still loved you."

Why hadn't he told her? Two months? And *nothing*?

"So you negotiate to sell our company behind my back? You love me so much that you'd hurt me like this?"

She was angry. And bitter. And sad. But mostly confused.

"I wanted to hear what Steven had to say. We're equal partners, Ellie. He offered to buy out my half. I said no. I wouldn't do that to you. I want *us* to sell."

"Why—how—do you think we can make marriage work? We failed before."

"Not marriage, unless that's what you want. I want *you* back. But we'll take it slow. Because the one thing you haven't said, every time we argue, is that you don't love me anymore."

"I . . . no. I mean . . . *shit*! Shit, shit, shit."

She paced, but the van was small. Two steps toward Marc. Two steps back to her chair. She wanted to get out, because she couldn't *think*, but Marc was blocking the exit. She'd have to touch him to get by him . . . and touching him might be the worst thing right now because she still found her ex attractive. Super hot, sometimes, because he knew her, knew what she loved, knew how to set her off in bed.

But she didn't want this conversation, now or ever. Things were good, right? Yes, she worked her ass off, but she *liked* it. And Marc knew she liked working. That she liked developing new products. He handled the finances and contracts and detail work and staff issues because she wasn't good at that. She could see a need and fill it; he made sure they got paid.

They'd hurt each other. When she found out he'd had an affair with their accountant, she'd slept with Steven Decker out of anger. And lust. Steven knew it, she knew it, and she regretted it because they had been friends, and sex put a big wedge in their friendship, even though they'd gotten back to where they'd been before. She knew immediately that what she felt with Steven wasn't what she'd felt with Marc, so she called it off pretty quick.

But could they even put all that behind them and work together? Maybe. Probably. It was sex, not love, and they both knew it. And Marc was right. They were all relatively friendly.

Yet . . . her business. What would she do with her life? She didn't relax well. Especially . . . well, what was she supposed to do? Retire at forty-five?

"Why now, Marc? We're introducing our biggest product in a year and you want to talk about our relationship?"

"Yeah, my timing sucks, I get that."

"I don't want to sell, Marc. I need something to do with my life, and you know it. You don't love me as I am, you love me as you want me to be."

"That's not true."

"Yes, it is. Because if you took me as I was, you'd accept me as a workaholic. You'd see that I love this company because I don't have kids to love. I don't have . . ."

Tears burned.

"Oh, baby, I love you so much. If you don't want to sell, we don't sell. But we have to make this work. We have to because I love you so much—and I know why you work eighty hours a week."

"Don't," she whispered. "Please don't."

She didn't want to think about her *five* miscarriages. Five. Five over eight years. They nearly killed her. Physically, emotionally, and yeah, she put everything into this business. Everything because this was something she could control. The more she worked, the better they did. Every product was like a child to her, her creation, and they didn't die.

The last time was the worst. Her baby survived . . . for sixty-three minutes. One hour of bittersweet heaven. And then she died in Ellen's arms. They called her Em because they didn't have a name picked out. No name because Ellen hadn't wanted to jinx anything.

After that, yes, she pushed Marc away. Because after Em, the doctor took her uterus, too. So even if she wanted to try again, she couldn't. Ever.

It wasn't Marc's fault . . . it wasn't anyone's fault. Except her. She couldn't carry a baby to term. She hadn't even wanted kids until she found out she was pregnant that first time. And the first miscarriage? It hurt . . . but that was when she realized she wanted a child, that she would make a great mother, that Marc would make a great father, so she was happy to try again.

Until.

Again. Again. Again.

Death. Nothing. Emptiness.

"I fucked up, Ellie," Marc said. "I fucked up big time and I don't blame you if you never forgive me. But I miss you, I love you, there will never be anyone for me except you. And I want us to make it work. Screw marriage. I just want you back in my life—and if I have to watch you kill yourself working eighty hours a week, so be it. I'll do that. Because my life sucks without you."

Ellen didn't know what to think. She *couldn't* think. This was coming out of nowhere. She didn't doubt that Marc believed every word he said, but for how long?

She'd been an emotional basket case after losing Em. She needed the company. And . . . fuck.

"Why?"

"Why what?"

"I don't know that I can fix this. I can't let go . . ." She didn't know if she was talking about her company or her grief.

Grief. Could she really have been grieving for the last five years?

"The biggest mistake I made was not seeing your pain, not knowing that letting you go was the worst thing for both of us," Marc said. "We'll find a way. Please."

She didn't know. "I need to do this test."

"Okay, let's get it done. What do you need from me?"

"I'll do it myself."

"I can help."

"I know, but—give me some space, please?"

He took the two steps toward her, looked in her eyes. She had loved Marc from the minute she'd met him, the day after she got her final discharge papers and they sat next to each other in a computer science class at Sac State. He was five years younger, so handsome, so funny and fun-loving. She was arrogant and jaded. He'd smiled at her and said, "Do you like ice cream?"

It had been unexpected and she said, "Yeah. I do."

"My treat, after class."

And that was it.

Until it was over.

It's never been over.

"I love you, Ellen, now and forever."

He leaned over and kissed her.

Slow, warm, reminding her of everything they had, everything they could still have, if she could get out of this funk, this grief, this pain . . .

"We'll talk later," he said.

She watched him wait for something, and she wasn't sure what.

Then he turned away.

"Marc."

He looked back at her.

I love you.

She couldn't say it, even though she knew it was true.

"Tomorrow, breakfast. Our place."

He smiled, and his eyes teared up. *Our place* wasn't their house—they'd sold it after the divorce, too many painful memories including a nursery that had never been used. But one of their favorite places was a small diner not far away, open only for lunch and breakfast, and they used to go there every Sunday morning when they were married.

They hadn't been there in years.

"Six a.m.?"

She nodded.

Then he left and she turned back to the work at hand, trying to push the conversation aside. It was still there tickling her in the back of her head, though, as she tried to make sense of everything. Maybe that was why she worked better with machines and equipment. There was always an answer, a fix, a solution.

People? Not so much.

Ellen programmed the drone to recon using night vision, which was built in—enabling the drone to be lighter and use multiple advancements. They had a built-in camera as well, but because sometimes they needed different types of tech, they could add a stronger lens with additional features.

She attached a high-end night cam so that she could capture the best images when they played this video tomorrow. She'd record now, then edit and narrate at the hotel. She lived only fifteen minutes away, but because she had her equipment here, and she wanted to be accessible for meeting with potential clients, she decided to get a room for the conference.

Earlier, she'd planted tech in the area to simulate drugs, weapons, and people, all within a quarter-mile radius of the hotel convention center, in order to show how sharp the surveillance could be.

She manipulated the drone—she had to admit, this was the fun part—taking notes as it moved smoothly, almost completely silent, over the area. There—a light, special paint on a box to simulate the heat signature of a recently fired gun. There were people walking down the street, but they didn't even look up at the drone. It was that quiet—a huge plus when law enforcement needed eyes but didn't necessarily want the bad guys knowing.

As she worked, she took notes, recorded, and mentally prepared for her presentation.

But in the back of her mind she was thinking about Marc.

She didn't want to sell the company. But Marc was right about one thing: When the drone tech took off, they could hire more staff. She wouldn't have to work every conference. She liked the work . . . but maybe she should think about her other needs. Like affection. A life outside of work. She and Marc used to go camping all the time. They had dreamed of visiting the Australian outback again. That's where they'd gone for their honeymoon, and maybe . . . just maybe . . . that's where they should go to see if they could reclaim what they'd once had.

She shook her head. Maybes, what-ifs—she needed to focus on her job, because if the drone tech didn't take off like they thought it would, nothing would matter.

Really? You don't want to sell . . . but why can't you have both? The company and *a man who loves you?*

Because Marc was right about one thing. She still loved him. She couldn't say it, and she didn't quite know why. It wasn't because he'd cheated on her—they'd both hurt each other that way. And it was just sex, not love. Not . . . someone who knew her, deep down. Who shared her pain and her joys.

She wanted that back.

She just didn't know how to get it. Could it really be this easy? Just tell Marc *okay*? Let's do it? Let's try again?

Maybe it was.

Something caught her eye on the camera, so she moved the drone back to check it out. Just to show the responsiveness of the unit, the ability of the tech to adapt to different situations, both user- and computer-controlled. Whatever she saw wasn't there, but she was recording everything, maybe she could use this as an example once she edited it and looked at the tape again.

Her phone beeped. She looked down at a text message from Marc.

Six a.m. I'm already hungry.

She laughed and sent him a bacon emoji, then went back to the test.

A flash on the recording startled her, then she frowned. What was that? She looked at the location—it seemed to be on the roof of the Sheraton Hotel. Most of the vendors were staying at the Hyatt, across the street. Both hotels were a block from the convention center, where she had the van parked.

She maneuvered the drone back around but didn't see anything that might explain the flash of light. No people on the roof. No machinery that might have reflected another light—though the drone should compensate for that.

She continued past the hotel to the cathedral to show the ability to get close to structures even at night, how the program compensated for different levels of light, and the details of the people and cars on the street. She magnified a few license plates to show the clarity, even from a hundred feet up.

Ellen had enough data, and she could edit it tonight in short order. She hit the HOME button, made a few notes, and when the computer beeped that the drone was overhead, she went out the back of the van to retrieve it.

She was looking up as the drone came down, smiling as she thought about Marc. He had always been the more romantic of the two of them. And she knew him well enough to know that he was serious.

It didn't hurt to talk things out, something she wasn't very good at. But time . . . well, she guessed the old adage was right. Time healed.

She reached up to take hold of the hovering drone, and out of the corner of her eye she saw two men in black emerge from the shadows of the convention center. She took three steps to the van as a scream bubbled up in her throat, but she didn't make it inside.

She saw a gun, then felt pain in her head so sharp she thought for sure she'd been shot, except she didn't hear anything . . .

And then she saw nothing as she fell to the ground.

Chapter Three

As soon as Jack left, Sean jumped in the rental car and started driving.

He didn't know where he was going; he just needed to get away. He felt like he was drowning. He'd felt like he'd been dying for weeks, barely able to keep his head above the water.

He headed east on Interstate 80. Toward Auburn, which wasn't that far from Jack's. He didn't have a plan. He used to drive this road all the time. The road to Tahoe. Skiing in the winter, boating in the summer. Gambling any time of year, until he got caught counting cards.

His life used to be simple. He had lots of friends, he had lots of girlfriends, he had a shitload of fun. He hadn't cared about the consequences. He had money because he knew how to make money, and he enjoyed spending it. Yeah, he'd made some really stupid decisions that could have gotten him killed or thrown in jail. But back then, he didn't take much of anything too seriously.

Because if he was going to be honest with himself, he *hadn't* cared about anything. He'd watched his parents die, he'd literally buried his parents after their plane crash, and he'd turned his teenage anger into *c'est la vie*. That's life, who cares, he was just going to have fun while he could because in the end he'd be dead.

Several things happened to steer him away from a selfish, wild, anger-filled existence. Partly, growing up. He'd gotten bored with the parties and fun and the hacking he did in college. He wanted to make a difference . . . and sometimes he did. His brother Kane had let him help on several of his missions. Sure, he always had to stay with the plane, but at least it was both fun and dangerous. It was helping Kane that made him want to work for Rogan-Caruso-Kincaid. It took some time to get Duke on board—Duke who would never quite see past Sean's wild youth.

Maybe that wasn't fair. They'd worked together better now that Sean was a principal of the company, now that he was integral to running the business.

Still . . . it was partly Kane, partly growing up, and mostly Lucy that had gotten him to this point. Because when he met Lucy, he knew she was the woman for him. From day one.

And yet . . . twenty-four hours with Senator Jonathan Paxton and he doubted everything he'd done, every decision he'd made, who he'd been, who he'd become.

Mostly, he was scared. Part of it was being tortured by his former best friend Colton Thayer. The hatred that poured off Colton when he locked Sean in a cage had gutted him. Colton knew what Sean feared—physically, psychologically—and used that to his greatest advantage. But Sean could get over the beating and the mind games and the sound of rats clawing behind walls. The truth of Sean's deep foreboding was Paxton, who had found his weakness, his greatest fear, and twisted it. And even though he *knew* that Paxton was twisting everything, there was a deeper truth that Sean couldn't shake.

"Every woman you ever claimed to care about is dead. Madison. Skye. Even your own mother. Killed because of

you. *I don't want Lucy to be next. And you know as well as I do that you are selfish, you have used women your entire life, and Lucy is only the last in a long line of smart young women who fell for your deadly charms. If you really loved her, you would leave her."*

A dozen times he'd almost told Lucy, but every time he opened his mouth, he couldn't speak. What could he say? He felt stupid. He knew, intellectually, that Paxton was wrong. But his pulse raced and he got light-headed at the thought of saying it out loud. It was like his body was reacting against logic. Nothing like this had happened to him before. When he tried to formulate his feelings into words, it sounded dumb.

If he told Lucy that Paxton had played on his fears of not being good enough for her . . . or his darkest fear that he would get her killed . . . that he'd used Sean's mistakes to point out that he maybe hadn't changed as much as he'd thought . . . she would say, *It's not true.* But he couldn't change the way he felt. Because while Sean intellectually could dismiss Paxton, there was a truth in the accusations, a truth that twisted him up so tight he couldn't think.

He'd always been logical! He was a computer guy, a nerd, a genius. He should damn well be able to talk his way out of his own head!

He needed to put it all in the past. To forget about it. To forget Paxton. The man was dead, and Sean didn't feel a moment of pity or sorrow. Why couldn't Sean just kill these feelings? Why couldn't he look at Lucy and remember she loved him? Instead of seeing the pain in her eyes. Pain she tried to hide.

Pain that he'd put there because of everything that happened four weeks ago.

You didn't put the pain there. Paxton did. Jimmy Hunt did. You were a victim.

He couldn't accept that he was a victim, was that the problem? Or was it that he couldn't *stop* feeling like a victim?

He slammed his fist on his steering wheel. Again. Again. He sped up, almost willed a cop to pull him over. Laughed when he thought there was never a cop around when you needed one . . . and they were always around when you didn't.

He sounded insane. Maybe he was. His pain was nothing compared with Lucy's. She had gone through far worse than he'd ever suffered, and she was strong. Determined. Whole. Why couldn't he be as strong as she was?

If he didn't even know what his problem was, how could he explain it to anyone? Dillon wanted him to talk; he couldn't. Jack pushed him this afternoon, but he had nothing to say. He had no words . . . just this deep, claustrophobic feeling like he was drowning. He couldn't even think anymore.

Sean didn't consciously drive to Lake Tahoe, but that's where he ended up. The sun had already set. He drove around the lake, knowing he needed to head back, but then he pulled into the Harrah's parking garage.

Almost as soon as he turned off the car, his phone beeped.

He looked down at where his phone was charging. It was a message from Lucy.

When will you be home? Jack and I just got back from the conference.

He didn't know. He felt . . . *lost.*

I'll be late. Don't wait up.

He left his phone in the car and walked to the door of the casino.

He looked back at the car, rubbed his eyes. Walked back, pulled out his phone.

I love you.

Then he locked the phone in the glove box and entered the casino.

* * *

Lucy woke up at four thirty in the morning and Sean wasn't there.

She immediately grabbed her phone, heart racing, fearing the worst. He'd texted her three hours ago.

Lost track of time. Sorry. Call you later.

No explanation of where he'd been, what he'd been doing, if he was coming home . . . she shook her head. She knew he was struggling, but how could she help him when he wouldn't let her in?

Lucy didn't want to disturb Jack and Megan, so she quietly moved about the kitchen with the aid of the dim light above the stove. Made a pot of coffee and watched as it dripped into the pot.

She hated not knowing how to fix a problem. But more, she didn't understand why Sean wouldn't talk to her. She knew Senator Paxton better than anyone; she knew the mind games he played. She understood every trick and justification for his devious acts.

Maybe it wasn't Paxton, but Sean's friend Colton Thayer. It had to hurt to know that his oldest friend had worked with Sean's greatest enemy to hurt him. To set him up for murder, kidnap him, torture him. But how? What had they done to Sean that had such a huge impact on him now, a month later? Paxton was dead and Colton was in prison. Sean had been completely exonerated.

She poured coffee, added cream and sugar, sipped. She loved her morning coffee, especially the first cup, but today she tasted nothing.

She sat at the kitchen table and closed her eyes. She hurt for Sean, but what hurt more was that he'd barely looked at her in a month. They hadn't even had sex . . . definitely not something she could talk about with people. The only person she felt comfortable talking about sex with was her husband, and yet she couldn't bring it up, not now.

Maybe she should have let him stay in San Antonio. Maybe he needed time away from her. Maybe he needed something she couldn't give him.

She didn't know what to do.

Before Jack said a word, she sensed him watching her.

"I made coffee."

"Strong, the way I like it."

She opened her eyes and watched as her brother poured coffee, black, into a mug and sat across from her.

"Sean didn't come home last night."

"This isn't about you, Lucy."

"It is. I don't know why, but he . . . he can't look at me."

"You've done nothing."

Jack was angry. He didn't understand what she meant, how could she explain?

"It's not what I've *done*, Jack. But this *is* about me. He can't talk to me, he can't look at me, he can't sleep with me . . . Paxton got into his head and is still there and I don't know how to fix it because I don't know *what* he said or did. I've never seen Sean like this."

Jack didn't say anything for a minute. He sipped his coffee. Put down the mug. Finally, "Did Paxton know anything about you that Sean might not be okay with?"

"I don't have secrets from Sean. And if he lied about something, Sean wouldn't believe him—or he'd ask me. That's who he is. This is different. He's not angry. He's . . . defeated. He's lost weight."

"I noticed."

"Somehow, Paxton figured out how to get to Sean. Or maybe Colton. Colton has known Sean half his life. They had once been close."

"Maybe it's simply about Sean. He wasn't a saint, we both know that. I don't care about his past, I don't think you do, either. To me, the man Sean has become far outweighs any crimes he committed. But maybe there's something deep down that he regrets, Paxton exploited that, and Sean can't figure out how to get past it."

Maybe, Lucy thought. But how did she convince Sean that no matter what it was, she wasn't leaving?

"You might need to let Sean figure this out on his own. I don't think we're helping."

She didn't like that answer.

"But Lucy—you need to call him on this. Not coming home. Making you worry? That's not acceptable. I think . . ."

He stopped talking.

"What? What were you going to say?"

"Don't coddle him."

"You think that's what I'm doing?"

"Yes. And me—last night, before I left for the conference, I talked around the situation. I let him steer the ship. We're enabling him to do shit like not come home, not call, and lie. He told both of us he was going to Duke's. He didn't, never planned to. You can't give him a pass. I sure as hell am not."

"What am I supposed to do? Kick him out? Leave him?"

"That's extreme."

"I don't know what you're thinking, Jack. I don't know that I can . . . push him like that."

"And you're the psychologist."

She stared at her brother. "I'm not going to abandon him when he's at his lowest."

"Of course not. But if you let him get away with this? He has to know there are consequences to his actions. Otherwise, when the going gets tough, he's going to run and try to figure it out himself."

"And if I give him an ultimatum and he walks away?"

"I didn't say give him an ultimatum, but if that's the direction it goes—you have to trust yourself. You know Sean better than anyone. He loves you. You'll find a way to get through to him, but whatever you've been doing hasn't helped. It's time to get tough."

"I don't know that I can."

"He knows you love him, but whatever is going on in his head, he can't reconcile it." He paused. "I don't know if that makes sense."

"I think I get it." She wanted to help Sean, but that was the thing—she didn't think she *could* help him. She didn't know how. And that hurt.

"I'll drive you to the conference, but first you need to eat. I'll cook. Go shower."

"Bossy," she mumbled.

"That's what big brothers are for." He got up and kissed the top of her head. "We are going to get Sean through this, whatever *this* is. I'm not going to abandon you, or him. I promise."

Chapter Four

Lucy and Jack walked into the ballroom before the scheduled drone presentation that morning and immediately a man in his early forties ran up to them and said, "Have you seen Ellen?"

He had a panicked expression.

"Marc, what happened?" Jack asked.

"We were supposed to have breakfast this morning. She didn't show. She's not answering her phone. She's not at her house, she's not in the room she has here at the hotel or in the vendor room. No one has seen her. This isn't like her, Jack, you know it."

"I saw the Pride Tactical van on J Street," Jack said.

"She has permission to park it there all week. Oh shit, I didn't think, that's where I saw her last night, she was working—but why wouldn't she answer her phone?"

Marc ran from the room.

Jack mumbled something under his breath that Lucy couldn't hear, then said, "Lucy, that's Marc Dupre, Ellen's partner. Ex-husband. Whatever. Just flash your badge and find out when Ellen Dupre used her hotel key last night. It's electronic, they'll have a record."

Lucy watched Jack run after Marc, then went over to the

reservation desk, showed her badge, and asked to speak with the manager.

Five minutes later she learned that Ellen hadn't entered her room since yesterday afternoon at five p.m.—Lucy had seen her at six thirty at the meet and greet.

"I need a card key," she told the manager.

He hesitated.

"We need to do a welfare check. She's missing."

"Of course. I'll take you right up."

Might be a slight fib, but Lucy was trusting Jack on this—and what he'd told her about Ellen Dupre was that not only was she a creature of habit, but she was punctual. If she wasn't where she was supposed to be and unreachable, she could be in trouble. A medical emergency most likely—but to know if she was ill or on meds Lucy would need to see her hotel room.

"When did Ms. Dupre check in?" Lucy asked.

"Monday. She lives locally but wanted a suite so she could meet with clients. She's been with us every year we've held the conference here—at least since I've been manager."

"You know her personally."

"Friendly, not friends. Ms. Dupre is very good to the staff, so we try to accommodate her on what she needs—such as a complimentary safe."

"Doesn't every room have a safe?"

"She needs a larger one. As you can imagine at a law enforcement conference, there are some items that need to be secured every night. Most vendors either bring their merchandise to their rooms or take equipment off-site, but because Ms. Dupre and Pride Tactical have been with us for so long, I make the larger hotel safe available for her use."

"Did she put anything in it last night?"

"Yes, when the vendor room closed, she put in her demo models. I expected her to retrieve them this morning, but then

I saw on the schedule that she was giving a presentation in the main ballroom, so figured she wouldn't open her booth until after."

They exited on the tenth floor, the concierge level. When they reached Ellen's door, the manager took out his master swipe and opened it. Lucy had him stand back and she entered, cautious, her hand on the butt of her gun.

The room was empty.

The bed was made, though it looked like someone had lain on the bedspread, a slight indention on both the cover and the pillow farthest from the door. Lucy looked in the closet—it was the closest door—no one. The bathroom was empty. She looked under the bed. It rested on a solid platform. She then motioned that the manager could enter, and she went into the bathroom to do a better search of Ellen's belongings, visual only—no searching of drawers or luggage.

She had no prescription bottles on the counter. Her toothbrush and toothpaste were laid out on top of a washcloth next to the sink. The clothes in the closet were hung perfectly—a dark-gray pantsuit and a black pantsuit—plus two polo shirts, one black and one dark purple, with the Pride Tactical logo on the pocket.

The suitcase was open on the suitcase stand, and had her underwear and workout clothes in it, all neatly folded. Black sneakers and low-heeled black boots were on the floor of the closet.

Lucy thought back to what Ellen had been wearing last night—dark jeans, black polo with a logo Lucy hadn't been able to fully see, and a dark blazer.

"Agent Kincaid?" the manager said, slightly apprehensive.

"When was this room last cleaned?"

He checked his tablet. "Yesterday, ten a.m."

She called Jack.

"Kincaid," he answered.

"It's Lucy. She's not in her room, didn't sleep here. She left at five p.m."

"She's not in the tactical van. Marc says it doesn't look like it's supposed to, but he's not a tech guy. He thinks something's missing, doesn't know what."

"Sean would know," she said.

"Call him."

"You call him. I need to do something." She ended the call before he argued with her. She didn't want to talk to Sean right now. She was angry with him, upset, and worried—and she didn't even know if he would answer her. She thought it would be worse if she needed to talk to him, about something important like this, and he declined her call.

She looked at the manager. "Can you please tell me about your security? I'd like to look at the footage from last night."

"Of course," he said and they walked out.

"Don't let anyone into Ms. Dupre's room—not housekeeping, not staff, no one until I clear it," she said.

"What happened to her?"

"I don't know, but I'll find out."

Sean almost sent Jack's call to voice mail, but he knew if he did he'd have worse to deal with later.

"Yep."

"We need you at the convention center."

"Sorry—I know, I was supposed to be there for Ellen's demo, I overslept."

"Ellen's missing, the tactical van may have been robbed but Marc can't tell for certain. The drone is gone."

"I'm coming."

"How long?"

He winced. It would come out anyway. "Two hours."

"Where the fuck are you?"

"Tahoe." He ended the call before Jack said anything else.

He hadn't overslept—he'd barely slept at all. He'd spent his first hour playing blackjack and parlayed a hundred bucks into two thousand. Then he went to a high-stakes poker table and ended up walking away eight hours later with over twenty thousand.

Winning was cathartic. He'd walked away when he was too tired to focus. But he didn't end up in bed until five that morning . . . and now Jack was calling him at eight.

He jumped in the shower to wake up, then dressed in the same clothes he'd come in wearing. He put a hundred-dollar bill on the pillow for housekeeping, then left.

Chapter Five

Detective John Black showed up at the hotel just after nine that morning.

He was a tall, imposing cop—over six and a half feet was Lucy's guess—and he clearly knew both Megan and Jack.

"John, thank you for coming," Megan said and shook his hand. "This is my sister-in-law Lucy Kincaid, from the San Antonio FBI office. She's here for the conference."

"Kincaid," John said with a nod. "You said possible missing person."

Megan said, "Ellen Dupre, owner of Pride Tactical. She missed a six o'clock meeting this morning and didn't show for her eight a.m. presentation of a new surveillance drone her company developed. The drone is also missing."

"I had the hotel manager let me into her hotel room for a welfare check," Lucy said. "She didn't sleep there last night. The last person to see her was her partner at approximately nine thirty last night."

"Partner—you mean her ex-husband."

Lucy forgot that everyone seemed to know one another.

"Did you take Marc's statement?" John continued.

"Just basic information."

Jack said, "Marc and I went to the tactical van this morning. Ellen wasn't there, and neither was the drone. He thinks that something else is wrong inside the van, but he doesn't know what's missing. I called my partner Sean Rogan, who helped Ellen develop the drone software. He's on his way here now."

"Okay. Let me know when he arrives, I want to walk with him through the van. No one goes inside it without me. Let's talk to Marc, get a firm time line, and I'll start the process to trace her phone."

Jack said, "We can do it faster."

"I'm aware that RCK has shortcuts, but we don't know what's going on here, Jack, so we use the system."

Megan said, "Lucy, you go with John—Jack and I have known Marc and Ellen for years, it's better to have an impartial cop work this."

Lucy didn't quite know what to make of that. Did they think there was a chance Marc was guilty of . . . something?

"Agreed," John said, and motioned for Lucy to lead the way to where Marc was pacing in the vendor room. A man was talking to Marc, but stopped and looked at them when she and John entered.

"Where's Jack and Megan?" Marc said.

John showed his badge. "Detective John Black, Sac PD. You've met FBI agent Lucy Kincaid." He looked at the man standing with Marc.

"Steven Decker," he said. "I'm with NorCal Tactical Gear, friends with Marc and Ellen."

John made a note.

"We need to look for Ellen!" Marc said. "This isn't like her. Tell them, Steven."

"Ellen is never late," Steven agreed.

"That's why I'm here," John said. He was calm and had a commanding presence.

"I told Jack and Megan everything," Marc said. "I shouldn't have to go over this again, we're wasting time."

"I'm a senior detective with Sacramento PD, and we're in the city of Sacramento. You want things to happen fast, talk to me. You want to delay, keep arguing."

Marc looked frantic, but he focused on John.

John said, "You last saw Ms. Dupre at nine thirty last night. Where?"

"In the tactical van. We were talking about the presentation today, and she stayed because she wanted to test the night-vision camera. We planned to meet at six this morning—she didn't show."

"You came here and she wasn't in her room?"

"No—breakfast near here. She was late—she's never late. I waited fifteen minutes, tried calling her, she didn't answer, so I went to her house in South Land Park. She wasn't there. I called her at least half a dozen times, called the office—we have a warehouse and office in West Sac. No answer. I came here, because she had a room here—but she didn't answer when I knocked. She didn't show up at her presentation. Something happened to her!"

"Did you go inside her house?"

He hesitated. "Yes, why?"

"Because I need to know whether to send an officer for a welfare check."

"I have a key."

Marc sounded defensive, and there wasn't a reason for that.

Lucy said, "Marc, Detective Black wants to help, but he needs all the information you have. It helps to know exact times, conversations, anything Ellen may have said that had you concerned. For example, did she say anything about being worried about security for the drone?"

Marc rubbed his eyes, took a deep breath, and said, "No.

I was late last night. Steven and I were in the bar talking and I lost track of time."

John looked at Steven for confirmation. He nodded, and John made a note. "Then you went to the van," he prompted Marc.

"Yes, I got there about nine ten. I was supposed to be there at nine, and Ellen was always of the mindset, *If you're not early, you're late*. I'm always late . . ." His voice trailed off.

"Anyway," he continued, "she was irritated, we were going to run the tests together. But we talked, and then she said she wanted to check a couple other things, and we planned the breakfast."

"What time did you leave the van?" John asked.

"About nine forty, take or leave five minutes. I got home at ten fifteen, and I live in Arden Park."

"What did you talk about in those thirty minutes?" John asked. "All business?"

"Does it matter?"

"Yes."

Why was Marc acting like he was hiding something?

"Some business. Um . . . about . . . I, um, told her I wanted us to talk about getting back together."

"Back together?" John asked.

"We were married. Divorced five years ago, but . . . it's complicated."

"You still own Pride Tactical?" John said.

"We're partners. How does this help find Ellen?"

"What was her mindset when you talked to her last night? When you told her you wanted to get back together?"

"Who cares?"

"Was she upset?" Lucy prompted. "Did this come out of left field or was it something you'd been discussing for a while?"

"She wasn't upset," Marc said, emphatic. "It was her idea that we go to breakfast this morning to talk about it. Just because we were divorced didn't mean we weren't still friends."

"I wasn't suggesting—"

"Yes, you were!"

Lucy said calmly, "Jack told me you were all friends, my point is that maybe Ellen needed time to process the information if it was unexpected."

"Not to the point that she would miss her presentation! Something's wrong. I know it."

"Was she worried about anything else?" John asked. "Maybe nervous about the presentation? Could she have uncovered a glitch and felt embarrassed or wanted to test it elsewhere?"

"No, it functioned as intended. The only thing she was doing last night was recording a demo with the night-vision camera. The tech is state-of-the-art—I mean, nothing that hasn't been done before, but different. I—I'm not the technical person. But I knew from talking to our clients that they were eager for something like this—light, quiet, extremely responsive—particularly when serving warrants. Our drone would save lives, both law enforcement and civilians."

Lucy asked, "Was she having problems with anyone? Maybe not work-related, but personally?"

"Not that she told me. And we talk every day."

"Is there someone else she might confide in?"

"Me!" Marc exclaimed. "Her best friend," he added quietly. "Grace Hotchkiss. She's a pediatric surgeon at Mercy. If anything was wrong, and Ellen didn't want to tell me, she'd talk to Grace."

"Do you have her contact information?"

"I'll call her."

"I need her number."

Marc clearly didn't like the direction of the conversation,

but he pulled out his phone and read off Grace's phone number.

"We'll contact hospitals," John said.

"I called the hospitals, she's not there!"

"We'll check again," John said. "In the meantime, I'm going to ask Megan to take you to Ellen's house. You said you have a key?"

"Yes—but I told you, she's not there."

"Megan can look for any clues as to where she might have gone."

"Oh. I—okay."

John sent Megan a text message, asked a couple more questions, then Megan came in and retrieved Marc, took him out of the room.

John turned his attention to Steven Decker. "You said you were friends with both Marc and Ellen."

"Yes."

"And you had drinks with Marc last night before he saw her."

"Yes. For about an hour. Here at the hotel."

"What did you talk about?"

"Business, mostly."

"You own a competing business."

"Not really. NorCal handles mass distribution of basic PPEs and required equipment. Vests, utility belts, the new Taser holsters that Sac PD bought last year. Pride Tactical is high-end, more expensive, sells in smaller qualities, usually for SWAT teams and private security details, some elite military units."

Steven looked from John to Lucy. "Look, Marc didn't say this, but he should have. I want to buy Pride. I talked to Ellen about it a while back, she flat out said no. But Marc and I have been talking quite a bit, and I told him I would keep their staff and Ellen could work as much as she wants. He was excited about the proposal—I knew he wanted to get back together with her, and he thinks she works too hard. Pride is everything to her—she has done an amazing job building the company. But if Ellen doesn't want to sell, Marc won't. Just to get it out there."

He had just handed them motive for murder—both Steven and Marc had reason to kill Ellen.

If she was dead.

By the slight shift in John's posture, he had thought the exact same thing.

John asked, "When was the last time you saw Ellen Dupre?"

"Yesterday, briefly, at the mixer. Then I had drinks with Steven—we met up at eight. Later, I went out with clients to the Esquire for a late dinner. Got back here about eleven fifteen or so."

John took down his contact information and thanked him.

John and Lucy left the vendor room. "What do you think?" John asked her.

"We need to find Ellen."

"And?"

"And he didn't have to tell us all that. It's almost as if he wanted to cast suspicion on Marc. Or—he thought because Marc didn't say anything, it would cast suspicion on him if it came out later."

John glanced at his phone. "One sec." He answered. "Marcie, I need a warrant to locate a cell phone. Missing person . . . No, she doesn't meet the criteria, but there are other circumstances . . . Yeah, I'll write it all up. I'm sending you her name, number, and provider. Thanks." He typed into his phone for a minute, then turned to Lucy. "It won't take long to get the warrant, it's limited. If her phone is on, we'll have a location shortly."

"You must have an in with the DA's office to get a warrant that fast and over the phone."

"I have a good relationship with the office."

"Do you know Megan from work?"

"We've had a couple of cases that overlapped. She's my favorite fed." He gave her a half smile. "So where's this tech guy Jack mentioned? Rogan? I assume the Rogan in Rogan-Caruso-Kincaid."

"One of them. Sean Rogan, my husband. He'll be here soon." She had no idea why he wasn't. He didn't tell her where he was, and Jack didn't tell her what he'd said, just that he was on his way. "I can call, get an ETA?"

"He'll be here when he's here. Let's talk to the security office. I'm going to want to see footage from last night, when everyone left, if Ellen came back in after she left the van. This could be a robbery or corporate espionage or Ellen ran away when she was bowled over by her ex declaring he still had feelings for her."

She'd thought the same thing, but Ellen didn't seem like the type of person to run from a commitment, like the drone presentation. Did she have plans last night, after Marc left?

John asked to speak to the security chief, then he got a call. He listened, thanked the caller, then turned to Lucy. "Ellen's cell phone is still on, and it pinged in the alley between 14th and 15th, off J Street. Not far from here." He waited until the chief arrived, told him what recordings he wanted to look at, and said they'd return shortly to view them.

Lucy's stomach fell. She had a really bad feeling about this.

They left the hotel, crossed the street toward the convention center, then turned the corner. The Pride Tactical van was parked with a SPECIAL EVENTS placard hanging from the mirror.

"SPD never should have given her a pass for three days," John said.

Lucy glanced at him.

He continued. "It's highly irregular, but the chief likes the gear and the Dupres always let SPD beta-test, then give us a discount."

"You know her, too?"

"Not as well as Jack, because Pride mostly caters to private security and military contractors, and I think your brother was in the army with her at one point. But I've met her once or twice."

A patrol car was parked behind the van. The officer stepped out when he saw John approach. "Detective."

"Riley. Any interest?"

"No. Megan—I mean, SSA Elliott—from the FBI came over and said no one in or out until you arrive with the tech."

"He's not here yet. You might know him—Rogan?"

"Sean Rogan? Yeah, of course. He and his brother were hired to protect my sister once."

"I'm sorry, we haven't met," Lucy said. "I'm Lucy Kincaid."

Riley grinned. "Riley Knight. I feel like I know you. My sister is Sonia Hooper."

Small, small world, Lucy thought. She'd just worked with Sonia on a case. She was married to the ASAC in Sacramento, Dean Hooper.

"Nice to meet you," she mumbled, feeling a bit out of sorts. She'd forgotten how well known Sean was here—he'd grown up in Sacramento, RCK started in Sacramento, he had friends all over the area.

John said, "If Rogan arrives before I get back, call me. No one is allowed to touch the van without me here, understood?"

"Of course," Riley said.

"Jack Kincaid and Dupre's partner already went in it this

morning, which ticks me off, but that was before they called it in."

John and Lucy continued walking another half block then turned left on 14th. The alley separated a block-long office building and a parking lot. The unstaffed parking lot had a machine where drivers pre-paid. The lot was about a third full.

"This is mostly for evening events," John explained. "The Memorial Auditorium, the community theater, Music Circus—all walking distance." He gestured to the building that took up half the block on the west side of 14th. "That's the AG's office."

"Security cameras?"

"Likely, don't know that they'd reach here. I'll have someone call."

He looked around the area. Neither of them saw anything out of the ordinary. They slowly walked down the alley. Three Dumpsters were lined up against the building on the right.

John pulled out his phone and dialed Ellen's number.

It rang in the Dumpster closest to the street.

John pulled on gloves and Lucy followed suit. He cautiously opened the Dumpster and they both looked in.

Ellen Dupre was lying faceup on top of the garbage.

"Fuck," John mumbled under his breath. He started to close the lid.

"Wait," Lucy said.

She smelled garbage, but she didn't smell decomp. If Ellen was dead since last night, there would be clear signs. But her body looked . . .

Lucy's heart raced. "I think she's alive! Help me climb in."

John pushed the top open. It hit the brick wall and stayed. Lucy pulled herself up, stepped into John's hands, and hoisted herself inside the Dumpster. There was only one layer of bags, some food but mostly paper and office garbage.

Carefully, she moved over to Ellen's neck and pressed her fingers on the main artery.

At first nothing. But her body was pliable, warm. If she was dead, she hadn't been dead long.

Then she felt a faint heartbeat.

"I have a pulse!" she said.

John was already calling for an ambulance.

Lucy wanted to remove her from the Dumpster but worried that Ellen might have a neck or back injury. She was fully clothed, shoes on. Dried blood matted her blond hair, on her right side. She could have been shot or hit or beaten. Her face was dirty, but unmarked.

There were no other visible signs of injuries.

She could have been here since last night, or since dawn. They needed a full time line of her night after her husband left the tactical van.

"Hold on, Ellen," she said.

It didn't take long for Lucy to hear an ambulance.

"What do you see, Kincaid?" John asked.

"Dried blood on her head, no other visible signs of injury. Her pulse is faint, but she is breathing on her own. I don't know why she's unconscious and unresponsive."

Only minutes later the paramedics arrived. One joined Lucy in the Dumpster, and Lucy assisted with putting a neck brace on Ellen and sliding the board under her body. Then Lucy jumped out while the two paramedics pulled Ellen up and out, onto a gurney. They were on the phone with the doctor at the hospital and immediately started an IV, checked her eyes, pulse, blood pressure—which was very low.

"We've got her, Detective," one of the paramedics said to John. "We're taking her to the Mercy trauma unit."

"Is Dr. Storm on duty?"

"That's who we're talking to now."

"Good. I'll be down as soon as I get this scene secured. Tell him this is my case."

The ambulance left, and John said to Lucy, "Gabriel Storm is my brother-in-law, heads the trauma department at Mercy."

"I swear, Sacramento is the smallest big city in the country."

John looked around the area, his face grim, his eyes seeing everything. "Why was she here?" He glanced at his phone. "Crime scene is on their way. I don't know what we're going to get from the Dumpster or the van, but if there's anything to find, my team will find it."

Chapter Six

Sean arrived downtown just after ten that morning. He couldn't park near the convention center; J Street was blocked at 13th Street, and a traffic cop directed traffic south on 13th. He'd expect this in a homicide investigation, not for an assault. He looked again at Lucy's message:

We found Ellen Dupre unconscious, unresponsive, but breathing in a Dumpster off 14th and J. She's en route to the hospital, awaiting status. Drone is missing.

That was thirty minutes ago.

He'd failed Ellen. He should have been here last night, running through the last tests with her. But his damn pride, his self-pity, his . . . what? He didn't know. All he knew was that he didn't want to be anywhere near the law enforcement conference. He didn't want to talk to people, to smile, to pretend like everything was normal.

And Ellen was in the hospital fighting for her life because he felt sorry for himself.

He sent Lucy a text message that he was parking in the hotel garage and would meet her at the van. She responded almost immediately that Detective John Black with Sacramento PD would meet him there.

Nothing more, nothing less.

He'd fucked up. Big time.

Sean parked at the top of the garage. He stood at the edge and looked down below at the corner of K Street and 13th, the convention center to the east, the police vehicles to the north. He had to pull it together.

Ellen was a visionary and got excited about new ideas like he did. He'd worked on her drone software project before he'd been arrested for murder; he had mixed feelings now working on anything that helped law enforcement track people. While on the one hand he knew that most cops would use it for lawful, warranted purposes . . . there were always a few bad cops out there.

He despised bad cops.

Sean shook the thoughts from his head. He wouldn't be able to help Ellen if he didn't focus on the task at hand. At doing what he was good at.

What, fucking things up? Because you really screwed things up with Lucy. You didn't come home last night. You didn't tell her where you were, what you were doing, just ran away like an asshole.

His fists clenched at his sides; why couldn't he just make this all stop? Was he so weak that he couldn't put the past in the past?

Or maybe he couldn't stop thinking about his failures because he knew that Jonathan Paxton was right.

His phone vibrated. He looked at the message. It was from Jack.

Are you coming?

Lucy must have told him he was here. Shit.

Sean walked down six flights of stairs and headed toward the van. Jack was standing near the corner of the convention center. From where he was, he might have seen Sean standing at the top of the parking garage. Sean wouldn't be surprised.

Sean straightened his spine. He didn't want to have it out with Jack now. His emotions were too raw, he would lash out in anger. This wasn't Jack's fault, but dammit, he didn't want to talk to him about it. Him or Dillon or Lucy or anyone. It would just make him seem weak. He felt weak, but he didn't want to share that with anyone.

Jack's face was blank as Sean approached. Without comment, Jack turned and walked toward the van as soon as Sean reached him. Sean saw Riley Knight, a cop he knew. Riley was a good guy, and Sean was almost relieved that he could work with someone easy-going who he liked. Crime scene tape surrounded the van, and a CSI tech was on her knees on the sidewalk inspecting something that Sean couldn't see.

Standing just outside the crime scene tape, Jack motioned toward a very tall, broad-shouldered detective. He came over and Jack said, "John Black, Sean Rogan. He worked with Ellen on the software, he'll know what's missing."

Sean said, "You didn't find the drone?"

"No, though we've broadened the search. But if this is a valuable piece of technology, it could be she was attacked for it."

"The drone isn't valuable—it's high-end, but someone could buy it for a thousand bucks. The software Ellen wrote is worth more, but that software is on a laptop that communicates with the drone. Even then, I don't see what they would gain from stealing it. Like I said, everything is available in different formats, and the software is open code. The only thing proprietary about the project was how Ellen packaged it."

John let Sean in under the crime scene tape. When Sean glanced back, Jack was already walking away.

"Ms. Robinson, correct?" John said to the CSI.

She looked up at him. "Yes?"

"Are you almost done? Can we go in the van?"

"We're done inside, but I'm collecting samples—I may have found a small amount of blood. Just stay on that side of the markers."

"Of course. Thank you."

She nodded and went back to inspecting the sidewalk.

"Marc Dupre gave me a basic rundown on the drone, but he wasn't all that helpful," John said. "Can you explain? In lay terms, please."

"One of the requests Ellen had from multiple law enforcement agencies was for a drone that was quiet and responsive. They would suggest something like a military drone without weapons, something to provide quality video to surveil an area of interest, specifically in urban areas. One SWAT team leader gave her a real-life scenario—they had a hostage situation, but they didn't know how many hostages or suspects, and the drones they had were too loud and didn't have the ability to incorporate other technology, like heat sensors or real-time video. All that tech is available, but putting it together in an easy-to-use system was Ellen's goal. An agency could purchase one package, Ellen would come in and train their tech people, and they'd be able to use it for any number of things—active shooter situations, looking for meth labs, assessing a hostage situation, high-risk traffic stops, and more. Ellen ran a scenario aimed at getting a handle on human trafficking along the Delta using drones to patrol the waterways—I'm sure you know that Sacramento has the second highest incidence of trafficking in the country."

"I'm unfortunately aware."

"Ellen is a true visionary, the way her brain works. If you can play video games, you can run her program, it was intuitive and responsive. I'm . . ." Sean shut up when his voice cracked. He was getting emotional, he had to rein it in. He cleared his throat. "Sorry, she's a friend. How is she?"

"I don't know yet, but the best trauma surgeon in Sacramento is working on her." John opened the rear doors of the van. "Did she have a major competitor? Someone who might be developing the same thing?"

"The tactical world is relatively small, and Pride caters to small units and private security. But I haven't heard of anyone developing something like this. It's sort of a niche market. It would be great for a business like Pride, but a big business like 531 or NorCal? Drop in the bucket."

"And you were hired to . . . ?"

"Test the software and work out the bugs."

John handed him gloves. "The van has been processed for prints, fibers, and blood—there was no blood. No prints. When we got Ellen out of the Dumpster, your wife assessed that she had been attacked, likely suffering from blunt force trauma, though she may have been shot. There was a lot of matted blood and they weren't in a position to fully assess the damage. No other visible wounds. Still—I don't know much of anything right now, other than that quick field assessment."

Sean pulled on the gloves John handed him. "No prints?"

"Someone wiped it down. We found prints in the cab—they match Ellen Dupre. And there were some prints on the back door of the van, they were all Ellen's and her ex-husband, Marc, but nothing in here." He gestured to the main command center.

Sean didn't need to look long to assess. "Her laptop is missing. It's the brains of the drone. Also the backup drive—it's supposed to be here." He gestured to an empty slot under the small desk. "But they're idiots."

"Explain."

"I can track the drone and her laptop from the Pride office. The backup drive is external, but it saves everything remotely to the main server in real time. I should be able to track what Ellen was doing last night—I mean, I know that she was testing the night-vision camera and creating a video presentation for today. It's the big selling feature. But I can find out exactly what the drone recorded."

"I suppose it would be too easy to have her attack on video."

Sean said, "Sometimes cases are easy."

"I'll have Officer Knight take you, if you don't mind?"

"Not at all. I've known Riley for years."

"Document everything. Don't talk to anyone except me—and of course Riley. I asked your wife if she would be willing to assist, so she's partnering with me on the case. Jack and Megan are friends with Marc Dupre, I can't have them involved any more than they already are. I can't figure out why Marc would attack his wife for her equipment. Unless he had a reason to kill her, and the robbery was a diversion. Did Ellen ever discuss with you whether she wanted to sell her company?"

"Sell Pride? No—she wouldn't. At least, my impression is she loved what she did. She worked her ass off to make Pride successful."

"And her ex-husband? Did he want to sell?"

"I get it. The ex is at the top of your list. I don't know Marc as well as Ellen, but I'll tell you one thing—he's great at marketing and sales, but he wouldn't know a backup drive from a dictionary."

"Agent Kincaid?"

A tall female officer younger than Lucy approached her. "Yes," Lucy said.

Lucy had been supervising the crime scene investigators in the alley looking for evidence, though she knew by their demeanor that they hadn't found anything of value. The only evidence might be in or on the Dumpster itself.

"Detective Black told me to report to you about our canvass."

She pulled out her phone so she could take notes. "Do you have a witness?"

"No, ma'am. My partner and I were tasked with locating all security cameras in the area. We found three that potentially had a view between the van and the Dumpster. One was close focus only, on a store front. One was outside the convention center, but angled away from the van. The third was there"—she gestured across the street—"on the Attorney General Building. It is aimed at the alley where delivery trucks come in, and may have an angle to the street. It's distorted, but they are copying the file from nine p.m. to midnight, per Detective Black."

"Great. There's nothing here on the parking lot?"

"No. But—I have one idea?"

"Tell me."

"Well, J Street is one-way. If anyone was walking on the sidewalk or driving to the van or away from the van, there are many businesses that have security cameras, and there are several police cameras on K Street and around the capitol building. It's a long shot—especially since we don't know exactly what to look for—but it might be worth looking into."

Lucy agreed. "Follow up, four-block radius, as well as checking the security from the two hotels across from the convention center. Do you know, is there any way to find out who was parked here last night during our window?"

"I can contact the parking company."

"That would be great."

"The only problem, it's all pre-pay—so you pull in, go to that machine"—she motioned—"and then pay. They can tell me when cars come in, but not when they leave."

Lucy considered. "We need to know all cars that were here between those hours. Someone might have seen something.

If the company can give us a list—I don't know if we need a warrant, or if there are any other jurisdictional issues."

"I'll ask. If they balk I'll bump it up to Detective Black."

"Perfect. Thank you, Officer . . . ?"

"Delacruz."

"Officer Delacruz." Lucy nodded and smiled, knowing how hard it was to be a young officer working a crime scene. Many times they received no appreciation from the people in charge, even though they were doing the bulk of the legwork.

Forensics was inspecting the area near the van as well as the alley and every place between the van and alley. Lucy turned her focus to the alley. It stood to reason that Ellen had been attacked last night and had been lying unconscious in the Dumpster for hours. Yet no one had heard anything. Was she attacked at her van or here in the alley? There was no blood evidence in the van, which told Lucy the attack likely happened when Ellen left the vehicle—though, according to John, the van had been wiped down. If the assault did happen in the alley, why was she here? She had a room in the hotel, which was in the opposite direction. She didn't have a car at the hotel—John had checked—she had driven the tactical van from Pride headquarters yesterday morning.

Lucy hadn't had much opportunity to inspect the wound before the paramedics rushed Ellen to the hospital, but it appeared to be blunt force trauma. She didn't see a gunshot wound, but she couldn't be certain. If Ellen had been shot, could someone have had a silencer? Silencers weren't completely silent, but they wouldn't echo on the street and possibly alert nearby residents. Had the killer thought she was dead, and that's why he put her body in the Dumpster, to avoid being discovered quickly? Or did he know she was still breathing and expect her to die before she was found? Either way, the shooter had a uniquely dark coldness about him.

Marc was a viable suspect only because he had motive—he wanted to sell the company, Ellen didn't. Or Steven Decker, the man who wanted to buy the company. Maybe he suspected she wouldn't sell . . . or went to talk to her after Marc left. Either of them could have attacked her, thought they had killed her . . .

Or had Marc attempted to kill her because she wouldn't get back together with him? Could he have taken the drone to throw off suspicion? Would he have left her breathing, especially if she would then identify him as her attacker?

Certainly possible. Greed was a common motive. Love turned easily to hate. But Ellen wasn't dead; she would be able to testify. *If* she survived

Then why the elaborate explanation that he wanted to get back together with her? Was it true? Or a convenient lie?

Or was it a truth that she rejected? Maybe greed wasn't the motive, but lust. Anger at being rejected.

That didn't feel right to her—clearly, they had been married, divorced, worked together. Why kill her now, five years after the divorce?

She's not dead. She could regain consciousness and tell the police everything. Including who attacked her.

She saw John walking toward her, talking on his phone, his face impassive. He ended the call and said to her, "That was the attorney general's office. He's supposed to speak this afternoon to the conference, and they want a threat assessment. His security wants to cancel, the AG doesn't."

"What's the likelihood that Ellen was attacked because of the AG?"

"My opinion, it has nothing to do with it, but I can't completely discount it. Political assassinations are rare in this country, so I think the AG's office is just being cautious—in case there's a personal reason for someone to come after the AG. He used to be a prosecutor, so that's possible."

"You want to talk to her ex-husband again."

"Yes, but he's at the hospital waiting to see her. I talked to Gabriel—Dr. Storm—a few minutes ago. Ellen has not regained consciousness. She was hit by something hard and likely metal."

"Coldcocked?"

"Distinct possibility. With enough force to crack her skull. She has a serious brain bleed, and fragments of her skull have moved into her brain. Gabriel is sending X-rays and photos to our crime lab for assessment as well, but if he says she was coldcocked, she was. He's called in the top neurosurgeon in Northern California for an assessment, and she'll likely be in surgery within the hour."

"So we talk to Dupre at the hospital."

John nodded. "He's there now. Megan is with him. I don't see him for this, but maybe a spur-of-the-moment attack, he panicked, put her in the Dumpster." He frowned.

"I can picture it—but if he wanted her dead wouldn't he have ensured she was dead?" Lucy said.

"He could have thought she was dead."

"Maybe she saw something, a crime in progress, a drug deal. Random attack."

"Then why dump her body? If it was spontaneous, wouldn't the attacker leave her where she fell? Robinson, the tech leading the forensic investigation, says that there was a small amount of blood outside the van, that it is likely Ellen's and that she was attacked there—near the rear of the van. She'll have it confirmed by the end of the day. Why move the body?"

Good question.

"Maybe whoever attacked her thought she was dead and panicked. Moved her to delay discovery."

"At this point, I'd believe almost anything," John said. He glanced at his watch. "Once we talk to Marc, we'll talk to

her staff. I'm told you have a presentation this afternoon—
I'll get you back here in time for that."

"I can skip it."

"No—it's hard to get on panels like this, and Megan says
it's the reason San Antonio sent you here—something about
a particular successful interrogation. The suspect thanked
you for sending him to prison or something?"

She laughed. "Not exactly, but close. I've had success with
interrogations, but I attribute that to my criminal psychology
background. When you understand what your suspect fears
the most, it's easier to get them to talk."

"Hmm. I hadn't thought of it like that, but I see how that
works."

"I haven't always been successful, but since I've gone
through hostage rescue training, I've adapted some of those
techniques to interrogation." She hadn't wanted to ask about
Sean, but she knew that he had assessed the van and Ellen's equipment, so she asked casually, "Was Sean helpful?"

"Yes. Laptop and backup drive are missing. Keys were
in the back of the van. Sean's going to Pride headquarters
with one of my officers to go through data—he says everything that the drone recorded should have been sent to their
server. I'm not tech-savvy, but it makes sense. Once we get
that data, maybe we'll have answers."

They walked to John's car. Lucy texted her brother that
she was going with John to the hospital and would be back
for her presentation at three that afternoon.

Mercy Hospital was only a few minutes away, on J Street,
on the east side of the freeway. John knew exactly where he
was going when he entered; he showed his badge and said,
"Dr. Storm is expecting us," and no one stopped him.

He turned into an office with DR. GABRIEL STORM on the
door. Marc was sitting in one of the two chairs across from

the doctor's desk; Megan was next to him. There wasn't much room for them, and Gabriel wasn't in the room.

Marc jumped up. "Do you know what happened? Who did this? She's in a coma—that's what the doctor said. She hasn't woken up. She may never wake up. Who would do this? For a drone?"

"Mr. Dupre, please sit back down. I know this is a difficult time, but I have a few more questions."

Megan nodded to Marc, and he sat. Megan put her hand on his arm, consoling him.

"We're just beginning our investigation," John said. He walked around to the doctor's desk and sat down. Lucy saw two photos on the narrow credenza behind the immaculate desk. The first was of two people she didn't recognize on their wedding day—presumably Dr. Storm and his wife, John's sister. Then another with the bride and groom along with John Black in a tuxedo and the maid of honor. Clearly John had no problem taking over his brother-in-law's space.

Lucy remained standing, observing more than participating. She focused on Marc Dupre and his mannerisms, the way he spoke, the way he answered questions. Sometimes detecting a lie was as much about observation as listening.

"The drone and the backup drive are missing," John said. "Sean Rogan is at Pride headquarters downloading data now—he believes he can retrieve anything the drone recorded last night. That may give us something to follow up on."

"Sean. Okay. He's good. I trust him. But—I don't understand what happened. She'd fight back. Is that why they hit her so hard? Because she fought them? There must be evidence. You'll find them. Right?"

"I talked to Dr. Storm. There are no signs of defensive wounds," John said, "but the doctors are focused right now on her brain scan. Did he come in and talk to you?"

Marc nodded. Megan said, "He explained the situation, but is waiting for a consult. They x-rayed her body and found no other injuries."

"So what happened?" Marc said. "You don't know Ellen like I do. She would have fought. She was in the army, for chrissakes. She was smart and disciplined and she would never be caught by surprise like that."

"Again, we'll know more soon. If she regains consciousness, Dr. Storm is going to ask her if she recognized the person who hit her. I want to interview her as soon as possible, but that's a no-go until after her surgery. But Gabriel agreed to find out what he could."

Sometimes, there was an antagonistic relationship between doctors and cops, mostly because of the doctor's need to take care of the patient's health, and the cop's need to solve a crime. But clearly John and Gabriel had a good working relationship.

Suddenly Marc broke down. The sob was long and painful and he put his head in his hands.

"She has to live. She just has to," he sobbed.

Megan said, "Marc, John is the best detective in Sacramento PD. He'll find out who attacked Ellen. You need to focus on being strong for Ellen."

"She may never regain consciousness. That means a coma . . . forever? I can't—I need her, Megan. I should never have agreed to the divorce! What was I doing? I love her so much."

"I know," Megan said. "If you can answer John's questions, it'll help."

"I did. I told you both everything. I—I have to find out what's going on. I have to see her."

"Gabriel will come talk to you when he knows something," John said. "Steven Decker told us that he made an offer for your company last night, that you were going to discuss it with Ellen. Did you?"

"Yes."

"What did Ellen say?"

"She doesn't want to sell. She just puts in so many hours . . . and she needs a break."

"But you wanted to sell."

"I wanted to sell because Ellen threw herself into the business after . . . well, it doesn't matter."

"It might."

"It *doesn't*. You wouldn't understand!"

Megan prompted, "It was after her last miscarriage."

"It wasn't a miscarriage! Em died in her arms. She was sixty-three minutes old. She lived sixty-three minutes. It—well, it's complicated. Ellen just . . . it's not important. That was over five years ago."

"You divorced after your baby died?" John asked.

"You weren't there," Marc snapped, angry. "You don't know how it affected Ellen, me, us, what we had, what we could have had back if we could work through the grief! I would never sell my half of the company without her blessing. Steven wanted to incorporate Pride into NorCal, as the elite tactical line. Ellen would still develop for the company, but we'd have more time to . . . find a way to be happy. That's all I wanted, and we were talking. That's why we were having breakfast today. It was another step toward getting back together and now she might die. If she dies . . . I can't think. I—I—I can't—can't . . ." He got up and walked out.

Megan looked from John to Lucy. "I've known Marc and Ellen for years. Since before the divorce. I don't see how he could be involved in this."

Lucy said, "Maybe he hired someone. Didn't expect her to be attacked. Maybe he just wanted to—I don't know—take the equipment, do something that would encourage her to sell."

"You don't know them. Ellen wasn't going to sell the company. I know you have to look at the ex-husband, I would do the same thing, but I know these people . . . it wasn't just losing the baby that tore them apart. Ellen had multiple miscarriages and she was in a very dark place. She and Marc hurt each other, they divorced, but they became friends again. I don't know how, but they did. Maybe because they never lost the deeper feelings they had? I don't know."

"I'm going to have to talk to him again," John said. "About any threats or enemies."

"I'll stick with him today, at least until we know how Ellen is doing."

"Thank you, Megan."

She left and Lucy sat down in the chair she vacated. "Motive."

"You think he has one?"

She shook her head. "I don't think he was faking the grief. I won't say never—I've interviewed too many sociopaths. But motive? If it's the sale of the company, yes, that's a strong motive. Maybe she said no, she'd never sell the company, and he hit her without thinking. But in the back of the head? Dumping her body in garbage? No. He loved her. Love and hate are opposite sides of the same coin, and I can see people snapping. But then cleaning up after the fact? Talking to us here? I didn't get the sense that he was lying about anything. His emotions were too raw."

"I don't think he's involved. Hiring someone?" John shook his head. "Still, I need to look into his finances to see if he's in some serious trouble where he needs her to sell the company. It's going to take a little time. I'm hoping she regains consciousness and can point to a suspect. At this point—considering we have no video yet, unless there's something on the drone footage—we don't have any other evidence."

"What about Steven Decker?" Lucy asked.

"What about him?"

"He also has motive. He knew where Ellen was. He wanted to buy the company. Maybe he called Marc last night, after Marc left Ellen, and asked about it, and Marc said Ellen doesn't want to sell. Maybe Steven went there to talk to her about it . . . convince her . . . and then attacked. Because he can convince Marc to sell with Ellen out of the way."

"Except he didn't kill her."

"Maybe he thought he did."

"That makes a lot more sense than Marc Dupre, but I don't want to be persuaded by his emotions right now."

"I watched him while he answered your questions. He's partly in shock, he's definitely worried about her health, and I don't see in his personality that he's violent. I mean—I do believe anyone, under the right circumstances, can turn violent. But under *these* circumstances?" She didn't see it, and she didn't think that John did, either.

John got on his phone and called his department. Lucy looked at her own phone, not for the first time. Sean hadn't called or texted her, and she was feeling a bit lost on how to handle this situation with her husband. She was angry with him for not coming home last night . . . but she was more worried than mad at him. Sean wasn't himself, and she didn't know what to do. Tough love, as Jack suggested? Maybe . . . because she couldn't ignore it. Could she? Could she actually just *forget* that he didn't come home last night, that she had no idea where he'd been or what he'd been doing?

John came back five minutes later. "I have someone pulling all the financial records and corporate filings for Pride Tactical as well as Decker's company. They're both incorporated, so it's just a matter of requesting the information. I'm also working with the DA on getting warrants where necessary."

A female doctor of about forty walked in. "I'm Dr. Grace Hotchkiss," she said. "I've been with Dr. Storm and the neurosurgeon from UC Davis he called in. Dr. Storm would have come here himself, but they're prepping for surgery and he asked me to fill you in, since I'm close to Ellen. I'm just—" She took a deep breath. "I love Ellen like a sister, and this is difficult. I know you want to ask me questions, but I need to be with Marc right now. Dr. Storm just told him that Ellen will die without immediate surgery, and even with the surgery her chances are not good. If someone had found her last night, the prognosis would have been much better. But Ellen is strong, and two of the best surgeons in the country are working on her."

"Did she regain consciousness?" John asked.

She shook her head.

"Sit down, please—we won't keep you long," Lucy said.

Grace took Dr. Storm's chair, looked at the photo on the desk. "I forgot, you're Selena's brother. You know Gabriel. You know that he'll move heaven and earth to save Ellen."

"Yes, he will," John said. "I'll keep this brief, I know you want to get back, but I have some questions that will help us. Did Ellen talk to you about anyone stalking her? Anyone who made her uncomfortable, someone wanting her drone technology? Anything that had her worried or scared?"

"No. Ellen and I talk every week, sometimes more. After she lost her baby—it wasn't her first loss—she was, I believe, clinically depressed. I wanted her to get professional help, but she's stubborn. She finally saw a therapist after her divorce, and that helped a little, but she always had this deep guilt inside about Em. The baby who lived an hour. It haunted her. Grief is a complicated process, especially for someone like Ellen who is as strong as anyone I've met. But the last year or so? She's been back to her old self. She works a lot, but so do I."

"Did she tell you that Marc wanted to get back together?"

"She texted me last night." She handed John her phone.

He read the text out loud: *"Marc and I are talking about reconciling. I still love him, even after everything. We're going to breakfast tomorrow. I'll call you later."*

Grace nodded. "And I responded to her. *It's about time.* Marc and Ellen are both stubborn, but they were good together."

"They divorced over losing the baby?" Lucy asked.

"It was more complicated than that. It was the catalyst. But after that Ellen didn't like herself. She blamed herself. She had an affair. Marc was furious, and he had an affair, too. They divorced, it was too fast and they should have seen a counselor, but neither of them listened to me."

"Were either of them involved with anyone recently?" John asked.

"Marc lived with a woman for the last year or so, but I knew they split several months ago. I don't know if Ellen knew—we didn't talk about it. I only met Marc's girlfriend a couple times, she's a teacher or something. A little young for Marc, but smart. Ellen hasn't seen anyone since Steven."

"Steven Decker?" John asked, surprised.

Grace nodded. "They were involved both before and after the divorce. There's a double standard in affairs. Marc cheats, he expects Ellen to forgive him. Ellen cheats, and Marc lost it."

"Yet Marc said that he and Decker are friends."

"They are. Look, I'm a pediatrician. Kids are simple and honest. Adults are far more complex, and I don't really understand them as well. As far as I know, the three of them were still friends. Now, I really need to get back to the waiting room—if that's okay? You have my contact information, you can call me anytime if you have more questions."

"One more," John said. "When did Ellen and Steven Decker split?"

"Years ago—pretty much right after her divorce was final. If you're thinking she had feelings for him, she didn't. They were friends before they slept together, and they remained friends."

"And Marc knew."

"Yes—they were surprisingly honest about that. But that's why I think Marc moved in with the teacher. He was hurt. But he didn't love Monica. He's never stopped loving Ellen."

"Thank you, Dr. Hotchkiss."

She left, and Lucy said, "This is a lot more complex now."

He was about to say something, then looked at his phone. "Officer Knight says your husband found something. We need to get to Pride, it's important. Maybe this will make the situation less complex. You still able to join me?"

Lucy looked at the time. "Yes, I have a few hours."

"I'll make sure you're back in time for your presentation—Pride offices aren't too far from here."

Chapter Seven

Sean wanted to see Lucy, but all morning he hoped she wouldn't come to Pride with Detective Black. No such luck.

As soon as she walked in, he saw the worry, anger, and disappointment in her expression. Then she locked down her emotions and all he saw was professional cop.

Riley had been chatting and asking questions the whole time, and while Sean responded, his heart wasn't in it. He had *some* answers about Ellen's attack, but he didn't have all the answers. He was stuck on the *why*. Theft? Nope, because he was pretty certain they destroyed the equipment. So if not theft, the only thing that made sense was that they thought she saw something . . . a crime in progress, maybe. And based on the drone footage, that's exactly what happened.

Except it didn't.

"Detective," Riley said. "Sean is a genius."

"If I were a genius, I'd know who attacked her, but at least I can show you what happened. How is she?"

"She's in surgery," John said. "It's going to be a long process."

Not for the first time, Sean wished he had been there. But he wasn't, so this was all he could do.

Sean dimmed the lights in the Pride IT office to give a

better visual. The screen he was using was state-of-the-art, high-res; clarity was sharp, but it was still dependent on the quality of the surveillance camera that Ellen had been using.

He said, "Ellen ran through two tests between eight fifteen and nine, one in daylight mode and one in nighttime mode. They were routine and nothing on the recordings looked out of place, but I made you a copy so you could review them yourself. She called the drone back to the van at nine oh one and recalibrated it, then put on the night camera for the third test, which she didn't start until nine forty-three p.m."

"Would it take her more than thirty minutes to recalibrate?"

"No. Two or three minutes."

John made a note, but Lucy knew he was thinking that Marc's statement was consistent, that he left a little after nine thirty. That would give Ellen time to recalibrate and send the drone up again.

Sean continued. "She tested the drone and camera, then ran through a simulation she'd set up—she had sprayed special paint on a few items in a three-block radius that would glow with the specialized camera and software, to simulate certain targets. You can see here"—Sean pointed to the screen—"that she was running the heat signature program through the recording. These are images in buildings of individuals. She would have edited a lot of this out—her presentation was going to be twenty minutes—but I guess she wanted as much footage as possible to highlight the capabilities of the drone and the software."

"It's pretty amazing," John said.

"It's standard, to be honest, but what Ellen did that takes this to the next level was anticipate the needs of law enforcement by having preset settings for different types of surveillance, very user-friendly, and she incorporated a bunch of bells and whistles that will help with admissibility in court, things like that. Geo-tags, alerts to tampering with footage, et cetera. It's pretty cool. Plus she had the drone built to her specs and it's one of the quietest I've ever worked with.

"Here's the one thing that seems unusual, knowing how these tests are usually run. Ellen went back over the roof of the Sheraton Hotel three times. She had set the drone on auto—again, a very cool feature because it automatically avoids collisions, maintains a preset range—but she took over manually at ten oh eight p.m. and went back to the roof. There was a brief flash on the camera, which is what I think caught her eye—not a bright light, but a reflection, like a low-intensity light reflecting off shiny metal. But it's off-screen—the flash is there, but whatever was reflected is not. I went through the entire video in slow motion, and found something else—a man in black on the roof. I think that movement, coupled with the flash, aroused her suspicions enough that she went back with the drone, but no one was there."

"Show me again," John said.

Sean went through the recording and stopped at one point. He pointed to an indistinct figure, a male all in black, with a hoodie obscuring his face. Only his profile—a partial profile at that—was distinct. He was Caucasian, but that was about all they could surmise.

"Hmm," John said.

"She thought it was suspicious—at least that's my guess based on her decision to go back to the roof and circle. He wasn't there or he was hiding from the drone—there are two places that the drone couldn't see, and she wasn't using the heat signature at that point in the demonstration. When she didn't see anything, she called the drone back home. It's a simple recall, and the drone immediately returns—'home' is set for the docking port, which was in the van. She put it on auto—which means it would lower at a predetermined speed and she could easily retrieve it without damage. If no one grabbed it, it would land safely on the ground and shut down."

"What's on the drone? Is there a copy of the data?"

"Yes and no," Sean said. "It can stream to the main computer—in this case Ellen's laptop—or it can save the data up to a certain limit on the flash drive in the camera itself. She could have done both."

"Could someone assume that the drone itself had the only copy of the data it collected?"

Sean frowned. "I suppose, but that would be a ridiculous assumption."

"Maybe someone not as tech-savvy as yourself. Like me," John said.

"Umm, maybe. But the average person has probably seen drones on the news and understands the basic principles. Which is why they stole the computer and hard drive. They made the correct assumption that the drone was sending data to a computer; what they didn't count on was that the backup drive shared in real time to an external server. But I need to show you the rest. Ellen didn't shut down the camera when she called the drone home."

"Is that standard?"

"It depends on the operator. She could have wanted to demonstrate how the homing feature worked."

"What exactly was your role with Pride?" John asked. "You seem to know this system well."

"Last year I was hired to test and debug the software. I had a prototype of the drone and full access to the system. I spent the better part of five weeks working on this project, so yeah, I know the system well. Here. You need to watch the rest."

Sean pressed PLAY. The image was of the ground, which

was the preset angle once the drone was called home. The van came into view. A few seconds later Ellen exited the rear of the van, stepped onto the sidewalk, and looked up at the drone. Sean's chest tightened as he focused on her face. He knew what was about to happen because he'd watched this three times already, but it still hurt.

The drone was descending toward Ellen. She was focused on the device. From behind her in the shadows of the convention center, two men dressed in black emerged. They had hoodies that obstructed their faces—just like the man on the roof. She didn't notice either man until they were only feet from her. She was reaching up to snag the drone when she hesitated and looked over her shoulder, as if she sensed or heard something. The man directly behind her grabbed her, while the other man reached for the drone. Something flashed in the hand of the man who held Ellen as he brought that hand to her head. The image wasn't as sharp as the earlier images because the camera lens didn't refocus automatically.

As the second man grabbed the drone, the image became even fuzzier, though it was clear to Sean that the man who held Ellen had a gun. Though the angle was tilted from the camera, the attacker's arm came down, gun in hand, hard behind Ellen's ear. She crumpled to the ground—at least that's what Sean guessed as she went out of view of the camera.

Then the feed went dead.

"They wore masks and hoodies," John said.

"I wanted you to see the raw video. I can enhance this a bit, but I don't think I can bring out any identifying characteristics."

John didn't say anything for a minute.

Lucy asked, almost too quietly, "Ellen locked onto a couple of license plates. Was she suspicious of those, or was that part of her demonstration?"

"Most likely the demonstration, to show that the computer was capable of digitally reading plates accurately even from a distance."

John said, "I need a copy of the raw data right now, and if you can enhance it send me that as well. I want all the license plates in the area, and enhance what Ellen circled around on the roof of the hotel."

"I have more," Sean said. "They likely destroyed the drone, or at a minimum found a way to disable it. Same with the laptop. I was able to trace them to the point that they became inoperable. They dumped everything into the American River at the 160 crossing. The railing there is low, it would be easy to roll down your window and throw the equipment out. While they likely physically destroyed the device, water is truly the best way to destroy electronics, and they probably knew that."

"But you're saying it doesn't matter," John said. "Because you have everything here."

"Correct. Unless the camera on the drone continued to record but the feed was interrupted—in that case, I might be able to extract data from it. But it's a very slim chance. You know forensics better than I do, but I don't think prints or other physical evidence would survive in the water. There are no cameras on that bridge."

"But," John said, "there's only one way to get there, from downtown, and there are several cameras between the convention center and that spot. A couple run by SPD, a couple traffic cameras, and several security cameras. It's a place to start. Do you have a time?"

Sean smiled. He couldn't help himself, because it was an easy question. "The drone stopped transmitting at ten twenty-five p.m. The laptop stopped functioning at eleven oh one p.m."

"Thirty-five minutes," Lucy said. "It took them thirty-five minutes to render Ellen unconscious, dump her body in the Dumpster half a block away, throw the laptop in the river. How long to drive to that spot?"

"At night? Five minutes tops," John said.

"So what were they doing for the rest of the time? Give them five minutes to search the van and clear out the equipment, five minutes to put Ellen's body in the Dumpster, and no one saw them. At ten thirty at night near a convention where four hundred cops are in attendance—going to bars and restaurants nearby—and no one saw anything."

"J Street is not heavily trafficked at night, especially on foot," John said. "We only saw two people on the camera, but there could be more. I don't think they carried her body— there was no sign of blood or other evidence between the van and dump site."

"Ellen was five foot six and one hundred thirty pounds," Lucy said. "A fit man could carry her to the Dumpster, but it might attract attention."

"There was a small amount of blood near the van, a small pool in the Dumpster," John said. "What if they thought they killed her, and dumped her to buy them a bit of time?"

"Possible," Lucy said. "Sean, would they have had time to review the video?"

"Not on the laptop—that has high-end security, and I can tell from here whether someone tampered with it. They didn't. But they could have easily reviewed the footage on the camera itself. They could have taken the memory chip and watched it elsewhere."

"We should assume that they did," Lucy said.

"Okay," John said, not sure what she was thinking, but Sean knew.

"They were up to something, thought Ellen saw them,

grabbed the drone, and if they view it, they'll know that we don't know shit about what they were doing on the roof of the Sheraton."

"Exactly," Lucy said.

"If the man on the roof was involved in this," John said. "That's a short time period for him to get down—not impossible, but dressed in black would arouse suspicion. The Sheraton is a swanky hotel."

"Can we get footage from their security?"

"That won't be a problem. Next stop." To Sean he asked, "How certain are you that the laptop and drone are in the water?"

"Almost one hundred percent."

"I'll talk to my boss about retrieving the equipment. I assume you can't track it anymore?" John asked Sean.

"No. It's dead. But unless they weighted down the equipment, the drone is light and has buoyancy and may float to shore. The laptop and external drive would sink. If they used a hammer on the equipment—to destroy it—there could be evidence in their vehicle, small pieces of plastic or chips."

John turned to Riley. "I want you to canvass every security camera on 12th and 16th—they likely used 16th Street to get to the river, but they could have backtracked to 12th. Pull feed during that window. I'll have the computer techs go over it, compare it with vehicles that the drone caught."

To Sean, he said, "If I need you, will you be available?"

"Of course. But if I may, I'd like to go with Riley—I have a lot of experience with security cameras and technology. It might make the process easier and faster."

"I don't have a problem with that, it's ultimately up to Officer Knight."

"I love having a ride-along," Riley said with a grin.

John looked at his watch, then said to Lucy, "Then I guess

you're with me, Kincaid. I need to interview the staff here, but it shouldn't take long."

Lucy looked at Sean, and he averted his eyes. He couldn't do this now. He needed to—he wanted to. He wanted to take Lucy away from all this and try to explain . . . but he didn't know what to say. What could he say? He fucked up . . . again.

"That's fine," Lucy said.

"I'll try to make it to your presentation," Sean said.

"If you can't, don't worry about it," she said.

She was giving him an out that he didn't want, but would probably take, because every time he looked at her he thought about how he'd hurt her.

Sean walked out with Riley. "Is something wrong?" Riley asked.

"No. Just tired."

"Just—well—I guess—nothing."

Great. Now other people saw the strain and Sean didn't know how to fix it.

Chapter Eight

Pride staff—a small, close group of people—were visibly upset about what had happened to Ellen, and were putting together shifts of people to go sit with Marc at the hospital. They didn't know who might want to hurt her, she had no enemies, there had been no threats, and they didn't have any pending lawsuits over their equipment. Two previous lawsuits had been settled years ago.

By the time John took Lucy back to the convention center, they had learned nothing more that could help.

"It goes back to that drone footage," John said. "Other than that person on the roof of the Sheraton, I didn't see anything suspicious."

"Maybe," Lucy said, "the killer *thought* the drone had caught them doing something. Or one of those cars the drone tagged is suspicious."

"I sent the plates to my boss, I'll have a report shortly." He glanced at his watch. "Do you want to join me talking to the folks at the Sheraton? I want to inspect the roof. The AG will be at the Hyatt later this afternoon, and there's no line of sight from the Sheraton to any of the rooms—except maybe the top floors—but even then, it would be next to impossible to plan an assassination."

"Assassination?" Lucy was surprised that that was where his mind had gone.

"The AG's security chief has been wanting a threat assessment on the AG and other dignitaries here for the conference—the DA, police chief, people like that. I don't want to downplay a threat, but I don't see it right now. And a room full of armed cops—it would be suicide. Bomb dogs already walked through the conference yesterday. They're going back today and doing a wider canvass, including both hotels as well as the convention center."

"Maybe there's something on the roof that will help us make sense of all this."

He glanced over at her as they walked through the main doors of the Sheraton. "I appreciate you helping me with this. You didn't have to spend your time off doing this."

"Ellen is a friend of Jack and Megan, I want to do whatever I can to help." Not to mention the vacation she thought she'd have with Sean had ended before it even began.

She didn't want to think about Sean now—she couldn't, not after last night. And he was so . . . *formal* at Pride. He knew Ellen, and that had to bother him, watching what happened to her. But he didn't reach out for Lucy, for support or anything . . . and she hadn't reached for him. She should have. She should have known that this was getting to him, in addition to all the other weight he was carrying. But she'd been hurt, and she let her anger and frustration take over when she saw him. Self-defense, maybe, but it shouldn't be like that, not with her husband.

She didn't know how she should have responded, and then wondered if that was part of her problem. Shouldn't she *instinctively* know how to help Sean? Not just because she loved him, but because she was a trained psychologist, she could see that he was in pain, that he was hiding something or holding back or . . . lying.

She didn't hold it against him, because he'd been through hell. She just wanted him to acknowledge that, to talk to her, to *let* her help him!

She didn't know how. If it was anyone else, what would she do?

Lucy couldn't answer that, because no one else was Sean. Everyone handled trauma in their own unique way. It was almost like Sean didn't trust her enough to tell her exactly what had happened with Jonathon Paxton. It was more than embarrassment . . . the fear ran much deeper than that.

She dismissed her anxiety—working helped. Working was definitely better than sitting around the convention center waiting for her panel to begin, or making small talk with other cops. She had been looking forward to the conference . . . but now it just didn't seem important.

John returned with the head of security, an older man named Ben. He took them up the service elevator to the top floor, then unlocked a maintenance door and they walked up to the roof.

"No one can get up here without a key," Ben said. "There was no scheduled maintenance last night, but that doesn't mean no one was on the roof. There's a/c units that sometimes have problems, vents, access to some of the systems. But it's not common." He paused. "Some of the staff come up here to smoke. It's not permitted, but we generally ignore it."

Lucy and John walked the perimeter of the roof, then stopped at the spot where the man in black had been spotted by the drone. There was nothing here—he'd been recorded halfway between the door and the corner of the building. The ledge was a little over two feet high.

The stone surface wouldn't hold prints, but the door would. John said, "Ben, I'm going to send up a crime scene tech to print the door, both sides, if you don't mind."

"Sure, but there could be employee fingerprints here."

"And if they come up here regularly, maybe they saw something out of order."

Lucy was staring at some marks on the southwest corner. "John?" she called out, and he approached. "What do you make of these? They look fresh."

They were scrapes in the cement that framed the roof, and a deep gouge near the floor.

"Don't know," he said. "I'll have the tech take pictures and samples—maybe someone will have an idea. But you're right, they look fresh." He asked Ben, but the security officer shrugged. He didn't know what they were, either.

"One more thing," John said. "I need you to send over a copy of all surveillance video from ten to midnight last night—everyone entering and exiting the hotel."

"I can do that. Give me a couple of hours."

"It's almost three, Kincaid. We'd better get you across the street for your panel."

Doug wanted to call off the entire job.

But there was a lot of money at stake.

He turned off the news. The woman wasn't dead. She was in surgery, hadn't regained consciousness, and the police spokesman said her status was critical.

He didn't *want* her to be dead, but being alive was worse.

He paced the hotel room. He hated waiting. He hated being indecisive!

They'd already taken money for the job. Money they couldn't easily give back.

Shit shit shit!

A key card in the door had his heart skipping a beat, then Beth walked in and he relaxed.

"Babe, I've been worried all day."

She kissed him and he felt better. "I told you, honey, it's fine."

"It's not fine! What if that woman dies? We'll be nabbed for a murder charge."

"We had nothing to do with that. We weren't even *there*. That was all your brother and Andy."

He bristled. He knew Frank had problems, but he was his brother. Doug loved him, and they needed him for this job.

"I'm going to fix this, Doug. You trust me, right?"

"Of course, but I've seen police here all day. And they blocked off the street, the alley—what if we missed something?"

"*I* didn't miss anything."

Now she was angry with him. Doug didn't want Beth to be mad, he was just worried. Worried for them, worried for Frank. His brother wasn't the sharpest tack. Andy was brilliant, but lazy. Frank was . . . well, he sometimes didn't think things through.

He said, "I think we should walk away."

"There's too much at stake. We can't back out now."

"I have a bad feeling, Beth. We've been doing this how long? Five years? No one has ever gotten hurt before. No one. And the news said that woman might die. I can't live with that guilt."

"She won't die."

"You don't know that!"

"Babe, please, calm down." She kissed him, then held his face in her hands. "I love you, Doug. We're going to get through this, and then we're done. At least with Frank and Andy. If we decide to take another job, it'll just be us, okay? Just like before."

Frank was his brother, and Doug knew that Beth had agreed to let him help with some of the jobs not just because they needed a third man, but because Frank couldn't hold down a job. Doug had always watched out for his big brother because Frank was . . . well, Doug thought he'd been dropped on his head. That was mean, he knew, but Frank didn't have a lot of social skills. He was the only family Doug had left, though—other than Beth, of course. Doug's dad had left the family when he was ten, and his mom had moved to Florida to live with a guy when Doug turned eighteen.

"I took care of you and Frankie when your dad ran off, I'm done."

Doug never heard from her anymore, not even a birthday card. He tried to pretend he didn't care.

But he did.

Andy was Doug's best friend. Andy was always the smart one. He'd gone to college, he had a job, he introduced Doug to Beth. Without Andy, Doug wasn't sure they would have gotten as far as they had, but maybe now was the time to cut off everyone. And not take any more jobs. Move, maybe. Out of California, lay low.

"You're thinking too much," Beth said.

"After this—we need to move. We'll have the money. Go to Nevada or something."

"I hate Nevada."

"Washington? Idaho?"

"I get it," Beth said. "You're worried. But this is just a hiccup, but it's not going to derail us. Everything is scheduled for tomorrow. I need you committed."

"I am committed. For you. For us. But—"

She kissed him to get him to stop talking. "Trust me. No one knows what we're doing. There's no way they can figure it out."

"What if they go up to the roof?"

"I took care of it already," she said. "They're not going to find anything because there's nothing to find. You need to have faith in me."

"I do."

She took his hand and led him to the bed. "I have a little time . . . an hour, two even if you're *really* good." She smiled and kissed him again, pushing him slowly down on the bed. She sat on top of him and took off her shirt.

He could never resist her. Five years of marriage and he loved her more now than he had when they said "*I do.*"

Chapter Nine

Late that afternoon, the attorney general's speech went off without a hitch. They'd more than doubled security and changed several details at the last minute in case his itinerary had been compromised. Once the AG was done, an officer assigned to his detail sent John a message, which he showed to Lucy as they sat down in the hotel bar after meeting up at the end of the speech.

AG secure, no trouble, doesn't seem that he was the target.

"We're back to square one," John said. "I'm off duty. Want a beer?"

"No, thank you," she said.

John motioned at the waitress and ordered a draft. Lucy asked for a Diet Coke.

"The idea that the AG was the target of an assassination was remote," Lucy said. "You said so yourself."

"Then what was that guy doing on the roof? Those marks could have been made by a sniper."

"Would a good sniper leave any trace of their presence?"

John conceded that they likely would not. His beer arrived and he paid for it, tipped well, and sipped. "I needed this. It's been a long day."

It was six thirty in the evening and Jack and Megan were
still at the hospital with Marc. Ellen had come out of surgery
not long ago and was in a medically induced coma. If she
made it through the next twenty-four hours, the doctors felt
she would recover, though permanent brain damage was still
a possibility.

"Ellen's attack has to be connected to her flying the drone
over the roof," John said. "The license plates didn't pan out,
and so far Riley and Sean haven't come up with anything on
security feeds in the area. I've gone through every event at
the Sheraton, thinking one of them might be a target, and
nothing is ringing my bells."

He sounded frustrated—the first real sign of frustration
that Lucy heard from her temporary partner.

"Do you have someone watching the hotel? Or the roof?"
Lucy asked.

"No. The crime techs I sent up there found nothing—well,
one interesting thing. The roof door had been wiped with a
disinfectant. No prints at all."

Lucy frowned. That didn't seem right. "If the man in black
wiped the door, there might not be many prints, but the security chief, Ben, he wasn't wearing gloves. He brought us
up and unlocked the door. His prints should have been on the
knob."

John straightened. "You're right. There was at least an
hour window from when I called in the techs until they got
up there."

"We were being watched," Lucy said. "Whoever is behind
this knew we were up there, and maybe thought they'd left
some evidence."

"There's no security on that door, only the elevators and
lobby."

"They could have been watching from the lobby."

Jack pulled out his notepad and looked at his notes from

the day. "We arrived at one fifty p.m. Left at two forty. That's a short window. I'll have Riley pull the feed from all public areas during that time frame. This might be a big break—though there are dozens, if not hundreds, of people going in and out of the lobby. Half the law enforcement conference is staying at the Sheraton, the other half at the Hyatt."

He sent a message. "I'm going to owe Riley a beer," John said. "He's already put in extra hours. His boss isn't happy, but since I tapped him as my officer-assistant for this investigation, I can get him the overtime. By the way, I enjoyed your presentation this afternoon. I'm sorry I missed the end of it, I needed to brief the AG's security detail before his speech."

"I'm glad you liked it." Sean hadn't come, but Lucy tried not to think about that. She hadn't talked to him since she and John left Pride early that afternoon.

"I liked how you showed clips from some of your interviews to illustrate your point, and then having the forensic psychiatrist show why a technique worked or didn't work was helpful."

"It took me forever to get permission to use those, I'm glad they were effective."

Lucy felt stuck. She wanted to go back to Jack's, but she didn't have a car. Sean had the rental, she'd driven this morning with Jack, and Megan had her own car.

She should have gotten a room at the hotel, but she didn't have any need before—and now it was likely full. Not to mention she didn't have any of her things.

John finished his beer. "I'm heading home. You need a ride someplace?"

Had she been that obvious? "I'm staying with Jack and Megan. I'll catch a ride with them when they're done at the hospital."

"All right. Thank you for everything, Kincaid. I appreciated your help on this. I don't know where we're going to be tomorrow morning in the investigation."

"If you need me, you have my number. I don't have any plans at the conference tomorrow, other than listening to a few panels. Dean Hooper, the ASAC, is giving a presentation that should be interesting. But anything you need, I'm happy to do."

"I don't like unanswered questions. The doc texted me that he thinks Ellen will make it—he's giving fifty–fifty right now, but he's more confident than the odds. We might have to wait until she regains consciousness before we get answers, and they're keeping her in a medically induced coma for at least the next twelve hours. Her attack doesn't feel random to me, but unless something pans out from the security feeds at the Sheraton, I don't have another direction."

John said goodbye and left, and Lucy sat staring at her watered-down soda. She looked at her phone. No messages from Sean. Was he still out with Riley? Had he gone home?

She texted Jack.

I'm at the Hyatt in the bar, ready to go home if you can leave. If not I can get an Uber. Let me know.

She felt . . . lonely. It wasn't a feeling she'd had in years. Maybe *lonely* was the wrong word.

No, it's the right word. Sean is your partner in everything . . . and he's MIA. And when he's here physically, he's gone mentally.

She realized she hadn't talked to Jesse since they'd arrived in Sacramento on Tuesday afternoon, when Sean called him as they were driving up to Jack's place, just to tell Jesse they'd arrived safely. What kind of stepmother was she that she hadn't called to check in for the last two days? She knew that Jesse was in good hands with Nate, but she missed him.

He answered on the second ring. "Hey, Lucy!"

He sounded happy to hear from her, which warmed her heart. "How is everything on the home front?" she asked.

"Good. Nate picked me up from soccer practice and we met Aggie for dinner at Tito's. I'm still stuffed."

Lucy laughed. "My favorite place." Aggie was the first of Nate's girlfriends that Lucy had met, and he seemed to have fallen hard, though getting anything personal out of her partner was next to impossible. Still, they seemed to spend all their free time together and Nate had already met her large family. Lucy was pleased. She liked the young DEA agent a lot; Aggie was good for Nate.

"Then after, we all went to visit Brad," Jesse said.

"How's he doing?"

"Miserable. I mean, he's fine, he says he's recovered, but I guess from what he told Nate he's being pressured to retire early or something. I guess there's something really wrong with his knee or something."

Lucy's heart went out to her friend. He had been tortured four weeks ago and nearly died, and it wasn't the first time. He was an effective DEA agent, and that made him a target for some of the cartels.

Jesse continued, "I guess his big boss is going to bat for him. But I heard him tell Nate that they want him to take over a slot at the DEA training academy, and he's thinking about it. Nate said it's a choice position, but I don't really know what it is."

"That would be good for him. He could train the next generation. I'll talk to him when we get back."

"He said to say hi. Is Dad there?"

"No, I'm still at the conference," she said. "We became involved in an investigation, and he's been helping the local police with some of the tech issues."

"What happened?"

Jesse sounded worried, and Lucy didn't want him to worry

about anything. He'd had enough fear in his young life. "A vendor here was attacked and robbed. Jack and Megan know her, so Sean and I are helping in the investigation."

"Is she okay?"

"She just got out of surgery. The doctor is optimistic, but we're not certain yet."

"That's awful."

"Yes, but we're going to find out what happened."

"Of course you are, because you're the best, Lucy."

"Thanks, Jess."

"Want to talk to Nate?"

"No, I'm sure he has everything taken care of there."

"He does. I'm almost done with my homework, then it's game time. But I promise—bed by ten thirty."

"You don't have a curfew."

"I know, but I'll never stay up past eleven on a school night. Remember last week when Dad and I were playing that new game? Dad said we could play as long as I wanted if I got up by seven for school. I didn't go to sleep until nearly three, and I was totally dead the next day. Not doing that again."

She laughed. It was a good lesson to learn, and sometimes you had to learn it through trial and error.

"You have fun with Nate, I love you."

"I love you, too, Lucy." He hung up.

She didn't know why she had tears in her eyes. Jesse wasn't her flesh and blood, but she couldn't love that kid any more if he were.

Sean was having a beer with Riley because he didn't want to go back to Jack's. He wanted to see Lucy, but how could he just text her as if he hadn't fucked up last night? He wanted to go back to San Antonio and have everything the way it was before Jonathan Paxton came back in his life.

His phone rang. It was Jack. He didn't want to answer, but he had to.

He excused himself from Riley and walked outside of the bar. "Yeah."

"I'm done with your bullshit, Sean," Jack said. "Lucy is waiting for someone to take her home. She asked me, not you. So you're going to get your fucking ass over to the Hyatt lobby and fix everything. *Now*. Not tomorrow, not next week, *tonight*. Do you think that none of us understand you went through hell? Do you think that we don't know Paxton fucked with your head? That Colton Thayer tortured you? You don't want to talk about it, that's fine. I get it. I don't talk about my shit, either. But I will not ever allow you to hurt Lucy because you can't deal with your own crap. Fix it *now*."

Jack didn't wait for Sean to respond. He had already hung up.

Sean went back inside. He was shaking. He was angry . . . he was scared . . . and he didn't want to lose Lucy.

He told Riley, "Lucy's done so I need to go pick her up."

"Yeah, John wants me to talk to the Sheraton about some security feeds from this afternoon. I'll walk back with you."

Sean wanted to be alone, but he didn't say anything. They were around the corner from the Hyatt—his car was still in the parking garage. Riley had parked his squad car near the convention center. One of the perks of being a cop was not having to worry about finding a parking place.

"You okay?" Riley asked as they walked.

"Not really. I don't want to talk about it, though."

"You have a lot of friends, Sean. You saved my sister's life, I'll never forget that. Dean says you're the smartest guy he's ever worked with, and coming from my brother-in-law, that's high praise 'cause he's the smartest guy I've ever met."

"Dean's a lot smarter than I am," Sean said.

"Just think how *I* feel." Riley laughed, cutting the tension.

They split up on K Street, and Sean went inside the Hyatt. He walked through the lobby, looking for Lucy.

She was in the bar. She wasn't alone; she was sitting with several cops from the conference. Everyone was drinking except Lucy. She only drank when she was completely relaxed, and preferred only having beer or wine at home. She looked attentive, listening and talking—maybe about her panel (that he'd missed) or about the conference or the speech by the attorney general or any number of things.

But she didn't look comfortable.

He should have been here. He should have done so many things differently.

Sean wanted everything to go back to the way it was before, but Jack made him realize that just wasn't possible. His life was different. It might have only been three days of hell, but those three days had affected him deeply.

Being accused of a crime he hadn't committed.

Being arrested; handcuffed; imprisoned.

Being kidnapped and framed for killing a cop. Knowing that if he *could* free himself, he was a wanted man with a target on his back.

All of that had affected him, but none of it destroyed him.

What truly gutted him was looking at himself through the eyes of Jonathon Paxton. Seeing himself as the one who hurt Lucy. Who put her in danger. Logic could only get him so far . . . there was a lot of truth behind Paxton's words. That Lucy would be safer without him in her life. Paxton had tapped into Sean's deepest fear: that had Lucy picked someone else to love, she would be happier and safer.

Sean didn't know what he had expected by running away to Tahoe for the night. Maybe he wanted to hurt Lucy so she would walk away—show her that he was everything Paxton said he was. Untrustworthy. Disloyal. Fun first, last, and always. A borderline criminal. Arrogant. Someone who would hurt Lucy because he couldn't change.

Jack said he had PTSD. Sean had thought that was bullshit. He wasn't a soldier. He wasn't a cop or a doctor who couldn't save someone. His feelings were hurt, and he had to get over it.

But Jack was right.

"You can't forget what happened. You have to accept it, acknowledge it, deal with it. Only then can you move forward."

Sean felt so damn weak! What he suffered was nothing compared with what Jack had suffered in the army. With what Kane had suffered in the Marines. With what Lucy had suffered at the hands of a psychotic rapist.

You can't compare your pain with the pain of others. There's no scale for suffering.

That advice came from Dillon Kincaid, Jack's twin brother. It was the only thing he'd said to Sean that had stuck with him. He couldn't reconcile that with how he viewed the world. Until now.

He had to fix it with Lucy. Now, not later.

He stepped away from the bar, pulled out his cell phone, and called Dean Hooper.

"Rogan? What's up?"

"Dean, I need a favor. I'll owe you big time." He explained what he wanted.

"I can make it happen. But you don't owe me anything, Sean. Ever. Give me five minutes."

He ended the call, and three minutes later Sean got the confirmation and a thumbs-up.

Chapter Ten

Lucy had seen Sean in the lobby looking at her. He seemed so lost that she wanted to go to him, to fix whatever was broken—but before she could, he turned and walked away. Her heart fell to the pit of her stomach, and she thought for the first time that maybe her life with Sean was truly in jeopardy. She almost couldn't breathe.

Jack still wasn't here to get her. She hadn't had time alone—within minutes of John walking away, two cops from San Francisco had come over to talk about her panel. A few minutes later another group came over to tell her they liked her presentation. Soon there were nine or ten agents and cops chatting about her interrogation techniques and laughing about some of their own antics. She liked hearing their stories, but her mind wasn't fully engaged. She didn't see Sean again, and she didn't know when Jack would be here.

"I have to go," she said finally, "my ride is here." The lie seemed to come easily, but maybe that was because these men and women didn't know her. She smiled, thanked them for their kind words about her panel, and headed for the main doors. She pulled her phone out to summon an Uber. It would cost a small fortune to go all the way to Jack's, but she didn't care—she just wanted to leave.

"Lucy."

She looked up from her phone and Sean was there.

She had no words. She thought he'd left.

He looked exhausted. And worried. Her heart nearly burst with love for him, and fear about what he was doing to himself.

"Hi," she said.

He leaned over and kissed her. She put a hand on his shoulder; he was tense, practically shaking.

She almost asked *Are you okay?* but knew that he wasn't, and she didn't know if he would lie to her . . . again. She couldn't handle it if he lied to her about what was going on with him. The professional in her might understand it and make excuses, but the woman who loved him couldn't, not anymore. She wanted to *make* him okay, and she couldn't do it. Knowing that she couldn't fix this hurt her, deep inside it hurt.

But she wasn't going to walk away.

He held up a plastic card. It took her a second, then she realized it was a card key for the hotel.

"Right now, all I want is to be alone with you. I need you, Lucy, and I'm sorry."

Tears dampened her eyes. "No apologies." She reached up to touch him. To kiss him.

"Yes." He took a deep breath, took her hand, and led her to the elevators.

They went up to the concierge level. "Is this where you were last night?" she asked.

"I was in Lake Tahoe."

She didn't know quite how to process that information. She had questions but didn't know where to start.

Sean opened the door at the far end of the hall. It was a suite—they walked into a sitting area. To the right was the bedroom.

"You got a suite?" she asked.

"I called in a favor and this was the only room available. But I won twenty thousand dollars in Tahoe, and figure this is a small way to start making up for it."

"You don't have to do this, Sean."

"I want to." He closed the door. "I know what you're going to say. That you forgive me, or that there's nothing to forgive. But there is a lot to forgive. I ran away last night. I didn't realize it at the time, but I did. I ran away from you, from Jack, from my failures, from everything. But I can't. I can't run away from me—I'm not making any sense."

He took a deep breath and crossed the room. He stared out the window. They were in the corner of the hotel, on the top floor.

Lucy didn't push. Sean wanted to talk. She could feel it in him, but he was struggling. She didn't want to put words in his mouth. She didn't want to tell him it would be okay. He *knew* that. He knew that she loved him. He was struggling, but it was with whatever Jonathon Paxton had said and done to him—and what Sean had done to himself, in his mind. She had to let him do this in his own way.

He wasn't looking at her, but that was okay, she realized. Maybe it was better for him this way.

"I remember when you first told me you loved me," he said.

She remembered, too, and shivered involuntarily. She had thought he'd been killed, that because she was torn up inside about what love was and wasn't, she hadn't told him how she felt out of fear—fear that if she said it out loud, something would break in their relationship. It didn't matter that he'd told her he loved her, it didn't matter that he'd showed her in his actions and words how much he loved her, she had this irrational panic that admitting how she felt would jeopardize everything.

Then she'd almost died in an abandoned mine. He'd saved

her life, and she admitted that she loved him and had been too scared to tell him. Scared of her feelings, of what they might gain—only to lose everything because of the lives they led.

She'd been a fool. Young, immature, terrified of loss because she'd already lost so much in her life.

"For a long time I didn't think I deserved you. Sometimes I still don't," he said, "but I love you and I know you love me, and everything that we've been through has just solidified that. Then I realized it wasn't what I *deserved* or didn't *deserve*. It was about me. The day you told me you loved me, you nearly died. I put you there."

"No, Sean, you didn't."

"Yes, I did. You went on that trip with me because it was my job, Lucy. You were in that situation—you nearly fell down a mine shaft, you still have a scar on your leg from where you were stabbed—because of my case."

"I would do it again to help the people of that town. To help that young boy who had lost everything. And I know you would, too."

Sean turned away from the window, looked at her. "I know it doesn't sound logical. And that's why I can't get this out of my head. It's all driven by emotion. Paxton used my deepest fears against me. But *knowing* that doesn't make the truth any less real. Everything I touch dies. My parents. I was flying the plane when it went down! My dad took over the controls but couldn't stop the crash. I killed them. I had to bury them, knowing that I was partly at fault."

"Sean—"

"Logically, I know that the plane had a major mechanical failure. That I didn't cause the failure, that my dad and I did everything we could to crash safely. But they are still dead. Skye Jansen, the first woman I loved, is dead. Why? Because I no longer loved her."

"She's dead because of her own actions," Lucy said.

"Logically, I know that. Emotionally I only feel that if I hadn't hurt her she might not have gone down that road. Jesse's mother is dead because I couldn't protect her."

Lucy knew where this was going and she wanted to hold Sean, to tell him he was wrong, but that wasn't going to fix how he felt deep inside. Calmly, she said, "Madison is dead because the man she married laundered money for a drug cartel."

"But I was supposed to protect her! Jesse—my son— nearly died that night. I'm terrified that because of something I do—or don't do—you're going to die. That because of *who I am*, Jesse is going to die. *Everyone I have ever loved is dead.* I can't stop thinking about it. I can tell myself that it's not true, I can tell myself that you are safe, but the fear is real, Lucy. It's paralyzing."

She understood fear. Nothing she said was going to take away Sean's pain. After she was raped ten years ago she dreaded her family trying to make things better. Some of them walked on eggshells around her. Some acted as if everything was normal. Some stopped talking mid-sentence, as if afraid they would upset her. The pity in their eyes . . . that was the worst. And while Jack's blunt, tough love had helped her more than anything—coupled with him training her to be stronger, better, faster—sometimes even he couldn't fix what was broken. Sometimes she just wanted someone to acknowledge that she had the right to be scared, that she had the right to be angry.

Time didn't fix everything, but time helped put fear and anger in perspective. It was always there—but she managed it. Most of the time.

She could tell Sean that, but he knew. He knew that his emotions had overwhelmed his logic, and for a guy as logic-driven as Sean, it had to be terrifying.

"I accepted my own mortality years ago, Sean. I don't want to die, but I know that the life handed to me—and the life I chose—is dangerous. It's not your job to protect me any more than it's my job to protect you. But we protect each other because we love each other. I know the fear and pain and doubt eating you up, and I hate Jonathon Paxton for putting that on your heart. But do you know *why* he did it?"

"This isn't about him—

"Yes, it is, Sean. Jonathon Paxton is dead. I have no remorse, no sorrow, only pity. Maybe not even that. Paxton fixated on me because I look like his dead daughter. He was twisted and half crazy and had it in his head that you weren't good enough for me—for the woman he believed in his warped mind was *his daughter*. So he took your *love* for me and turned it into *fear for me*. Because he knew that you have a big heart, he knew that you would do anything to protect me. If you think that loving me will cause me to die in some unknown future, you're letting that bastard win. You can*not* let him win, Sean. I don't know how to fix this—but we have to do this together. I refuse to let that man come between us."

Sean stared at her, tears in his eyes, then he stepped forward and she ran into his arms. He hugged her so tightly she almost couldn't breathe. But she didn't let go. She needed Sean as much as he needed her.

Sean picked her up, something that always made her a little nervous because she wasn't all that short or light, but he carried her with ease to the bedroom and put her on the bed. "I love you so much, Lucy."

She kissed him. Over and over. "Show me, Sean. Show me how much you love me."

Lucy slept like a rock for four hours, then woke up, alert, almost forgetting where she was.

Hotel. Right. They were at the Hyatt, in a suite.

And she was starving.

It was eleven thirty, and she was on the tail end of room service. She ordered food for her and Sean, though she wouldn't wake him to eat.

The situation wasn't fixed, but they were beginning to repair the damage that Jonathan Paxton had done to Sean. A huge weight had fallen from her shoulders. Now she understood and together they would find a way to get beyond Sean's emotional pain.

She looked at her phone. A text from Jack, which came in two hours before, was simple.

?

So Jack.

She replied: *Sean and I are staying at the Hyatt tonight. Can you or Megan bring our luggage in the morning?*

She wasn't sure Jack was still awake, but he responded immediately.

With a smiley-face emoji.

Lucy laughed out loud.

The suite had two robes in the closet, so that's what she was wearing when room service arrived. The late-night menu wasn't expansive, so she'd ordered burgers and fries.

Sean stepped out of the bedroom as soon as she closed the door. He wore his boxers.

"It didn't even occur to me that you hadn't eaten," he said.

She kissed him.

"I got enough for both of us." She put the tray on the coffee table and sat down.

He sat next to her and kissed her. He looked like he wanted to say something, but then he kissed her again and said, "I love you."

"I love you. And food." She took off the lids and started eating.

After a few minutes, she started talking about the case. She missed bouncing ideas off Sean. He was so good at seeing the whole picture, and asking the right questions to help solve cases.

He didn't comment. Maybe she was pushing for normalcy too quickly, but he seemed interested in what she was telling him.

She said, "You heard that Ellen made it out of surgery. That's good news."

"Yeah, great news." He glanced at her. "Ellen wanted me there to help her test the drone. I told her I had plans. I lied. I should have been there."

"She is a smart, capable woman who didn't need you to help her," Lucy said. "Don't go down that path, Sean. It never ends well, as we both know."

He didn't say anything, ate some fries, then said, "Yeah. You're right."

"Did you and Riley find anything interesting?"

"No. There's some data to go through, but I don't think anything is going to be there. I think whoever attacked her knew about the cameras and went a route to avoid them."

"What are they up to?" Lucy wondered out loud. "It can't be for the equipment, since they destroyed it. If they wanted her dead, they would have made sure that they killed her. I can't imagine they didn't know that she was alive when they put her in the Dumpster, but if they thought she was dead, it didn't seem from the video that her murder was the goal."

"They didn't know what she saw with the drone. I think the man in black, on the roof, was doing something illegal up there and didn't know if the video caught him doing it. And you found nothing up on the roof?"

"The door was wiped clean, but we think it was done after John and I went up there, because the Sheraton security chief's prints weren't on the knob and we know he touched it."

"They were watching you."

"That's my guess. There were some odd scrapes that appeared fresh on the corner of the roof. There's a nearly three-foot ledge all around."

"Do you have a picture?"

Lucy looked through her phone, showed the marks to Sean. He stared at them for a short minute, then said, "I know exactly what those are from." He took her phone and opened the browser, did a search, then showed her a picture of a multipronged hook.

"What's that for?"

"It's a grappling hook. Mountain climbing."

"They climbed up the side of the hotel? Someone would have noticed."

He frowned, then did another search and brought up Google Earth. "I wish I had my laptop, but this gives us a perspective. There are a couple of buildings that could be reached from the Sheraton roof."

"Sounds like a thief."

Sean was thinking. She loved watching him while he thought deeply, because his mind was like a computer. He was running through a bunch of scenarios quickly, trying to put together facts he knew with the evidence that presented itself.

"I think you're right," he said. "A heist. It makes sense. Multiple people involved—at least three. Using the roof as access. Maybe to rob someone in the hotel—and leaving this way? Or going across to . . . this building. The Ban Roll-on building."

"The *what*?"

"It's what we called it when I was a kid. It's round, like Ban Roll-on."

She laughed.

"See here?" He pointed to the satellite image. "It's flat on this side. There's a helicopter pad. A way to access the building from the roof. Either they're going from the Sheraton to that building, or vice versa."

"They did this Wednesday night. They thought Ellen had seen them, so they grabbed the drone. Whatever they got, they're probably long gone."

"I haven't heard of a major theft, but maybe it hasn't gotten out, or it hasn't been publicized. Or they were doing recon. If they knew you went to the roof and then went up to erase any evidence, they were still in the hotel."

It made sense, but Lucy thought this seemed elaborate for a theft. "Maybe they're looking to rob the Sheraton. There are events there—not the law enforcement conference, but other conferences, meetings."

"It's worth looking into, but then why a grappling hook? I think they have a plan to do something *from* the roof."

Sean definitely thought outside the box when it came to these sort of things, so she nodded. "We can't do anything about it now, it's midnight," Lucy said. "But I'll email John and Megan and we should discuss this in the morning."

"I agree. Early. The police will want to talk to each of the businesses and have them check for any thefts. It could be something was taken and no one noticed. Files, an account that was emptied. Probably not the bank—they would have a far more elaborate security system than the businesses upstairs."

"Bank?" Lucy asked, not sure she was following.

Sean walked over to the window in the corner and looked out. She followed and stood at his side. He wrapped one arm around her, held her close, and pointed across the way.

"That's the Ban Roll-on building. There's a bank on the bottom floor, a twenty-four-hour security desk, several financial services companies, some nonprofits, some lawyers."

"You know a lot about who works there."

"RCK has some clients in the building. A few that could be targets, but we would have heard if their system was breached. I hope—if they followed our protocols, they would be alerted immediately."

"Maybe the man in black was doing recon, like you said. Didn't actually break into anything yet. Or maybe they were just after information and didn't actually *take* anything."

"Possible. Definitely possible."

Sean turned and pulled Lucy into his arms. "Send your email, I want to take you back to bed."

"Bossy, aren't we?"

"I have to make up for lost time."

"I'll send the email on one condition."

He raised an eyebrow. "Now who's bossy?"

"I noticed in the bathroom that there's a big bathtub. Big enough for two."

"You noticed that, did you?"

"Fill it up. And you might just find a bottle of champagne in the mini fridge."

"You ordered champagne?"

"I did."

"What are we celebrating?"

She stared into Sean's deep-blue eyes. She loved him so much, and she would make sure he knew it every single day. She kissed him lightly. "Us."

Chapter Eleven

Lucy was grateful that Megan and Jack arrived early and brought her suitcase. She changed into fresh clothes and came out just as John Black arrived.

"Your email intrigued me, Kincaid—if I wasn't completely crashed when it came in after midnight, I might have come over then."

"Eat," Sean said. "I ordered up breakfast."

That was an understatement. There was enough for ten people, not just the five who were there.

"I never say no to free food," John said.

Jack had already started to eat. He hadn't said much since he came in. While Jack not talking wasn't generally a cause for alarm, she sensed the tension between Jack and Sean and wished she hadn't talked to Jack about her problems. Except . . . Jack was one of the few people she trusted completely, and the only person she felt comfortable talking to about anything personal. Weird, she supposed, since he was her brother.

Lucy hoped that Jack and Sean mended fences. She would be distraught if they had a falling-out. She loved both her brother and her husband so much, and their friendship meant a lot to her—and to them.

Lucy didn't want to ask what the suite was costing Sean—the living quarters had a conference table that could seat eight, as well as a desk, a cabinet with whiteboard and television, two couches and two chairs, and a bar. But he'd told her he made twenty thousand dollars playing blackjack and poker, and he didn't feel good about the winnings.

"I didn't have as much fun as I used to . . . and I knew that I was just avoiding going home. So I want to do this. We can stay all weekend."

They'd agreed to stay at least until Saturday, when Jack and Megan were having a party and expected them to be there.

Sean motioned for them to sit at the conference table. "I don't have a formal presentation, but I set up my laptop so I can show you a couple of slides I created this morning about why I think I'm right—or close to right."

He opened the television, and what was on his laptop was projected onto the screen. It was the photo Lucy had taken on her cell phone on the roof of the Sheraton.

"These marks," he said, "are from a type of grappling hook. They are used by mountain climbers, but they're also used for zip lines. This"—he pointed to a deeper mark—"is a specialized hook. If something slips, it'll flip out and secure on a lip. This roof has a lip that works for just this type of device."

"Our crime scene techs couldn't find anything comparable in the database," John said.

"It's very difficult to match these up, not unless you're familiar with exactly what to look for. I don't have access to all the types of hooks and devices that might cause these exact marks, but if you found the equipment, your forensics team could match it up."

"Okay, I can buy into that." John sounded a bit skeptical, but he was clearly interested.

"When Lucy and I were talking last night, we were running through all the possibilities why someone would be on the roof and not want anyone to know they were there—thus going after the drone. Most obvious is an illegal motive—theft is clearly the most logical. The Sheraton itself is a possible target, but I only have a list of their public events. There could be private events I don't know about. They have a small reinsurers' conference going on, with only a hundred people registered. They have a wedding reception tomorrow night and a graduation party tonight. I would assume that many of the cops registered for the law enforcement conference are at the Sheraton."

"Half the hotel is law enforcement this week," Megan said. "Same with the Hyatt."

John said, "I actually talked to the Sheraton going down that same train of thought, Sean. Other than the events you mentioned, there's a retirement dinner for the CEO of a pharmaceutical company tonight. I talked to the director, the guy has no known threats. There's also a big nonprofit fundraiser and auction on Sunday. No known dignitaries, but that doesn't mean much—I considered that there might be something valuable at the auction, but I looked at the list of items on the block, and it's things like tickets to a River Cats game, a week in Lake Tahoe, a wine-of-the-month club. Nothing of great value, though I can't get the guest list—not without a warrant."

"Did you go through the security footage?" Megan asked.

John nodded. "We're still looking at it during the window before and after Ellen was attacked, but no one stands out. We're also looking at the footage during the time Lucy and I were at the Sheraton. Someone went up to the roof after we left but before my techs got there because the door was wiped clean. Lucy pointed out that the security chief, at a minimum, would have had prints on the door because he let us in."

"You should ask them to run a comparison," Lucy said, "if they can."

"Of what?"

"All adult males under fifty who were in the first section of surveillance tape—from Wednesday night—and the second section, when we were there."

John nodded. "Good idea." He texted someone on his phone. "Consider it done."

"Two people attacked Ellen," Megan said. "There's nothing to make us believe that there were *only* two people involved."

"That's pretty much what Lucy and I thought," John said. "The timing would be too close for the man on the roof to also be one of the two men downstairs who attacked Ellen— not impossible, but nearly. I'm pretty certain we're looking for three men at this point. Maybe more, but at least three." John looked back at Sean. "I sense that you don't think anyone at the Sheraton is a target."

"I don't, but I can be convinced someone is. I also think we should look at the Hyatt, because there are so many people going back and forth between the two hotels, and the convention center, that it's not suspicious. But I think the real target is a business in the Ban Roll-on building."

John laughed. "You are a native."

Sean grinned. "I had to look up the actual name of the building, and it's boring: 1201K? What kind of name is that? At least the sleek building next door is called the Esquire."

"The police union has an office at 1201K," John said.

"So do several RCK clients," Jack said.

"There are several potential targets," Sean said. "But looking at the trajectory—" He clicked his computer and another slide came up, from Google Earth, showing the satellite image of the Sheraton and 1201K. "The roof of the Sheraton is almost level with the roof of 1201K. The corner that the grappling marks were found points to that building—I would have to get on the roof to know exactly how they might breach the structure, but it would be much easier at night from the roof than trying to bypass security downstairs—especially since there is a twenty-four seven guard at the desk.

"The Sheraton is eighteen floors. The Esquire building is taller, and there's no access point at a level lower than the Sheraton. Meaning, no balconies. But again, the Ban Roll-on building—1201K Tower—is near level."

"Okay, now you lost me, Rogan," John said.

"There are two reasons why someone would be on that roof. One, assassination. From that nest, they could target someone primarily on K Street, and part of J. For 12th Street, the angle is wrong, and most of 13th Street is blocked by the Esquire building. To me, that's too narrow a coverage area, plus escape would be much more difficult. The other reason to be there is for a robbery. Getting in from the roof at 1201K would be child's play for anyone with moderate to advanced skills. Elevators are locked, stairwells are locked—but being locked just means you need a key. Or you can use the vents, which are accessible from the roof. Most of the time ventilation systems aren't good for breaching a facility—they're smaller than most people think—but the access points are larger, and they just need it big enough to get into the building, not move around inside."

"You keep saying accessible," Megan said, "but they don't adjoin."

"It's less than fifty feet from this corner"—he pointed on the satellite image—"to the roof of 1201K. Easy to hook up a zip line. They would certainly be able to secure it here, and from my view of the 1201K roof, it can be secured there as well. If there are corresponding marks, that would tell us that they either already completed their theft or did a dry run.

If there's nothing on the other building, it could be a simple scaling of the wall, but I can't figure out why they'd go up or down on the outside. They'd be too visible—except maybe in the middle of the night. Same with a zip line."

No one said anything. Then John asked, "Assuming you're right—who? What's of value?"

"Information. Technology." Sean clicked his mouse and the image changed. "Here's the list of every lease in the building. I highlighted three that I think are the most vulnerable. First, a tech company that's developing high-end encryption software for financial institutions. If you can steal their specs, once the software is rolled out, it's vulnerable to hackers. If you can steal it without anyone knowing, that is. The second, a law firm that's representing a pharmaceutical company in a major, multimillion-dollar wrongful death class-action suit. They also have several other high-profile clients. Getting access to those records could mean blackmail, fraud, any number of things. The third is of course the bank on the main floor."

"Which would be doubly protected."

"Yes, except for the fact that their executive offices are on a different floor with a private elevator that goes down to the main bank. Get into the executive offices and you can access the system *or* the vault. If you have the skills."

"A bank robbery," John muttered.

"Other businesses may be vulnerable as well—there are several that I don't know what they do—and information is as valuable as cash," Sean said. "One of those would go to the top of our list if they deal in finance or information, but I need more time to research."

"Omni Inc.," Jack said.

Sean looked at the list. "I'm not familiar with them."

"They used to be Golden State Investing," Jack said. "RCK handles background checks on their employees, which is why they jumped out at me. Sean, you tested their security system a year or two ago, if I remember correctly."

"You're right, I remember that," Sean said. "Yes, they need to be high on the list because they handle tens of millions of dollars in high-end transactions every week. Hacking from the outside would be next to impossible—not without them being alerted. In financial crimes you often look at catfishing, or maybe malware being downloaded on their computers—but if they followed RCK protocols, that would be next to impossible. Still, it only takes one employee to click on an external link, even with the best virus protection software, and a sharp hacker can worm his way in."

"Then why would a thief need to be on-site?" John asked.

"If they couldn't get anyone to bite on a link, they can download malware directly by placing a small flash drive in the back of a hard drive, by actually opening up the hard drive itself and inserting a chip—there are several ways to do it if you have control over the physical computer. If they know what they want and have the passcodes, they can log in on-site. Even without passcodes, a talented hacker might be able to break into the system, but it would have to be someone as good as or better than me. Or—maybe they don't need a hacker, if they're going solely after information. Even in this day and age, some financial information is still on paper. Either way, they'd need to be in the office to access any of that. But if they did it Wednesday or Thursday night, they could have already gotten what they wanted and no one may know."

"Is that something you can determine?" Jack asked.

Sean nodded. "If the computer network was breached. If someone looked at or copied physical data, I don't know how anyone would know until that information was used."

"I need to contact all businesses at 1201K," John said. "Maybe they don't know they were robbed."

"I'd like to talk to Omni myself," Jack said. "They run RCK computer security on-site, and I know the CFO personally. Richard Lesko."

"That's fine. I'd like to be there," John said. "If it turns out Sean's theory is right and someone is attempting a heist, I need to make sure SPD has a clear chain of evidence."

"Maybe we should bring in the forensics unit," Lucy said. "They may be able to analyze the 1201K roof as well as any possible way they can get inside."

"Good idea," John said. "But I don't think I'm going to get approval for that without more evidence. I'll talk to my boss, see how far I can push on this."

Sean said, "We need to get access to Omni's client list, Jack. Find out if any of their clients had any unusually large transactions going through this week, or early next week. These types of financial transactions aren't going to sit in an escrow account for long—but it's not unusual for a major real estate transaction or stock buy to take twenty-four to forty-eight hours to clear."

"How long would it take for someone to steal money electronically?" John asked. "I assume that's what you're thinking, that this heist is about cleaning out some bank accounts."

"Minutes," Sean said. "They will probably spend more time getting into the building than getting into the computer system—*if* they have passcodes and know exactly what they're looking for. A good hacker? Ten to fifteen minutes. The more time, the greater chance of being caught on either end."

Chapter Twelve

While the rest of them finished breakfast, John Black spent twenty minutes talking to his boss on the phone about Sean's theory. He was getting some pushback because there was no solid evidence that a heist was planned, and the target of 1201K Street was a guess, at best. But by the end he gave John the okay to investigate and noted that if there was evidence someone had illegally accessed the building, then he would authorize additional resources.

John shared that information the group. "It's as much as I hoped. I didn't think he would approve crime techs, not for something this vague. I also have Officer Knight and another detective coming down to help canvass the businesses. It's nearly nine, we should go over there and talk to security."

Megan tapped her watch. "Lucy and I have a meeting, we need to go."

"I almost forgot." Lucy turned to Sean. "It's the SAC of Sacramento FBI talking to all agents at the conference. I don't *have* to go, but I should."

"Go," he said, then leaned over and kissed her. "We came here for the conference. We'll meet up later."

John said, "Thanks for the breakfast, it hit the spot."

"That was all Sean's idea. I would have been happy with coffee."

After Megan and Lucy left for the conference center, Sean walked with John and Jack across the street to the 1201K Tower. Riley Knight was standing outside with a detective John introduced as Stan. John explained the theory, and then went inside to talk to security. It didn't take long before they were all cleared. Riley and Stan started at the bottom, and John took Jack and Sean up to the top floor where Omni was located.

After they gave a brief explanation for their visit at the front desk, Richard Lesko came out and greeted them. He was a large, imposing man in his sixties who dressed impeccably with subtle wealth. The kind of man you would think of as an old-time banker, and one you would automatically trust with your money.

"Jack, Sean. I'm glad you're here." He shook each of their hands firmly. "Good to meet you, Detective. Please, come to my office."

Most of the staff members were already at work, not unusual for a business that ran on Eastern Time, even on the West Coast. Omni filled the top floor and had a staff of more than fifty—investors, portfolio managers, accountants, support personnel. It was one of the top investment companies in the country, with offices in Sacramento and New York.

Richard led them to his corner office, which was a misnomer. Because the building was round, his office was round. He looked out at the K Street Mall and they could even see the capitol building two blocks over. Though Richard was the CFO and not the president of Omni, he clearly had the best office.

He motioned for them to sit at a conference table.

"You told my assistant we may have a security breach."

John described Ellen Dupre's assault and why SPD was investigating, and then let Sean take over to explain his theory on why someone had been on the roof.

When Sean was done, Richard said, "Our accounts are all in order, but you are welcome to check for any attempted hacks."

"Thank you," Sean said. "May I use your computer?"

"Of course."

"While Sean does his thing," Jack said, "Detective Black and I are going to the roof to look for evidence that anyone unauthorized was up there."

They left, and Sean worked. Richard stayed with him but didn't ask questions—which helped Sean work faster. He logged into the admin account that was set up specifically for RCK to manage their clients. He started running security logs, looking for anything out of the ordinary. There were of course standard attempts from bots trying to hack in, but those were all bounced back. He could find no malware hiding in the system, but he would need to run additional reports on individual computers to ensure that no one accidentally downloaded a virus to their own hard drive.

By the time John and Jack came back, Sean had completed a good analysis of the system. Before he could say anything, John said, "You were right, Rogan. The same marks are on this roof. I called my boss, and he's going to send a crime scene team over to look for trace, but it might be too late."

Richard looked worried. "We have a security system over and above building security. We follow all the protocols your firm established."

Sean said, "I can see that, but as we said then, nothing is a hundred percent foolproof. The good news is that there are no external threats to your system. I verified that the firewall is solid. It prevented anyone from getting in from the outside. There is no malware on the network. I'll want to run a virus scan on each computer, however, in case it's hiding on an individual hard drive to be deployed later."

"It sounds like a military operation."

"Exactly," Sean said. "Computer viruses can be dormant and virtually undetectable until a certain time, or until they are activated by a third party. But based on what I'm seeing here, the only way that someone can hack into your escrow accounts is through one of five accounts—you, the assistant CFO, the two accountants, and the vice president."

"Correct."

"Meaning, from my perspective, I believe that one of these passcodes will be used, if you're in fact the target."

"Are you implying that one of my most trusted staff members is trying to steal from our clients?"

"No. But one of their logins would be used. Or yours."

"Impossible."

Nothing was impossible, but Sean didn't state the obvious.

"Your office may not be the target," John said. "We're talking to every business here."

That didn't appease Richard; he still looked concerned.

Jack asked, "Is there a client who will have an unusually large sum of money in escrow tonight?"

"I can't divulge confidential client data."

"I'm not asking who, just if."

Sean said, "If Omni is the target, the thieves know that there will be money in a specific escrow account tonight. They may know the client and be planning to steal the money. For example, a relative or employee or someone with access to client information."

Sean didn't contradict Jack, but they needed the client list to determine who in that person's life might have cause to steal from them. A disgruntled employee. An ex-spouse. A grown child left out of an inheritance. A colleague.

"I can get a warrant," John said.

Richard was skeptical. "I understand you're doing your job, but I have to protect my clients' privacy. With all due respect, I don't think you have enough to get a warrant. Is there any way you can protect our system without violating privacy laws?"

"Set up a sting," Sean said.

"What?" John said. "Did you say a *sting*?"

"Whatever you want to call it. But someone can be waiting here, inside."

Richard nodded. "I'll hire a security officer."

"Jack and I should do it," Sean said. "These people are determined. They put an innocent civilian in a coma because they thought she might have seen something. A standard security guard isn't going to cut it."

"I agree," Jack said.

"I'm okay with that," Richard said. "I'll be at the Hyatt tonight for my daughter's wedding—the rehearsal dinner. Her wedding is tomorrow at the cathedral."

"I don't think that's a coincidence," Jack said.

Richard frowned. "I don't understand."

"You're going to be across the street and Omni may be a target for theft?"

"I don't see what one has to do with the other. This wedding and the rehearsal have been planned for months."

"Like I said," Sean said, "a great hacker might be able to get into your escrow accounts, but it'll be difficult. Your passcode will cut the time from potentially hours to minutes. Do you have your passcode written on anything in your office or on your person? Like in your wallet?"

"No—well, yes. But we secure them in my assistant's office."

"Nothing is foolproof," Sean said.

"It's a safe."

"Fingerprint?"

"No, there's a code."

"I guarantee I can break into that safe in five minutes or less."

Richard was skeptical. Jack said, "Richard, I believe RCK is still contracted with Omni for security maintenance."

"That's correct," he said. "What does that have to do with anything?"

"We signed confidentiality statements when you hired us to update your security. I think Sean's right—we need to know who may be the target. We need to look at the client list and every client who has a large transaction going through tonight or Monday."

"I hadn't thought of that. Give me five minutes, I'm going to run it by our counsel, she's just down the hall."

Richard left. John asked, "You think you can make that determination? Just by looking at a list of names?"

"We can narrow it down," Jack said, "but it's also about asking questions—once we see who is potentially a target, Richard might have more information."

John said, "My techs are here, I'm going to take them to the roof. I shouldn't be long." He left, and only a few minutes later Richard returned.

"Our lawyer verified that your agreement is still valid." Richard handed Jack a folder. "Based on what you said, I printed out a list of each client who currently has more than one million in escrow. Most of those funds will be transferred or invested by Monday morning."

Sean immediately homed in. "Why does the name Feliciano sound familiar?" he asked.

Richard looked surprised at the question. "Nick Feliciano is my daughter's fiancé."

"There's a fifteen-million-dollar transaction scheduled for Monday. What's that?"

"His trust fund," Richard said. "The money was put into

escrow this morning, and he receives it once they are married. He asked that Omni manage the trust. I won't be in charge of the funds—Nick and Laura interviewed three financial advisers here and picked who they wanted to work with."

"What happens if the wedding is canceled?" Sean asked.

"It won't be," Richard said emphatically. "Laura and Nick have been together for three years now. And—" He hesitated.

"And what?" Jack pushed.

"Laura's ten weeks pregnant. No one knows—she and Nick told me last weekend when we went over some final wedding details. They said they would be telling Nick's family after the honeymoon—Nick isn't as close to his family. They are deeply in love, and Nick is ecstatic about the baby. He treats Laura like every father wants their daughter to be treated. He's my son in every way but blood."

"Was anyone upset that Nick moved his trust fund for Omni to manage?"

"I wouldn't know. It's Nick's decision. He received control of his trust when he was twenty-five, but kept it with the family because he didn't care much about the management end. But he had some questions about some of their investments and he wasn't pleased with the answers. He asked if Omni would take over management, and I said yes, and they chose Desiree Holden to manage their account. We set this up months ago, it's not a surprise to anyone."

"But the money was just transferred this morning."

"Correct."

Sean looked over at Jack, who nodded. They were thinking the same thing.

"We need more information about the Feliciano family and Nick's trust fund," Sean said.

At that moment John Black came back in. "My techs are

up on the roof, but we can't figure out how they plan to come in. The door has a secure key card system."

"Easy to steal," Jack said.

"But it's alarmed after hours."

"Easy to bypass," Sean said.

"And the ventilation system is too small for a person bigger than a child to pass through."

"Sean and I are going to be here," Jack said. "But in case we're wrong, we need someone on Richard, his daughter, and her fiancé tonight."

"Is that really necessary?" Richard asked.

"Yes," Sean and Jack said simultaneously. Sean continued, "Someone has gone to a lot of trouble to get into this building, and Omni is a ripe target."

"There are other businesses here," Richard said.

"We're talking to all of them," John said. "But right now, you're the most likely target."

Reluctantly, Richard agreed. "But I don't want Nick or Laura knowing what's going on. If you're right and someone plans to steal Nick's trust fund, it'll put undue stress on my daughter and a cloud over their entire wedding."

Jack said, "My wife and sister are FBI agents. Can they pose as guests?"

"It's a wedding rehearsal, only two dozen people—wedding party and significant others."

"They can't be staff," Sean said. "They would be distracted."

Richard frowned. "I have an idea, for one person," he said.

"We're listening."

"Brandy is my older daughter. She's a wedding planner, and she's been putting this all together for Laura. She's also the maid of honor. I can talk to her, explain the situation, and she'll understand. She can tell Laura that one of your people is her assistant. Laura won't question it."

"That works. Lucy will be with Brandy and Laura, and Megan can act as a staff manager or support with the hotel, just observing," Jack said. "Back Lucy up if necessary."

"Do you really think my daughter is in danger?"

"No," John said, "but at this point, we don't know exactly what their plan is or how they intend to access these accounts, so it's best to cover all our bases."

Doug saw his life flash before his eyes.

They were fucked.

"Did you hear me?" Beth said.

"We're dead."

"I have a plan."

"We can't go through with this, Beth. The police are everywhere. They must have figured it out. We have to disappear."

"They haven't figured it out, and we don't have the money to disappear."

Beth needed to realize that this was serious! "We leave, go to Canada maybe, lay low for a while. We have enough money for new identities."

"What about Frank?"

His stomach tightened. He must have an ulcer by now, he was tense all the time. Why had they agreed to this job? They'd never done anything this big before. Or for someone who had the money to hunt them down if they failed.

"I have a plan," Beth repeated. "It'll work. Then we disappear. Disappear with enough money that *no one* will find us."

"How?"

"Richard Lesko will take us inside."

He knew exactly what she was thinking, but he couldn't do that. He couldn't put someone at risk—even if he knew they'd never hurt them. What would be the penalties if they were caught kidnapping? Far greater, that's for sure. They already had an assault—or maybe an attempted murder charge—because of the drone lady. Kidnapping the CFO? That was . . . "No," he repeated.

"The police were all over the roof, they're talking to everyone in the building. My guess is they'll have someone on the roof of both the Sheraton and Omni. Probably inside as well. I can convince Lesko to go in after hours and transfer the money. He'll do it, he'll make it believable, even if there's a cop sitting in his office. Remember, he's a widower. I'll be there with him."

"What? How?"

"I'll pose as his girlfriend. He'll know I'm serious."

"Someone might recognize you. You can't do that."

"No one really sees me, Doug, and I'll make sure I look completely different. Hair down, makeup, nice clothes. No one will recognize me."

"It's far too risky."

"We can't get in the way we planned, we have to do it this way. You know it, I know it."

"No one gets hurt."

"Agreed."

His stomach flopped. He didn't believe her.

Chapter Thirteen

Putting together the Friday night operation took time and detailed planning. John Black and Riley Knight were situated on the roof of 1201K. An unmarked car with two plainclothes officers was parked on J and 12th. Two other plainclothes were in the lobby of the Hyatt to back up Megan and Lucy, if necessary. Jack and Sean were in the Omni offices. Sean had modified the security system so that if and when the thieves came, they wouldn't see anything different than what they expected, but Sean and Jack could move around freely inside. Sean had already worked with the FBI and the bank to get a lock on the escrow account—no one could touch it for seventy-two hours. Just in case they were wrong and the hackers had found a way to access the account from outside the network.

Sean didn't think he was wrong, but he didn't want to take the risk, not with that kind of money at stake.

At the Hyatt, the wedding rehearsal dinner started at six that evening, beginning with a cocktail party. Brandy Lesko was an amazing planner, Lucy realized—someone she would have been happy having organize her own wedding, though Sean had done an amazing job. Brandy made it seem so easy.

Brandy was on board with the plan from the beginning,

and Laura didn't even question Lucy's presence when Brandy introduced her as her assistant and said, "So I can enjoy tonight."

The dinner was a buffet and the food was plentiful. Lucy made a point of identifying each of the guests. Most were either mutual friends of the bride and groom, or Laura's family. The only person from the groom's family who came was his mother. She asked Brandy about it—out of Laura's earshot, but where she could keep an eye on Laura.

Brandy scowled. "I don't know where Nick came from, because he is nothing like his family. They're stuffy hypocrites. His sister is in Europe, can't be bothered to come for his wedding; his brother is in rehab—not because he wants to quit drinking and drugs, but because he was arrested for drunk driving and got rehab over community service and jail time. Nick's dad will be at the wedding, but isn't flying in until tomorrow morning. I doubt he'll make it on time. Nick's mom is okay, I guess. Kind of regal and queenlike, but she's the only one who's actually been nice to Laura. And then his uncles—they are just jerks. He didn't want to invite them to the wedding, but his mom and I convinced him that not inviting close relatives would create more problems for the family down the road. Sometimes we do things we don't want to do to keep the peace. But fortunately, this party is just close friends." She looked at Lucy—practically glared. "Do you really think that my sister could be in danger?"

Lucy had been listening to Brandy, but she was also keeping an eye on Laura. She was mingling, separate from Nick, but every time they looked at each other they grinned, like they were sharing a secret joke.

"We're here as a precaution," Lucy said.

Brandy glanced around, then leaned closer to Lucy and whispered, "When my dad told me that Nick's money might be the target, I remembered something Laura told me a couple of weeks ago. Nick thinks that the trust—which was managed by a law firm that his uncle works for—has been mismanaged. He'd asked for an audit last year and it took what he thought was far too long to get him the results, and when he tried to ask questions, the accountancy firm was unavailable. It was weird, he said, and one of the reasons he wanted to move his money to my dad's company."

Warning bells went off. Greed as a motive seemed so crass to Lucy, even though it was common. But if there was something else—say, if the trust didn't have the money—the motive might be much stronger.

"How big is the trust supposed to be?"

"I have no idea, but every heir—there are six, Nick and his siblings, and then three cousins—gets a guaranteed fifteen million on their twenty-fifth birthday. It was set up by Nick's grandfather, who made all his money in land. If they don't take it out, they get an allowance every month. Nick put his allowance in an investment fund because he can live off his earnings—he's an architect. So is Laura—it's how they met, they were hired to give competing bids for a project and ended up doing the job together because the client liked some of each plan. When they get back from their honeymoon, they're starting their own company together. They've been renovating a house in South Land Park, near the zoo, where they'll have their office as well so they can stay home with the *baby*." She whispered *baby*, clearly because few people knew about the pregnancy.

Laura approached them at that moment and hugged her sister. "Brandy, this is amazing. Just amazing." She then hugged Lucy. "Sorry, I'm just so happy!"

"I'm happy you're happy," Brandy said. "How's the buffet? Do we have enough food?"

"*Too* much! And the desserts? That chocolate mousse?

OMG, I'm going to gain ten pounds tonight. But I don't care!" She grinned.

"Chocolate mousse, my favorite." Lucy loved chocolate.

"You'll have to get one—or two!—when my slave-driving sister lets you take a break." She laughed, then said in a loud stage whisper, "I'll bring you one."

Lucy smiled. "Congratulations, Ms. Lesko."

"Soon to be *Mrs. Feliciano*."

The bride sighed again and looked over at Nick; he sensed her watching and glanced up from where he was talking to his mom. He winked at her and Laura beamed. "I just could *not* be happier. Where's Dad? I haven't seen him for a while."

Megan was keeping an eye on Richard Lesko, but he wasn't in the room. And neither was Megan.

Lucy needed to find him, but she was responsible for Laura. She glanced at Brandy, and the older sister picked up immediately on her dilemma.

"I'll find Dad for you, Laura, you sit and take it easy."

"Can I take Lucy here and get some chocolate mousse? She deserves it."

"Absolutely, but save some for me and Dad."

"No promises!" Laura called as she pulled Lucy over to the dessert table.

They ate and Laura was right—the mousse tasted even better than it looked. "I'm in heaven," Lucy said.

"I know, right?"

Nick came over and kissed Laura lightly. "Sixteen hours," he said.

"It can't come soon enough."

"Where are you going for your honeymoon?" Lucy asked.

"The Cascade Mountains," Nick said. "I rented a cabin for two weeks. I don't think either of us has ever had two weeks off in a row."

"It's perfect," Laura concurred. "We can hike, we have privacy, there's even a hot tub with an amazing view where we can watch the sunset. And I can sleep as late as I want. Not to mention we're renovating our house in South Land Park, and I don't really want to be around while they finish painting and installing the floors."

"Brandy is more than capable of managing the crew," Nick said. "Your sister can move mountains."

"My husband and I honeymooned in Vail, away from everything. Couldn't even see another cabin." It wasn't as relaxing as they'd planned, but murder seemed to follow Lucy and Sean wherever they went. "We went back for our one-year anniversary, last October, and it was even better."

"That's a great idea," Nick said. "I'll make sure to reserve the same place next year."

"I need to use the ladies' room," Laura said, "if you'll excuse me!"

Lucy said, "If you don't mind, I'll join you."

She didn't see Brandy or Richard, and that marginally worried her. But Megan was also gone, so she could be with him.

She checked her phone. Sean had sent a message that all was quiet across the street.

She texted Megan and asked for a status. Megan responded immediately that Lesko was in the lobby.

He's called Jack three times already. He's worried, and told me he didn't want Laura to sense his worry. I'm trying to convince him that we have this under control.

Maybe they were wrong. Maybe no one was planning on breaking into Omni at all. Though John and his team had talked to every business, and no one had been robbed, maybe there was another reason for the marks on the roof— another heist planned, or some extreme stunt.

Then why attack Ellen Dupre and leave her for dead?

Lucy concurred with the others that *something* was

planned directly related to what Ellen had recorded on the drone. John had convinced building security to bring in another guard and to change the pattern of how they monitored security feeds to keep eyes on each floor as much as possible.

Laura was chatty and happy, and Lucy hoped she never had to learn about the potential threat so she could fully enjoy her wedding.

Being around Laura and Nick reminded Lucy why she loved Sean. Having someone in your corner always, having someone to confide in, to share with, to cry on. A best friend, a lover, a soul mate. She had never believed it was possible before Sean; she couldn't imagine not having him in her life. Maybe that's why his reticence to talk about what happened with Paxton had hurt her so deeply—because when things were difficult, when they were the hardest, you should be able to trust the one person who has your back.

She realized now that his fear ran deeper than that, and that his hesitation wasn't because of her, but because of everyone he'd lost and his deep-seated feelings of guilt. Paxton had always been good at psychological manipulation—so good that you could end up believing up was down, wrong was right, justice was injustice.

But Sean was on his way back to his old self, and they would overcome this crisis like they had overcome everything else life had thrown at them.

Lucy finished washing her hands then smiled at Laura. "You know, I wouldn't object to a second chocolate mousse."

"Oh God yes, let's," Laura said with a wide smile.

Lucy tried to step in front of Laura as they left the bathroom, but Laura was chatting and giddy at the same time.

A large man stepped into their path. He revealed a gun in his waistband and said, "If you want to see your sister alive, do not say a word, come with me."

"No," Lucy said. "Laura, don't move."

She tried to bring Laura back into the bathroom so that she wasn't between Lucy and the stranger, and then Lucy would be able to pull her weapon and keep Laura out of harm's way. But the stranger grabbed Laura by the arm and pulled her to him. She yelped. The bathrooms were down the hall and around the corner from the lounge where the party was. No one else was nearby.

"Don't fight me. *Look*."

He pulled out his cell phone and showed them a photo of Brandy in the back of what appeared to be a limo. Brandy looked both scared and angry.

"Who are you? What do you want?"

"Come now or you won't like what happens to her."

Lucy had to act now. She was worried about Brandy, but her job was to protect Laura and there was no way she was letting Laura go with this man.

Fortunately, the stranger's attention was on Laura, not Lucy. Simultaneously, she grabbed Laura, pushed the door shut, and pulled her own gun. "I'm FBI, get in the stall now!"

Laura was stunned to see the gun but she obeyed.

The stranger pushed against the door so hard that Lucy's full body slammed against the tile wall. Her vision clouded, but she shook her head to refocus.

As soon as the man entered, gun drawn, she kicked up and out, startling him enough that he turned his focus to her and not Laura, who was closing the stall door.

"FBI," Lucy said, "drop the weapon or I'll shoot."

He did neither. He ran.

Lucy had to pursue, but she couldn't leave Laura alone. She ran out of the bathroom to see where he was going. He was heading for the staircase.

At that moment, Nick came out of the lounge. "I thought I heard a scream. Where's Laura?"

Lucy pulled her badge out from under her shirt, where it

had been concealed on a chain, and said, "Agent Kincaid, FBI, Laura's in the bathroom, get her secured and call SPD now."

She ran after the man while she pulled out her phone and hit REDIAL. Megan answered.

"I'm in pursuit of an armed Caucasian male, running down the east staircase. Six foot three, thirties, wearing dark khaki pants, dark blazer, gray shirt. Secure Lesko."

"I'll come to you."

"Secure Lesko! They have Brandy, Laura is safe."

She ended the call because she couldn't run, talk, and maintain control of her weapon. If they had more time they could have checked out radios.

She saw the suspect three floors down and watched as he hopped over the railing, putting even more distance between them.

Lucy picked up speed, grateful that she'd worn black tennis shoes with the black slacks and white blouse "uniform" she and Brandy had decided on. Her blazer flapped behind her and she supported herself with the railing as she ran faster.

She didn't know the layout of the hotel well, but there were two floors the suspect could exit the building from—the mezzanine level that went into the parking garage, and the lobby level, with multiple exits.

She was slowly gaining on the suspect, but there were too many floors between them. She tried to keep eyes on him but it was difficult to run and keep him in sight below. She heard a door open and looked—he was in the lobby.

He could easily exit through multiple doors on the east side of the building.

She called Megan again, but there was no answer. By the time Lucy reached the ground floor she didn't see anyone.

Not her suspect.
Not Megan.
Not Richard Lesko.
She called John Black.

Megan ended the call with Lucy and went over to where Richard Lesko was talking with a woman in her thirties. They were walking toward the entrance of the hotel—the woman looked familiar, but Megan couldn't place her. Maybe hotel security?

"Mr. Lesko," Megan called out to get his attention.

He didn't look at her, didn't even acknowledge that he'd heard her. He walked out of the hotel and she knew something was wrong.

She needed to back up Lucy, but Lesko was in trouble. She followed Lesko and the woman, then called out again, "Lesko! Stop!"

The woman had Lesko by the arm and was pulling him out of the lobby, but he wasn't resisting her.

Megan suspected that the woman had told Lesko his daughter was being held and to come with her, but Megan couldn't let him be taken as well. They had a greater chance of getting Brandy out of this if they didn't have Lesko in the crosshairs.

She pulled her badge out from under her blouse, let it drop on the chain around her neck, and called, "FBI, stop!"

Lesko looked back, but the woman pushed him forward.

The bellhop at the front door looked at Lesko, then at Megan. She didn't want anyone to get hurt, so she didn't ask him to get involved, but he clearly understood the situation.

He approached Lesko to help, then stopped and put his hands up.

That's when Megan saw the gun in the woman's hand.

Shit.

She pulled her own gun and followed them through the doors.

"Stop," she said. "Let him go, you haven't hurt anyone yet."

The woman didn't comment, but opened the door of the limo. Megan couldn't shoot her, not with so many people around, and not with Lesko as a shield.

The bellhop suddenly yelled, "Watch out!" And pointed behind her.

Megan turned, trying to keep Lesko in view while assessing the new threat, but a large man hit her over the head with his gun and she fell to her knees. She whipped her gun up, but her vision was blurred and she didn't trust she wouldn't hit an innocent bystander.

Then she was off her feet and being carried to the limo.

"Leave her!" the woman shouted.

"Go, another one is coming!"

Megan was pushed to the floor of the limo and disarmed. Her worst nightmare. She had trained for this over and over and over . . . but when the situation was happening in real time, seconds mattered, and she hadn't been able to watch her own back.

The door slammed shut and the limo lurched forward, then into traffic.

"She's a federal agent!" the woman said.

"She's a good hostage, then. The police aren't going to shoot at one of their own."

"The police aren't going to shoot at anyone, dammit! You made this ten times worse than it would have been."

Megan shook her head and opened her eyes, her head still pounding. But her vision was better. She reached up and felt blood on the back of her head and realized that if she'd been hit on the side like Ellen, she, too, could have been knocked out cold. The bastard had a wallop—and based on his build, she was sure it was the same guy who had attacked Ellen.

The woman cuffed Megan's right wrist to Brandy's ankle, then searched her. Found her backup weapon, her knife— she'd never carried a knife until Jack had trained her to use it—and her identification.

"Megan Elliott. Elliott? Shit, you idiot! This is the *district attorney's* fucking *sister!*"

How did she know that? Who was this woman? Why did she look familiar? Megan knew she'd seen her before, but she couldn't remember where.

"We get the money, we leave," the brute said. "Just like we planned."

"Nothing has gone like we planned," the woman said. "They brought in some security specialist who fucked us over, but that's why we have more than one plan, right? So listen to me: I take Lesko up. If anyone tries to stop me, I'll leverage the situation. I'll do the job, then we release the hostages when we're free and clear. But no one gets hurt unless they make a move first. No one, understand?"

"I'm not an idiot," the man said.

Lesko asked Megan, clearly worried, "Is Laura okay?"

"Yes. She's safe."

"Shut up, Agent Elliott. No talking. No planning anything, no trouble, and you and the girl won't be hurt. Play nice, don't try anything stupid."

The limo stopped only a minute or two after they left the hotel. When the door opened, the woman put her gun on Lesko. "Out. I don't want to hurt anyone, but I will if I have to."

Lesko got out. In the dark, Megan realized they were outside the 1201K Tower.

Jack and Sean were inside. John was on the roof. They would figure this out. Lucy would have alerted them by now.

The woman closed the door, but then Megan heard the passenger front door open. She listened carefully but caught only part of the conversation.

A man was driving. He said something like, "Let's just go."

The woman was indistinct, then Megan heard, ". . . promise. Okay? Just do what I said, okay?"

"I love you. Don't get hurt. Please."

"I'll be okay. I promise." The woman closed the door, and the limo sped off.

Megan needed to use that information, but how?

Jack Kincaid ended the call with Lucy.

"They have Megan," he said quietly. Calmly. Because he was always calm in action, even when the woman he loved was in danger.

Megan is smart, trained, capable.

He could tell himself that a hundred times, but she was still at risk from an unknown threat and he would not be at peace until he could touch her.

"Lucy thinks they're coming here," he continued. "She's on her way, coming in through the back to avoid detection."

"They got to the bride?"

"Her sister. Used her as bait to lure Richard Lesko into a limo after they couldn't get to Laura. The bride is secure, in a room with her groom and hotel security."

"They have to know their plan isn't going to work. That if we know, we secured the money."

"Maybe they'll order Richard to steal from other clients. Whatever it is, can you stop them?"

"Then you won't have backup."

"I will. Lucy's on her way, Black is aware of the situation. You need to secure yourself and do your thing."

Jack didn't understand half of what Sean did, but he trusted that he would be able to stop a major cyber-theft.

"Go, Sean," Jack said, "we don't have time to argue."

Sean reluctantly went into Omni's IT office and secured the door, as they had planned. Because they didn't have all the information they needed, Sean had mirrored Lesko's account onto the main IT computer so that he could monitor everything that Richard did on his computer, diverting money if necessary but still making it seem as if the transfer went through. The only problem was if the suspect had someone on the outside who was capable of watching the end account in real time, outside the Omni network. But they had to buy time, and this was the best way to do so.

Omni was a large office that took up most of the top floor, but because there was also a cafeteria here and a small administrative office, they had both a main entrance and a "rear" entrance. Jack looked at his vibrating phone and saw a message from Lucy that she was at the rear entrance.

He let her in.

"They're on their way up. When I got here, I told security to let them up and text me. He unlocked the elevator just now. Lesko is with a woman."

"Only one?"

"There's at least two more involved. I chased one of the suspects, but he had a head start and I couldn't catch up. Then I heard commotion in the lobby. By the time I got there, a witness told me that Megan and Lesko were forced into a limo along with a woman and a large man. Another woman was in the limo, and I'm guessing that was Brandy Lesko. A third suspect was driving. I cut through the Hyatt parking garage in order to beat the limo here—the benefit of one-way streets is that they had to go all the way around three square blocks."

"Megan?"

"She's okay. She was hit on the head, but was conscious and talking, according to the witness."

That didn't make him feel better, especially knowing what had happened to Ellen two days ago.

"Sean's in place," he said, "but I need you to talk these people down."

"We need Sean to track Megan's phone."

Why hadn't he thought of that?

"I'll tell him, then hide—but I'll have my eyes on you, okay? You good?"

"Yes. As soon as Sean knows where Megan is, John has a team ready to go after them. I'm going to buy us time. Tell Sean I'm turning on my speaker; he knows how to access my phone."

Jack slipped away seconds before he heard the door unlock.

Lucy positioned herself in Lesko's office. She put her phone on the table so she could see messages that came through—as soon as she knew that Megan and Brandy were safe, she would change tactics. She planted her backup weapon in a drawer at the conference table. She wasn't certain how she was going to handle the situation, but if the suspect disarmed her she needed to know where a second weapon was in case things went south.

Preventing the theft was important, but saving Richard Lesko's life—and Megan and Brandy—was the priority.

She forced her heart rate to slow. The attack in the bathroom, the race down the stairs, running over to the building— her adrenaline level was high. But she had to have all her senses alert, and listening to the blood pump behind her ears wasn't going to help her sense any nuances.

She heard a male voice outside the office. "Don't hurt my daughter, please."

"You cooperate and no one gets hurt. I promise, okay? We're just going to get the money."

The woman sounded nervous. Because their original plan had been thwarted? Because she expected a trap?

They stepped into Lesko's office, Richard first. The lights weren't on, save for a faint security light coming from each corner of the room. The woman had a gun on him. Lucy kept her hands visible.

As soon as the woman was in full view, Lucy knew she'd seen her before.

The woman locked eyes with Lucy. Confused.

"What?" The woman glanced all over the room, looking for others but Lucy was here alone.

"Robinson," Lucy said.

The crime scene tech.

She'd processed Ellen's crime scene.

She'd processed the Sheraton roof—where all the prints had been wiped from the door.

She'd processed the roof of 1201K.

She had been privy to information. John would have talked around her, not realizing that one of his own techs was in a criminal gang. She must have learned that they suspected 1201K would be robbed, and she would have known that Omni was at the top of the list.

Yet she still went through with the plan. Deviated from the original strategy of coming in at night through the roof. But still went through with it.

That told Lucy she was desperate. She would know that John would have people in the building. She would know that she couldn't get away with it, that they would learn her identity soon enough. Hotel security cameras. Lesko's testimony. Unless she planned to kill everyone.

Murder was a lot harder to run away from.

"Agent Kincaid." Robinson sounded surprised. "How— you were in the hotel."

"Let's talk."

"No time to talk. I'm sure you're not the only one here, but I hold the cards." She led Lesko to his desk, sat him down, and stood behind him, putting him between her and Lucy. "Do it," she said. "Exactly what I told you in the elevator."

"And Brandy will be safe."

"I give you my word."

"Your word?" Lucy said. "Is it good?"

"I'll be taking Mr. Lesko back with me. As soon as we get out of the city, I'll release everyone, and we'll be on our way. This isn't personal. It's just a job."

"Your partner nearly killed a woman Wednesday night. She's in a coma. They don't know if she'll ever come out of it."

"It was an accident. He didn't mean to hit her so hard, and her prognosis is good."

"You checked." Lucy wasn't surprised.

"I didn't have to. Detective Black has been calling over to his brother-in-law asking for status updates. It was pretty easy to figure it out."

"You're in law enforcement. Why?"

"Why this?" She turned to Lesko. "Do it, Richard. I don't have time. Good." She watched what he was typing. "Keep going." She pulled out a notebook and put it down next to him. "That account. You have two minutes. I know it doesn't take longer."

"Robinson," Lucy said, trying to keep her going. "You haven't hurt anyone. Your partner, yes—but not you. You share with us who hired you, cooperate fully, and maybe you'll get off easy."

She laughed. "Really? Easy? You don't know John Black very well, do you?"

"John's not here. It's you and me."

"You across the room, me here. And that's the way it's going to stay. One minute, Richard. Tick tock."

"I know your original plan didn't have any innocent bystanders involved. You were going to slip in, transfer the money, slip out."

"Black brought in a security consultant, some genius who figured everything out. Based on a couple of scratches on the roof? What the fuck? But yeah, I didn't want to bring in anyone else. I don't want to hurt anyone, but I promise you, I will. If I have to, I will do anything for my family."

Family. That helped. She wouldn't want to die if she was trying to protect her family. She wouldn't want them to die.

But family could also make people desperate, and desperate people could make bad decisions.

Lucy had turned off vibration on her phone, but a faint shift in the color told her a text had come in.

From Jack.

Located Megan. ETA five minutes.

Lucy didn't know if she could keep Robinson occupied for five minutes.

"I'm Lucy," she said. "What's your first name? Calling you *Robinson* seems awkward."

"Beth. I'm sure John will tell you when you talk to him. I know he's on the roof."

"Yes, with Officer Knight. Riley."

"How do you know him? You're not even from here."

"I met him. His brother-in-law is the ASAC of Sacramento FBI, I'm in the San Antonio office."

"Fuck me," Beth muttered. "I swear, I never should've taken this job."

"Why did you? If this was so far out of your comfort zone."

"It wasn't the job—it was the bastard who . . . never mind. Not important."

"Who hired you, Beth? Who are you risking your freedom for?"

"Richard, it's been more than two minutes. The money is not in my account."

Beth was holding a phone.

"It's going. I swear. I did everything right."

Richard knew the plan, and that the money was frozen, but he was playing along.

"Please," he begged. "Don't hurt my daughters. I'm doing everything you said. I don't care about the money, I only care about Brandy and Laura."

"Then what is going on?"

"Look—it says it's transferring. I don't know why it's taking so long."

Lucy glanced down at her phone.

Sean is going to fake the transfer, he says. He's in her phone. May not work. Buy time.

She trusted that Sean knew what he was doing.

"Do you want me to help?" Lucy said.

"Stay there. Do not move. I don't want to kill you, but I don't have a lot to lose right now."

"I'm not moving. I'm staying right here, behind the conference table, giving you space." She needed to make sure that Jack and Sean knew exactly where everyone was if they felt the need to breach the room.

Beth stared at Lucy, as if to make sure she stood still. Then she turned back to Richard.

"Is it locked up? Did you do something? Alert someone?"

"No," Richard said. "I logged into the account and went through all the security questions. I answered them right—you saw that. And now it's showing the transfer icon. You saw that I typed in the numbers correct!"

Beth frowned, then she turned off her phone. "The money had better be there."

Lucy practically held her breath while Beth logged back into her account. Thirty very long seconds later, Beth smiled. "Thank you, Richard. That wasn't that hard, was it? And no one has to get hurt." She called someone.

The person didn't answer. She called again.

"No, no, no."

Lucy glanced down at her phone. A message from Sean. *Have Megan, Brandy. No injuries. Jack, John outside door.*

"Beth," Lucy said. "The police have your partners in custody."

"I don't believe you!"

Sean texted, *Beth's husband Doug and his brother Frank.*

Lucy said, "Doug and Frank are in custody, uninjured. Put the gun down and step away from Mr. Lesko. It's over, Beth. You're not going to get out of this building. And you don't want a violent end. You don't want to never see your husband again."

"How are you communicating? What are you doing?"

Then Beth saw the phone on the table and frowned. "What's going on?"

"Everything you said and did was sent through speaker to John Black. We tracked Megan Elliott's phone, followed the limo. This isn't worth losing your life, Beth. The more you cooperate, the greater the chances you'll get out with minimal time. No one died, and that's a good thing."

Beth looked torn. "No one was supposed to get hurt at all. In five years, we never hurt *anyone*."

"I believe you. Who hired you, Beth?"

"It's too late. He has the money. He'll be long gone."

"He doesn't have the money."

"He does—I saw the account."

"The genius you mentioned? He's a computer security expert. He mirrored the account so you would think that the money was transferred. The Feliciano trust fund was never at risk—the escrow account has been locked."

"No. You're wrong."

"I'm telling you the truth. So even if you get out of here—which you won't—you won't have your money, and I suspect the person who hired you will track you down. Let me guess. If I'm right, put down your gun."

"Let me think!" Beth was torn, but she knew that she wasn't getting away. She was a crime scene technician, she knew what the police would do. She knew that she wasn't going to be able to run forever, even if she got out of the building.

"It's Nick Feliciano's uncle." Lucy remembered what Brandy said earlier. "Right? He didn't want Nick to move the money because he did something with the trust. Lost money, maybe replaced it with someone else's money to pay Nick this week. And you were hired to get it back. But it's not going to go back to him, and you're not going to be paid. Either you put the gun down or you're going to be killed leaving this building. You and I both know that."

"How the hell did you guess that?"

"Something Brandy Lesko said to me earlier about Nick's family. I had a hunch."

Beth put her gun down on Richard's desk and put her hands on top of her head.

"Thank you, Beth, you made the right decision," Lucy said. "Richard, please step away."

As Lucy spoke, John and Jack came into the room, guns drawn. Jack glanced at Lucy, nodded. Richard left his office, pulling out his phone at the same time.

John approached Beth, read her the Miranda rights, then cuffed her. "Get a lawyer, Beth."

"Is that what you say to all the criminals you arrest?"

"Only the ones I think are remorseful."

"Is Doug okay? Really?"

"Yes. He didn't put up a fight. He's in custody. His brother resisted, but we had an agent inside who helped take him down. Bumps and bruises."

"Can I see Doug? I know it's not protocol, but . . . I will cooperate. I promise, full cooperation. Doug didn't even want to do this, I talked him into it."

"No promises, Beth, but I'll see what I can do."

John escorted Beth out, and Sean ran in and hugged Lucy. "You did great."

"I agree," Jack said. "You good?"

"Yes."

"Then I'm leaving. Megan hates the hospital, but she needs to get checked out, so I'm taking her whether she wants to go or not."

Lucy turned to Sean, kissed him. Surprisingly, they were alone, at least for the moment. "We're going to have to give our statements. Then I'm ready for bed."

He frowned. "You have a bruise on your cheek. And here—you're bleeding. What happened?"

She looked at where Sean was pulling at her blouse. She hadn't noticed the blood before. "The door in the bathroom," she said. "When Frank—I assume it was the brother-in-law— tried to grab Laura, he hit me with the door. I thought it was just my head. I'm fine."

"I'll be the judge of that."

She put her arms around him. "You'll just have to inspect every inch of my body and make sure I'm a hundred percent okay."

"Tough job, but I'm up for it." He grinned and kissed her. "I love you, Lucy Kincaid Rogan."

"Love you more."

Chapter Fourteen

Sean and Lucy arrived at Jack and Megan's late Saturday afternoon, hours after the party started. Neither of them felt guilty—they agreed that they needed the morning to relax after the stressful night.

"Do you want beer or wine?" Sean asked.

She shook her head. "I'd fall asleep. I'm going to the kitchen to make a pot of coffee. But you have a beer or two, I'll drive back to the hotel." She smiled and kissed him, and he watched her go into the kitchen. He was the luckiest man on the planet.

The tension and fear Sean had been feeling for the last month had been fading since his heart-to-heart with Lucy Thursday night. He still was apprehensive about the future, but it wasn't all-consuming, and he finally could see the light. He might talk to someone, but not Dillon the shrink, even though he liked him. And not Jack, even though he respected him. They were Lucy's brothers, and while they treated Sean as their own family, there were some things he'd feel awkward discussing with them.

But Kane . . . Sean needed his own brother now. He'd called him this morning, while Lucy was sleeping.

Sean realized how much Kane had changed in the last two years when he answered his phone on the second ring.

"Hey."

"It's Sean."

"Do you think I'd pick up the damn phone if I didn't know who it was?"

Good point.

"You still in Sac?" Kane asked.

"Yeah. We're flying back tomorrow. Commercial. I was wondering if you were in the middle of something."

"What do you need?"

What did he need? "I don't know. I thought if you and Siobhan wanted to come up and visit for a couple of days. Jesse has his eighth-grade graduation Friday, I know you planned to come for that, but . . ."

"We'll be there Monday afternoon. Good?"

"Good."

He hadn't had to explain anything, and that told Sean he made the right call. That between him and Kane, they would figure out how to get Sean past this.

Yes, he would get through this. He finally believed it.

Jack came up to him, handed him a beer, and clapped him on the back. "Where's Luce?"

"Making coffee." He sipped. "How's Megan?"

Jack's face darkened. "She's fine. Her head hurts, but she won't take painkillers. Concussion, but I'm keeping an eye on her. I convinced her to relax on the back porch—people can come to her, she doesn't have to entertain anyone."

"We're not going to stay long."

"I wanted to cancel, but Megan didn't. And we won this one, so I'm going to let her celebrate. But we wouldn't have been offended if you didn't come."

"We wanted to. We're leaving tomorrow, and, well, I'm sorry. About everything."

Jack looked him in the eye. "No apologies. I've been where you are, Sean. You're a good man. None of us are good at talking about our shit. But you have one of the finest women I know as your wife, and I knew you'd find a way to get back to her."

"You kicked me in the ass when I needed it."

"It's the past, Sean. We're good, okay?"

"Thank you."

"You should talk to Duke before you go."

"Where is he?"

"At the grill. He's a control freak."

Sean laughed. "He is."

"But at least I don't have to cook."

Sean went out back and talked to his brother Duke and his sister-in-law Nora. Molly, who'd turned two in March, was running from person to person showing off a giant stuffed purple bunny. As Sean watched, JT Caruso—one of the principals of RCK—scooped Molly up with the bunny and turned her upside down. She screamed out laughter. When JT righted her and put her on his shoulders, she shouted, "Again! Again! Upsies downsies!"

It was good to visit. Sean was going to have to do it more often.

But he couldn't wait to go home and see his son, Jesse.

After catching up with Duke, Sean saw John Black talking with Jack on the back porch. He excused himself and went over to talk to them. John said, "I was just telling Jack that I was late because I was at the hospital. Ellen Dupre is out of her coma and gave her statement."

"She's okay? Really okay?"

"Yes—they expect a full recovery, though they'll be monitoring her closely for the next forty-eight hours."

"What did she say about the attack?" Jack asked.

"She saw the man on the roof and thought it was fishy, so

she went back with the drone. She planned to enhance the tape and turn it over to authorities, and admitted she was preoccupied when she stepped out of the van to retrieve the drone. She didn't see who attacked her and doesn't remember getting hit. She remembers nothing until waking up last night."

"Is she up for visitors?" Sean asked.

"Call Marc. I'm sure she'd love it."

"Lucy and I will stop by tomorrow morning on our way to the airport."

"You nailed it, Rogan."

Jack smiled. "Sean's really good at making us mere mortals feel inferior."

"I'm just glad that no one got seriously hurt," Sean said. "You have them all in custody, right?"

"No one slipped away. Beth Robinson is being held separately. Though she was a crime scene technician, she's still law enforcement, we want to make sure she's safe. The DA is concerned about her previous cases, so he's going to interview her himself on Monday—what we don't want is every case she worked to be a potential reversal. I don't think it'll happen—from what she said, she and her husband kept their thieving separate from her work. They were hired thieves. She's going to make a full statement in exchange for leniency, but they'll all be doing some time. I'm going to talk to the DA. If they agree to testify against Feliciano's uncle, they'll probably do three to five. Frank Robinson, Doug's brother, will do additional time for the assault on Ellen. No less than ten years."

"What kind of things did they steal? They weren't just embezzling?"

"They started in corporate espionage. Doug used to work for a computer software company, which is where he met Andy Ralston, the fourth partner. The company paid Doug

and Andy to hack into a new competitor's system to retrieve proprietary data. They discovered they were good at
it. Doug told Beth—he apparently felt guilty—and she way-
laid his fears, and started seeking out other jobs. During a
divorce case she stole jewelry from the wife to give back to
the husband. Made ten thousand on that. Another time they
stole an heirloom given to one kid in the parents' will, the
other kid was jealous. In fact, most of their crimes paid between five and ten thousand, usually personal things, personal griefs. Andy was good at breaking security systems,
Doug was better at computer hacking and planning. But
none of their crimes would have jump-started a major investigation because the dollar amounts weren't all that high.
Probably could have done it for years. Then they brought
Doug's brother Frank aboard, and he got them several big
jobs. I think they got greedy, so when Nick Feliciano's uncle
hired them to steal Nick's trust—and paid a half million up
front—they didn't think it through."

"Did you find Ralston?" Jack asked.

"Yep, when they changed the plan from hacking the system on-site to using Lesko, Ralston wasn't needed. We arrested him while he was binge-watching Netflix. We don't
have much on him, other than Beth's statement, but when we
ran his prints we learned he's wanted by the FBI for cyber-
crimes. The FBI will take custody of him on Monday."

"Sounds like a win all around," Jack said.

"It is. I owe you both. And your wife, Sean. She was a
great partner on this case. I already told her that, and will be
sending a note to her office for her file."

"She would appreciate that. Thank you."

Sean excused himself and tracked down Lucy, who was
talking to Dean Hooper. Dean said, "What a night you two
had. I'm surprised you made it out here today."

"We're going back to San Antonio tomorrow, and we

wanted to see everyone before we left. But I'm actually taking my wife away from all this."

"You're not staying?"

"Like you said, we had a night. I think early to bed is on the schedule." He looked at Lucy.

"I completely agree," she said.

They said their goodbyes to everyone and left.

"You're not upset that we bailed early, are you?" Sean asked.

"Not at all. I like everyone there, but we did the rounds, and all I want is to relax. And isn't there a rooftop hot tub on the concierge level?"

"Yes, there is."

"Sounds like heaven."

"Are you still sore?"

"Nothing that the hot tub, a glass of champagne, and making love to my husband won't fix."

He leaned over and kissed her. "Your wish is my command."

Afterword

The Lucy Kincaid series is near and dear to my heart, and I hope you've enjoyed these novellas as much as I enjoyed writing them.

If you missed any books, here's a brief summary of the series as it stands in January 2022. I hope to add more stories in the near future!

In *Love Me to Death,* Lucy was a suspect in the murder of one of her rapists who, unknown to her, had been released early from prison and found executed only miles from where she lived in Washington, DC. When she found out her family lied in a failed effort to protect her, she turned to private investigator Sean Rogan for help. In *Kiss Me, Kill Me,* while Sean and Lucy are in New York City looking for Sean's missing teenage cousin, they end up helping the FBI solve the case of the Cinderella Strangler. After these adventures, Sean and Lucy take a vacation in *If I Should Die,* where they uncover dark secrets in a small Adirondacks town.

Lucy is thrilled when she's finally accepted into the FBI Academy! While she's waiting for her session to start, she works as an analyst under the watchful eye of Special Agent Noah Armstrong. When the mistress of a congressman ends up dead, Lucy connects the murder with the deaths of several prostitutes in *Silenced.* Finally at the FBI Academy in Quantico, Lucy's mentor asks her to help with a cold case in *Stalked*—that may be connected to the murder of a true crime writer who was looking into Lucy's own tragic past. In *Stolen,* Sean risks his reputation and his life when he agrees to go undercover for the FBI—by stepping back into his old shoes of computer hacking with his former college friends.

In *Cold Snap,* the Kincaid family Christmas reunion is threatened by murder . . . Patrick takes center stage in the first of three mysteries when he helps a family friend track down a missing teenager. Lucy, Sean, Kate, and Dillon are stuck in a Denver hotel during a blizzard—with a dead body. And back home in San Diego, Carina Kincaid is taken hostage by a grieving soldier who believes someone killed his sister, and needs help to prove it.

It's been fourteen months since Lucy and Sean's first adventure, and now she's a sworn FBI agent assigned to the San Antonio FBI office in *Dead Heat.* One of her first major assignments is a joint task force running Operation Heatwave, a major interagency warrant sweep headed up by the DEA. But when one of their targets bolts and they uncover a virtual prison in the basement of his home, it's clear there's something far more insidious going on.

Lucy's been a rookie agent for six months when she's assigned to work with a by-the-book senior agent to investigate the suspicious death of a congresswoman's husband in *Best Laid Plans.* Still haunted by the events in *Dead Heat,* Lucy realizes there's more going on that connects Operation Heatwave to her current case. When a corrupt DEA agent agrees to turn state's evidence in a plea bargain, the final card is played in *No Good Deed* when the agent escapes and seeks retribution on everyone who put her in prison . . . or are the bodies she's dropping only a smoke screen for her real plan?

Lucy's fiancé, Sean, learns he has a son when the mother of his child begs for him to help find the boy and his missing stepfather in Mexico in *The Lost Girls.* In the meantime, Lucy is working a particularly difficult case of human trafficking and black-market babies with her mentor, Noah Armstrong, who has temporarily taken over running the San Antonio field office. Four weeks after the events in *The Lost Girls,* Sean and Lucy are finally preparing for their wedding . . . when Sean's estranged sister seeks to make amends in *Make Them Pay.* But Eden Rogan is a pathological liar, and her lies put Lucy's life in grave danger.

Though *Shattered* is the fourth book in the Maxine Revere cold case series, it's also a Lucy Kincaid story. Lucy agrees to help Max, an investigative crime reporter, look into the cold case murder of Lucy's nephew Justin Stanton when Max develops a theory that Justin was the first of four victims . . . and there may be another young boy in danger.

Breaking Point introduces JT Caruso's sister, Bella, who is working deep undercover in a human trafficking organization . . . and Lucy may be the only person who can find her before her cover is blown. But Bella doesn't *want* to be found.

Five months after *Breaking Point,* Sean finally has a relationship with his son, Jesse . . . only to learn in *Too Far Gone* that Jesse's stepfather will do anything to prevent it, even if it puts Jesse's life in danger. While Sean tries to protect his son, Lucy is looking into a hostage taker who until a month before his criminal act, had been a respected, law-abiding citizen.

While Sean and Jesse recover from the events in *Too Far Gone,* Lucy works with the Bexar County Sheriff's Department on a possible serial killer case in *Nothing to Hide.*

Three married men are dead, all in the same way, with no connection to each other . . . or is there? And in *Cut and Run,* Lucy teams up again with Max to solve a cold case that involves a missing child . . . only to uncover a conspiracy that is still leaving dead bodies in its wake.

Multiple characters from the past come back in *Cold As Ice,* when Sean is arrested for a murder he didn't commit, his brother Kane goes missing in Mexico, and Lucy's partner, Nate Dunning, is detained for drug trafficking. And that's only the beginning.

For the most up-to-date information about the Lucy Kincaid series, as well as my other thrillers, please visit allisonbrennan.com.